MORAL TREATMENT

MORAL TREATMENT

a novel

STEPHANIE CARPENTER

Moral Treatment: A Novel copyright © 2025 by Stephanie Carpenter

Anspach Hall
Central Michigan University
Mount Pleasant, MI 48859
cmichpress.com

Chapter One of this novel previously appeared, in different form, in *MidAmerica: The Journal of the Society for the Study of Midwestern Literature.*

ISBN 979-8-9910646-0-6 (paperback)
ISBN 979-8-9910646-1-3 (ebook)

Library of Congress Control Number: 2024942099

Book design by Erin Smith
Cover art image adapted from "View of Michigan Asylum for the Insane. Kalamazoo." Map of Kalamazoo Co., Michigan. Philadelphia: Geil & Harley, 1861. Library of Congress. Original daguerreotype taken by Schuyler Colfax Baldwin (1822-1900).

Author photo by Adam Johnson, brockit inc.

First Edition: February 2025

For my family

Prologue

D R. FOLEY DRIVES HIS CART along the bluff road. He's been called out to the Underwood place. It's a warm September evening; what trees haven't been felled by the lumber company blush red and orange. On autumn nights in past years, young men drove this road with their sweethearts and Foley had hoped one day to do the same. Now it seems that the hardwoods will all be harvested before he manages to court anyone. He's gained another ten pounds since last September, piled another year of timidity atop the rest. He's arrived at another autumn alone behind Dobbins, whose dun rump undulates before him, whose blond tail lifts as if in contempt.

At least the view to the west is compelling. The bluff drops down to Lake Michigan and the sun fades far out over the still, silver water. Perhaps in another year he will have someone to admire this with him. For the present, there is his work—and just ahead, set against a lingering stand of trees, there is the lumber agent's rambling new Queen Anne. Dr. Foley has come to see the Underwood girl. He has been called to determine whether or not she is insane.

Foley silently reviews the directions he studied that afternoon, after unearthing his student copy of E.C. Spitzka's *Insanity: Its Classification, Diagnosis, and Treatment*. He may not have cracked this book before, but Spitzka presents things clearly enough, explaining how the physician should conduct himself, what indications he should look for, how he ought to go about winnowing down the possibilities until he arrives at the best diagnosis. Lodged in Foley's memory, however, is the final, impossible sentence of the chapter on examining patients. 'Where the diagnosis of a special form of insanity cannot be made,' the doctor 'must test for psychical weakness in the abstract, for abnormal irritability, logical perverseness, abulia, hyperbulia, lack of reaction, and abnormal emotional states, *whose characters language cannot portray*, so that they can be appreciated in the living subject only.' The italics are a flourish of Foley's imagination, the typographical equivalent of the sweat that trickles now down his back. He's been in practice four years; he just barely meets the state's minimum requirement to act as a certifying physician. He has never before been called in a case like this, never been called to assess emotional states that defy description. If there's any room at all to say that the girl is sane, he's resolved: he will say it. Instead, Spitzka seems to give him infinite leeway to say otherwise.

Drawing nearer, Dr. Foley sees Mr. Underwood emerge from his barn. Foley hasn't yet been introduced to the man, but he recognizes Underwood's gait—tense about the shoulders and stiff in the legs—as well as his dark moustache and long frame. No matter that the town is booming, a newcomer is conspicuous, and as a relative newcomer himself, Foley is grateful for those like Underwood, come more lately. The lumber agent lifts his hand and Foley responds—hello!—before realizing that the gesture is only directional. Dobbins breaks into a jog, whiffing hay; Foley draws back on the reins. There's no cause for hurry. His practice is still small, his reputation uncertain. He's only here today because the law requires two certificates of insanity. The Underwoods, like most of their neighbors, take their everyday illnesses to Dr. Gibson, the town's sole physician for the last forty years.

After they've tended the horse, after a gruff handshake—no pleasantries, no welcome at all in Underwood's ice-blue eyes—Underwood leads him into the turreted hulk of a house. Lamps are burning already in its wide entryway. From halltree to houseplants, everything is so new that Foley can only guess at the inhabitants' character, and he is being guided quickly, too, not toward the intimacy of a bedchamber but, mercifully, toward the front parlor. He nearly sighs in relief. The Underwood girl is old enough to make a bedside visit awkward, if her condition doesn't require it, and Dr. Gibson had at least told him that much: the girl is not enfeebled, not hysterical. Or wasn't, when the older doctor made his examination earlier in the week. Now, following Underwood into the parlor, Foley finds a grown girl with her father's dark hair, slumped sideways on a plush settee. There is a family history, Gibson had said—to go along with this pronounced family resemblance. But it is not Mr. Underwood who seems ill.

Looking at the girl side-by-side with her stepmother, Foley appreciates how one might make the mistake that Spitzka cautions against: guessing wrongly which is the afflicted person, offending the whole family through a simple blunder. In this case the error would be in guessing that *both* women were unwell, though in different ways. Mrs. Underwood is thin and pale, with blond hair dressed in a high roll and features too large for her angular face. She sits bolt upright, an almost electric tension in her bearing, an air of 'nervous complaint' about her taut forehead and compressed lips. Per Spitzka, this might be melancholia, paranoia—or anemia, insomnia, one of the ailments that Foley understands. Miss Underwood, meanwhile, is costumed like an insane person in an amateur theatrical, in a much-mended calico and with her brown hair hanging snarled and greasy around her scab-crusted face. The expression she shares with her father is difficult to read. Square-jawed like him, she wears his incipient grimace—eyes squinted, teeth clenched—which seems neither quite like the angry expression of the *maniac*, nor the blank face of the *stuporously insane*. Dr. Foley feels another twinge of panic: the condition of the facial muscles is supposed to reveal much, to a trained alienist.

Good evening, he says to Mrs. and Miss Underwood. The woman nods in reply; the girl remains silent. She shakes her hair farther forward but looks up at him through it. I've come to speak to Miss Underwood—

To *examine* her, says Mrs. Underwood. Her voice is low in pitch and slightly foreign in inflection. Please, let us be plain.

Of course. The parlor is crowded with the trappings of their up-and-coming social station—hectic rugs, porcelain curios, literary annuals fanned across low tables—and Dr. Foley handles his bag carefully, making his way toward the patient. With your permission, Miss Underwood, I'd like to check some of your functions.

The girl looks to her father, who leans in the doorway. I saw that fat doctor.

Today you're seeing this one, says Mr. Underwood. His wife rises from the settee to take a wing chair just at Foley's back.

Dr. Foley crouches in the small space afforded him, aware of how his clothes gap and pull in such a pose. He is not yet as rotund as Gibson, but...he shakes his head, concentrates on assembling his ophthalmoscope. As he screws the lens and dial onto their ivory handle, he glances at the girl. Her pupils are dilated. Because of the dimness of the room, or due to her illness? Perhaps the condition of her optic disks will tell him something. But she closes her eyes when he draws closer.

Come now, Miss Underwood, it's only a matter of our looking at each other through this little glass. His free hand rises toward her, falls away. If the girl will not respond, Foley cannot very well pry her eyelids open. Will you let me measure your pulse-trace? I can measure your father's, too, if you like.

The sphygmograph clanks as he withdraws it from his bag, and, at the sound, the girl folds her arms behind her. Foley does not bother to retrieve his thermometer or his aethesiometer. A melancholic may fear strange instruments, according to Spitzka. Maybe, then, her reactions to his tools are of more value than the measurements he hoped to take. Anyway, there's nothing definitive in physical symptoms, not in this matter. He cannot trust the evidences of his normal practice.

Amy was examined by our regular doctor to ensure that she hadn't been…harmed…last month by one of my work crews, says Mr. Underwood. I assume Gibson told you about all that?

Dr. Gibson had told him that the girl was running off with men. She has not the look of it, not as Spitzka accounts: 'the nymphomaniac betrays her condition, if not in every gesture, in every glance.' Dr. Foley blushes thinking about that passage. Is it possible that he is so inexperienced as not to recognize those gestures? He is desperately inexperienced, though of course now is not the time to think about such matters. Not when he is crouched at the feet of a girl who could be a sex maniac. What if she were to sniff out his virginity, with the heightened senses of the insane? But Foley nods in response to Mr. Underwood's question: Gibson had said that the girl showed no signs of recent sexual activity. It's a good thing Foley hasn't been asked to repeat *that* examination. And now perhaps the girl is assessing him, waiting to spring. What if she is violent? What if she is perfectly sane, and he can't see it?

Foley hoists himself onto a tasseled ottoman, hitching around so he can see all three of the Underwoods.

Your parents have asked me to come here and speak with you, Miss Underwood—about your illness. Do you understand?

She shakes her head.

No? Well, tell me, ah…do you have any trouble sleeping?

The girl doesn't respond, but Mrs. Underwood nods vigorously. I hear her dashing about her room at night, says the stepmother. Rattling the door and windows.

Are these kept—? Dr. Foley loses his voice for a moment.

Locked, affirms Mr. Underwood. To prevent her from harming herself.

Is it somnambulism? Have you ever found yourself awake in a different room of the house, Miss Underwood, without knowing how you came to be there?

The girl looks at her hands—and, following her gaze, Foley shudders. The backs of both are webbed with angry scratches; her nails are filthy stubs. Mrs. Underwood sighs loudly.

She is not a sleepwalker, doctor. It is her running off during the day that causes us to act so at night.

It's not safe, we know, says Mr. Underwood. Fires and whatnot. The point is that she's not safe here anymore.

Miss Underwood, says Dr. Foley. Your parents are concerned about your whereabouts and your well-being. Why do you leave the house without telling them where you've gone?

She shakes her head. They put me here.

Yes, well…it seems a very comfortable place to be, from the looks of it and—well, what is it that you do when you leave?

The girl pulls the ends of her hair under her chin, tight against her neck like the strings of a bonnet. She doesn't answer.

Do you pay visits—see friends?

Every soul she knows is back in Ionia, says Mr. Underwood. She's got no one to visit.

Foley nods, heartened by this reminder that he's better established in the area than the Underwoods. And the mention of friends seems to have roused the girl. She's watching him with her pale blue eyes. He has seen eyes like the Underwoods', eyes of the same color and cool flatness; he has seen them on an Eskimo sled dog, in a circus show. Those dogs tear apart animals not of their pack. But he won't be unnerved.

Ionia is a long ways off. You must miss your friends?

The girl blinks at him. She opens her mouth, stops.

She is forever running off into the woods, says Mrs. Underwood. As her mother used to. Her mother—

Ask her about the whiskey, says Mr. Underwood, frowning at his wife.

Are you fond of whiskey? Foley asks, grateful for the prompt.

The girl glances at her father. No.

Foley wipes his forehead. Do your friends give you whiskey, there in the woods?

Amy, says Mrs. Underwood. The girl wriggles back in her seat. Tell the doctor how you stole from those girls, at Miss Carter's School.

I didn't!

You took Lucy Sewall's Christmas annual, says her stepmother. You took a set of handkerchiefs from that Smith girl. You fought

Miss Carter when she tried to take those things back. She drew blood, doctor, biting.

Like a dog, Foley thinks. He swells and deflates, vindicated, uneasy. May I ask about the family history?

Again the Underwoods glance at each other. Amy, says Mr. Underwood, would you bring in coffee for Dr. Foley?

And cake, urges Mrs. Underwood, stretching out her pale hand for the girl's ravaged one. It is a transparent ploy, but Miss Underwood doesn't resist, even seems eager to be led from the room.

As soon as they are gone, Mr. Underwood drops into the empty wing chair. He balances on the edge of the seat, leaning near Foley.

What's your opinion, doctor?

I, ah…I still need to hear the family history, and with the women gone—

The first Mrs. Underwood was a suicide. Mr. Underwood rubs his forehead. There's your history. She had spells like Amy's of wandering off. After Amy was born, she wasn't ever right.

Oh, dear. Foley's collar sticks even closer to his neck. Does the girl know?

Would you tell her? That sort of thing passes in the blood, doesn't it?

Foley closes his eyes, recalling the close-set pages of Spitzka. Maternal influences have been found to be significant, in the transmission of insanity. But illness after pregnancy is also very common…a disorder unto itself.

She cut her own throat, doctor. Do you call that common? And now here's Amy, wandering off and coming back with her dress torn and whiskey on her breath. I didn't know enough to help my wife, Dr. Foley. I'm wiser now.

I am very sorry, says Foley—and wasn't he always, when in medical school their cadavers came to them with 'suicide' as cause of death? A terrible waste! Still, Mr. Underwood, if your late wife suffered from *puerperal* insanity—

Amy has run away from or ruined every situation we've put her in. She made a mess of school; she wouldn't take the water cure or sit still for any of the treatments we tried downstate. My wife has gone in for everything—but doctor, it's wearing on Mrs. Underwood, to spend every minute wrangling a girl Amy's size.

Foley nods. Mrs. Underwood's nerves must be under terrible strain....

That's just what Gibson said. He said if she could only restore her nerves, her other functions would steady. Her reproductive functions, for example.

You have hopes, then—despite.... Dr. Foley waves his hands, reluctant to reiterate all of the bad luck that childbirth has brought the Underwoods.

We've had lots of hopes, doctor, but they don't come to term. Something always happens to spoil them. You could help with that.

Foley meets Underwood's gaze, full of suffering and self-interest. The man's daughter is plainly peculiar. But—Foley clears his throat. Is Miss Underwood violent toward others? That is, you mentioned that she bit this Miss Carter. Has she ever assaulted you, or your wife?

Assaulted us? Mr. Underwood raises his eyebrows. She's only a girl, doctor.

It is a painful question, I'm sure, but if Miss Underwood poses a threat to those around her, that makes a very good case for commitment. So...think well, sir. I can wait.

Do you need me to say yes? Underwood's lips tighten. Is that it? Why don't you just take another look at her and make up your mind? Rose! Come back in.

The two women re-enter without even the pretext of a coffee tray, though crumbs of something linger on the girl's lips. An apple strudel, maybe—if Mrs. Underwood is as German as she sounds—and Foley's disobedient stomach grumbles. Now is not the time to pine for sweets, not with the two women facing him again from the settee. Hovering between them, Foley imagines a third, who tugs at her loose hair as Miss Underwood does, who stares at him as the girl does, half dazed. Foley must question them both: mother and daughter. He clears his throat, tries to smile.

Miss Underwood, I know young people can be restless and impulsive. I remember those feelings myself. But tell me: do you ever try to stop yourself when you have the impulse to run away, or to steal? Do you think of the consequences?

The girl bites her chapped lower lip; it cracks to blood. She touches the spot with her tongue. Dry and pale, that tongue should be a clue.

Miss Underwood, who tells you to do these naughty things? Is it your friends? Or—he shifts his weight, closes his eyes—is it your mother?

Mrs. Underwood gasps and *Sir!* her husband says, rising from the wing chair.

But the girl blinks at him. Her face is covered in scabs, and he knows that the insane are capable of far greater self-harm than this. Her pupils are dilated, her nostrils flare: she is plainly excited by his question, but she does not stir from her seat. She nods her head sharply, folding her hair again around her face. The gesture obscures her features; does it answer his question?

To the rest of his inquiries, Miss Underwood makes no reply.

If only she would! But what he has seen is enough, according to Spitzka—and according to the Underwoods. The girl is deluded as to the whereabouts of her friends; possessed by imperative impulses to run off, steal, take spirits and disrupt her own person; and subject to emotional disturbances—anger, anxiousness. She seems on the whole secretive, perhaps paranoid; and, in all likelihood, mentally weak. Add to that the hereditary strain—maybe. He could fashion from these symptoms a diagnosis of mania…or even of melancholia. Insanity of pubescence remains also a possibility. Are hers shallow and sham emotions? Is she liable to behave in a silly and changeable way? Foley has not seen enough to know. Knowing the girl better, Dr. Gibson might be able to say for sure. How much simpler it would be to simply corroborate whatever diagnosis Gibson made! But, instead, Dr. Foley is tasked with assessing the girl on his own. This is not like making a diagnosis of 'flu or fever; it is rather more like detecting a cancer, without being able to precisely state its size or prognosis.

Dr. Foley holds the physician's certificate in his hands, with the blank fields where he is to insert his name, place of residence, qualifications—and rationale. 'The said _____ is insane, and a proper person for care and treatment.' 'I further certify that I have formed this opinion upon the following ground, viz.:*__________________ __________________ *Here insert delusions, insane conduct, or other evidences of insanity.' Her parents have called upon him to do this. In her wordless way, maybe the child has, too.

Dr. Foley draws a pen from his pocket. If Dr. Gibson, her family doctor, has prepared such a document—surely that man must know! And if Foley doesn't give them *his* certificate, it's not as though they will drop the matter. No. In refusing, he would only set them the challenge of finding another qualified physician in this thinly populated corner of the state. A person not related to them or involved with the operations of the admitting hospital. How much of Foley's practice will consist of such examinations? How many such certificates will he submit to the probate judge, over the course of his career? He will have to write as small as he can to fit his evidence into this form. He has not been given room to elaborate on her case. It is not, he understands, his place.

I, <u>Lysander Foley</u>, a permanent resident of Petoskey, [permanent? he fights the impulse to strike the word] *in the County aforesaid, being a graduate of* <u>Western Reserve University</u>, *and having practiced as a Physician* <u>4</u> *years, hereby certify under oath that on the* <u>10</u>th *day of* <u>September</u>, *18*<u>89</u>, *I personally visited and examined* <u>Amy Aurelia Underwood</u>, *of* <u>Petoskey</u>, *a* <u>female</u> *aged* <u>17</u> *years, by occupation a* <u>none</u>, *and that the said* <u>Amy Aurelia Underwood</u> *is insane, and a proper person for care and treatment.*

Dr. Foley signs his name to the form and writes himself out of the girl's story.

Chapter One

THE DOCTOR IS A MAN trained in the old system, the system of moral treatment. He has staked his career on the therapeutic power of a well-ordered environment: on pure food, adequate rest, wholesome influences, wholesome occupations. These will cure the disorders of the ordinary brain, those strains of mania or melancholia brought on by wear or shock. To the patients who will not be cured, who suffer from organic or degenerate diseases of the brain—dementia, epilepsy, alcoholism, hysteria, syphilis, senility, paranoia, delirium—his hospital offers a generous refuge.

His hospital is a public institution, built in 1885 after Dr. Kirkbride's linear plan. At the center of the main building lie the administrative offices, the pharmacy, the kitchen, and the doctors' apartments. The men's and women's wards extend north and south in symmetrical stepped wings. Convalescent patients are housed nearest to center, then intermediate, and, at the farthest removes, the most disturbed. The hospital is the largest institution in this part of the state; five years after its erection, it remains the most modern, with forced-air ventilation, indoor toilets, a telephone system, electric lights. Stumbling upon its vast grounds, a stranger might think himself in an arboretum, or, approached from other angles, a dairy farm, an apple orchard, the kitchen garden of a small city. The stranger might mistake the hospital *for* a small city, built of clean yellow brick, thriving and self-contained.

There are nearly 700 patients at the hospital, and the doctor knows every one of them by name. He can recite their histories; he corresponds with their loved ones. He is the superintendent of the hospital's affairs, and he is its final authority in every course of treatment. Even his wife is involved in his work. She pays visits to the wards, invites women upstairs for tea. Most of the female patients are in their middle age—her age. Many of them have been ill-treated. 'Domestic infelicity' is a common exciting cause of their insanity, as is 'grief, care and anxiety.' There are many women with whom the doctor's wife cannot converse. They are Swedish or Finnish or Dutch. They are farmer's wives and farmer's widows. They shake with palsy; they cannot sit up for the pain of breathing. They were found delirious in a boarding house downtown; they were discovered waist-deep in the lake. They see things; they hear things; they speak in tongues.

The patients come from all walks of life, but the humblest walks are best represented. For most, the wards are more comfortable than the homes they have left. There are oriental carpets on the floors, potted plants hanging from the ceiling beams. On every ward, a piano or an organ, and always fresh flowers from the greenhouses. The patients are fed nourishing foods and kept clean and warm. Restraints are rarely used. The doctor has found that this manner of living—separate from society but not degraded, in the borderland between the town and the country—will elevate even the most debased patients.

The doctor advises that patients be brought to his hospital in full knowledge of where they are headed. He meets all but the most dangerous in the receiving room, at the center of the main building. They come with their spouses or their siblings, their off-spring or their neighbors. They come in the grip of their father and their stepmother.

The father, Mr. Underwood, manages the northern interest of the local lumber baron. Even in a tailored sack coat, he carries a whiff of pine sap about him; he sits the couch like a man better used to horseback than to horsehair cushions. His fair wife is corseted, tucked, gathered, and bustled into a blue traveling suit. She looks too young to have mothered the girl they hold between them.

The girl, Amy, is seventeen. Her medical history includes the usual childhood diseases and the onset of menstruation at age fourteen, roughly coincident with her psychic troubles. Over the past three years, her behavior has become erratic, her attachments shallow. Indifferent toward her family, she is swayed by strangers and prone to running away. She is destructive at times and has grown, of late, increasingly careless of her person. The parents have chronicled too the hapless efforts of their family doctor: cups to the back of the neck, mustard casts, draughts of quinine with iron. Most recently, they tried a water cure. A relic, the doctor might himself say, damp quackery. But he spares them his censure as he sits opposite them, reviewing their two requisite certificates of insanity. The referring doctors cite 'pubescence' as the probable exciting cause of the girl's illness; one makes note of delusions.

We had to cut short the water cure, Mr. Underwood says. She got ahold of whiskey.

The doctor nods. And her schooling?

Country schools until she was fourteen, and, last year, a term at my late wife's alma mater. She was expelled in December for stealing.

It isn't a case of the wicked stepmother, says the stepmother. I have loved this child since she was born.

My late wife and Mrs. Underwood were first cousins, explains Mr. Underwood. On their paternal sides, that is. Amy and Rose here were brought up together, by Amy's grandmother that was Rose's aunt. That's before Rose and I married.

I see, says the doctor; he will untangle that knot later. Now he takes the girl's wrist in his hand. Her pulse is normal, her fingers warm and limp. She does not have the poor circulation indicative of chronic masturbation—that enervating habit so often found with pubescent insanity. Still, her expression is apathetic; her complexion is oily and inflamed.

In our climate, the nervous organization of a young girl is very sensitive. He smiles at the girl. Do you know where you are, my dear?

She looks at the carpet. These are ugly.

But durable. He scuffs his feet against the nap. Can you tell me what kind of place this is?

She knows why she's here, her father says. The girl bends forward, propping her chin on her knees to study the rug. Mr. Underwood's low forehead and flat-bridged nose are repeated on her face; her dark hair and pale eyes are like his. But in her mental weakness, she does not take after him: her documents note no hereditary taint on the father's side. The late mother is another story: suicide following puerperal insanity. Was this due to sepsis, or something else? The doctor regards the stepmother, the dead woman's cousin. She does not meet his gaze.

She gives me no peace, says Mrs. Underwood. Amy was a dear child, and we hoped to keep her home through these troubles… but I cannot manage her.

My wife is delicate, says Mr. Underwood. She's been advised to avoid strain.

I would have advised the same, the doctor says. He resists the urge to advise more: that Mrs. Underwood give up her corsets. I hope the trip wasn't too hard on your nerves?

It was perfectly comfortable. I look forward to—Amy! Stop!

Pulled upright by her stepmother, the girl offers a blank face, dropping the strand she's worked loose from the rug. A burgundy thread, which, tugged, has left a long pucker in the rug's (admittedly, ugly) design.

I am very sorry, says Mrs. Underwood. Apologize, Amy!

I am very sorry, the doctor says, smiling, to have offended Miss Underwood's sensibilities. You'll find no such eyesores in your room, Miss Underwood. Shall I show you there now, before your parents leave?

He guides the girl and her parents from the reception room down the broad tiled corridor at the building's center. They pass the marble staircase that stretches up to the doctors' quarters; they pass through a locked door into the service stairwell, then up a dim flight, through another firedoor, and on to the long, carpet-strewn hall of convalescent ward seven. No one sits at this hour in the rocking chairs that stand between the open bedrooms. The ward is quiet.

Where is everyone? Mr. Underwood nudges an empty rocker. Have you cured them all?

The doctor smiles over his shoulder, leading them along. The women leave the ward for two walks daily and calisthenics several times a week. Those unable to take exercise will be in the dayroom, just around this corner—ah, good afternoon, ladies!

Good afternoon, the women chorus, and their attendant sets

aside the novel from which she's been reading aloud. The group is clustered around a bay window, beneath the ward's cherished arbor of philodendron. Afternoon light makes the glossy leaves glow, brightening the faces of the invalid women. Here is Mrs. Heffron, who suffers from kidney disease and melancholia; Miss Roosa, whose religious delusions emanate now and then from the cancer on her cheek; Mrs. Stigar, widowed and calm in her wheeled chair. They are chronic patients, women whose physical conditions excited their psychic troubles and prevent their leaving. All three are also gossips, sneaking glances now at young Miss Underwood, but they still manage to respond cordially to the doctor's inquiries. The scene is cheerful, the women contented—yet Mrs. Underwood remains unimpressed.

They are so still, she whispers, just out of the patients' earshot. Her long fingers wrap tightly about her stepdaughter's upper arm and her large features quiver, as fragile as porcelain. She is a crane-like woman, beside whom the girl seems a goose: plain, solid, cross.

They are unwell, the doctor reminds her. If they had been brought here sooner, they might be stronger. It's best to treat *any* illness at its onset.

Best not to wait, echoes Mr. Underwood. My wife can appreciate that, doctor. Which of these is Amy's room?

Miss Underwood will be on the middle intermediate ward, the next ward over.

What does that mean? the stepmother asks, her voice rising. Why won't she stay here?

My practice is to introduce patients onto the intermediate wards and adjust that assignment as necessary. The doctor smiles: it's natural that the family should be nervous. Come, he says. Ward nine is very comfortable, too.

The whispering Underwoods follow him past a dining room and an empty visiting parlor, through the firedoor between wards. They cross the landing of another service stairwell, pass through another locked door onto intermediate ward nine. A long hall like the last one, ward nine extends to their right, but Mrs. Underwood stops with Amy just over the threshold, beside French doors admitting to a sun porch. The two look out at the chapel, the laundry, the shop building: the doctor identifies each for them. As they watch, female patients wearing kerchiefs and aprons pour from the laundry. The women take spots leaning against the sunny wall of the building, talking and laughing, on break from their afternoon shift. Some of those women come from this ward, he tells them.

Doctor, says Mrs. Underwood, Amy will not need to work for her keep. And I wonder, should she be kept among those that do?

Work is a therapy, ma'am, not a form of payment. The doctor locks and tests the firedoor, proceeding carefully. We are by design a mixed institution, so you can expect Amy to be in regular contact with indigent patients.

But…there *are* private hospitals? Mrs. Underwood straightens Amy's skirt, straightens it again.

At greater cost and farther away. That decision is yours, Mrs. Underwood—yours and your husband's.

This is where she belongs, says Mr. Underwood. As if oblivious to the conversation, the girl stares out the window, worrying a cluster of scabs on her chin. Stop it, her father says, seizing her forearm. No more of that now.

She shreds her hair, too, says Mrs. Underwood. And bites her fingernails down past the quick. What do these things mean, doctor?

He shakes his head. Anxiety, boredom…it is too soon to say. We all have our habits, ma'am, and not all of them symptoms.

Let him study her for himself, says Mr. Underwood. But the frown-lines that mark the man's face come out more decidedly as he catches the girl's hand again, clasps it between his own.

Miss Underwood's room is a narrow chamber, identical to all the others. The doctor makes a quick survey before standing aside to let the Underwoods pass. All is as it should be: an iron bedstead, a small table, a straight-backed chair. The plaster walls have been freshly washed, the polished plank floor is still damp from the mop, and a new black wool blanket has been laid out in anticipation of the girl's arrival.

Mr. Underwood strides straight to the window. He tugs at its fixed sash, then turns, nodding, to the doctor. Good—but how is she to get fresh air?

The attendants have keys. See here. The doctor shows him where a little turnkey enters the window frame. And the wards are very well ventilated by air ducts. Have you not noted the cleanness of the air?

It is like a prison cell, says the stepmother. Planted in the doorway, she trembles so that the girl, whose arm she still grips, seems to tremble, too.

The rooms are simple, the doctor says. Intended for rest, not for morbid isolation. And of course the patients are allowed personal items, to make the rooms more home-like. We ask that you consider the risks associated with the things you send, but there's no reason Miss Underwood shouldn't have comforts.

Mr. Underwood shakes the bed frame; bolted to the floor, it doesn't budge. She won't have a roommate, then?

The doctor shakes his head. This ward is made up of a dozen private rooms and a six-bed dormitory. The dormitory is very comfortable for some of our patients, but not what I would recommend for a young lady like Miss Underwood.

Young *lady*, Mr. Underwood repeats. The girl's topknot has fallen and she is splitting her dark hair from the ends up. Torn in two, the strands that frame her face frizz wildly. Is this a true compulsion—or a strategy for irritating her parents?

Begging your pardon, the girl will learn by example how to better herself. Would you care to go over the grounds?

We'll see them soon enough, I'm sure, says Mrs. Underwood. Our train….

Of course. The doctor draws the admission forms from his coat pocket, unfolds them on the bedside table. You can sign these right now, if you like.

Mr. Underwood waves away the doctor's pen and removes his own from a rich leather case, embossed with the lumber company's seal. His wife releases the girl long enough to sign her line on the payment bond, and then Underwood produces a check, as required by law, for thirteen weeks of Amy's care. When the ink has dried, the doctor folds the forms away again and guides the party back down the ward.

Here? The stepmother tries the door to the sun porch.

No, says the doctor, but he admits them anyway. The girl rushes immediately to the porch's wooden railing, pushing her face against the heavy screen that makes it impossible for her to jump. Mrs. Underwood draws her index finger across the screen and lifts it, black.

Ugh, she says, taking hold of her stepdaughter's waist. Filthy, Amy. Stop. From her handbag she draws a handkerchief and a bottle of toilet water, and wipes the girl's forehead. The girl receives this attention passively. Write to me, Mrs. Underwood says. I will write to you every day.

The doctor clears his throat. You will appreciate, ma'am, that a patient's adjustment to the hospital is vital to her recovery. Letters from home can sometimes impede this process. Why not wait a while and see how Miss Underwood progresses?

The stepmother glances quickly at her husband. I *will* write to my child.

Let's let the doctor direct Amy's treatment, says Mr. Underwood. At least for the time being. He pushes his daughter's loose hair away from her face and kisses her cheek. Be good, Amy.

It's only for now, says the stepmother. Only till you're better. She hugs the girl tightly. Remember that we love you.

The girl turns her back to them and presses her just-cleaned cheek to the sooty porch screen. So this is how they get on with each other. But if the Underwoods will catch their train, there is not time to repeat the ritual of cleaning her face, not time to coax her into a sweeter mood or to risk the tears that might follow. Instead, the doctor assumes a sympathetic expression and ushers the parents from the porch, nodding to an attendant to see to the girl. Over the course of his career he has been witness to many parting scenes and markedly fewer reconciliations. He observes a respectful silence now as he unlocks Mr. and Mrs. Underwood into the stairwell. Time will tell whether their daughter's disease is curable or not, whether her symptoms will progress or be arrested, reversed. But neither parent seems interested in discussing the case further. They rush silently down the service stairs, and, once unlocked into the building's center, offer him only the most perfunctory goodbye. So intense are they in their actions, so abrupt, suddenly, in their mannerisms, that they might be taken for patients themselves—paranoiacs, maniacs. They startle the receptionists as they hurry through the lobby. Is it the suggestiveness of the environment that provokes this behavior, or the difficulty of the decision they have just made? The doctor would assure them of the prudence of their decision, the therapeutic properties of this hospital to which they have committed their child. He would explain to them in greater detail the efficacies of the moral treatment—if they were not already gone.

During the first hours Amy is left to herself and no one will speak to her. The other women sit silently in their rockers; they are all old. This is a hospital, not a school—these women the sorts who call out from the poorhouse yard, fenced in and in rags. They are harmless there. Here, they rock and seem not to see her. They are unwell, she knows.

The women in white shirtwaists are attendants—in charge. They order the others into line, they unlock the doors, and they walk at the front and back of the line down the stairs and out the building and onto the grounds. Behind the building are hills and trees; in front of the building is a lawn scabbed with stumps. In another direction are fields and there are men working far off and cows grazing nearer. The only fence is that holding the animals. Amy follows the attendants down a broad lane, matching her pace to the woman's beside her.

Where are we going? she asks.

Nowhere.

How long will we walk?

Till the attendants have tired.

They pass the hospital three times. The fourth time, the attendants say stop. The attendants count the women again and again until the larger one says—this new girl. This new girl is making the count odd. Why didn't you say something? she asks. She is taller than most men and speaks with a strange accent. I didn't know, Amy answers. But the attendant has turned away. She wears all the keys like a corsage at her waist; when she unlocks the door, the women file up the stairs and back to their ward. There are women who fall at once onto the thick chairs that line the walls, and there are women who fall to chores.

What do I do? asks Amy. The women, rocking, do not respond.

A woman passing with a bucket and brush says, Come with me. This woman's face is white in places where the skin is dead. Everywhere else it is very red. She stands in front of Amy until Amy stands too and then leads her to the end of the ward, to a door marked water closet. An outhouse smell comes through the door.

The woman gives Amy her bucket and brush. Go scrub them floors and bowls.

A poor woman does that.

No, you do.

The mottled woman waits and Amy pulls the door open. Skirts pool beneath the two closed half-doors inside. The bucket is empty and it is too big to fill from the washbasins. She slips back into the hall and sees, opposite, a door marked bath. Against the far wall of this room stand three iron bathtubs and, between them, two straight-backed chairs. Her bucket fits easily under the nearest tub's faucet but there is a cage built over its handles; her fingers will not fit between the wires. The floors in this room are tiled, slick; one wall is lined with closed cupboards. The two tall windows run with condensation. Amy sits down on a damp chair. She does not know how long she will be made to stay here. She was left for three months at Miss Carter's School for Girls.

Amy listens to the creak and thump of the rocking chairs in the hall. Listens to birds on the other side of the clouded closed windows. Their strange silhouettes jump on the windowsills. She rises to tap on the glass and the birds fly away. Wiping a pane clear she looks out at tangled gray trees. A trail of smoke over the treetops makes her think of a train cutting through the woods. A different train than the one that brought her here.

Humid air drags at her heavy dress. Sitting again, she sees an opening in the back of the faucet's metal cage. She slides her wrist between the wall and the wires and twists the hot water handle. Water spills into the bucket. It is loud, and the door opens outward, and the smaller attendant comes through. The attendant is quick; one arm holds Amy to the chair, and the other turns off the water.

How did you get in here?

The door was open.

The door is never open. How did you get in here?

I don't know!

The attendant grasps the back of Amy's dress and heaves. The dress is made of thick strong material that does not give but catches Amy under the chin, hoisting her from the chair and onto her toes. Her head is slung in heavy fabric and she cannot see the attendant, who forces her legs to move forward and catches hold of her wrists when her hands rise up toward her neck. Amy's throat is constricted and her mouth dry and open as the small attendant propels her across the tile and out the door. Their feet on the floor are suddenly silent, and then there are patches of black in her eyes, and these patches rush toward each other and block out everything.

Get up, the attendant is saying. Go and sit with the others.

Amy cannot speak. She is lying in the hallway on the runner.

Go and sit, the attendant repeats. There's water in the dayroom.

I was told to clean.

Go and sit! The attendant is almost as small as Amy, but, leaning over her, she seems larger. Amy scuttles backward but not quickly enough; she is caught by her forearms, lifted to her feet, and pushed toward the dayroom.

Among the others she finds an empty chair. Her feet are sore and her head and stomach ache for want of food. The women rock but all keep their eyes closed against her. She closes hers and opens them at the sound of a gong and of the women lining up.

All the way down the hall the smell of stewed meat grows stronger until they reach the dining room. There, silver and plates mark the places, and the women rush for spots at tables of four. Amy is shoved into an empty spot. It is like a restaurant just for women, all standing now with hands clasped in front of them. At *Amen*, they scrape back their chairs and sit. Amy is beside a woman who will not speak and across from a woman who will not eat. The attendants lean with plates in the corners of the room, gobbling their portions. The woman who will not eat watches Amy. Her hair is sparse and gray and her gray eyes are huge and red-rimmed in her wasted face.

Gluttony is a sin, the woman says. Covetousness is a grievous sin. I am talking to you, child. Take heed.

The others at their table eat quickly.

I'm hungry, Amy says, taking a bite of bread and butter.

The woman smiles. I was hungry once, too. Now I am full with the Lord.

Amy eats faster.

The Lord called upon me once to fast for thirty days. You must have seen the newspapers? They called me the Walking Skeleton of Charlevoix.

Amy shakes her head.

Heretics called it trick photography.

Aren't you going to eat your bread?

It wasn't a trick.

May I have your meat?

I was half my present weight.

Amy switches her empty plate with the full plate across from her. She eats two portions of meat, two portions of vegetables. She drinks both their glasses of milk. The thin woman does not interfere but folds her hands and watches.

Gluttony is a sin, the woman says for a second time. It is also against the rules.

No one saw.

Save Him who sees all. Here we eat only from our own plates.

An attendant bangs the small gong on the sideboard, and the patients rise and begin to clear the dishes. They stack their dirty plates and glasses on trays and send them down a dumbwaiter. Some women begin to scrub the tables and others to sweep the floor. The rest are rounded up by the large attendant. Amy shuffles with them back to the day room.

In a half hour there will be an evening program, and the fasting woman plays the organ to pass the time. The rest sit quietly. They are much older than Amy, older by years and years even than her stepmother. Maybe there will be other girls at the evening program; maybe she will be allowed to sit near them. Amy closes her eyes to wait but as soon as she does, the women are commanded to stand. The others begin to line up, but the small attendant says no.

Someone took a knife tonight. Either that person will step forward, or none of you will have your lantern show.

No one moves. Both attendants take hold of the woman nearest to them and run their hands over her body. She is the woman who wouldn't speak at the dinner table. She is silent as they shake her flannel skirt, paw through her apron pockets, peel down her wool stockings.

The rest of you will save us some time by undressing yourselves.

I will not have you handle me in such a manner, says the fasting woman. That child there is a born thief. That child's conduct is not in keeping with the Christian conduct of our ward.

What's that? says the large attendant. She jerks Amy's arm and a knife clatters to the floor.

This will not do, the fasting woman says. We are a God-fearing ward.

I didn't take it! says Amy.

Not much you didn't, says the smaller attendant. You mind yourself, or you won't be up here long.

Are we all to miss the program? asks the fasting woman.

Line up now! says the large attendant.

Not you, the smaller one says, and Amy gasps as again the attendant takes hold of her collar, her forearm against Amy's backbone, and pushes her down the hall, across the threshold of one of the bedrooms. The attendant presses her knees into the backs of Amy's to make her kneel on the bed. She keeps one hand hard on Amy's shoulder, undressing her.

I'll be back with your nightclothes, she says. Then the door locks from the outside, shaking slightly when it is tested. Amy is left alone and naked in the high narrow room. A black, rank blanket to wrap herself in. There is no light in the room but what comes in around the door. The window is a blank in the darkness. Through it, she cannot make out cows or fields. There is nothing homely here, no one here whose name she knows. For all she strains her ears, there is no sound from the ward; the other women have left. At home, at night, the trees make noise in the wind, and her parents' voices rise up through the vents:

Will you look at this dress! Why should I bother to mend such a rag?

Her father gave his low whistle: How'd she manage all that?

She claims she fell down the bluff. I could almost believe it.

It's true, Amy had whispered—but she didn't call down the air-shaft, didn't tell *them* that she knew how to fall. Back in Ionia she had fallen and fallen. It was hot and flat where they'd lived then, and everybody had a farm except her father, who had a lumber-yard. All the girls would bunch together at the mid-day recess, and, one at a time, they'd drop backward—a quick rush and hitch, caught just before the crash. She loved better to fall than to catch the others, though she loved that too, their weight straining her arms. Later all the girls linked elbows to walk home from school. Sometimes her father's lumber cart would pull up behind them, the big horses blowing. Everybody liked Amy best because he rode all the girls home. Her father smiled more, then; her stepmother smiled more and played dolls with her sometimes when they were supposed to be doing the mending.

Now they live in a town without any girls, where it's only hot at the dead end of the summer. The rest of the year, the wind off the lake makes their big house moan and the trees that sweep from the bottom of their yard to the edge of the lake sigh and fall against each other when the winds rise. They fall against each other and Amy fell through them, all down the bluff. She ran as hard as she could with the low branches catching at her and every time she tripped, she let herself fall, the branches tearing her clothes but catching her before she hit the ground. It was harder to fall face first than it had been to fall backwards. She ran and fell and was caught until she reached the place where the trees ended and the lake began. From their house they could see over the trees to the lake and the boats making the long trip to Chicago. They could watch the sunset through all the west-facing windows. At the bottom of the bluff, the lake lapped her toes. It came and went with pebbles in its waves that hit the shore and were drawn back out. Standing on the shore she let the cool water cover her boots, drawing her deeper. Sometimes she went with it, to her knees, to her hips. It was hard to pull her wet feet up the slippery hill home.

Did you see her poor face? Her arms are just the same, torn to bits. It's a wonder she hasn't broken any bones.

Well, she can't be playing around in those woods much longer. There's a crew coming in to clear out the hardwoods.

Not *our* trees? And Amy had felt herself falling, uncaught, as if the trees were already gone. Her father droned on in his business voice, flattening her stepmother's protests, until, at last, her stepmother's voice rose again, sharply: And how am I to *keep* her from the forest?

She's a girl: tell her to stay inside. Lock her up if you have to, but I don't want her underfoot. Her father had laughed. You'll be spared all this mending, at any rate.

If you knew how I worry, Nathan—that she might hurt herself—you would not joke.

Didn't you just say she fell down the bluff? You're making a big fuss over an accident.

I don't call it an accident. She does this to herself, these terrible scratches. You've seen her making them.

It's her age, Rose. Be firm and she'll come around.

What if she can't? What if she is like her mother?

She isn't! her father had shouted that night. He had ended the conversation, as he always did when Amy's mother was mentioned. Just once had Amy heard them say more. She listens for it, now, her mother's story, but no voices echo through the hospital vents. The ward is quiet. Amy slides her fingers over her scabbed face, works her fingernails across her cheeks. She has no idea of a way out of this place, no idea of the way back to her green trees or to those girls downstate. Only the map of her face is familiar—and the sting of each scab torn loose, the thrill of air across raw skin. In the bare room she finds a comfort.

Chapter Two

IT HAS BEEN ALMOST HALF a century since the doctor left his parents' farm, but he has never lost their habit of early rising. At four-thirty or five o'clock, he's simply awake, jolted sometimes by the childhood dread of oversleeping. His father never yelled those mornings that he came late to the barn, but neither would he speak to him directly for the duration of chores. Even now, a dream of his father's disappointment causes the doctor to hurry through his toilette, as though already behind on the day. The doctor's wife has never known such concerns; she sleeps habitually until eight o'clock. Her maid sleeps late, too. In the predawn hours, the only trace around the apartment of another waking person is a pot of coffee, sent steaming up the dumbwaiter. Every morning, the doctor drinks a strong cup before lacing his boots and heading outdoors.

As he begins his morning walk, the watchmen are finishing their night rounds. It will be another hour before the main building is fully awake, but lights burn in the basement where breakfast is being prepared. The spice of dying leaves tinges the dark air, together with the ripe stench of manure, the soft vegetable taint of the marsh at the hospital's southern edge. Underlying it all is the cool exhalation of the lake, a quarter mile to the north. Breathing deeply, the doctor crosses the hospital's front lawn, wending his way between stumps. He skirts the men's wing of the main building and passes the dark cottages of the tuberculoids and the senilics. He follows the side lane past the carriage house and the horse barn, whose inhabitants nicker softly at his footfalls. Ahead, the farmhouse is already empty. The doctor passes the tool shed and the breeding pen and nears the dairy barn. Its doors stand open; inside, electric bulbs burn. It is a huge brick building, with a haymow twice the size of the hospital's calistheneum. It is a tribute to the hospital's self-sufficiency; it is a wonder.

Standing in the doorway, the doctor looks out over the glossy backs of thirty stanchioned Holsteins. More cows bellow in the barnyard, waiting to be milked, waiting to feed the patients still sleeping on the wards. The hospital's herd is already famous for its productivity—and if the patients on this work crew do not all recover from their illnesses, they rarely worsen, braced up by their good, familiar work. In the bustling barn, the doctor cannot even be sure which men are the patients and which the supervisors. Only when men pass him, carrying full buckets to the milk house, does he recognize them by name and diagnosis: acute alcoholism, hypochondrical insanity, melancholia with delusions of persecution. All are too busy to say more than hello, and the doctor remembers his youth in this way, as a period of work so intense that it precluded any other considerations. But he found his calling elsewhere than in a dairy barn.

James the Brain, his schoolmates had called him. For their parts, his parents usually called him by another brother's name: Pete—no, Johnny—no…Jim! The fourth of five sons, he'd been the only one to leave the farm. He had forged through high school and medical college without drawing objection or even memorable comment from his father—who, after all, still had the other boys at home to help. The doctor had taken his degree at Penn, had interned at the Pennsylvania Hospital for the Insane under Dr. Kirkbride, the father of the moral treatment. He had begun his career in Philadelphia and then, seeking a more intimate setting, spent nearly a decade tending the health resorts that ringed that city.

From time to time over those years, he'd driven back to Berks County to visit the home place, interrupting chores with news about his doings. He doesn't fault his folks for always turning the conversation back to cows or politics—subjects they knew something about. In '61 the two brothers bracketing him in age had both enlisted—men already in their thirties, but bachelors yet in the family's own tradition of early industry and late marriage. The doctor had decided to remain in civilian practice, going west in '63 to an open position at the Kalamazoo asylum. If his family understood that his medical work was a war in itself, they had not been proud of him for waging it—or particularly interested in the frail girl he wed before departing. He and Diana disappeared 'clear across the country,' and not once in the years since have any of his family members come to look for them. Nor has the doctor had much time to go back, except in hasty visits, carved out of medical conferences and subordinated to the demands of Diana's people. His soldier brothers were lost at Vicksburg and Fort Sanders; his parents are gone now, too—and only his two eldest brothers are left, widowed septuagenarians still working the farm. If he sees them again in this lifetime, it will be at his own instigation.

Now the doctor steps outside of his barn. The chickens have just been released into their yard opposite and cluck nervously in the half-light, stretching their sleep-stiffened wings. They scatter when he walks past—and then past the blacksmith's shop, where the forge is heating, through the first row of the ripe apple orchard and back toward the main building. The sun begins to rise as he nears the protrusion of the chapel. Standing in its lee, he looks up at the hospital's glowing windows and the sky turning blue above them. He has approved the morning use of electric lights on the wards, so long as it is not recommenced until relatively late in the evening. He's like his father in at least this respect, vigilant against waste.

The first bell sounds, rousing the patients. The doctor lets himself in through the chapel's side door and makes his way to the front of the large, dark room. Electric lights are well enough for others—therapeutic, even, for the patients—but he does not need light to find his way. He knows the hospital's hallways and tunnels by memory, and he knew them this well before he had ever set foot here, so perfect an example is this hospital of the linear plan. Anyone familiar with Dr. Kirkbride's architectural model would be as well-oriented here: placed in the scullery and asked to find his way to the most-disturbed wards, a doctor from the Pennsylvania Hospital, the Danvers State Hospital, the Hudson River State Hospital (and how many others?) would not falter in his course. New asylum designs have sprung up in the last decades; debates have raged among superintendents about the best means of caring for the insane, and even about the possibility of cure at present, without means of intervention *at the cellular level*. New language, which the doctor greets with interest—and skepticism. If insanity were simply a disease of the body, he would join the camp of the young men, the dogged somaticists, who insist on physical causes and physical cures. But their position discounts the role of the mind—that intangible organ—which cannot be reduced to just the grey folds of the brain. A well-ordered environment and positive moral influences *are* often curatives, as Dr. Kirkbride knew, as the doctor knows, as the men in his dairy barns are daily proving. Sometimes the cure is amazingly simple: removal from a troubling environment.

Early in the morning, there is a sound like a fire alarm and then the sound of someone crying. Huddled under the black blanket, Amy presses her face to her mattress and closes her eyes. The alarm stops but the crying continues. Then a door opens outside the darkness she's made and her blanket is pulled back to bright electric lights.

Get up, says the small attendant. Didn't you hear the bugle? What did you do with your nightgown? The attendant's hands clamp around Amy's shoulders, pulling her off her stomach and onto her knees. Amy wraps her arms around her bare chest. Well, here then, says the attendant. Here's your things for today. If you're as modest as that, why didn't you stay in your nightgown? She strips the blanket from the bed. As Amy shivers into her chemise and drawers, the attendant looks under the mattress, under the chair, under the table. There's nothing there. The attendant rubs her temples, stares. Where did it get to? she says.

I never had one, says Amy. She tugs up her hose, knit from something coarser than what she's used to. The underskirt is strange, too.

You must have. The attendant shakes her head.

No one came, says Amy. She finishes buttoning her dress, but it comes out unevenly. There's no mirror in her room. Please, she says. The attendant does not hear.

You'd better not have torn that mattress, says the attendant.

You'll learn quick that we don't stand for tricks around here. Now get to the dayroom. It's time for breakfast. The attendant stays in the room after Amy leaves, searching.

Down the hall past empty rooms to the dayroom and the women waiting for an order to line up. Some seem still asleep, but when the order is given, they rise and file down the hallway to the room full of tables. They take their places, standing each behind a chair; they pray, they sit. There is oatmeal and coffee or chocolate. Around Amy, women eat, but when she takes her seat, the Walking Skeleton takes the seat opposite. The Skeleton sips her coffee black and watches as Amy stirs and stirs her cereal. When Amy raises her spoon, the Skeleton kicks her sharply in the shin, and Amy does not cry out, but she does not try to eat again, either. The gong is struck and she has not tasted her breakfast. Then the others push back their chairs and, left sitting, she lifts her bowl to her lips. Her mouth is filled with the cold, flavorless cereal when the Skeleton lunges across the table. Thin hands reaching for her face—she topples her chair backward to escape them.

Careful, says the larger attendant, pulling her to her feet. Four legs on the floor. The attendant is mild this morning, and Amy clings for a moment to her forearm, her eyes watering from the pain of swallowing unwillingly. Let's have that bowl, now, the attendant says. Come on. She prizes it from Amy's fingers and, with its rim, scrapes oatmeal from Amy's bodice before passing it across the table. On the other side, the Skeleton slops Amy's uneaten cereal into a bucket, stacking the bowl to send down the dumbwaiter.

It is an effort to walk to the dayroom. Once there, like the others, Amy sleeps.

The attendants wake the women for the morning walk. Three times around the lane, the women straggling and stumbling. There are men in the distance in the fields, and men nearer, working on the lawns. A group of men walks the lane in the opposite direction; the women, walking faster, pass them many times. All but two of the men are very old and unkempt; the young tidy ones hail the female attendants. By the third time they pass, they are using each other's first names: Hello, Jenny. Hello, Frank. Hello, say some of the patients to the young men, but as if struck deaf, the men do not respond. Though the group of old men is allowed to sit on the lawn, the women are counted and taken back inside, where half of them vanish. The attendants sit at a table together with *Godey's* magazine and some of the women sit near them, begging to see the pictures.

Do you care for these things? asks the woman sitting beside Amy. The cuffs of her dress are very plain and very white.

Amy shakes her head no.

Then you are more sensible than the rest of them. My name is Mrs. Edward Littleton. What business is your father in?

He's a woodcutter.

Oh!

When does the doctor come, please?

Mrs. Littleton laughs. The doctor has already been here today!

He hasn't!

He sent me his wife's regards this very morning. You were probably asleep—like the rest.

When does the mail come, then?

The matron brings it.

When will she be here?

Mrs. Littleton laughs again. She comes before the doctors, of course!

Amy stands and the larger attendant looks up. Where's my letter? Amy asks.

Shh, says the attendant. Might be you'll have one tomorrow.

I have to use the toilet, Amy says. She's heard other women say this when they leave the room, but instead she walks the length of the hall. She walks back and forth, past all the doors standing open outward. Every day at Miss Carter's School she had a letter. Every day, even when her stepmother could only manage a paragraph. Most of those letters were about meals and chores, but sometimes they told memories of the old times, when the two of them were younger—Amy and Rose, both cared for by Amy's grandmother. Amy was a baby then; Rose was fourteen, fifteen—not her stepmother yet. Amy's mother was dead, and her father was at the lumberyard, and only her stepmother can tell her about those days with her grandmother who is dead now, too. If there's no letter, does this mean that Rose has died? Amy walks to the sun porch, rattles its locked door, walks back. No one rocks in the hallway at this time of day, though, in some of the rooms, women are mopping. The mottled-faced woman is on her knees in one room, scrubbing. Another woman washes walls. No one speaks to Amy or tells her what to do.

Some of the open bedrooms are very clean. She enters one of these; at first, she is not sure that it isn't her own, so alike are the furnishings. But there's a book lying on the table, and, beside it, a hairbrush. She doesn't have anything of her own here—she was left without anything! The dress she's wearing is not even hers; brown calico, it's plainer than anything her stepmother would choose and too large in the bodice. Before, when they sent her off, they sent along books and brushes. This time, her father told her to put on her coat—and that was all he told her until their train drew near this city.

She sits down on the bed that's just like the one in her room. It is equally as hard and the black blanket is just as rough and strange. Even so, she knows that this is someone else's blanket, someone else's bed—and on the table, someone else's book. She draws the book onto her lap and opens it. On the front page is written *To Violet Minor on the occasion of her Confirmation, St. Paul's Lutheran Church, 1872*. This is the year Amy was born, the year her mother died. Under her fingers, the page begins to pull loose from its binding. It wrinkles in the middle, torn free at the top and bottom. She holds the page between her first finger and thumb until it comes apart entirely from the book. It is just the size of her apron pocket and thin and crisp, rustling faintly when she walks. *To Violet*. A note written to a flower. From a flower? From…Rose? Walking up and down the hallway, Amy heeds the soft crackle of paper in her pocket. Before she can decipher it, the gong rings for dinner, and they all line up.

The doctor tells his medical officers that, by their unwavering enthusiasm, they will set an example for the attendants. He knows, however, that this is not the only instruction his attendants need. At Kalamazoo, there had been infractions now and then: patients made to wrestle for the attendants' amusement or forced to care for one another while their caretakers loafed. Feeding tubes, restraints, sedatives used punitively rather than therapeutically. No attendant here has ever been accused of abuse, but the thought of it sometimes makes him walk more quickly on his rounds. The attendants are robust young people, associating all day with the infirm. They have not often had prior nursing experience; such work can have a depressing effect on the spirits. The doctor makes it a policy never to revoke a Sunday off, a free evening. He has set up a training school for those recently hired or seeking better positions.

Since the doctor himself cannot be spared, his three assistant physicians—West, Meijer, and Ingstrom—share the teaching. Classes are held in the chapel after morning rounds; the doctor occasionally observes from the back of the room. On this day, young Ingstrom is at the lectern, addressing a class of female attendants. It is rare that Ingstrom interacts with women in his hospital duties. With Dr. West, the oldest member of the hospital's medical staff and its chief pathologist, Ingstrom has primary responsibility for the men's wards. The doctor deemed this ward assignment prudent, in light both of Ingstrom's training and of the younger man's uncommonly good looks. Tall, dark, and impeccably groomed, Ingstrom and his moustache always cause a flutter at the patients' evening programs. It is doubtful whether Ingstrom could successfully conduct routine examinations of the female patients, let alone the kind of gynecological examination he's evidently lecturing about today. Now Ingstrom has situated a wheeled blackboard in the middle of the stage and positioned one of his students before it. A broad-shouldered girl, she holds a stick of chalk but does not write. Ingstrom addresses the others:

While we await Miss Breithaupt's drawing, who can name three symptoms of pelvic inflammation? Don't be shy—you are all learning.

Chairs creak and no one offers an answer. These are good girls, the doctor knows—embarrassed, perhaps, by these lessons.

One symptom, then? Even a child could name *one* symptom— could she not? Can no one draw from her reading or her own observations to name one symptom?

A girl near the front raises her hand. Discomfort? she says softly.

Discomfort? I am discomforted right now by the confusion I see—ought we to suspect that I have a pelvic inflammation?

No, sir, I mean discomfort of the uterus…burning and the like.

The poor girl is nearly whispering, and the doctor steps forward slightly, into a fall of light from the stained-glass windows. Seeing him, Ingstrom nods.

Very well, miss—you have at least the advantage of frankness over your classmates, if not the advantage of specificity. Miss Breithaupt, finally—can you draw the female reproductive system, or can't you?

She turns toward him, her long face made longer by vexation. The two curved lines she's drawn are vaguely reminiscent of ram's horns or fallopian tubes. I know it's not right, she says. But I can't do any better.

So I see. Ingstrom holds out his hand for the chalk; when she yields it, he sketches the organs with quick and expert strokes. You may take your seat, Miss Breithaupt, unless you've anything to add.

Her expression doesn't change, but she nods her head, watching as he shades and stipples his drawing. This Miss Breithaupt is older than some of the others, the doctor sees, silver veining the dull gold of her hair. The older women, having been working longer, often receive correction less meekly than do the younger girls. Now Miss Breithaupt strides to the edge of the stage and jumps off, her skirts lifting with the two-foot drop. The chapel echoes when her feet slap the floor, and Ingstrom, still embellishing his organ, winces. The other women lean toward one another, whispering.

Ingstrom brushes chalk dust from his hands and clears his throat, facing them. The group of you aspires to be nurse attendants. Very well. But whether from squeamishness or some ridiculous Victorian nicety, you are not devoting yourselves carefully enough to your studies. Our female patients very rarely present normal gynecological symptoms, and we doctors are sorely overworked.

The women grumble—you *doctors* are?—but Ingstrom continues: We are reliant on attendants for good information about patient symptoms. If you aren't capable of observing and recording such information, you simply aren't capable of succeeding as an attendant. I see here quite a few faces, in other words, destined for the scullery.

Miss Breithaupt raises her hand but speaks without waiting. How many years did you go to school, Mr. Ingstrom? And how many weeks is it now with us?

Good morning! the doctor calls before Ingstrom can respond. The doctor walks quickly down the long center aisle. Forgive my interruption, Dr. Ingstrom, class.

The women all scramble to their feet, recognizing him as he mounts the steps, takes the stage beside Ingstrom.

It is beyond me how we are to use them, Ingstrom mutters— barely under his breath.

You have done enough for today, sir, the doctor replies. He looks over the class, their plain faces inclined toward him. They are good girls, who want more than to clean house or scrub clothes. But what does Ingstrom know about any of that? His everyday suit is finer than the doctor's very best.

Allow me to commend you on entering the training school, the doctor says to the women. As Dr. Ingstrom just remarked, the role of the attendant is a vital one. All the persons under your care are invalids; no matter how physically sound some may seem, you must always remember that your patients are diseased in one of the body's most delicate organs. They are often quite incapable of judging whether they are receiving good or harm from their exertions. Thus, the attendants' ward notes must be minutely detailed, so that the doctors can tell what is to be done next.

The doctor pauses, caught between Ingstrom's impatient and the women's grateful gazes. Remember that care and compassion will save lives, he says. And trust that what we ask of you here is in the best interests of a very vulnerable population. And in *your* best interests, too, if you desire to better yourselves—as I can see that you all do. I thank you for this. My colleague, Dr. Ingstrom, also thanks you.

The women clap for him and he bows. Good morning to you, he says. You are dismissed.

Ingstrom takes the doctor's arm as the women file from the room. They are lazy, he hisses. And you have condoned it!

We are not training them to be doctors, sir. The doctor pulls away from Ingstrom's well-tended hand. In essence, they function as observing chaperones. We cannot expect them to study like medical students. It is of more importance that they know *where* the key organs are than that they can draw them.

But without trained nurses, how can this hospital make clinical advances?

The doctor smiles. I count it as an advance if we retain our attendants and teach them to treat the patients with kindness.

Ingstrom throws up his hands. If you will doom yourself to obsolescence, it is your own business. I am only the executor of your will.

Ingstrom's is a false humility that the doctor resents—but this pose does not surprise him in a doctor so young.

You are well-intentioned, I know, says the doctor. But think of the precedent you set by treating these women harshly. Be kind, Dr. Ingstrom, and try to be patient.

Of course. Ingstrom exhales loudly. Will that be all?

I won't keep you. You'll want a rest before your afternoon rounds.

I leave *that* privilege to my elders. Returning to the lectern, Ingstrom shuffles his notes into a neat stack and tucks them into a leather folio. He doesn't look again at the doctor as he strides from the stage. Morning light slashes briefly across the room when Ingstrom passes through the side door, onto the hospital's back yard.

Only when his assistant is out of range does the doctor allow himself to sigh. Ingstrom is willful, but he's careful and correct in his work, a favorite among the male patients and a favorite with the doctor's wife. But such petulant displays of temper throw everything else into question. The boy is plainly not suited for a superintendency, but does Ingstrom have the composure and character necessary even for an assistant physician? He's been in his position for nearly two years; surely this is long enough to settle in?

Turning, the doctor is startled by the chalk figure beside him: Ingstrom's reproductive system, disembodied and perfect. If disconcerting to him, how much more so to the congregants for the next morning's church service? But it's too exquisite to erase. The doctor wheels the chalkboard behind the stage's velvet curtain, to take its place alongside the magic lantern, the player piano, the crates of white tapers for Sunday services. All therapeutic tools, diversions meant to bolster the patients—as every element of this hospital will, so long as it is properly arranged.

At dinner Amy manages to eat: a full portion of meat and two potatoes. But at the evening meal, she's seated beside the Walking Skeleton, who eats using her left hand and continually bumps

Amy's right. Knocking Amy's fork on the floor, bruising her knuckles with a butter knife. The Skeleton reaches her thin arm under Amy's and snatches food from her plate—bread and butter, carrots. The Skeleton swallows both portions herself. Amy's food disappears before she can reclaim it, and the woman to her left has finished eating. Little remains but a basket of rolls on the sideboard, and Amy pushes back her chair, but the Skeleton is just as quick. Amy knocks her chair into the older woman's shins—dashes for the side of the room—bony hands scrabbling at her waist. Thin hands on her shoulders, pulling her back as she reaches the basket. She stuffs a bun into her mouth just as the attendants grab them both—the smaller attendant, as always, grasping Amy by the collar and the larger one pinning the Skeleton's arms to her sides. Spit it out, says the smaller attendant, tugging Amy's collar. Spit it out! But somehow, she manages to swallow, and she opens her empty mouth and smiles.

The patients clear the tables and file to the dayroom; there, a middle-aged woman in a dark wool dress sits sewing. Good evening, ladies, she says, and some of the women rush toward her. How do you do? she says to Amy, standing. I am Mrs. Morris, the matron. Would you care for a book? The woman hands her a copy of *Eight Cousins*. I will bring it back for you every week, she says. She passes out games and books to the other women and begins to read softly aloud to those nearest her. She shows the pictures around when she comes to them. Though it is a thick book—*Oliver Twist*—there seem to be many pictures. The matron's voice is like none that Amy knows, but moving gently over the words, it makes her throat hurt.

Amy doesn't realize the attendants have been absent until they are back, on either side of her. Get up please, the larger one says. Time for your bath. There's another patient with them, an old woman who squirms in the smaller attendant's grip. Come on, says the larger attendant. She takes Amy by the arm and the four of them walk down the hallway. They pass through the door marked bath, and the other patient, the old woman, immediately begins to undress. Beneath her graying underclothes, her bare arms are loose, her breasts long. Her shins are purple, black, and brown. There are bruises on the points of her hipbones, too. Amy stares at her nakedness.

Come on, the smaller attendant says. It doesn't make any difference to us. She reaches around Amy's waist to unfasten her apron, and Amy stands still, holding her breath—the hands like her stepmother's, tending to her. But rather than continue, the attendant gives Amy a little shove—Do it yourself, can't you? I'm not your maid—and Amy takes off her dress, her skirt, her prickly hose. She holds her clothes in front of her; when the attendant takes them away, she does not look at the old woman.

The tiled floor is slopped all over with muddy water and the tubs are full to their brims. The larger attendant rolls up her sleeve and pulls the stoppers out of both tubs. Amy stands with her arms crossed and watches the gray water drop, exposing layers of rings around the enamel. This room did not seem so dirty the day before. When the tubs have drained a quarter of the way, the attendant puts the stoppers back in place and runs new water, back up to the brims.

Get in, now, says the smaller attendant, and the old woman quickly does, settling with her back to the caged faucets, up to her chin in water. Amy puts her hand in the nearer tub. The water is not hot, and the room is cold, too.

Please, she says. I bathed the day before yesterday.

Please get in, says the smaller attendant and steps toward her. Amy lifts her leg high over the side of the tub and stands for a moment halfway in. She can feel grit on the bottom, can barely see her foot. All the way, miss. She brings the other leg in, too. Sits like the old woman, submerged, her body lost from the neck down. She has taken the curing waters—not so long ago—last month? Mineral-rich, hygienic…those waters were not like these. At the cure, she was made to drink a half a dozen tumblers of icy water in an hour's time. She was made to sit in cold water with her feet in hot water. She was wrapped for entire afternoons in wet sheets, kept wet by nurses with buckets and ladles. She drank water and was doused and douched with water until she felt sick without it and cold all the time, as though that were her natural state. Her stepmother would come every afternoon from another part of the resort—having had the sulfur baths and Swedish massage, having bathed in the lake and drunk ginger tonics. She would sit beside Amy and drink her own tumbler of water and say, I feel so much better. I feel my nerves entirely restored. Things will be better now, won't they, she would say. Her stepmother roamed the grounds freely while Amy took forced hikes at dawn. After her stepmother's visits, Amy shook in her wet sheets until one day, the woman next to her, a middle-aged woman, ruddy-complexioned, said, I have something better to drink. What they drank while the nurses weren't looking made Amy feel warmer and better; it made her relax as the doctors had advised her to. There was an afternoon when it relaxed her so completely that, swaddled like an infant, she lost her self-control. When the nurses realized the cause, they stood her beneath the ten-foot shower and let cold water fall over her until she was clean and stinging and crying for them to stop. Where did you get the whiskey? they asked, and, finally, she told them. Her stepmother came that afternoon to find Amy waiting in dry clothes. The fabric chafed after days of wetness and she cried all the way home, as the train's motion rubbed her skin raw. Her stepmother wept, too, repeating, what choice is left?

Sit up, says the small attendant, because Amy's mouth is beneath the bath water. The attendant holds her by the shoulder, and, with one hand, works borax into her scalp. Scrubs her neck and shoulders. Raise your arms, she says, and scrubs beneath them, quickly. Hold your breath. And she dips a bucket of water out of the tub, pours it over Amy's head. Presses a towel to Amy's face and helps her to stand. Dry yourself and put on your nightdress. When the old lady is dressed, too, they are walked back to the dayroom, where the matron is still reading. The attendants take the Skeleton next, the two of them to the one of her as she protests: to bathe through submersion is to profane the sacrament of baptism! But a plate of gingerbread is being passed around. The fire has been lit and the gingerbread is warm. Amy drowses near the matron until the attendants return and, lining the women up, give each a dose to drink, before locking them in their rooms for the night.

Chapter Three

IN HER ROOM, AMY LIES with her eyes open, her black blanket thrown back. Her nightgown is damp under the arms and around the neck, a wet oval across the small of her back, another over her stomach. Her legs stick together and she does not sleep. It might have been hours since she was put to bed; there is no moon to gauge by. It might have been minutes. The room is dark except for a yellow blur above the door.

Amy lies on her back with her hands folded over her stomach and just this slight pressure makes her stomach ache. She needs the toilet. The other side of the room seems farther away in the dark, but she's there before she expects to be, stumbling, stubbing her toe against the doorjamb. The doorknob does not turn; the door does not open. She knocks and there is no reply. She knocks, then reaches over her head, her fingertips just touching the transom window. The window doesn't tilt when she pushes it; she isn't tall enough to tap on the glass or to smash it. She isn't tall enough, even though she stretches.

While she's on her toes, something warm begins moving up her legs—a draft come under the door? It is as warm and heavy as a person's hands on her knees; it spreads steadily up the front and back of her. A feeling like warm hands or like warm water, and she stumbles, topples off her toes and against the door. She grasps the doorknob for support but there's nothing to support. The transom window recedes as she slides to the floor—slowly, it isn't a swoon. But her joints are suddenly weak, as though something has eaten them away…eaten them away or replaced them with velvet. Her body crumples like a heap of soft fabric. She can't get out of this room and though she needed to, badly, when she got up from bed, she doesn't mind, now, that she can't. That she can't get out matters less than the warmth that pulses in the small of her back. It feels nothing like taking spirits. Holding onto the doorknob, she shivers against the door. Her kneecaps grind into the floorboards. Her nightdress now is wet through. She closes her eyes, which won't focus on the square of light above, and she has never felt like this before. She has never felt such bliss. It does not stop, and she remains on her knees, receiving it.

When the alarm sounds, Amy's fingers unclench. She topples sideways, her head glancing off the floor. The floor, the door… her limbs are dead with sleep as she tries to work out where she is. Not at home, not at anyplace she's called home. Not at school. Her right hand is numb, cold, the fingers flexing life back into themselves only when she concentrates. Pins and needles pierce her calves and feet. Pricks of pain everywhere and she shivers, in her nightdress on the floor. A blanket—there is a black blanket on the bed behind her, and she drags herself toward it, struggling with her good left arm and the tops of her knees. Then, a key scratches in the lock; the door opens outward. She is a worm inching across the earth and the attendant is a bird that rushes down at her and lifts her up to the edge of the cot. The attendant presses on her legs; electric twinges explode under her skin. Amy screams: she knows where she is.

What's the matter with you? the small attendant says. What have you done to yourself? She pulls Amy, gasping, to her feet. Did you take a fit? Say so! Did they know about this when they brung you? There ain't nothing about that in your records. The attendant lifts the hem of Amy's nightdress, prodding her calves. Hold that up and take a step now. That's good—good. Now, what's the matter? What's the matter with you?

I was on my knees.

Praying?

No. Amy looks down at her swollen kneecaps.

Well, why then?

Amy shakes her head. I don't know.

The attendant sighs. You're supposed to stay in your bed.

I'm cold.

Here then. Here's your under-things. Your folks sent good, warm clothes for you, lucky girl. And here's your nice dress.

That isn't mine, Amy says. The attendant has brought the same large, plain calico as the day before.

Sure it is. See?

On the inside of the collar are stitched the letters AAU—her initials.

It's not mine!

It come straight from your trunk. Look how nice and new it is.

It doesn't fit me! Amy steps away from the bed, so that the open door is at her back. Her legs still tingle, but only a little.

The attendant's mouth is angry but her voice is calm. Come here, she says, and when Amy leaps for the hall, the attendant follows, one arm catching Amy's waist, the other pulling the door closed tight, so that the two of them are shut together in the room.

You'll wear what we bring you, miss. Now put on your dress.

Amy shakes her head, but the small attendant winds her arms quick around Amy's midsection and lifts her, just high enough to set her down in the center of the too-large skirt. She pulls the dress up fast and begins buttoning it, trapping Amy's arms against her chest.

Stop!

Will you be good then and get dressed?

Yes. And when the attendant releases her, she puts her arms where they belong and finishes the buttons herself.

See, the small attendant says, tugging at the dress's shoulders. It's only a little bit big. Could be you'll grow into it. Now will you go sit in the dayroom like a nice girl? The attendant follows Amy from the room and locks the door behind them.

In the dayroom, Amy sits with the other unkempt women and at breakfast, she is not hungry. The same meal sits before her that did the previous morning; she lifts her spoon and puts it down, though this time there is no one near interested in how or what she eats. The Skeleton sips coffee at the next table, taking no notice of Amy—not even when Amy waves, not even when she shouts hello. Not even then seeming to recognize her or care that Amy is eating a spoonful of cereal, then another…but somehow, this is all that she can manage to eat. Her stomach twists at the sight and smell of the oatmeal gruel. She pushes all the cereal to one side of the bowl and hurries away from her place when the gong sounds.

After breakfast, the women walk; after their walk, they return to their chairs. Though Amy tries to make herself stay awake for the doctor's visit, she sleeps like the rest. She sleeps and wakes when the gong rings at noon; she eats a few bites and then walks and sleeps again. She takes her supper, takes her evening entertainment, and like the rest, she takes a drink and is put to bed. The feelings come as soon as she starts to look for them. Again, a spreading warmth as she rolls onto her stomach, rolls over the edge of her mattress. The fall is over in an instant, but the sensation lasts and lasts—of falling and being caught, by limbs, by hands. It is exhausting, exhilarating, and, when the morning bell rings, she cannot tell how long she has been lying on the floor, in the aftermath.

The attendant only says, Get up, and Amy dresses and takes her place with the others.

In the dayroom, in the dining room, the women are all drawn and tired. They slouch with their faces just over their cereal bowls; they do not drink their water. The water is too cold, but Amy drinks her coffee to the bottom, where most of the sugar has settled. She scoops up the sugar sludge with her spoon and adds a morsel of cereal to it. She eats this and another bite, gritty and sweet. When the gong rings, she switches her nearly full bowl with her neighbor's empty one.

Drizzle taps against the tall windows and the attendants bring out wraps before the morning walk; the cloak initialed with AAU looks like something Amy's stepmother used to own—how long ago? Deep red in color, it's cut for a taller woman and the raised hood smells faintly of lavender water. Rain makes the cloak heavier and it winds about Amy's ankles as they circle the lane four times, as always. The lawns are bright in the wet, but behind the hospital, the hills have faded to brown. Back on the ward, the attendants build up the fire and call to the basement for hot drinks;

there were not enough coats to go around. Amy is already warm, pacing up and down the hall. The doctor hasn't come.

Where's the doctor? she asks the small attendant.

They were here this morning.

But I didn't see him.

Well, there's nothing the matter with you, then.

My stomach hurts.

Eat more oatmeal. It helps with digestion.

The large attendant comes into the dayroom with a bottle in her hands—the medicine bottle. She moves among the women and gives drinks to some, in small wooden cups like those used at night. She wakes the Walking Skeleton by tapping her on the shoulder. She gives a dose to Mrs. Littleton.

What's that? Amy asks the smaller attendant.

It's a—what do you call them?—aperitif. The small attendant smiles. For those ladies who don't eat as they should.

My stomach hurts.

You get your dose at night.

So do they!

The attendant smiles again. Some people's stomachs need more help than others'.

Amy watches the women take their medicine, wincing as its bitterness touches their tongues. Did my letter come?

I do have something for you. The attendant produces a silver-embossed card from her apron pocket. The doctor's wife sent it down.

Amy turns it in her hands. It's an invitation to tea.

That's an honor, you know.

When is this?

Days from now. Do you want to hit the gong?

Amy shakes her head, and the small attendant hits it herself; the women stand up and make a line for the dining room.

At the table, Amy chooses a seat across from the Walking Skeleton. The old woman sits quietly while the food is passed around. Her forehead is moist. When Amy cuts into her meat, the Skeleton leans toward her.

Repent, she says. Let us live on locusts and wild honey.

The meat is gray and its juices are clear. I'm not hungry, Amy says. It is the same food every day. Carrots, potatoes, and meat cooked together, sometimes with cabbage, always with bread and butter on the side. The gingerbread was nicer, on bath night. The thought of it makes her mouth water. She pushes her plate aside.

Do you want your spud? asks the woman beside her.

No, Amy says, and the Skeleton nods. Amy puts her hands over her stomach, pressing against the ache that does not go away. I wish I had some of your stomach medicine.

Beg pardon? The Skeleton sips her water, squinting across the table at Amy.

The stomach medicine they gave you before.

The Skeleton pats her mouth with her napkin. That was nerve medicine they gave me, child. Tincture of morphia. Poor stuff next to what my own druggist used to mix.

Is that what I have at night-time?

I imagine so, yes. For what good it does.

I'll have yours next time.

Oh no, the Skeleton says, smiling. I must have something.

If you'll give me yours, I'll stop eating altogether.

The Skeleton is still smiling. No.

Why not?

It is a sin against God to impede his will and every day I am here, I am sinned upon. The prophets fasted, but I am made to eat…you have seen, have you not? My nerves could not bear it without assistance. I know that these attendants could be good girls, but the doctor is a prideful and ungodly man.

The gong rings; the women push back their chairs. The Walking Skeleton comes around the table and slips her hand through Amy's arm, so they are as close as two girls, walking.

Be sure of this: the wicked will not go unpunished, but those who are righteous will go free.

Amy nods. The liver-spotted hand on her sleeve could be a grandmother's. Is that the Bible?

I have thought, the Skeleton says, I have thought that if we all were to rise up against him at once, we would be victorious. Then we would run from this place to our freedom, and no man could bring us back. That is why for now, you should eat. The Lord has given you appetite. Your strength may be the salvation of us all.

Amy nods. They will leave this place, the old woman is saying. Together.

Amy nods again: I can eat.

The Skeleton slides her arm free and touches her dry hand to Amy's cheek.

My child, she says. You are a true Christian.

It rains for days and the women are kept indoors. Amy paces the screened porch where last she saw her parents. Every day she looks for them, come to reclaim her, but the only one to lay claim to her now is the Walking Skeleton. She nods to Amy at mealtimes but disappears into her Bible all day. The rain strips the dead leaves from the trees, making every day grayer than the last, and if Amy's trees are still standing at home, up north, they must be standing like this, too, wet and bare and piercing. The women cannot have walks in the gray and the wet; at walk times they are herded to the calistheneum, a large, low room beneath the chapel. There, the attendants teach them to throw leather balls and use their muscles. They are given more baths; they are marched to evening programs, Sunday services. Then the rain stops and the women rush outside again.

After days like this, the drink blurring everything together, the small attendant comes to Amy. Damping a handkerchief with her tongue, she wipes Amy's face.

Do you have a comb? she asks.

No, Amy says. She lost hers the day she arrived and nobody since has bothered her to put up her hair. The small attendant rummages through her own pockets until she finds a broken one.

Hold still, she says, and runs it as best she can through Amy's snarls. The attendant quickly plaits Amy's hair and pins it up with the comb. Don't fuss and it'll hold, she says. She beats at Amy's dusty skirt with her hands. Well, that'll have to do, too. Mind yourself in the doctor's apartment.

A neatly dressed woman waits to take Amy through the locked door at the end of the ward, the door marked no admittance. The woman doesn't direct Amy down the service stairs but passes her through the stairwell, onto ward seven. Amy has been here before, with her parents. It may be that her parents are here now, but the woman who escorts her walks so quickly that Amy can't look for them. The woman keeps her hand on Amy's elbow and says, when you're better, miss, this is where you'll be. There is the woman in the wheeled chair and the woman with the growth on her face. There are books and pianos, stillness. A 'good' ward—it is like a tomb—and the fingers of Amy's free hand rise. It is not until they reach the end of this hall, the other side of another locked door, that the escort looks Amy in the face.

Mercy, you're bleeding! They are in the center of the building now; her voice rings off the white, clean walls.

What's that? A man puts his head out a nearby doorway. Seeing him, Amy slides her right hand beneath her apron—the hand with blood under its fingernails.

The escort is breathless, flushed. I'm sorry to have disturbed you, Dr. Ingstrom. As you see, this young lady is injured. The blood startled me. She was fine only a moment ago.

The man steps into the hallway. He's tall and young; he has dark hair and dark eyes—the very opposite of the white-haired grandfather that admitted Amy. Standing before her, this young doctor smells like clean linen and she smells like a hired man. He gestures for her to tilt her face toward him. He doesn't touch her.

Here. He hands the escort a wad of cotton gauze from his pocket. It's nothing much. Have her press this to the scratch until the bleeding stops.

Thank you, Dr. Ingstrom.

The man nods, glancing at Amy. You should be more careful, Miss—

Underwood, says the escort, when Amy doesn't answer. Amy Underwood, a new patient on ward nine. On her way upstairs to tea.

Ah. The young doctor looks at Amy more closely. She shakes her head, but the broken comb holds; she lifts her hands toward her face, then remembers her nails and hides them again. The doctor's lips curve beneath his dark moustache.

I won't delay you further, he says. He nods, stepping back into his office. You must give my regards to your hostess, Miss Underwood.

Of course, sir, says the escort, pulling Amy away. You press that hard to your face, miss, and no more bothering the doctors.

There are other doctors behind the other doors, then—and maybe the old doctor is here, hiding a hoard of letters for Amy— but the escort hurries Amy past these doors and up a polished staircase to the third floor. Here are only two doors, on either side of the open stairwell, which turns and heads up again, higher than the rest of the hospital—leading where? But the escort holds Amy's arm to keep her from climbing farther. She raps quickly on the right-hand door before unlocking it herself. Behind is a foyer, lit by sidelights and yielding onto a narrow hallway. Its walls are not plastered like those on the wards but papered in blue, like walls in a regular house. The escort leads Amy a few steps down this hallway before knocking on a chamber door. From inside, a woman answers: Come in.

The escort takes the blood-spotted gauze from Amy before pushing her gently through the doorway. The room inside is also like something plucked out of a regular house: cluttered and cozy, a parlor just the size of her stepmother's parlor up north. Not a great gaping room with bulky furniture—not a ward. And waiting on a horsehair settee is a tiny woman all by herself. A woman who looks like the old doctor, white-haired, smiling. When she stands to greet Amy, she is as thin as the Walking Skeleton and pink in the face.

I am so glad you could come, my dear, says the woman—the doctor's wife. Please, have a seat. She pats the place beside her. When Amy sits, she is aware again of her own sharp odor.

Oh! says the doctor's wife. You've a cut beside your nose. Fetch the resin, please, Matilda.

Is the doctor here? asks Amy.

No, but my maid will doctor you nicely. The doctor's wife smiles. Her dress is the brown-gold shade of an autumn leaf and she wears a white silk kerchief at her neck. She rustles like a crisp, clean leaf as she pats Amy's hand. How are you settling in? Is there anything you need?

My stomach hurts, says Amy. They won't give me medicine for it.

No? asks the doctor's wife. Well, we'll see if Matilda can't find some syrup for you before you go. Are you otherwise comfortable?

The same woman who escorted Amy up tells her to close her eyes and tilt back her head. A powder sprinkles onto her face and the woman pats off the excess with a damp cloth.

I can imagine your spirits must be depressed, says the doctor's wife. When I was a girl, I was sent away from home and it was very hard.

Where did they send you?

Where? The doctor's wife crosses her ankles. It was a health resort, she says.

I've been to one of those, Amy says.

Oh—no, says the doctor's wife. I was an invalid. My brother was weak, too, as a boy. Have you any brothers or sisters?

No.

Then perhaps you are more resourceful than I was, at your age. They say only children are their own best friends. And of course you are from the north, are you not? That must have made you very resourceful, indeed!

Amy shakes her head. We came up three winters ago. I knew lots of girls, back home.

The doctor's wife pats Amy's hand. We came here ourselves only five years ago, when this place was built. I know very well, Miss Underwood, the difficulty of parting with friends.

Amy doesn't answer. The maid has rolled a cart into the room, with a tea service and covered dishes. She positions it beside the doctor's wife.

Are you very hungry, my dear? I hope your stomach can handle such nice things. I think mine is better constituted for sweets than for sensible foods.

The old woman serves Amy a baked apple and a slice of cake, pours her a cup of tea and adds cream and sugar.

I like a bit of cream over my apple—will you have some? When Amy nods, the doctor's wife pours for her. The apple is tender and full of cinnamon and nutmeg; Amy cuts big bites. Now that the offering isn't stewed meat, she finds the appetite that the Walking Skeleton willed her. Amy finishes her apple quickly, spooning up all the cream from her saucer. Then the cake, which is light and lemon-flavored, and which the doctor's wife replaces as soon as Amy finishes her first piece. She could eat the entire cake, if it weren't for the sharp twinges coming from her aching stomach.

The doctor's wife nibbles thin cookies and watches her. She has small, even teeth and sky-blue eyes that open and shut like a china doll's.

What are your interests, Miss Underwood? Do you sew? Sing? Play? Do you like to read? Write? Draw?

To each of these questions Amy answers no. She has *no aptitude*, as Miss Carter had said, as her stepmother had agreed.

Perhaps you will learn to care for these things later on, says the doctor's wife, when you are married. My interests have been great comforts to me. She calls the maid to bring her workbasket, full of lace and baby's clothes. She bids the maid bring her paint box and shows Amy half-finished watercolors of the lake by moonlight.

I don't want to get married, Amy says. So many small stitches and brushstrokes; so much time.

No? The old woman smiles. You may change your mind. But a single girl is even better served by her talents. You might teach, for instance.

No, says Amy. No! Her mother had been a teacher, before she married, before she died. I don't want to!

Well. The doctor's wife blinks, smiling. You are still young, of course. Surely you enjoy albums? She nods, and her maid brings them: autograph albums and card photographs, poems clipped from newspapers. One book is filled with small, full-length portraits, many of young men in uniforms. Most of the men are standing in front of the same backdrop: a military camp. They gaze past Amy.

This was my brother's keepsake, says the doctor's wife. His college classmates, before they all marched away. There are very many of them, I know, but my brother was a great favorite. And, of course, we are from Pennsylvania—where the War actually happened. She shifts half of the album onto her own lap, points to a picture. This one is my brother himself, on the day of his college graduation. And there is a photo of the doctor—my husband—when he was at the sanatorium. It is just how he looked back then—so stiff and serious!

Amy looks at the small, grave face, with its dark bushy eyebrows and dense side-whiskers. I haven't seen him.

The doctor's wife tilts her head. You must have: a handsome

older man, slight, with silver hair and a full moustache? He visits the women's wards every morning. He and good Dr. Meijer, who you can't have missed—a behemoth, as kind as he is big.

He only comes when I'm sleeping, Amy says. Can I see him now?

You may see Dr. Meijer tomorrow, but my husband is away this week, at a medical convention in Detroit. See? Here are some cards he's brought me from the places he travels.

The doctor's wife shows her photographs of New York and Washington, Saint Louis and Toronto. There are no more pictures of soldiers.

Where's your brother? Amy asks, turning the pages.

The doctor's wife coughs. He died of tuberculosis, on January the 27th, 1862. He had just begun practicing law, but he was never meant for such work. I have a better picture of him—hand me what's in that drawer beside you.

Amy opens a small, shallow drawer in the octagonal side table. Lying alone inside of it is a molded leather case the length of her palm and less than its width. It looks like a cigarette case. The doctor's wife takes it carefully from her and opens it like a book, with both hands.

This is a likeness of him when he was very young, she says. Before he went away to school. See? She tilts it toward Amy, a silvery blur within a brass frame. Go ahead, says the doctor's wife. You may hold it.

When it is in her hands, Amy makes out a boy in old-fashioned clothes, photographed from the waist up. The image is smaller than the old woman's *cartes* and held in place by thin glass. Even so, every detail is precise: the loose curls of the boy's light hair, the lone pockmark on his forehead, the tiger's-eye pattern in the buttons of his coat. The boy sits in a high-backed chair, his head inclined slightly to the right, his eyes looking directly forward. His mouth is a wavering line—as though he would like to smile. He catches the light like a looking-glass and she can see her scabbed face on top of his clear one. She has never had a brother.

He looks nice, Amy says.

Yes, says the doctor's wife. Gone, now. She closes the case. Must keep this out of the light, she says. Light and air degrade daguerreotypes. Put him back for me, please, dear.

Amy turns to close the drawer, then takes a cookie from the tray. She eats it as the old woman did, in tiny nibbles. Crumbs spray her skirt.

Where is Matilda? asks the doctor's wife. You'll be missed back on the ward.

I'm sorry for your loss, says Amy.

That's very kind of you. It has been many years, and of course I still have my sisters. The doctor's wife smiles, dimpling like a girl. You must remember me at the evening events—now that we are good friends.

Tell the doctor to come and see me, says Amy. Tell him to bring me my letters.

Your letters? Have they been lost?

My stepmother writes to me every week.

Oh, says the doctor's wife. Have patience, my dear. When the doctor sees that you are well enough, then there will be news from home. And the maid gives Amy a dose of cherry syrup before walking her back to the ward.

In her room, in the darkness, Amy opens the case and sets it beside her bed. It picks up every hint of light in the room; it fairly glows, though the boy's face is lost to her. His silvered skin, his iridescent irises, his pupils smaller than pinpricks. She shuts and opens the case, exposing him, protecting him, savoring the creak of the tiny hinges. She shuts and opens the case over and over again. The leather is cool in her hands and the boy's face is dark in the darkness but there is a smudge of light, still, across the surface of the picture. She stands the case like a tent over the bridge of her nose, rests with his image above her eye, the velvet lining of the case soft against her skin. You are a great comfort to me, she whispers, in the old lady's careful voice. In the daytime she will keep the case closed and she will keep him close to her. If they find she has taken this thing, they will take it back, but in return, surely, they will give her something else—a dose of medicine in the afternoon, or, if they are very angry, a ticket back home.

Chapter Four

THE WALLS OF THE WOMEN'S wards are emblazoned with mottos from the *Lady's Book of Axioms*. The doctor's wife chose them: *Veni, Vedi, Vici*; *After Clouds, Sunshine*; *Kindness Keeps Friends*. Painted on the walls in large, flowing script, these phrases encourage the patients. Today, they also serve as signposts for the doctor. Each motto he reads brings him one ward closer to the end of morning rounds, one ward closer to rest. He drags after Meijer, no match for the big man's energy.

The doctor's trip to the state medical society meeting was itself stimulating. He heard remarkable papers read, learned of great breakthroughs in galvanism and anesthetics. During the train ride back north, he had been consumed by these ideas—but upon arrival at the hospital, he was met by a more familiar medical problem. In the few days of his absence, Diana managed to strain her nerves by sketching in the damp, over-indulging in patent tonics, sleeping one warm night in a silk rather than a flannel gown. During such spells as these, she seems to court the tuberculosis she dreads. Sitting up with her, the doctor replaced her chloral drops with valerian tea, held her wrist instead of her quivering hand. He has occasionally found his medical texts left open to telling chapters—on dyspnoea, phthisis, pulmonary consumption—but last night, his wife was unscientific. You shouldn't leave me here, she'd repeated, you shouldn't leave me here when you go. It is fear talking, or boredom: they both know that in thirty years of marriage she has never been dangerously ill. She will apologize for her behavior later on; she will remember herself and rise (for the time being) to heroic displays of rationality. The doctor worries that she goes too much among the patients, but she swears she feels stronger at the asylum than she ever did at sanatoriums.

The doctor is sleep-deprived, slow, as he circulates the wards, but he remembers the young girl's name when he reaches ward nine. Amy Underwood, the lumber-agent's daughter: she's usually sound asleep when he visits. Awake, her eyes are rheum-crusted; the abrasions on her face are many and fresh. A common compulsion, this picking at one's person. She holds her hands now behind her back, regarding him with an expression that is distrustful but not dull. Undaunted, the doctor smiles.

How are you this morning, Miss Underwood? Won't you give me your hand, say hello?

She shakes her head. The small one said you were bringing the mitts.

I've brought nothing of the sort. Which attendant said such a thing?

The small one.

Well, she shouldn't have. I've brought only my bag—as you see—no mitts, or any other sort of restraints. This little mallet checks your reflexes; this contraption—a sphygmograph—will measure your pulse. May I?

She allows him to bring her left arm forward but watches him closely, flinching as he draws each new instrument from his kit.

Though she is plainly nervous, her reflexes are good, her pupils responsive, her ears, throat, and lungs all normal. Only her pulse is of concern: slightly deficient in amplitude, as is common among melancholics. And the state of her face…she risks infection from the filthy fingernails that she hides now beneath her apron. The doctor notes all of this in his ledger and smiles again at the child.

As to this question of mitts, he says, I'd rather make use of your hands than bundle them up. You have my permission to sit in the afternoons on the next ward over. The ladies there have a sewing circle. Doesn't that sound nice?

She picks at the nap of her apron and her loose hair falls forward. Has my mother written?

Your mother? The doctor has not forgotten the girl's history and what her mother was.

My stepmother, Rose—who left me here?

Patients seldom receive letters right away, he says, relieved. You must get settled first. Perhaps you would like to go driving this afternoon with the ladies from ward three? Join the Bible study?

I would like a dose at noon, she says. I would like my own clothes!

She begins to weep, shifting quietly from composure to tears. He can't be sure whether her spirits truly are depressed or whether she has taken this mannerism from those around her. The attendants note nothing unusual: they write that she eats well, sleeps well and seldom speaks. They write that she takes her morphine willingly and does not pose a threat to the others. However, they write similarly of almost every woman on the ward. Looking now at Miss Underwood, the doctor resolves to insist on greater specificity. It will be a blessing when more of the attendants have graduated the training school.

There, Miss Underwood, he says, it's to be expected that you should be lonesome at first. Sewing will be just what you need. And friends—which you will naturally make, if you will only take a little trouble to make yourself pleasant.

The girl's tears track around the scabs on her cheeks; she does not answer him. Except when provoked by delusions, such emotionality is more characteristic of melancholia than of pubescent insanity. Her pulse corroborates this diagnosis. If melancholic, it may be that the girl is undermedicated—or, if the original diagnosis of pubescent insanity holds true, over-medicated. The effects of illness and those of drugs can occasionally be difficult to distinguish; where the patient is young and slight, the difficulty is exacerbated. The doctor instructs more vigorous toweling after her bath, a milder dose of sedative at night. Better to unduly weaken than strengthen a dose, and he instructs milder doses for every woman on ward nine, against the possibility that the attendants here have been dosing too generously. Medication can be as cruel a restraint as straps or padded mitts, and he reminds the attendants that all therapeutic tools are to be used sparingly, with the support of detailed, careful ward notes. The best tool of all is an attendant's compassionate yet firm disposition.

When the doctor finishes his rounds, he calls for his driver and carriage. He has a photographer's appointment this afternoon in town. It is regrettable that the appointment falls on this weary day; he washes his eyes with cold water, pats the skin beneath them with witch hazel. He sits for his portrait annually. He orders fifty prints at a time, to exchange with his colleagues in the Association of Medical Superintendents of American Institutions for the Insane. Prints to send to his former patients. They write: Send me a picture, doctor, so that my family can know my greatest friend. Send me a picture of yourself, and one of the hospital. It would do me good to see that place every day, as I used to. Such requests come mostly from women. They write: You are the wood-cutter who found me lost in the woods. You are the shepherd who kept me from the wolves. Send me a picture of yourself, with that expression of yours that led me out of my darkness. The doctor is happy to comply, to keep his friends with kindness. He finds that women in general make better patients than men. They are more receptive to influence, to cure.

His driver urges the horses quickly down the city streets—this city younger and humbler than the one he just visited. Its shade trees are shorter but its lake more vast. The doctor is greeted by almost everyone he passes and greets them in return. Then, his carriage pulls up before the photographer's studio. Pasted to the window are advertisements for collectible photographs: studio cards, of which his wife has many. There are photos of the West—Yellowstone and Yosemite. There are photos of Norway and of President Harrison. There are photos of local celebrities: the lumber baron, the mayor, and, in last year's pose, the doctor himself. He is gazing to the far right of the camera, in the same pose as the other great men. Like them, he is standing beside a pillar made from marbleized plaster but appearing solid and strong. This time, he thinks, he'd prefer to sit down. His legs look stumpy in full view. And this time, if it is possible, he'd like to look directly at the camera. His patients should feel that he is still looking after them, with concern.

Night after night Amy is given the drink—like the others—and the others, in their rooms, must experience this same warm feeling, this state that is not quite sleep, a long drift that leaves them bleary in the mornings, clumsy at their walks but able to circle the lane again and again. They are untiring but, like her, they doze sitting up in their thin-cushioned rockers. They doze and startle when the gong sounds for mealtimes. Amy eats only because the Walking Skeleton is there to prompt her. The Walking Skeleton can't say yet what God will use Amy for, but she assures Amy daily: He has a plan.

Letters still do not come from her stepmother, and she doesn't know what has happened. Her father is always in his office in town—her father busies himself with ordering men to cut down trees; it's possible he doesn't even notice she's gone. At the end of his day, if there are only two women in his house, his wife and the hired woman, he may not remember that once there was a third. But her stepmother had promised and now that she's alone…what could she be doing, if not writing letters? What fills her day now, except silence—not writing? Why hasn't she, Amy asks the attendants, why haven't I heard anything from my stepmother? If both her parents died, there would be no one to tell her—or if they moved farther north, chasing the tree line, it would take longer for a letter to arrive. But it never could take this long. There is no place they could have gone where the mail could be this slow. *To Violet*, she reads, over and over, but the words don't reveal their message—and, one day on the afternoon walk, she opens her fist, and the torn page blows away.

The days repeat. She's jolted awake every morning; always, she reaches first for the boy, shutting his case, sliding him safely beneath her mattress. The attendant comes with a dress that doesn't fit, and, every morning, Amy says, please turn your back, as she is taking off her nightgown. Sometimes the attendant will; then, she slips the boy into her apron pocket. If the attendant won't turn, won't take her eyes off Amy as she dresses, then Amy sneaks back after breakfast—quickly, before the women who clean have made their start—and rescues the boy from his hiding place. In her pocket, during the day, he bumps against her leg as she walks; she does not know his name. She counts the days: Sunday, Monday, Tuesday, bath night; Thursday, Friday, bath night again—hiding him after supper, under her mattress, when she counts that the attendants will be taking her clothes from the bathroom. This image of the boy is so exact, not hazy-edged like the other photos the doctor's wife showed her, not gray-fleshed and black-eyed, but made up of colors she does not have names for, which reflect and entice, fooling her into pressing her fingers to his face, as if to a reflection in water that could be stirred up or could point her to the boy himself. When she leaves the case open, he is in the room with her, this boy that the doctor's wife kept buried. A glowing boy, more real than the other photos the old woman claimed were of him, more real than the old woman herself. The boy is a boy forever and when Amy looks at him, her own reflection looks back: she's a child again, too.

The small attendant takes her one afternoon through the door marked no admittance, onto ward seven. The frail women she's seen twice before are there still, sitting in a circle now with other strange women, able-bodied. With them is Mrs. Morris, the kind woman who comes on bath nights. My dear, Mrs. Morris says, and smiles sweetly. The small attendant catches Amy's hand rising up toward her cheeks; the small attendant folds Amy's fingers and holds them closed, tightly.

Mitts, she says softly, and louder, Miss, you'll stay here with these ladies. Someone will come for you later. She lets go of Amy's hand—and Amy reaches after her. Behave yourself, the small attendant says, and she pushes Amy by the shoulders into a chair.

The chair is strange and fine, upholstered in velvet. The air here is fresher than on her own ward. The eight women in the sewing circle hold fancywork, stretched taut in round frames. A sampler of the Lord's Prayer. A bouquet of flowers that spills out of its frame.

What have you brought to work on, dear?

Nothing, Amy says. I don't have anything.

Miss Underwood, says Mrs. Morris. You must get started. She gives her a needle, and Amy licks her thread but frays it wide, trying to pass it through the needle's eye. Mrs. Morris cuts the thread off lower—and lower and lower.

I can't, says Amy, and the other women look up from their beautiful work, frowning.

Shh, Mrs. Morris says, and she threads the needle for her. Put this on your thumb like so. This is just a pillow, so your stitches won't matter much. Keep them as small and close together as you can—like this, in and out—and mind that you only sew up three sides of this square. Let me see you do it—good. Now just sit quietly and keep working. I will continue. She takes up *Harper's* and begins to read aloud about winter fashions.

Amy's thumb grows moist under its metal cap, but she presses the needle back and forth through the fabric. The other women watch her out the corners of their eyes: the woman with orange skin, the woman in the wheeled chair. There are no girls here. All of those surrounding her are middle-aged and efficient, working patterns into cloth and watching as she stitches shut one side of a square. They are old, but their glances are like girls'—like those of the staring, whispering girls at Miss Carter's School. Amy tucks her chin against her chest; when she looks back up, they all look away.

Stop it, she says, and they do stop, these women who live on the other side of the door marked no admittance. They stop working. They hold their needles in their clean hands and stare at her openly.

Ladies, says Mrs. Morris, may I continue? The other women nod, beginning again with their needles, but Mrs. Morris is looking at Amy. Amy pushes her needle again through the cloth—too wide of a stitch and the fabric puckers. She pulls tighter, so that it puckers more. The old doctor sent her here, to be gaped at. She cannot take comfort from the boy under these women's wrinkle-eyed scrutiny. Ladies? says Mrs. Morris, and Amy begins to imitate the sewing gestures of the others, squinting and motioning with her wrist. But beneath the square of fabric, she works her thumb out of its metal cap and with every pass of her needle, she pricks herself purposefully. The needle pokes the pad of her thumb, her cuticle. The women are still watching, she knows, so she pulls loose the broken comb, letting her hair hang around her. Hidden, she pricks herself repeatedly. It doesn't hurt; she only bleeds because her hands are chapped, her fingertips chewed. She only bleeds a little, but she presses the fabric to her thumb until the pillow's border is dotted with small red spots.

Child, says Mrs. Morris, let me see your progress. She pushes Amy's hair behind her shoulders and takes the empty pillow from her hands. You seem a bit clumsy with the needle, dear. Watch that you don't give yourself blood-poisoning! She smiles, and Amy puts her thumb in her mouth. This will do for today, Mrs. Morris says. Mrs. Bailey, please walk Miss Underwood back to her ward. Here are my keys; this one will let you through the firedoors. Take care to shut one before you open the next.

The large attendant and the small attendant guard their keys so carefully that they are impossible to take or touch. But Mrs. Morris has handed her key ring to a plump little woman—a patient!—as though this were the most natural thing in the world. And the woman sets aside her sewing, unsurprised. She turns her dumpling face to Amy. Come along.

Amy stays in her chair.

It's all right, croons the woman.

She isn't an attendant, says Amy. She tears a cuticle with her teeth and blood wells around the bed of her thumbnail.

No, Mrs. Morris says. Several of the women were struck with pneumonia. The attendants are with them. Please, Miss Underwood, go with Mrs. Bailey.

All the sewers are staring, so Amy stands and, like Mrs. Bailey, shakes lint from her skirt. The boy's case beats against her leg as she does so: *I am here.* She follows Mrs. Bailey through the circle of chairs and down the hall. The plump woman walks quickly, pitched forward at the waist and with her right hand stretched before her. In it she grips the key ring, with one key held apart from the rest. The key ring might be a lantern, guiding their way; they might be fugitives, racing down the ward. Amy trots to keep up. Mrs. Bailey unlocks the first door and they pass through. She remembers to lock it behind them. She unlocks the second door and pushes it open for Amy. The keys jingle in her dimpled hand. The key ring looks like the attendants', like the doctors'. Those keys are the way out. Doesn't Mrs. Bailey know that?

Are those yours?

Mrs. Bailey tilts her head and smiles. You just saw Mrs. Morris give them to me.

Please—let me see them. Please?

I had better not. Go along, now. Mrs. Bailey steps back, so that she is in the stairwell between the two wards, while Amy stands in the open doorway of ward nine. Mrs. Bailey clearly has a good appetite; she is not like the Walking Skeleton, not godly. Could she be strong—like Amy?

Please. Amy reaches for the keys.

No! Mrs. Bailey bats at Amy as weakly as a child and tries to pull the door shut. But Amy catches the door with the side of her boot; she ducks under Mrs. Bailey's outstretched left arm to snatch the key ring, clutched to the other woman's heart. The keys slip easily from Mrs. Bailey's short fingers, and Amy jumps back onto her ward and throws herself hard at the door. Simultaneous with its slam, with the thump of Mrs. Bailey being knocked back, comes a jangle of metal—the keys hitting the floor of the stairwell. Though Amy felt metal against her fingertips, felt Mrs. Bailey's soft grip yield, she doesn't hold the key ring now. Here are tiny scrapes, frayed skin on the tips of her fingers—but the keys are behind the door, clanging and scraping now against the far lock. She puts her eye to the keyhole, sees Mrs. Bailey's dark form trying key after key from the enormous jumbled ring.

Help, the woman sobs. She presses her front to the ward seven door, like a dog, desperate to get into a house. Go down the stairs, Amy whispers—though, new as she is to this place, she knows there's another locked door at the bottom. Without the right key, the stairs are a dead end. And Mrs. Bailey can't calm herself to find the right key. But couldn't Amy? *Then we would run from this place to our freedom, and no man could bring us back.*

There's no one behind Amy in the corridor, no one coming down ward nine in response to the slammed door, the sobbing in the stairwell. Amy edges her door open. Mrs. Bailey shrieks when its hinges creak. She flings the key ring at Amy's door and it clatters again to the floor. But then a voice speaks from inside ward seven. Shh, it says, we are here.

The voice continues, murmuring so that Amy can't make out its words, and Mrs. Bailey continues to cower, as though afraid that *something* might catch her alone in the stairwell. Then a key turns and Mrs. Bailey falls sobbing into a square of light, onto her ward. Darkness again, quiet. Slowly, Amy cracks her door. The oily sheen of metal is just visible on the tile floor. Those keys, the matron's keys, must surely open every door in the hospital. Amy edges into the stairwell. The keys are only an arm's length away, a gift she can share with the Walking Skeleton. Together they could unlock all the rooms, free all the women, and—

—Where do you think you're going? The small attendant's strong hand closes on Amy's shoulder, hauling her upright, away from the keys. Who's brought you back and left this door open? Come with me now, miss. And the attendant pulls her back onto the ward, locking the door marked no admittance.

With the last hour of his day, after the evening program, the doctor works on his annual report to the State Legislature—an exhaustive, exhausting document. The asylum's year ends on the 30th of September; for two months afterward, he compiles figures as mandated in the hospital's charter with the state and composes his remarks germane. There's not enough time for sleep in this season.

From the steward, the doctor will receive an account of the hospital's output: the amount of milk given and hay harvested, the gardens' yields, the pounds of beef and pork butchered, the number of brooms and brushes and beds manufactured. The matron will prepare a list of all the items made in the sewing room—hundreds of aprons and pairs of drawers, countless sheets, shrouds, doilies, dish towels. The head carpenter will give him a list of all repairs made to the hospital in the last year. The treasurer will provide a careful reckoning of credits and debits.

The doctor's own figures are of a different sort. He charts the assigned causes of insanity. The moral causes: religious excitement, seduction, shock. The physical causes: injury, pregnancy, privation, fever, drug abuse, tippling, influenza, old age, lactation, masturbation, venereal disease. There are hereditary cases, and there are cases of congenital defect. There are those few—one in one hundred patients—who are discovered after their admittance not to be insane.

The doctor studies the rates of admittance, recovery and death in the past year, subdividing patients along the lines of their illnesses. If seventy were admitted with acute melancholia, and thirty-two were released while fourteen died—then, there is another figure that he is not required to comment upon: the twenty-four melancholics who remain in the hospital, alongside scores of others left over from previous years. This—the remainder—is the figure that depresses some of his colleagues. The somaticists envision the perfect hospital as a factory, manufacturing sound minds and shipping them away.

It is an unhelpful metaphor, in the doctor's opinion. It makes the low cure rate an indicator of failure, rather than a sign that the wretched have found refuge. The hospital is more aptly analogized to a home, where prodigal children are received, cared for, and kept, for as long as necessary. This is no more than the state's responsibility to its citizens or man's responsibility to man.

Now, the doctor charts cure rates after patients' first, second and third admissions—the likelihood of cure dropping with every re-admission. This is only natural. Returning to the hospital after intervals with their families, the patients are often dispirited, having fallen away from the stabilizing routine of ward life. They are less willing to leave when next the doctor pronounces them cured; they make themselves ill with apprehension. The hospital has been in operation for five years; the average patient has been in residence for three-and-a-half. They are veterans, immigrants, vagrants, widows. By accident or design, they *will* return to the hospital…and some will die here. The doctor condenses West's autopsy notes into his report, striking some of the colorful details—calcified ribs, fat-blanketed organs, cerebral arteries that snap like pipe stems—in order to present the essentials:

> Male, aged 71, native of Ohio, admitted December, 1888. The patient was greatly demented and suffered from religious delusions, believing all those around him to be Indians and claiming that he had come North to convert the 'savages' in the name of Yahweh. In the weeks following his admission, he had several paralytic seizures—raptures, in his own terminology—passing on February 3rd into a comatose state from which he never recovered.

> Female, aged 28, native of Michigan, an inmate since July 7, 1886. The patient was an epileptic and had suffered convulsions since the age of two. In the year preceding her death, she had about four attacks per week and was watched constantly by nurse attendants. Her death occurred during a series of convulsions lasting ten or eleven hours. In the post-mortem examination, the motor zone of the left hemisphere was very much congested.

> Male, aged 65, indigent, native of Pennsylvania, an inmate since August 1885. Suffered from senile dementia, requiring assistance in bathing, dressing, eating, etc. Exhaustion due to old age is assigned as the cause of death, as no organic disease was discovered during autopsy.

Each autopsy report describes an individual, not a disease—and how can the doctor put aside his pen without doing justice to each? But he has a stronger obligation to his living patients than the dead, and he forces himself to rest, even though, often, he can count on one hand the hours of sleep he claims for himself.

The doctor is securing his apartment door from the inside when the clock strikes: midnight, already. An asylum doctor cannot afford superstition and yet, he must swallow a yelp when he turns to find his wife at the top of the hall, just visible in the scant light falling in from the stairwell. Her white hair drapes her shoulders, thick like quilt batting.

He is lost, she says, and the doctor steps slowly toward her, not sure whether she's dreaming or awake.

Who, he asks, who is lost?

She clasps his wrists, her hot fingers working under his shirt cuffs, squeezing against his bones. Pulling him into the parlor, she points to an empty drawer in the side table. Empty of her daguerreotype, he remembers.

Charles, she says. Gone.

Where have you looked? he asks. I'll look again.

I have lost him, she says. He will never forgive me.

It's too late to look now, he tells her. I'll find it in the morning.

He's gone, she says, but she does not weep. His wife, who cries easily, is stolid, staring at him.

In the morning, he says. We'll be able to find it, together. Why don't I give you something, to sleep?

She nods. Morphia?

Valerian should be more than enough.

I'll wake you if it's not.

Fine, he says, and, freeing his wrists from her fingers, steps into the hall, pushes the light switch. Would you like me to sleep in your room?

I'd only bother you with my tossing. She rubs her eyes; electric light troubles her at night. I'd rather be alone.

Fine, he says, crossing to his study to mix her a dose. Her footsteps fade toward the bedrooms; he unlocks his medical cabinet, rests his forehead against a shelf. He needs sleep, too, but anxiety about her—about all of them!—tingles in his veins. Three drops of tincture into a vial; he'll mix it with water from her drinking pitcher. For himself—he tilts back his head, releases the tincture directly onto his tongue. The acrid herb might as well be a match tossed into his mouth, burning and terrible, but taking it like so is preferable to drugging himself in front of his wife, his patient.

As the days grow colder, the women are kept indoors more often. Shawls cut from old blankets are passed out in the afternoons; Amy wraps herself in a black wool triangle and shivers whenever she sits still. Sometimes there are squabbles over the largest and least worn of these shawls, and the rougher women tug blankets from each other's shoulders. At walk times, the attendants make them pace up and down the ward or lead them through the building to play London Bells in the calistheneum. The Walking Skeleton is left bundled beside the fire during such excursions, become frail again from fasting.

Whatever else she is doing, Amy scratches her head. Around her the others do the same, both the sloppy women and the neat. Tidy Mrs. Littleton scratches her scalp with the blunt end of a knitting needle, then applies the sharp end until blood trickles from her chignon. The large attendant takes the needle from her and uses it to push and part her hair, at the nape of her neck and the top of her head.

Oh, the attendant says. She looks at the rest of their heads, those who will permit their heads to be touched. Her large hands on Amy's head are warm, firm; Amy likes the tickle of the knitting needle on her scalp. But the large attendant keeps saying oh. Then she says, Come with me, please, and beckons for Amy to stand. Amy and Mrs. Littleton follow down the hall with the large attendant; when she stops at the door marked bath, Amy's hand closes around the solid rectangle in her apron pocket. Has she lost track of the days? But it's still light out, not bath night, and the boy, her brother, should be safe here with her on the ward.

Take off your clothes, Amy is told, once admitted to the bath room. She rushes to the door, locked tight. Water is already flowing into both tubs. Here, says the attendant, coming up behind her to unfasten Amy's apron. She tries to strip Amy of the garment.

No, Amy shouts.

It's dirty, the attendant says, with bugs. Do you want bugs? She pulls at the apron while Amy clutches its pocket—and the pocket tears free—a square of fabric blanketing the boy, who Amy holds now in her hand.

What's this about? Cigarettes? The large attendant peels Amy's fingers back like the skin of a fruit. When she opens the case, she smiles.

This is an old one! Is that your pa, then? What a nice boy he was, nice-looking—like you. See? I'm putting him right here on the windowsill. She sets the case on its end, so that the boy is looking at them with his perfect small eyes. Take off your dress, now, miss.

Shut that!

Are you as shy as all that? He can't see you. Just take off your dress and get in the tub.

Shut it, Amy says. She tries to find a way around the attendant.

Mrs. Littleton, naked, steps to the window and snaps the case closed.

You can't treat a daguerreotype like a common photograph, she says. The girl is right to be cautious.

Get in the tubs, the attendant says, pushing them both back from the window. She slams the doors to the cabinets, dragging out bottles and jars of ointment. The water is hotter and clearer than on bath nights, the attendant's hands more zealous, slathering Amy in strong carbolic soap, scrubbing her scalp, dousing her, dunking her, and repeating the process before toweling her roughly. Amy's skin burns even as her head still itches. The dress marked with her initials is bagged up with Mrs. Littleton's things and thrown down the laundry chute, and she must either wear what the attendant gives her—a shapeless chemise and chintzy drawers—or nothing at all. Dressed like this, still damp from the bath, she is positioned astraddle a straight-backed chair. The attendant arranges a sheet over Amy's shoulders and begins combing through her hair with close, careful strokes. The comb stops every time near the base of Amy's skull. The bulk of her hair is a wet tangle down her back.

Just sit still, and you'll get your photo back quicker, the attendant says. This'll grow in again before you know. A sound like metal teeth grinds beside Amy's ear, and, immediately, there's a loud splash from Mrs. Littleton's tub, the sound of wet feet slapping to the locked door. Mrs. Littleton begins to shout but Amy doesn't move as long snarled hanks tumble down the front of the sheet, into her lap. When the shears have chewed around from ear to ear, the attendant's comb begins to move again over her head, her hair weightless now, and the attendant's fingers plucking and picking across her scalp. Finally, the attendant shakes the sheet clear, brushes stray strands from Amy's bare arms. She helps her into an ugly, hospital-issue dress. Wet and naked in the corner, Mrs. Littleton stares.

You were a brave girl, the attendant says. If your pa had really been here, he would have been proud. Don't forget his picture, now. She walks Amy to the door, cracks it just enough for one person to squeeze through, and locks it quickly. From the other side, Amy hears the thud and sob of Mrs. Littleton trying to get out, desperate like Mrs. Bailey had been when she was trapped between wards. The sounds coming from Mrs. Littleton are like those Amy herself made earlier, when she feared for the boy. But the large attendant hadn't recognized him; she'd even thought he looked like Amy. Maybe. Amy touches her damp hair, slick and reeking of alcohol. Strands stick strangely to her forehead and cheeks. When she rounds the corner, she'll see herself reflected in the pier glass: thin and boyish, dressed like a charity case and shorn like a sheep. Let the other women stare if they choose; now that the boy is her father, no one will take him away from her.

With the excitement of the doctor's return and the trauma of losing her brother's photograph, the doctor's wife demands to be by his side in the evenings. Being useful, she calls it: I sleep so ill, anyway, James—let me be your secretary. Better to foster this bright mood, this chirpiness, than to risk one of her slides into dejection. Thus, the doctor invites Diana after dinner to his office on the hospital's second floor, where she claims his favorite chair as her own. Young Ingstrom, it is apparent, is working late, too—his office next door is lit when they arrive at eight o'clock. No doubt, the boy is working on his always-impeccable ward notes…or planning another torturous lesson for the students of the training school. But the sound of a pen scratching can't penetrate the hospital's thick walls, and the doctor resolves likewise to keep thoughts of Ingstrom from his mind. Diana peruses the finished pages of the annual report as he prepares its finishing touch: his letter to the hospital's 'Esteemed Board of Managers'.

The six men whom the doctor addresses are among the founders of this still-young city. Civic-minded businessmen, the managers lobbied for the hospital's erection and capitalized on its tremendous need for land, bricks, wood, plaster, cement. They served, too, on the selection committee that chose the doctor as medical superintendent. Though removed now from the day-to-day operations of the hospital, they appear at intervals to tour the wards or review the hospital's accounts. They will convene shortly to consider the doctor's requests, the treasurer's and steward's reports, and deduce their own estimates for next year's budget. They will take the report out of the doctor's hands, these managers, and pay to have it typeset and bound; they will deliver the completed document to their good friends in the state legislature. No large-scale improvements can be made without additional allocations from the state; as the treasurer's figures show, every bit of the hospital's money is budgeted somewhere, on coal or carriages, newspaper subscriptions or scalpels. If the managers are to persuade the legislature, the doctor must first persuade them, by making a convincing show of want.

How do you come along? his wife asks, popping up from his chair. She shakes her head when he passes her what he's written.

The facts are good, I'm sure—and heaven knows we do need new cottages and grading on the roads—but your prose is very dry. Have pity on these poor men, dear. After all, they are only making a hobby of asylum-keeping.

The doctor smiles and scribbles for a moment, until she has seated herself again. He writes his name, strikes it out, writes: 'The hospital is, architecturally, the perfection of its type. Success is only a matter of making sure that its operations are strictly regulated.'

It is duller yet; he's sure of it. He glances at Diana, starts over: 'The brain revealed is like the stone of a fruit, bored through sometimes as though by worms. One day, perhaps, there will be more refined means of excising disease from the living tissue. However, many of our patients do not suffer from diseases of the brain, nor from diseases of the body. This class of patient, the morally insane, is highly sensitive to rational influences. It is imperative, therefore, that the hospital has a large enough medical staff to keep up doctors' twice-daily rounds while staffing the training school.' That's better: a nod to the somaticists while making his own case. He continues:

'It will always be a struggle for any man to regulate his senses and sensibilities. The hospital is a training ground for self-control. I, myself, have envied the patients their peaceful routines, which allow them respite from everyday worries, an opportunity to resume responsibilities slowly and slowly recuperate their old selves.'

He hesitates over the bald appearance of *I*. '*We* might envy'? Yes, better so: 'We are happily aware that our facility is in far better condition than the state's older hospitals. However, our need for repairs and improvements is not made less serious by theirs being greater. We must continue to invest in buildings, staff, and equipment. Nor do we hold that attendants should be above the common need for food and sleep or that they should be so invested in their charges not to mind privations. We do not see the high rate of attendant resignations as a sign of the moral failings of the lower classes. Instead, we see the need for shorter shifts and higher pay. Our best-paid attendant earns one-third the average prison-keeper's salary. This is appalling. The attendants are caretakers, not swine-keepers, and we must remunerate them accordingly.'

His index finger cramps when he finishes the paragraph; his pen, half-dry, has made knifelike incisions into the paper. He has climbed astride his hobby-horses—too stridently? Perhaps meekness better suits the occasion. But his wife tugs the pages from under his hand.

A metaphor! she exclaims. 'The stone of a fruit'—quite poetical, James! A perfect note to end on, for the night.

He shakes his head. He has not yet given credit to all of the donors or written his appeals for more of everything. The steward fears that the hospital's water intake is too close to its sewer output. The plumber says that major improvements must be made to the pipes, if even a minimum standard of sanitation is to be met. And these improvements must be made quickly: all estimates suggest that the rate of insanity is increasing yearly, as is their state's population. The hospital must grow exponentially in order to keep up; it must have more medicine and more money. Briefly, the doctor describes these problems and passes the scored page back to Diana. He is perspiring, he realizes, dehydrating himself just before bed. He can't risk a headache tomorrow. Yet if he drinks too much water now, there will be a night full of bathroom trips ahead.

That's lovely, James, his wife murmurs, reading through to the end. Very good. But don't forget about the two of us. Here— She rises, taking his pen from its stand and bending over the letter. In a hand that nearly matches his own, she adds, 'The superintendent's apartment must have new carpets if a semblance of decency is to be maintained.'

I will not recopy this part, says the doctor, not this year.

Well, perhaps *I* will. Don't gape that way, James—it makes you look like an old man. You'll have to wait and see how I make my own appeals to the managers. We're both finished for tonight. His wife screws the cap onto his ink bottle, resting her hand atop it until he rises, relenting. She extinguishes the light before he's even donned his suit coat.

A bulb shines yet in Ingstrom's office. As the doctor locks his office, his wife raps her knuckles on the frosted glass of Ingstrom's door. Genius burns, Dr. Ingstrom! Take care that you get some sleep!

Goodnight, ma'am, the boy calls back. A natural exchange, easy, yet one that the doctor cannot bring himself to mimic. Not even with his wife's example can he behave warmly toward his prickly young colleague. Diana squeezes his arm, forgives him. She is in many ways still the charming girl who agreed to marry him and move, of all places, to Michigan.

To bed, she says, quietly, and he lets her lead him. But how can he let himself sleep, when, implicit in all of his requests to the managers, is the hospital's clamoring need for more of *him*?

Chapter Five

ATURDAYS, SOME WOMEN ARE CALLED to the visiting parlor. They return with baskets of apples or baked goods, packets of letters from back home. Amy has not been summoned since she arrived. Instead, on Saturdays, she is allowed to sit unattended in her bedroom. She sits by the window, holding a book borrowed from Mrs. Morris, holding inside the book, the open daguerreotype case. The boy with his fine features, undimmed. She takes care to keep him in the shadow of her book. It is *Eight Cousins*, still. The story of an orphaned girl named Rose, raised by her father's relatives. Amy's own cousins are far off in Ionia—all except one: her stepmother, named Rose. Her stepmother was her mother's cousin. Things are much simpler in the book. Everyone loves the orphaned girl because she is pretty and good, like her dead mother was before her. They don't say what killed her mother. It is a children's book, after all.

I don't have cousins, Amy tells the boy. No mother. He looks back at her, half-smiling. She touches her fingernail to his thumb-sized face. She doesn't mar him.

The ward is quiet, but there's activity outside, below her window. The stumps have been torn from the lawn and a crew is leveling the ground with rakes and spades. The white-haired doctor is with them. She watches him walking, stopping, stooping. He's gathering stones from the fresh dirt. When his hands are full, he casts the stones back to the ground. Then he waves and a man with a wheelbarrow comes to him. He points at the stones. The man takes small trees from the wheelbarrow, peels burlap from around the trees' roots, and plants a tree wherever there is a rock. Tiny trees go into the ground where tall trees were. Tall trees turned now into tables or pulped into paper. Planed into planks and sold at lumberyards. When she was small, the stacks of wood rose far over her head, and she scaled their sides when her father wasn't watching. You'll be crushed if you're not careful, he would say. She had never seen a forest until they moved north or imagined a lake so big she couldn't see across it—that lake now a blue line on the horizon. Before, her father had sold beams as broad as his shoulders and told her that, in the north, there were yet impassable forests. Now, she looks out at the hospital lawn leveled, and she lays her hand over the boy's perfect face, preserving him.

The men working below are like the men who worked for her father. Lumberjacks, who wore thick flannel shirts and sat where the trees ended and the lake began. Her father had said she would need to stay out of the woods beneath their house; she'd heard him say it when she listened through the air vent. But June turned into July and still, no one stopped her; there was no one but her in all the green woods. In August, her stepmother took to bed with heat headaches, made worse by their week at the water cure; she didn't notice that Amy's dress was falling apart. The leaves on the trees grew brittle and the dress more tattered, so that there was less to stop Amy as she ran down the hill, slipping on the dry duff and sometimes clasping the branches like hands to break her fall. She reached the bottom of the hill faster every time, out of breath and with her face smeared green.

There was no voice in the woods but hers, panting, no sounds of axes or of men—until one day there they were, six lumberjacks, sitting on the rocks where the lake began. They were passing metal bottles back and forth.

She walked out of the woods, toward them.

Hello! they shouted, and their axes were propped against the rocks. Come here, girl. Where did you come from?

Up there, she told them as she came closer.

Nice to meet you, they said, and she smiled. Their beards were stained brown with tobacco, but they seemed friendly.

Did you follow us from town?

You look a little banged-up.

You got a name, little girl?

The men had laughed when she'd asked for a drink, but they passed her a bottle. The metal on her tongue had a thick taste like tar, but the drink cut through it, ashes and sugar. It was what had warmed her at the water cure.

You're a thirsty one!

How old are you, girl?

Did you come down here to take a dip?

We'll watch your clothes for you….

She drank more. One of the men took her hand and pulled her down on his knee. His clothes smelled of sweat and sap, and he laughed and held her by the hips when she tried to jump up.

We met some nice gals last night! Did they send you out here?

Have another swig? There's a good girl.

You ain't got a husband chasing you?

No pimp hiding 'round about?

She shook her head, feeling the drink in her stomach. What's a pimp?

The man who held her laughed, his breath on her neck. Oh—he's a feller who'd charge us money…just for a little cuddle. So, I'm awful glad to hear that ain't how it is.

She'd felt the heat of his body at her back, the eyes of the other men on her shirt front, where the buttons of her dress had been torn away by branches. She'd pulled the placket together, covering her chemise. Until that day, there had been nobody but her in the woods.

Scootch back a little, darlin', just relax. I like a girl who doesn't wear a corset!

There's something familiar about you, little girl—you been following the camp?

It's them eyes—I like a gal with blue eyes like yours.

The man beneath her shifted, jogging her up and down. One of his broad hands settled on her stomach; the other rummaged between his legs.

Tell us where you came from?

Up there, she said, twisting to point. You can see the house. See?

They looked where she pointed, and some of them frowned.

You don't mean *that* house?

Keep squirming like that, gal.

You're the hired girl, then?

She shook her head. My father said stop. He doesn't want you to cut down these trees.

Yeah? What'd your *mother* say?

My mother is dead.

Who's your father to us?

Just keep wiggling….

He runs the lumber company. Nathan Underwood.

There's a joke!

He said to stop lumbering.

Prove it, they said, and she'd shown them her handkerchief, marked with AAU. Proof enough that their faces went slack. The man with the grayest beard pulled her to her feet: Did you take that from your mistress? When she shook her head, he frowned: I heard his daughter was touched. One of the others emptied his metal bottle into the sand. The man who'd held her swore and fastened up his pants, and Amy saw how close she'd been to the red thing he tucked away—close enough that it might have touched her. She ran from the men toward their axes. It took both her hands to lift one, to drag it to the edge of the water, away from the trees. It was too heavy for her to hurl. She waded with it until the oldest man caught her—her dress only wet to the knees.

Your father wouldn't like you down here, he said. Rinse your mouth. I'll take you home. He walked her up a trail the men had cut and her stepmother opened the door to the two of them. Found her by the lake, said the man. She seems confused. Her stepmother gave him money before she pulled Amy through the door and up the stairs. Shook her by the shoulders—what did you do? Put on your nightgown—get into bed. Did you think I wouldn't smell that rotgut? She gave Amy a strong dose of ipecac and stripped her drawers from her, examining them under the lamp. You must tell me if you've done something with those men—you must tell me now and not later. And, when Amy wouldn't answer, her stepmother left her alone—locked in the room where the windows wouldn't open—her stomach heaving with heat and purgatives. Over the days to follow there would be doctors come to look at her and then the trip by train.

At the end of the train, this hospital.

Amy lifts her hand and looks now at the boy—his gleaming, immobile eyes. His mouth that wants to move but can't. There was a game, she tells him, where we fell backwards into each other's arms. We rolled hoops down the street with sticks. There were other girls then.

The boy is beautiful and perfectly still. She closes the photo case to keep him inside.

At supper that night, something is strange. The breadbasket is passed more often than usual. Conversation is high-pitched and halting. Amy sits across from a stranger; the Walking Skeleton is not in her usual seat. She takes a bite of meat and cabbage, then another. No one comments on her eating. She looks around the tables, at all the familiar, nameless faces. The Walking Skeleton is not among them.

Where is she? Amy asks. Where is that thin woman?

Nobody answers, but all the women look up. Their plates are full, their mouths empty.

Where is she? Amy asks, louder, and strikes her plate with her spoon. The large attendant sets her own supper on the sideboard and hurries to Amy's side.

There, she says, laying her hand over Amy's. Quiet, now.

Where is that thin woman? Amy repeats.

Mrs. Lovelace?

The Walking Skeleton.

She's fine. She was taken away this afternoon by her husband. Now, will you be quiet and eat your supper?

Amy slips her hand free, and the large attendant goes back to her food.

She come around the dayroom saying goodbye, says the woman beside Amy—the mottled-faced woman. Her husband come around with her. Wearing his collar. A preacher, she says he is.

Where has she gone? Amy says, craning her neck to look again around the room. Where has she gone!

He come took her home. I expect he thought she'd been here long enough.

How? Why did he take her?

My husband come for me last time without sending word aforehand. He'll likely do the same next time.

But how did he know you were better?

The woman is patting her boiled potato flat. He brung me back when the haying was done.

The gong is struck and the women push back their chairs. The large attendant puts her hand on Amy's shoulder. You'll scrape the plates now.

I don't know how, Amy says.

Like this, the attendant says. She slops beef fat and potato skin from the nearest plate into the bucket. Then you stack them together.

When is she coming back? Amy asks. Mrs. Lovelace.

Shh, says the attendant. She's gone back home now. If you work hard to get better, you'll go home, too. Go ahead.

She stands waiting until Amy picks up a plate. It is slick to its edges with thin gravy. Amy tilts it over the slop bucket and the uneaten food slides off; the plate slides from her fingers. It lodges at the bottom of the bucket—almost an exact fit. The large attendant, counting silver, doesn't notice. Amy slops the other dishes until the plate is nearly buried in greasy leavings. She wipes her hands on a dishrag and starts toward the dayroom.

Come back here, calls the small attendant. You're one plate short. Somebody left today.

I thought of that already. What did you do with it?

Amy shakes her head. The Walking Skeleton has been kidnapped or has managed to rise up without Amy's help, to break out of this place where they are kept locked. The Walking Skeleton is gone without her.

The small attendant takes the slop bucket by the handle and leans it on its side.

Reach in and pull that out, she says.

No.

Reach in and pull out that plate, miss.

No!

The small attendant grabs Amy above the elbow and shoves her hand into the clotted mess of wet bread crusts, leftover milk, gristle. Amy lets her arm go slack, limp in the attendant's tight grasp. The attendant shakes her, and Amy's fingertips meet the edge of the plate. It tilts into her open hand, and her fingers close around it. She pulls it up from the bottom of the bucket, covered in scrapings, and flings it toward the attendant. Her wrist is still in the attendant's hand; the gesture is wild. Carrots, cabbage, potato flesh fall on the floor, on their feet.

You think you're too fine for chores? You'll wipe up that mess!

It's the thin woman's job!

Mrs. Lovelace is gone now. Wipe it up!

No! She pulls her slippery hand free, but the attendant catches her by a swath of skirt. The attendant wraps her arms around the tops of Amy's, her fists beneath Amy's ribs, making her kneel as before by pressing her own sharp kneecap to the back of Amy's knee. With the dishtowel, she swaddles Amy's fists, then forces her onto her elbows, dragging the girl's bound hands over the spill until it is cleaned up. Amy is breathless, dizzied by the fast, forced motion, held up by the hard hands that work her forearms back and forth.

Let me go!

You'll learn to do chores like everyone else!

No! My father is coming to get me!

Oh? The attendant lets go of Amy and crouches beside her. Just when is he coming?

Amy shakes her head. The Walking Skeleton will come back for me.

You'll be here a long time if that's what you're waiting for. Now get up.

The attendant hoists Amy by the armpits and rubs a dishtowel roughly across the bodice of her dress, where grease spots have already set into the dark fabric. Holding Amy by the arm, the attendant pulls her down the hall, through the dayroom, into her own room where it is dark and cold. When the attendant shoves her into the bed frame, as she does whenever she's angry, Amy falls forward, casting the photo case under the bed. When the attendant takes her clothing, takes her blankets, leaving her without the drink, alone—she has just the boy to shiver with beneath the mattress. Her cold fingers take comfort not from him, but from her own yielding face.

The doctor has come to recognize the air of an agitated ward. He is rarely surprised when the attendants tell him there has been a fight, a suicide attempt, a minor rebellion. Such incidents leave traces upon the other patients. On ward nine, the women walk in circles about the dayroom, pound silently on the airless organ. Some of the houseplants have been shredded.

The attendants bring him their ward notes, brief copperplate jottings. In the previous days, half of the ward has stopped eating, half has stopped sleeping, and several have acted out. All of this because a patient has been released; their small community has been disrupted. It is a sign of how far these women must still come, that they cannot bear such a commonplace loss. Even the loss of a favorite—a celebrity like the reverend's wife—should not seem extraordinary, in this place where people come and go with frequency. But the doctor has seen it happen often, that a patient improves upon taking an interest in another person's case and, conversely, relapses if the object of interest is removed. The doctor cautions the attendants against responding to this crisis with increased doses of sedatives: tranquility must be restored here through reason, not contrivances.

He goes to those patients who will not come out of their rooms—those who look up hopefully at his knock and sigh to see it is only him. They are brown-haired women with Bibles. They clasp their hands and pray with him that they will see their friend again, outside of this place.

The lumber agent's daughter is more distraught than the others, having lost not just a friend, it is to be supposed, but a surrogate mother. The girl has been confined to her room for three days, having fought with the attendants, having scratched her own face bloody.

The doctor knocks on her door before unlocking it. The girl sits in her chair, by the window. She wears a rough shift, like the patients do on the very worst wards, and her cropped hair is greasy. She's holding a book, which she shuts when he enters. Something shoved between its pages strains the spine. The air reeks of the girl's unwashed body and an unemptied chamber pot.

Hello, he says. May I sit with you for a while?

She stares at him, as if frozen.

He stands beside her chair, looking out the window. The object in the book could be anything—a knife, a razor. It could be nothing. He smiles calmly. It's a nice view from here, isn't it? You have the advantage of seeing my landscape design from above. He wipes the windowsill with his handkerchief and leans against it. I hope the view pleases you?

She slides her book beneath her, so that she's boosted several inches higher in her seat. She nods her head.

The attendants tell me that you haven't been well, Miss Underwood. They tell me you don't like to do your chores. I am certain you would cooperate if you understood that small tasks like these are part of your cure.

She looks down at her torn hands. No one writes to me.

The doctor studies her sad, scabbed face. When you were admitted, I instructed your parents not to write without my leave. That way, we can be sure that the environmental causes of your illness have been eliminated.

They left me, she says. Everyone left me.

There, there, Miss Underwood. I write to your father regularly, and you may be assured that I keep him well-informed of your condition. Right now, I am sorry to say, I could not report progress. But if you'll try to follow the attendants' orders, I am sure you will come along nicely.

She left me here, the girl says, beginning to cry.

Your parents had your best interests in mind, my dear, and they are acting in your best interests now. I know it's difficult to see others leave, but you will leave too, in time.

He lays his hand on her shoulder, and she startles so violently that her book shoots out from beneath her, falling, open, to the floor. Something else hits the floor, too, a small rectangular object that skids into the baseboard beneath the window. The doctor picks it up, a case of some kind, and the girl leaps from her seat. She tears at his hands, her bitten fingernails raking jaggedly across his knuckles. A flash of pain; she has drawn blood.

Miss Underwood! he exclaims. When he steps away from her, she comes after him, so that he must lift the case high over his head. Sit down, he commands her, sit down!

Her expression doesn't change: mouth open, eyes narrowed. She jumps for his raised left hand, grunting with effort and dragging at his arm with all her weight. But she is a slender girl, unguarded in her movements. So intent is she on the object he holds that he is able to catch her around the waist with his free arm. She thrashes against him as he hauls her to the straight-backed chair. The doctor has not the attendants' daily practice at subduing patients, but he manages to press her onto the seat. He sheds his suit coat just quickly enough to throw it around her, the back across her torso, straitening her. The heavy wool strains as he knots the coat's arms behind the chair's slats. What's in this case that has made her so desperate?

He opens it—and finds his brother-in-law.

Miss Underwood, he says. You are excited. I understand why. You know that you have done wrong. He's panting, pauses to quiet himself.

This doesn't belong to you, he says. It belongs to someone else— my wife—who values it very highly. Do you understand?

She wiggles her shoulders, working her arms loose of his improvised restraint. He seizes her left wrist, holding it behind her back. Her pulse jumps under his fingers.

Miss Underwood, stealing is not tolerated at this hospital. I am responsible for the interests of all the patients here—as you know. It is my opinion that this is not the proper ward assignment for you. I cannot risk your disturbing those around you, who are fighting their own battles with self-control. You will be moved to ward fifteen. The atmosphere there will suit you better.

An attendant will be in shortly. We will talk when you are calmer about the gravity of what you've done. My wife did you a kindness, and you have responded quite ungratefully.

He releases her wrist, and, when she doesn't fight, he unties the savaged arms of his coat. As soon as he's lifted it away, the girl falls forward, forehead to knees. He backs to the door, but she takes no notice of him. Her shoulders shake; she weeps in a high wordless whine as he locks the door from the other side. The doctor's heart is still pounding; he isn't often assaulted by patients, especially not women. The scratches on his hands will need to be dressed. His stretched coat may necessitate a trip to the tailor's. What he holds, though—the lost treasure—will make up for the discomfort, will make his morbid wife smile again.

He holds the daguerreotype behind his back, like a bouquet of flowers in his bandaged hand. Diana's white rug has been spoiled by hospital dust, but he wipes his feet at the door, this time, before tiptoeing to the threshold of the sitting room. She isn't there. There's no fire lit, no tea laid out. She is not in her bedroom, or in his study, either. He calls her name quietly—like a boy, playing hide and seek. He searches the second bedroom, the dining room, the pantry. Diana, he repeats, opening all of the doors. An hour until supper; must he wait that long to surprise her? He calls out, hello! but not even the maid answers.

Defeated, he sits down in the room where he finds himself—the parlor, where his wife receives patients. The horsehair couch is stiff from disuse, the air musty with the odor of hair wreaths, circlets of brown roses gone brittle. His wife began treating these with camphor after mice ate through their outer loops. He pushes his hand between the sofa's cushion and its stiff arm, making sure the same mice haven't nested in the furniture. He finds an ivory button, a scrap of paper. He turns the button between his fingers, pressing its carved pattern into the pad of his thumb. He does not wish for his wife to dislike or fear his patients. Living under the same roof, eating sometimes at the same table—she should not see them as morally degenerate. Deceitful, perhaps. But not despicable.

The doctor waits on the couch until the stairwell begins to echo with the voices of his wife and her maid. He waits for the sound of her key in the lock, her skirt brushing the walls of their narrow hallway. Her exclamation: has someone been in the parlor, Matilda? His wife is in the doorway, and he rises from the couch, smiling, saying look what I've found! Offers it to her in the palm of his hand.

Diana drops her parcels and snatches up the case, kissing it, kissing the image, and then kissing the doctor's cheek.

Where have you been? she asks the image of her brother. She glances reproachfully at her maid, who's gathering the dropped shopping.

I'll put these in your room, ma'am. Matilda rushes away, and the doctor lays his hand on his wife's arm.

He was only tucked in the couch; don't blame Matilda. Let me show you a safer place. He leads her across the hall to his study, unlocks his medical cabinet. Within it gleams his household collection of vials.

Diana touches the stoppers of the tinctures and powders. These won't hurt him?

The doctor wraps the daguerreotype in his handkerchief and lays it on the bottom shelf. They are airtight, he says.

Thank you, she says, and, before the maid spies them, she shuts and locks the cabinet door.

In her room Amy is alone in the dark. Her face is wet; the boy is gone. No hands reach out to catch her as she falls.

Then the door opens.

She doesn't make it out.

The attendants push her onto the bed. She tries to curl closed but the small attendant grabs her wrists and crosses them, forcing Amy onto her back, forcing her arms to her chest. The large attendant grips Amy's ankles.

Lie still, they tell her, none of your tricks with us. Lie still!

Amy writhes and arcs but she's anchored by the women's weight. The large attendant clambers astride her shins and Amy feels but can't see straps tightening around her ankles, fixing her to the iron bedstead. Then the large attendant climbs off and comes to the head of the bed. Her rough hands take over holding Amy's crossed arms.

The small one ties a handkerchief around the large attendant's nose and mouth and then one around her own face. They look like bandits, like cowboys out West—what do they mean to do?

Stop your wailing, the small attendant says, drawing a bottle from her apron pocket. You always like your medicine, don't you?

Amy shakes her head, trying to burrow into the mattress. The large attendant presses her palm to Amy's forehead, pinning her.

When the bottle opens beneath Amy's nostrils, there's a sick-ly sweet smell. She tries to hold her breath but laughter loosens in her, like bubbles rising through soda water. Stop tickling! she gasps, but both attendants have turned their faces away. The doctor's face was hot and dry; it felt the way his wife's skin looks: feverish. Amy's ears buzz and burn—feverish, too?

We had horses, she says, Quince and Duster, and Papa would come along after school and give us all rides home.

Did the attendants know her, back then? What were they like, as girls? Why are they hiding their faces, now?

Her arms and legs are not just restrained but leaden when she tries to squirm. How can two women weigh so much? Or is it the air of this place? Sneaking in through the transom, under the door, pressing her down down down....

There she goes, the large attendant says. Good girl.

Where am I going? Amy asks—and then she is gone.

Chapter Six

THE DOCTOR'S DESK IS COVERED in correspondences. During his weeks of report writing, he responded only to urgent matters, but now that the report has been signed, sent to the board of managers, he must work through these stacks of unanswered letters. He does so in merciful solitude, the novelty of office work having worn off for his wife. Nor in her absence does he engage a proper secretary. Let his nights be foreshortened; this is his work to do. When he finally closes his eyes, he sees his handwriting spooling across hospital stationery, the familiar, polite language of the letters keeping him awake. But he will not again answer those letters with morphia.

The weather has turned; the holidays are fast approaching. The doctor writes permissions for patients to leave the hospital at Thanksgiving and at Christmas. He answers inquiries about relatives' health—this one suffers from chronic constipation, that one has developed an abscess on his leg, another has developed a fear of crows. The accounts of several private patients are now delinquent, and he writes notes to accompany the treasurer's statements. The responsible parties must either remit payment or prove indigence before a probate judge, so that the costs of care can be transferred to the county. But the negligent parties know that their loved ones won't be turned out on the street, as they might at private hospitals—and the doctor perceives in some cases of nonpayment a gradual abdication of responsibility. Families distancing themselves from their troublesome kin, willing such relatives to disappear. In this era of 'progress,' how many families share this wish? He responds almost by rote to questions about the commitment process: two certificates of insanity are required, signed by two licensed doctors. Enclosed is a list of items that your daughter will need. Please be sure to label everything with her initials.

The doctor reads apologetic notes, as well: We regret that we have not visited this past year, but John's condition is most distressing to his mother. There is no history of such problems in her family or mine…. It is with chagrin that I must ask you to stop posting Matthew's letters home. They do more harm to their recipients than good to him, I am sure…. Please tell Amy that our absence is due not to neglect but to my own indisposition. It is vexing not to write to her directly, but I am sure she understands that this, too, is part of her cure…. Tell Pete his ma died Tuesday. Its too far to come get him for the funral.

To most letters, the doctor makes brief, consoling replies. You have your own health and the health of your family to attend to. Your son, brother, sister, daughter is being cared for here. Duty is often best met by placing a loved one in a hospital; home care leads too often to neglect, abuse, or suicide. But when it does seem practical to keep a patient at home, he writes in a different voice: Have you really no room for a sick woman who is quiet and neat? Your nephew is the ablest worker on our farm; won't you give him a chance? With the doctor's approval, the law allows for the trial removal of unrecovered patients, but few families make this experiment. To the constant funerary announcements, the doctor replies with condolences, assurances that he will carefully convey the news. He tends to give lowest priority to these black-bordered notes, their contents being least urgent and their imperatives often most distressing to the patients.

The doctor pauses now in his letter-writing to unearth from the piled envelopes a cardboard box with the photographer's imprint on its side. He opens the box to a stack of his own likenesses. A relaxed, frank expression; posture straight but not stiff—he smiles to find the picture a success. His hair has absorbed the studio's lights and is pure white against the red-gone-gray background. In the photograph, he appears distinct, distinguished, as he hopes always to be.

He lifts the top photograph from the box, by its edges, and signs the back, then takes a fresh piece of stationery from his desk drawer. Dear Sirs: Enclosed you will find my most recent portrait, just now delivered by the studio. Please include in the report as usual. Write directly if you have need of more. He addresses the envelope to the secretary of the board of managers, folds the note carefully around his image. He turns the box of photographs over, lifting it to leave an upside-down stack standing on his desk. He autographs the back of every one.

When Amy wakes, her hands have gone dead, flung between the bars of the bed frame. She flexes her fingers, as she's learned to do since coming here, since waking so often in strange positions. As the blood comes back, she becomes aware of leather straps around her wrists, raw patches at the bone. She does not struggle but lies still and looks at the ceiling. Her bed is now on the opposite side of the room. The chair is on the other side of the window; the table seems taller. She cannot tuck her feet to her chest; they are strapped down, too.

The room is full of sunlight. They have left her long past the alarm. The other women may have been told that she has gone home. They might be sitting in the dayroom or circling the lane while she lies forgotten. They are eating their oatmeal and she is hungry. Her feet are cold and her calves cramped. When she shifts her legs, the buckles of the restraints clank against the bedposts. She cannot move freely, begins to shout.

The door opens; strangers come in. Two women wearing attendants' shirtwaists, who are not the attendants. They are solid women with yellow hair and matching faces. They stand side by side beside her bed, and one repeats, Be quiet, Miss Underwood, be a good girl now. They look down at her as she yells: no. She has never seen them before and the word flows out of her again and again, as at night she hears it howling from others on the ward: no no no!

One of the women pulls the pillow from beneath Amy's head. Will you be quiet? Amy twists her limbs—a clamor of metal. The woman waits, holding the pillow in front of her chest. When Amy shouts again—no!—the woman presses the pillow down over her nose and mouth. Amy can't push back with her bound hands, can't buck the attendant's weight from her face and neck. The sour mass of the pillow holds her jaw open, filling the space where air should be. She can't find a breath—electric bolts striking her stuck body. The woman has thin pink lips that open: well? We can't have you setting off the rest of them.

Blink, the second woman says, blink if you'll be quiet now. She leans over the bed, her long blond face beside the smothering woman's, blinking herself, slowly. Amy's frenzied muscles twitch, her eyelids flicker wildly. When they do, the pressure stops immediately. The pillow lifts. Her eyes water when she opens them again; her chest burns as she gulps air.

This must seem strange for you, says the smothering woman, tucking the pillow back beneath Amy's head. You was brung here this morning.

Don't carry on, says the other. You're just one floor up. I'm Lil, and she's Klara.

Amy has never known the name of an attendant. She doesn't know if that's what these women are.

Stay with her, says the smothering woman, Klara. I'll get a tray.

Lil sits down in the straight-backed chair, now on the other side of the window.

The doctor left you some books, she says. You can look at them after you've ate. He left you something else, too, a picture. There, now, hold still. We'll unstrap you when your dinner's come.

It can all be borne if the boy is on the table, in her pocket—*with* her again. Amy lies still and closes her eyes.

Klara brings a wooden tray with a covered plate and a glass of milk. She sets it on the table, and the attendants face each other from the ends of the bed. They begin to unfasten Amy's restraints, her feet first and then one wrist. They help her sit up; they rub her legs. They set the tray over her lap and watch while she eats. She is too hungry to leave the boiled turnips or the bread crusts.

You'll stay here the rest of the day, says one. If you're good and quiet, tomorrow noon we'll let you take a meal with the others. There's a pot under the bed. We'll look in now and again.

The smothering woman removes the last of the straps and both attendants back toward the door. Amy sits on the edge of the bed until the lock turns.

On the table are books—*The Young Ladies' Guide*, *A Girl's Companion*. She pushes them aside. The leather case isn't there. But there's something thin and flat. They will ruin him if they treat him like this. She picks up the photograph quickly, covers it with her hands. She makes a tent around him with her fingers and looks in.

He is not the same. Air and light must have gotten to him, her boy, her brother, turning him into this white-haired horror—an old man.

But no. As she looks closer, she understands the difference. This isn't the boy at all, that dear boy with the earnest expression and the tiger's eye buttons. It is a photo of the old doctor, smirking.

The photograph flies from her twisting hands, spinning into the wall from the force of her effort to tear it in half. She picks it up, creased but not ripped, and rakes her nails across the old man's face and body. An edge turns up; she works it loose. The old man becomes a gray curl of paper that she rips smaller and smaller. The taste of him is bitter. She chews and spits and pushes the wet bits of the photo through the heating grate, then the cardboard, too, with his signature scrawled across it. She pushes the doctor from her room…and still the boy is missing, a captive of the feverish old woman. A captive of the old doctor, who has left her here with these stupid books. She opens the cover of the nearest one. It is a thick book, not from words but from margins two fingers wide. She tears out the title page, the table of contents, then grasps pages by the fistful and rips them from the book's spine.

It is fully dark in the room when the attendants return. The door's draft pulls scraps of paper into the hall. Hall-light shines in on pages covering her floor. The two women are not as strong as her old attendants but still, she is made to pick up the mess on hands and knees, made to lie back on the bed, strapped.

They keep her alone in the days that follow. The attendants Lil and Klara bring her trays of food, doses of the drink at night. They strap her to her bed before the lights go out, and, in the cramped dark, she finds no rapture but only a restlessness that does not abate. The girls back home, her father, her stepmother, the Walking Skeleton, the boy: she lies on her back, and none of them come to her. She is not able, like this, to go to them. In the afternoons, the matron visits to read from *Eight Cousins* and recite lessons about stealing, violence. The old doctor comes with his prying questions: why did you want that photograph, Miss Underwood? Who is that boy to you? Sometimes the stout doctor comes, instead. She will not speak to any of them.

Finally, the attendants bring one of her initialed dresses. They dress her; they walk her between them down the hall. It looks like the hall below, matches the old ward door for door. In the dayroom, though, the paintings are different. Different women sit in the chairs. Amy rubs the heels of her hands against the sealed scabs on her cheeks. Across the room, three women make guttural noises—like the country German her stepmother uses with the hired girls. A poor woman's language, which Klara and Lil begin speaking, too. Amy covers her ears and sits. The gong is struck; she eats supper with these new women and, afterward, files downstairs with them to the chapel, where liquid pictures of mountains and rivers project onto the wall. Her former wardmates walk past to their seats, and none of them notices her. She does not bother to call out, stand up—knowing that if she does there will be a punishment and knowing, too, that there is no one among them who she would care to see. The Walking Skeleton is gone, like the boy, and neither of them will try to find her.

* * *

In mid-afternoon, his rounds complete, his dinner consumed, the doctor habitually retreats to his private study for a half-hour's rest. He has settled into his favorite armchair when Matilda alerts him: That *man* is here, sir.

The doctor blinks for a moment, startled by this break from routine. It takes only another moment for him to guess what guest his well-trained maid would announce so pertly. Berthold Humphries. The most voluble of the hospital's managers, a widower, a glad-hander, Humphries is the owner of the brickyard from which the hospital's buildings were born. He is the visitor that the doctor most dreads. Even if Humphries has come alone, he will declare himself the visiting committee, will demand the managers' privilege of a tour of the wards; he will want to 'talk shop;' he may have already pinched a female attendant.

Before the doctor can button his jacket (last year's, outdated but serviceable until the tailor is through mending his abused suit coat), Humphries has joined Matilda in the doorway. The brickman's bulk forces the maid into the room. She wheels like a trapped cat before squeezing somehow past him and away.

James! With one stride Humphries crosses the carpet, taking the doctor's hand in both of his giant paws. I had business in town—thought I'd drop in.

Good afternoon, the doctor says, freeing himself.

I can't stay for your evening show but thought I might pay respects to the missus after we've had our talk. Humphries lowers himself into one of the doctor's armchairs, red-faced, his red hair dark with pomade. His greased head immediately spoils the antimacassar.

The doctor steps to his desk. Shall I notify her that you'll be staying for supper?

Please! The grub here just suits me. 'Bertie,' my friends tell me, 'visit the loonie bin if you must, but don't eat the food!' That's fool superstition, I tell them, the food's the best blessed part—though, of course, a widower like me can't complain.

No, agrees the doctor. His handwriting is pinched from late overuse as he writes to his wife: B.H. for supper.

So—Humphries rubs his great hands together—Let me see what you've been up to. It's a damned cold day out, but I wouldn't mind an indoor stroll, through the wards.

Of course, says the doctor, rising. Overcrowding is still troublesome on the men's wards—if you'll follow me?

Oh, ho, Humphries protests. We're all alert to the need for more beds up here, but I call it damned unchivalrous to overlook the ladies. Why not head in that direction for once?

The doctor closes his eyes, briefly. His hospital is not Bedlam, to be opened for the public's enjoyment. Still, this man has a deep and vested interest in the hospital's work.

Of course, the women would be delighted by your visit, Mr. Humphries, but perhaps you'd like to tour the new men's cottage? The patients there are living quite independently, and we already see great improvement in some of our milder chronic cases.

Humphries chuckles. You nearly cottage-d me to death last year, what with the plans and the groundbreaking and the open house. No, if you're determined to steer me, take me through the main building—show me the damage from these bad roofs. And, this time, let me see the worst of the bunch. It's always the same couple of loons playing checkers when I visit.

The doctor closes his fingers tightly around his ring of keys. I won't make a spectacle of my patients, sir.

Yours, are they? I'd sooner call them *ours*. And I think I've a right to see how they're being treated. Come now, Jim—let's be friends.

In their democratic essence, Humphries's sentiments are the same as the doctor's own, but no matter how he reminds himself of this, the brickman's hand on his back feels like an invasion.

This way, the doctor says and prays for forbearance.

The doctor leads his guest to the firedoor between his apartment and the south service stairs. Beyond this is the men's third-floor convalescent ward, the lowest class of the most promising patients. He unlocks and locks with Humphries close behind him. It is the smoking hour; Humphries follows the smell of tobacco down the ward to the dayroom. There, as he'd predicted, a pair of wizened checker-players face each other across the board. Other patients set aside their newspapers when they recognize the doctor. The attendants in their rough dark suits look at each other sideways and, laying down their hands, rise from the card table.

Who's winning? Humphries laughs, hikes up his pants. Tell me, boys, how many have you on this ward?

Twenty-two at present, sir, answers the taller of the two attendants. Both attendants have soft, mustachioed faces, and the doctor recollects that they are brothers, come from downstate.

You're over capacity, then?

Yes, sir. We've got ten in the dormitory, right now, ruther than six. The beds are tight, but we manage.

Ten to a room? Humphries turns to the doctor.

We've found that some patients are calmed by having others nearby at night, Mr. Humphries, and, then, of course, there are economic advantages to housing the indigent patients like so. And you'll recall that dormitories are used exclusively in our new cottages—a plan that's proved very successful at other institutions. If you'd like to tour those cottages….

All of us board members have read up on the cottage plan—I follow the idea right along. Still, James, I have to wonder whether it's wholesome to let them bed together like that. Considering—well, what we all know—they aren't natural to begin with, or they wouldn't be here.

Those with vicious habits are treated on the most disturbed wards, says the doctor carefully. Isolation and reflection calm their over-stimulated minds.

Over-stimulated *minds?* Humphries raises his eyebrows. Those aren't the parts I'd worry about, with all of them together in the dark.

The attendants glance at the doctor, then at the floor. They tug at their moustaches, trying not to smile.

The doctor clears his throat. You will forgive me if I cannot see the humor in sexual delusions. He turns to the attendants; he has made himself ridiculous. Dr. Ingstrom and Dr. West were here this morning?

Yes, sir.

And have there been any unusual problems of late?

Only that some of them have been more excited. The crowding is chafing them, sir.

Chafing—a bawdy word in the context of Humphries's joke, a little flare of insurrection from the attendant—but the doctor chooses to ignore the brothers' badly-hidden smirks. He turns to Humphries: Now, if we could have a building appropriation—

His guest has already drifted to the checkers table. More build-ings, you say? My brickyard won't argue with that, James. Look here, friend, why don't you take those? Humphries leans over the red player's shoulder, tracing out a triple-jump. When it is done, he thumps his champion on the back, as he often thumps the doctor. The red player thumps Humphries in return, as the doctor never does. Even the black player grins—and, after showing *him* a play, Humphries gestures to the doctor: carry on, carry on.

Deeper on the ward, water stains creep down the outside walls of the bedrooms. The pitch of the roof has proved too low, and the work of shoveling and scraping in winter is both dangerous and ineffective; water *will* seep in. The allocation needed to fix the problem would add nothing to the day-to-day efficiency of the hospital, but safety and sanitation demand the repair. Whether Humphries is listening, the doctor cannot be sure, distracted as he clearly is at being in the patients' rooms. Humphries picks up the photos and hair wax tins littering their side tables; he inhales in quick, steady puffs the mingled scents of sweat and tobacco that mark the men's wards. Surely, it must trouble the brickman to think of a bad roof damaging his good yellow bricks—bricks that hold up this building and half of their growing town. But Humphries's small eyes move restlessly, as though he's looking for something else. The doctor can never be certain what Humphries sees on these tours, nor what to guard against his seeing.

They pass through the firedoors onto the adjacent intermediate ward. In the dayroom, three old men crowd onto a battered sofa, a thick pad placed between them and the cushions. The room smells faintly of their urine, strongly of chewing tobacco; the cuspidor is full. An attendant is washing the windows with ammonia and newspaper. He tears off his apron when he sees the doctor.

A woman used to come, but she don't come no more. The man flushes red; he balls the apron in his fists.

Humphries steps to the window and rubs the pane with his

handkerchief—laughing when it comes away dingy, laughing at the attendant's expression.

It's all right, Frank, the doctor says. You're doing a fine job. He shakes the attendant's hand, as dry and tough as a charwoman's. From the couch, the senilics giggle, the sound drawing Humphries like a magnet.

There's little to remark on this ward. If it is not as clean as the convalescent ward, it is nonetheless passable. The three old men present are neither dirty nor deranged; they are insane in the most mundane sense, rendered so by old age. Their able-bodied ward-mates are in the fields, the workrooms. *Trainable*, Humphries calls the absent men, and, rather than quibbling over language, the doctor agrees, adding that these men have had bad luck, either with fortune or heredity.

Those who have had worse luck, those who have no real hope of leaving this hospital—except to go to another one—are housed on the next ward. It is the ward farthest from the administrative offices, highest from the ground. It is the hospital's worst ward, put bluntly. The doctor waits for his guest, who lingers now, folding his handkerchief into the shape of a dove. When Humphries flicks his wrist, the bird hangs free for a moment in the air before turning again into a square of fabric and fluttering to the floor. The old men clap. Humphries folds the handkerchief back into his pocket, bows, and nods down the hallway.

The doctor hesitates in the service stairwell before unlocking the last door. To the men on the other side, he is of no more use than Humphries. The violent cases, the chronically deranged, recover by chance and relapse just as unexpectedly. After death, autopsy will uncover lesions and tumors upon the brain, degeneration of the frontal lobes—hidden diseases hinted at now by the patients' faltering motor control, erratic moods, violent and filthy behaviors. Old injuries that the body has not forgotten. The families of these chronic cases could no longer make excuses for them. Those families put their faith in the doctor, on the doctor. On him rest their hopes that their sons' lives will be salvaged—that they will be restored to full citizenship in this country where anything is possible. But the men on the other side of the firedoor are not able even to work in the fields. The doctor opens the door and steps through first, first to catch the stench of shit, the din of sundered voices.

Humphries swears, bringing his dusty handkerchief to his nose; the doctor takes his heavy arm.

It can't be helped, he says. Will you turn back?

Humphries shrugs loose. Not before I see what you're doing here, he says. That's the bottom line. He strides quickly past closed chamber doors, toward the brightness of the corridor's bay window. There are no proper dayrooms on the worst wards.

The ward's two attendants emerge from the short hall at the far end of the wing. Two young patients trail behind them, like children after pied pipers.

Dr. Ingstrom and Dr. West was just here, sir, says one of the attendants. We ain't got anybody sick right now. Behind him, the patients quarrel over a bulky rocker. They are dressed alike in hospital-issue pajamas. Humphries stops short when he sees them, taking in their small features, their smooth, mild faces.

We're here on a tour, the doctor reassures the attendants. Go on with your business. We won't be long.

Already, in fact, Humphries seems anxious to leave, shifting from foot to foot. He has less to study in these stark surroundings—floors tiled, windows bare. There is no visiting parlor here; ward eighteen does not often receive visitors. No potted plants or card tables to look over, but only bracing mottos painted on the walls: *Valor consists in self-recovery; Nothing can bring you peace but yourself.* Truncated adages from Emerson.

Humphries coughs. Not as homey as the others, is it? I can see why the men keep to their rooms. He steps from the doctor's side to peer into the nearest bedroom. The round grate in the closed door is smaller in circumference than the brickman's broad face. Humphries swears: This fellow can't be thirty!

Mr. N's is a case of general paralysis, the doctor says, joining Humphries at the door. The patient inside sits on the edge of his bed. His head hangs forward, his face slack. One of the most common diseases among our male patients.

Humphries chews the ends of his moustache. What's being done for him?

We keep such patients clean, feed them nourishing foods, allow them plenty of rest. But the disease is progressive and, as far as we know, irreversible.

The disease is syphilis—isn't that right? Humphries turns to face the doctor directly. Poor fool probably paid for the privilege of getting it, and here he sits paying for it some more.

The doctor studies Mr. N rather than Humphries. The cause of GP isn't always clear, or the diagnosis itself perfectly reliable—a brain tumor can cause similar effects. But we do treat these cases as we would syphilis, with iodide of potassium and mercury.

Humphries nods, his expression dour. And with locking him up like an animal.

Mr. N has failed physically since his admission, but he's still capable of violence. He suffers from a delusion that those around him are siphoning his vital forces—the fact that he's growing weaker only increases the strength of this delusion. He's attacked the attendants, his fellow patients—he attacked his own family before they brought him to us.

At the word *family*, Humphries raises his eyebrows, and the doctor nods.

He leaves a wife and three young sons.

Hereditary cases in the making. Humphries coughs into his handkerchief. It ought not to be so, he says firmly. That such a man has propagated when you and I have not. It's the decline of the race, is what it is.

Let's not exaggerate the problem, the doctor says. All around you, you see hale, hearty young people, who—

Who might crack up at any moment, Humphries finishes. If it happens to me, Jim, I've got my pistol handy. No cages for me—and you can't tell me that *he's* better off, either. To say nothing of the impact that this sort has on the rest of your patients. The chronics are just eating up resources that might be used on curable cases—and where's the good in that? The economics of the thing are rotten, and I say so as a citizen, not just as a businessman.

I understand your frustration, the doctor says. But we're not a private hospital that can admit its patients selectively. There's a pressing need in the state for custodial care.

Is that how you explain *them* being here? Humphries gestures to the two young patients, still squabbling over the rocking chair. Our charter expressly forbids admitting idiots—and you know it, James. I imagine that's why you're hiding them back here.

The doctor shakes his head. Where else can they be sent, Mr. Humphries? A sanitation officer found them at a mining camp in Hancock—preyed upon, without protection. I've written to the Governor, the Board of Charities, the Commission on Lunacy—

and I will keep these boys here until the State provides a more suitable accommodation.

And, thus, your recovery rate remains at ten percent, says Humphries. Well, better they're in here than out in the world, spawning—but I'm bound to tell the other board members about this at our next meeting. We've all agreed to the rules, James—even you. He extends his hand for the keys. I've seen enough for now.

It's closer to twenty percent, the doctor cannot help himself from saying. Our recovery rate. If you factor those released as improved.

But, keys in hand, Humphries has already thundered off. The doctor lingers a moment longer.

These two orphan boys are reminders of all the other feeble-minded patients the doctor has had to turn away, as not properly the responsibility of a hospital such as his. Meanwhile, Mr. N is a reminder of something else. He is Thomas Nickerson, properly speaking: once a law clerk and now the resident of an insane asylum. Like the others here, Nickerson is a man to whom the doctor is beholden, a man to whom he has made an implicit promise. His word that he will effect changes for the better—and who but blowhard Humphries would deny that the doctor has *kept* his word, by providing the man comfortable and humane accommodations, constant care? Who would dismiss that achievement, except Humphries, the young somaticists…and Mrs. Thomas Nickerson?

The doctor calls softly: Mr. Nickerson! and the man inside the room lowers his head farther, until his forehead touches his knees. The doctor calls again, but Mr. Nickerson does not look up. The doctor would go into the room—wouldn't he?—but Humphries has his key ring.

Jim! Humphries shouts. He's holding the firedoor open with his wide foot. Come on, unless you're ready to be locked in!

The doctor obliges his guest; he follows the brickman off the ward.

The center of the building is brighter than usual this night, readied for the party that Diana has managed to throw together. On the ground floor, the officers' dining room has been opened, lamps lit in the foreign, formal room. The hospital's two receptionists have stayed for the evening to help serve. Guests file in after Matilda announces the meal: women from the receiving room, men from the managers' parlor. Eight extra bodies to shield the doctor from proximity to Humphries. Here are the first, second, and third assistant physicians, along with Mrs. West and Mrs. Meijer. Dr. Ingstrom is a bachelor; he and Humphries sit opposite each other, at the bottom of the table, with the doctor's wife at the end. She has invited two of the women from ward one to balance the party. They are women who can properly return a man's gaze and who laugh at the right pitch when Humphries makes his jokes. Miss Williamson has auburn hair and made herself ill with overstudy. Mrs. Sherman is the most beautiful woman at the hospital, though there was a time when she could not recognize herself in a mirror. The doctor's wife has placed Humphries beside Mrs. Sherman; he passes her the relish dishes before she asks for them. She slices small bites from her pickled beets, covers her mouth with her hand when she chews. Across the table, Miss Williamson is flanked by Ingstrom and Meijer, the two physicians who attend the men's wards.

The doctor, at the head of the table, chats quietly with his colleagues' wives and watches what could be courtship. Ingstrom shapes his fingers into a tent, opening his eyes wide, and the doctor's wife laughs, the patients laugh when the finger-tent flies apart. The doctor pours more wine for Mrs. West and carves for plump Mrs. Meijer. The meat is a pork roast, which the doctor dislikes.

After apple cake, coffee, the doctor lets Humphries fill the managers' parlor with clouds of cigar smoke. The women have gone to the chapel for the evening entertainment, escorted by the other doctors.

Another fine meal, says Humphries. Blowing smoke rings and smiling, he stands beneath a handsome lithograph of his own brick factory. All local?

Everything was raised and prepared on the premises.

It's impressive, what they can be taught to do—those boys on the middle wards. And the women—well, the women tonight certainly seemed a likely pair.

The recovery rate for female patients is slightly higher than that for males, says the doctor. Of course, tonight, you've seen the very fittest of the women.

A balm after what we saw earlier. Don't scowl at me, Jim—you know it's confounding to see men like that. Humphries stubs out his cigar and reaches into his breast pocket, withdrawing a check. Maybe this will help you to keep up with the times.

The doctor shakes his head, seeing the figure: $3000. You shouldn't do this. We're grateful for your time and advocacy—it's too much to accept gifts, as well.

I'm all alone—let me share what I have. And in return, why don't you have me back for dinner once in a while? I like that Ingstrom better every time I sit down with him, and West and Meijer have always suited me. We'll make it a regular event—you might bring in the same ladies every time and all the rest, too.

The doctor holds the check in both hands. It's enough money to pay sixteen attendants for the year, build a new icehouse, dig a new well....

It's very generous of you. But if I accept this, it must be to use at my discretion—in consultation with the managers, of course.

Yes, yes—I'm not trying to run the place, James—that's your line. But if my money can help you to catch up with the times—with neurology, you know, and these surgeries they've been trying—trephining, even, from what young Ingstrom was telling me earlier—well, it would please me tremendously, to think that I'd helped to raise the recovery rate.

The doctor extends the check toward Humphries. Three thousand dollars won't turn us into a research hospital, Mr. Humphries.

No, no. Humphries pushes the money back. But it could change *something*, couldn't it? Don't look so mournful, James, not when I've just made you a gift. 'Thank you' is what I'd say—that would be gracious of you, don't you know.

And I *do* thank you, says the doctor. You mustn't mistake my concern for ingratitude.

All right then, I won't. Now, phone over for my buggy, would you? I'm due at the club. That's fine—I can see myself out. Humphries takes his coat from the tree, swings its great folds over his shoulders, and fairly breaks the doctor's hand in shaking it. The doctor can hear the brickman's steps ringing down the corridor, his guttural voice singing. He looks at the thin piece of paper Humphries has left behind.

Three thousand dollars. A considerable gift—yet it will go nowhere toward addressing the overcrowding they've seen today. It cannot pay for the necessary repairs to the roofs or fix the hospital's plumbing problems. It might purchase some of the land adjacent to the hospital, fence more of what they already own. Above all, the gift will make its donor feel as though he has contributed to progress.

It would be a great relief, the doctor suspects, to believe like Humphries that the brain can be serviced like a clogged steam engine: vented, fixed. The doctor himself holds a more realistic view—of Mr. N, for instance. If this patient's skull were trephined, his brain relieved of fluid pressure, his disease would only have more room to grow. What would such an experiment add to the poor man's comfort? And who on his staff would be qualified to perform it? Isn't it more compassionate to care for him than to exploit him?

The doctor tucks Humphries's check into his vest pocket. He'll forward it to the hospital's treasurer tomorrow. But it seems to him less a gift than another obligation, and, though he had eventually managed a *thank you*, in truth, he would rather have torn the check into pieces.

Chapter Seven

FROM THE WINDOWS OF THE new ward, Amy can see the lake plain and the long barges taking on logs at the dock. She can see smoke rising from all the houses in town. The lawn is lower now and when she looks down, she sometimes feels as if she is falling forward from the window—the window through which she could never pass, its panes doubled by a set of bars. When the sash is raised, an iron grid is still in place. A girl could put her arm through the pane-like bars but not her head, never her shoulders.

Amy stands often at the windows because she is forbidden to sit alone in her room or to handle books. She does not knit, as some of the others do, and she does not care to listen when Lil and Klara try to read aloud. The doctors come but they can't make her talk. She is not made to clean, though there is always dust blowing along the baseboard on this ward. Always handprints on the windows, long hairs matted into the rugs. She takes more care of her dress now that there are messes to be avoided.

Many of the women are missing, days on this ward. They return with loud voices in the late afternoons. Coming into the dayroom, they disrupt their sleeping wardmates; even when she happens to be awake, Amy cannot bear their conversations. She turns her back to all of them, pressing closer to the window—standing so close to it that the lamplight fringes her reflection. Her face becomes a blank that swallows up the others when they pass behind her. This is a comfort: though solid women move about the dayroom, they are only shades on the dark glass. Smaller than her and unreal. They let her alone, unseen, unbothered. Until, one afternoon, another reflection appears beside hers, as suddenly as a ghost. Someone else slight and featureless: another girl.

Amy shudders as the girl grows larger in the window. Growing too is a sharp odor of sweat and lye soap from the laundry. The girl's body is a surge of heat, close by.

The girl stops abreast of Amy and leans her head against the glass. She rolls her brow from side to side, leaving a smear on the pane. Says, That's nice, ain't it?

Amy holds her breath. She can see only a sliver of the girl, out of the very corner of her eye: a red-brown frizz of hair, a hospital-issue calico.

I'm Letitia, the girl says. She closes her hand softly around Amy's wrist and lets go. Her touch leaves its feeling behind on Amy's skin: rough and dry and hot, the pad of a dog's foot. Amy breathes out, slowly. She turns from the window to face the other girl directly. The girl holds out her hand and Amy takes it.

The girl Letitia smiles and her mouth is full of sharp gray stones. Jagged teeth that tilt toward one another, broken. Remnants of teeth, and it is as though the dentist's file is in Amy's mouth, laying her nerves open to the raw air. She brings her hands to her cheeks, dropping Letitia's hand, stepping back, looking away. Looking at the rug, at the yellow chrysanthemums on the mantle—and back at Letitia's ghoulish smile. Cold water tingles across her knees until Letitia closes her mouth and puts her hand in front of her face.

Ain't they hideous? she asks. Her great brown eyes widen.

Amy shakes her head.

I wouldn't take my medicine.

Did they beat you?

Four sat on my chest while another stuck a wedge between my lips. I had the tube for a week afterward.

Who? Amy glances around the room for the attendants sitting at their table in the corner.

Letitia shakes her head. It was when I was at Pontiac.

Amy looks at the girl again—at her cheeks, pink and smooth but nipping in near the corners of her ruined mouth. Doesn't it hurt?

Sometimes. But then Lil gives me a rag with ammonia to suck on. You should fake toothache sometime—it's that nice.

Can you eat?

Most things. They grind the rest up for me. Dr. Ingstrom's going to send me to a dentist to get false ones.

Your father should get you some.

My father is a madman.

Your mother's father, then, says Amy, blushing.

Letitia shakes her head. He doesn't know I'm here.

Your mother should tell him!

I wish she could.

Mine is dead.

They had mine at Pontiac. I walked there. She wasn't there, but they tried to keep me, so I ran off. Then a farmer caught me stealing potatoes and they locked me up again and I got my teeth all broke. I was at Kalamazoo for a while, too, but she wasn't there.

Dr. Ingstrom says they might have sent her to Illinois. He's the tall one with the black moustache.

There's a boat that goes to Chicago.

Letitia nods. A train, too. He's twenty-nine. He wants me to go away with him. He wants to give me special treatment.

My mother is dead, Amy repeats. She cannot bring herself to say more.

Letitia sniffs. Are you here because of grief?

Amy shakes her head. I ran off, too.

At my other hospitals they had little kids but here I thought I was the youngest. Letitia stares at Amy and then smiles with her mouth closed. Do you want me to tell you about the crib?

What's that?

It's a box like a bed. They strap you in by your waist and your feet and hands and close the lid tight on top of you. The whole thing is made of wire like a chicken coop and cuts into you terrible. You can barely turn your head and you're held so tight you can't hardly breathe. If you want anything, you have to hope a nurse is coming and not the one that put you in, because she'll beat you with her keys and put the tube down your neck.

Amy leans closer to Letitia. Is there one here?

Here! This is a holiday compared to the other places I've been.

How long have you been here? Amy asks. The smell from Letitia's mouth is discomposing.

I come up on the train with the doctors when it opened.

But how long ago?

Letitia uses her fingers. Five or six years, I believe.

Amy sits down on the floor. There are old woman sitting near the fire, old women sitting on the ward below. Letitia crouches beside her. The other girl was taller, standing, but their shoulders are level now. Letitia's thin face is freckled; her eyes are asters full-blown. Her mouth is an old woman's. She closes her fingers again around Amy's wrist. Amy clenches her jaw and breathes.

The doctor's wife begins lighting candles on the first day of December. Her Advent observance has become more elaborate in the years since they moved north. Whereas once she marked only the Sundays of the season—purple candles in an evergreen wreath—now she celebrates each day, anticipating Christmas like a latter-day magi. It may be the heavy snow, the fir trees, the coziness of their current home that inspire her behavior, or perhaps all of this is tied to the hobbymania she has developed since her change in life. Whichever the case, watching her prepare for the holiday, the doctor regrets that the only nativity she has experienced is this symbolic one. Advent is, for him, a season of self-reproach. He failed to give her a real child. He failed to work that miracle.

His wife is more than usually involved in planning the evening programs, this month. Nights are full of carols—'O Come O Come Emmanuel,' anticipatory, wavering. While the doctor repeats his daily routine, his wife sleighs through the woods with the groundskeeper, collecting holly and pine boughs, searching for a tree to fell on Christmas Eve. Once the chapel is thoroughly decorated, she turns to their apartment. Every room is garlanded, gilded; there are crèches on every open surface. His wife makes him kiss even Matilda's cheek, if they pass each other under the mistletoe.

Her fevers flare, despite the falling temperature. The doctor administers sulfur baths and cold compresses and warns her not to over-exert herself. But her enthusiasms, once upon her, cannot be curbed. She crochets delicate stars and snowflakes, straining her eyes. She cuts cookies as thin as pasteboard, stamped with elaborate Scandinavian patterns. She strings popcorn and cranberries, forgetting to stop for tea. Her once-orderly afternoons devolve into shopping frenzies; everything *New for Christmas!* is heaped in brown parcels in the parlor. She has hinted and hinted her own Christmas wish for one of the new box cameras. He will indulge her, of course; if the thing can be gotten, she will have it. And, yet he cringes already, imagining the ardor this gift will (temporarily) excite in her. She will tyrannize him with requests to pose or demand his company on scenic afternoon drives. The doctor imagines his wife stumbling home after a day of snapping as she stumbles now, walking to her bedroom, worn out by her holiday exertions. He shares his wife's bed, nights when she is very ill, endeavoring to warm her shivering body. If his limbs should touch hers, she begins to twitch and talk in her sleep. Fever shakes her frame, shakes the mattress.

Accustomed as he is to sleep-deprivation, the doctor cannot bear his wife's thrashing, which erupts every time he's almost asleep. Yet neither can he leave her, for what if this were the night that a low fever finally gave way to something worse?

He creeps from his wife's bed with sick-room footsteps, opening the door so slowly that the latch does not click. Down the hall, quietly, to his study, where he retrieves his key ring from his top desk drawer. He mutes the keys' rattle against his palm, searching out the smallest. Normally, he could mix a draught with his eyes closed, but he switches on the overhead light, sleep-starved as he is. The electric beam shines on his rust- and dust-colored powders, his droppers, pincers, beakers. It shines on one of his monogrammed handkerchiefs, folded into a neat bundle. Like an archaeologist, the doctor slowly exhumes the small mummy inside.

Inside the handkerchief, the molded leather case, sarcophagal. Beneath its velvet-lined lid, his brother-in-law's face, enshrined.

Though familiar, it is still a disquieting find—the image of a young boy with his hair in long curls—his wife's treasure. The child's androgynous beauty provokes in the doctor a sort of schoolyard contempt; his brother-in-law was, by all accounts, a ninny. Studying in bed, coughing, coddled, subjected to one faddish treatment after another. It's a wonder the boy was ever let up, sent off to school, set up with a legal practice. His mother's paranoia borne out: it was tuberculosis, after all. Charles was dead before the doctor was brought into the family. In all these years since, the doctor has never heard him referred to as a living brother but only as a sort of icon—a tubercular saint whom his sisters revere and whose symptoms they adopt, more or less convincingly. On occasion, the doctor has even seen blood on his wife's handkerchief.

But Diana's imitation is, overall, unpersuasive. Her lungs are no weaker now than when they met, those years ago at the sanatorium. He had listened then to the shallow intake in her chest, measured the slow, soft pulse of her blood. Then, her physician and not her husband, he called her ailment neurasthenia: nervous exhaustion. Based on his tentative gynecological inquiries, he had considered it unlikely that she would ever bear children. A dropped and small uterus, periods that came either heavily or not at all. She was not constituted for motherhood. He hadn't, however, predicted her other problems. She complains here of what sound like heart symptoms, there of digestive troubles. After all these years, his present diagnosis is no more precise than the original: her ailment is not the wasting disease that she regards as a birthright but something else, that, recurring, prostrates her—and renders her prone, like his patients, to bouts of acute melancholy.

He closes the daguerreotype case before mixing a dose. He doesn't dare give Diana more morphia, but valerian has lately had no effect. What can he do, then, except drug himself, again? He wraps the handkerchief around the daguerreotype before swallowing his bitter draught. No palliatives for him—none of the wine and cinnamon that make for a laudanum addict. Let this taste sting like an embarrassment.

Slipping back into the bedroom, he stands inside the doorway in the dark. Afterimages from the electric light burn before his eyes, and he cannot hear her breathing. Cannot hear her breathing, and rushes to the bedside, to find her quiet and still—sound asleep.

It becomes a habit for Amy to stand at the window in the late afternoon, not hiding but waiting. Staring at the room reflected, she never misses Letitia's entrance. She does not spoil the other girl's game, but stands still, as if unsuspecting, while Letitia sneaks along the wainscoting. Boo, Letitia whispers, seizing Amy's from behind, and her fingers span Amy's abdomen like an extra set of ribs. The smell of Letitia's mouth is like camphor and rot when she laughs.

Together they find chairs or a sofa; they sit on the floor rather than sit apart. Letitia tells Amy about her day in the laundry. The lazy laundry-attendants, the men who operate the machinery, the men who fold drawers and undershirts at the table adjacent.

The way they stare at us! And don't they move fast if they see you with your hands full—let me and may I. They're old men! It's silly to have them there at all. As though I haven't touched men's drawers before.

You have? asks Amy.

Back when I was home and had all the chores to do. You haven't had to wash, I 'spose?

Amy shakes her head. She cannot imagine handling her father's underclothes.

Think of it—I might've been your washwoman, if you'd lived downstate.

Amy opens her mouth to tell Letitia about the lumber mill, the other girls, the dry grass underfoot where she used to live, but Letitia is still talking.

The man who runs the mangle, he's what I call handsome. Nice broad shoulders and hair as black as Ingstrom's. 'Course he don't speak to any of the rest of us—and I don't know but that he can't. The laundry-attendants are the only ones who talk to him, all the day long. But sometimes I catch him looking around, and I look right back at him, too. We don't wear our collars, in there—it's that hot—and I know why he's looking. Somebody said he came from Russia.

Amy glances quickly at Letitia's bosom, full beneath her worn dress. Have you ever seen a wolf? she asks. It is all she knows of Russia.

No—but I was chased by wild dogs once, when I eloped from Pontiac. They were in the woods near the train tracks and came out after me, a whole pack of them. I made it up a tree but not before they tore my skirt to shreds. I was up there for hours before they went away.

Were you…naked?

No, not even, but I looked like a savage when they were through with me. I had to beg for a blanket when I come out of the tree. Well, the old woman gave me one of her worn-out shifts and a blanket, besides, but she had a hired man who come out to the barn after she went to bed, and he got terrible rough. My ma told me if anything like it ever happened to eat wild carrot root just as soon as I could, so I did, and it gave me terrible stomach pains, but it brought on my bleeding. Think of where I'd be if I hadn't known what to do!

Oh, says Amy, and she puts her arm around Letitia's shoulder, carefully, as though there were still bruises there. She has been given purgatives, she might tell Letitia. A lumberjack once held her on his lap. But what is that to Letitia's story?

Letitia sniffs. I've had a hard time of it—and that ain't even the worst.

Yes, says Amy, quickly.

I'm an orphan, I think.

Me, too.

You ain't either.

My mother is dead.

But you still have your pa.

No, Amy says. It has been months, now, or something like a year since he left her at this place. She no longer looks for letters.

If you're lying, I'll know. I'll know soon.

How?

Pretty soon they'll start taking ladies away.

Amy's arm tightens around Letitia. She is not thinking of bruises now. Where?

For Christmas. Most leave for at least a week. There's Christmas dinner with the doctors for those that stay. Last year I pulled poppers with Dr. Ingstrom.

Will they tell us, when they take us?

If you're an orphan, nobody'll come for you. You'll have to stay here. Letitia sniffs. You said you were.

I am, says Amy.

I am, too. Letitia smiles sadly, without parting her lips. She casts her eyes down and then up, and for Amy there's suddenly a flash—of night in her room and the drink in her head. The same loose feeling in her joints when she looks too long at Letitia's eyes. Later she will return to this moment: grit against her palms, when she pushed herself off the floor; shadows falling across their laps; a hollow sound when she laid her ear to the wall. The room of women, before them, unaware, and Letitia's brown-and-gold eyes—so beautiful they eclipse her broken mouth entirely.

On the sixth of December, the hospital celebrates Saint Nicholas's Day, with fiddle music in the chapel and windmill cookies in honor of the Low Countries. The steward, as Saint Nicholas, wears a glad red robe; the groundskeeper soils his face with soot and wears tattered clothes, taken from the tailor's shop. He shakes a thorny locust branch, carries a large potato sack; he is Knecht Ruprecht, the elf whose grimaces provoke truthfulness. This pair circulates, asking each person whether they've been good this year. (Those who might not understand such games are kept back on their wards). The patients, perhaps more truthful than children, answer yes and no in equal numbers. Saint Nicholas praises and consoles, annotating his list of names. In the morning, the patients will find encouraging notes tucked into the toes of their shoes. The handwriting will resemble the doctor's; the notes will be skewered shut by peppermint sticks. Meanwhile, tonight, a band from the second ward plays German folk songs. The first Advent candle burns on the altar; the attendants ladle wassail into punch glasses. In the center of the room, women dance, together and with the men.

The doctor stands with Humphries, his now-chronic guest. Humphries clenches a fourth glass of diluted wassail, the proportions of which he's grumbled about all evening. Dr. West and Dr.

Meijer keep the wives company; Dr. Ingstrom stands on Humphries's far side, alone. Ingstrom's fiancée was killed in a riding accident; the doctor's wife has described the girl's miniature, which Ingstrom carries inside his pocket watch. He still writes to her family every week. Now, he strokes his silky moustache and, cued by Humphries's own laughter, chuckles at the brickman's commentary. But even in a holiday mood, the doctor can't humor a blowhard.

Instead, he turns his attention toward the chapel floor, where excited patients jumble each figure the fiddlers call. As though cracked from the whip on a skating pond, women are slung into the laps of wallflowers. Errant dancers careen the wrong way through the lines. Gentle Mr. Burgoyne from ward four trips over the wheeled chair of Mrs. Stigar, from ward seven. Children might conduct themselves this way—though with less vigor—and the doctor steps forward, waving for the attention of the band leader. He cannot risk anyone's safety for the sake of a pleasant evening.

But the doctor's gesture is upstaged by Ingstrom's. Ingstrom strides from the side of the room to the center of the dance. With a tap on the shoulder, a practiced bow, he frees the auburn-haired Miss Williamson from her heavy-browed partner. The doctor can see her flushed face clearly, as her look of consternation is replaced by one of delight: here, a partner competent to lead her through the unfamiliar dance steps. Following Ingstrom's example, Humphries begins to dance with Mrs. Sherman, the most beautiful woman on ward one. His own coarseness seems amplified by contrast, his clumsiness only a small improvement over her previous partner's. The scene becomes calmer, though—the wheeling patients, steadied by these gentlemen, find their way more surely through the set. The folk tune ends, a waltz begins, and the lovely, delicate women are still held by the doctor's peers.

Waltz me, the doctor's wife says, and he sees that big Meijer and even rheumatic West have taken to the floor with their spouses. Everyone is following Ingstrom's lead. The doctor lays his hand against Diana's narrow waist and guides her into the turning crowd. But his eyes still follow Ingstrom. The boy behaved with an authority rightfully belonging to *him*, as superintendent; Ingstrom took to the floor without even glancing at the doctor for approval. Another illustration of the arrogance of youth. No matter that, this time, arrogance has been rewarded with success: the attitude itself threatens the hospital's careful hierarchy. The doctor shakes himself, jarred by a sharp heel on his toe. Why must he regard the younger man in such a light, in such a season? A superintendent must be broad-minded, must allow for holiday spirits at holiday moments.

Diana smiles up at him—It's good to dance, isn't it, James?—and all around them spin dancers who seem equally happy. This is the goal, of course: that the patients lose themselves in ordinary pleasures, like ordinary men and women. What if the doctor *is* bumped and trampled by those dancing nearest to him; aren't these the ordinary hazards of a dance? What if the doctor *is* upstaged by his assistant? He has always been overly sensitive. See how everyone is pushed, how the patients smile and keep dancing. The doctor will keep dancing, too. It won't be for lack of effort, if he fails to actually make merry.

A man costumed in red had stopped Letitia and Amy at the cookie tray. This man, rouged and strange, spoke to them brazenly. Have you been good, he'd said, and Amy hadn't answered. Then another, dressed shabbily and covered in filth, had contorted himself at them, so that Letitia had laughed, but Amy had shuddered. Tell the truth, the dirty man had jeered. Answer Saint Nicholas.

And red-suit, again, had asked his question. I don't know, Amy had said, while Letitia held her by the waist. She hadn't been so good that they'd kept her at home but not so bad, either, as some she'd met at this place. Then the man in the red cape had asked her, What good deeds have you done? and Letitia, laughing, said, we're both good, goose.

Now Amy looks over Letitia's shoulder, watching the room revolve as the taller girl guides her. They turn quickly to the music, their hands damping each other's waists. The insides of their elbows press together, their hands clasp to make a box, and they gaze through a window made of their arms and giggle. Letitia is taller, stronger; she leads so quickly that Amy's feet leave the floor, black spots coming and going before her eyes. When the music slows, she is spent and clutches Letitia through the next song. The swaying movement of the music draws her up on her toes, where she braces her collarbone against Letitia's. Their skirts stick together, wool to calico. Then a new song begins, its melody just as brisk as the last. Amy's feet have all but mastered the steps when a man touches Letitia on the shoulder. It is the tall, dark doctor, asking for a dance. Letitia's hand is gone in an instant from Amy's waist; her fingers slip willingly from Amy's. She takes the woman's pose and twirls away. A fat man grabs Amy, his swollen hand around her elbow. He wears fancy clothes—he's not a patient but something else—and he pulls her toward him before asking, May I? His huge pink face is in front of hers, his breath glazed with whiskey, and she twists, flees from his grip to the side of the room, beyond the row of wheeled chairs, behind the plain women with their folded hands. She is panting, crouched against the chapel wall; the man, having caught a different woman, doesn't follow her. He doesn't care which of them he catches.

Someone else is watching her, though—one of the women she ran past. The woman has turned around in her seat to stare at Amy. Her iron-gray hair makes a small bun at the nape of her neck; the collar of her dress is higher than anyone else's. Her face is familiar in its gauntness. Amy shakes her head, rubs her knuckles hard against her eyes. It is the Walking Skeleton, returned.

I am eating, Amy whispers, crawling quickly to the Walking Skeleton's chair. She grips its backrest. Every day, like you said.

The Walking Skeleton turns in her seat, away from Amy. She doesn't respond. Amy squeezes between the chairs again to stand in front of the old woman. The Skeleton's skin is sallow and dry, her big eyes webbed with red veins.

You said I should eat, Amy repeats. For strength, you said—do you remember?

No, says the Walking Skeleton.

You said we would all rise up—

No! says the Walking Skeleton.

They took you away, then. Do you remember? Your husband. Old doctor says he's a minister.

You are mistaken, says the Walking Skeleton. I'm sure I've never spoken to you in my life.

We were on the same hall! Amy says. The one with the painting of rabbits? There was a big attendant and a small attendant.

Child, says the Walking Skeleton, you are making a nuisance of yourself. If you don't care to dance, sit quietly. Leave me be.

But we were on the same ward, Amy says. You told me I could eat.

The Walking Skeleton looks at her once more, with her great red eyes. Who am I to tell you such a thing? She stands and walks past the attendants and out of the chapel.

Amy takes the chair the Skeleton vacated. Its seat is barely warm. It was the Walking Skeleton; it is impossible that it wasn't—impossible that two people could be so alike. She presses her fingers hard to her ears, closes her eyes. She leans forward, cheeks against kneecaps. She has been forgotten, denied. She is forgotten regularly. It is almost Christmas, and no one remembers her. Snow drifts high around the hospital already and around the house up north it must be even higher. There will be frost lacing all of the windows and a tree cut by her father's men braced upright in the parlor. The smell of hot wax when the candles are lit, and, if Amy were there, her stepmother's hand would rest firmly on Amy's shoulder, holding her back from the tree. She knocked it over only once, but her stepmother doesn't forget. Her father would read St. Luke in his monotone, and three presents, one for each, would be arranged on the tree skirt. In the morning, icicles would drop like daggers from the eaves and they would drive to church to see the other young ladies in their neat velvets. They looked very different than Amy. Her stepmother always wept all the way home. Will she cry, this year?

Something butts against the crown of her head, and Amy opens her eyes to see Letitia, squatting in front of her, flushed, her hair curling from exertion. The black has widened over her radiant irises. Her lips, a-sheen with petroleum salve, have less of a raw look than usual. She presses her mouth to Amy's cheek quickly. Jubilantly.

I danced with Dr. Ingstrom, she says. Did you see? Twice!

There was a woman, Amy says. She can't say more for her twitching lips.

Letitia takes her hand, pulls her to her feet. Don't mind any of them, she says. Come on, let's go. Did you see me with Dr. Ingstrom?

Amy shakes her head, watching Letitia's mobile mouth. She can feel the spot of salve it left on her cheek.

He said he'd see about a better position for me and that sometimes patients earn wages. And he said I seemed in fine spirits and that dancing agreed with me. So *I* said he shouldn't have wasted so much time before asking me—did you *see* that girl he was with?—but he said it was pretty to watch the two of us. He asked if you were on my ward and why—he's a real gentleman, isn't he?

Your t-teeth, Amy says. The Walking Skeleton hasn't come back.

Oh, I couldn't pester him at a dance. He's going to have a new dress sent for me—just gray wool like yours, but this one's too skimpy for winter and almost in pieces. Did you see how handsome he is? He said his new treatment would get rid of my headaches for good, and then I could leave—any time I pleased. Ouch! Don't you trim your nails? Turn me loose!

Letitia's hand is welted with half-moons.

I'm sorry, Amy says. She wipes her eyes with her sleeves.

Letitia frowns. Never mind. Did you think I would lose you? She takes Amy's hand, leading her through the crowd in the chapel. Strange bodies press upon them from all sides. When a familiar face passes—the old doctor, the small attendant, the woman with the mottled face—Amy averts her eyes. All but one familiarity now seems treacherous. She holds fast to her friend until they file down the halls and back to their ward.

Chapter Eight

SNOW FALLS THROUGH THE FIRST weeks of the new year: 1890. Mornings, the doctor looks over the blank lawns and cannot distinguish his saplings from broken twigs blown across the snow. The men's work crew will find traces of yesterday's paths and redraw them against the possibility that it will be warm enough today for the women to walk outside. It has not been warm enough since mid-December.

Winter is the hospital's dormant phase. The rate of admittance falls off due to the difficulty of travel; the field work is over; the annual report has been completed and sent. It is possible now for the doctor to spell his assistants. Meijer is just back from a New Year's trip to Chicago; Ingstrom left on the 9th to visit his fiancée's family, like the son-in-law he would have been. The doctor takes up each of their loads in turn.

He calls after breakfast at West's office, finding the first assistant physician amid a dusty jumble of trade journals and loose papers. The uppermost of these relate to West's pet project: Lincoln's brain injury, a diagnostic puzzle about which West corresponds with a wide circle of doctors and physiognomists. The former president's crooked face, his history of migraine, his renowned melancholia—

congenital, or the results of some forgotten head trauma? It's a harmless interest, but perhaps a key to West's particular inertia: he is more engaged with the medical mysteries of the past than those of the present. West has been an asylum doctor for longer than the doctor himself, without apparent interest in a superintendency. He has been with this hospital since the day it opened, running the pathology laboratory and seeing to the men's wards. He will be here, in all likelihood, until he's no longer fit to make rounds or stand for hours over his corpses. Already rheumatism has settled into his knees. West limps along beside the doctor now, offering here a compliment on the Christmas Eve service, there an observation on the St. Nicholas Ball. Together, they make their way slowly down the stairs, through the wards. The patients ask again and again after Ingstrom; he's well-liked, and the doctor, in this new year, is glad to know it. Maybe Ingstrom could succeed him, after all—or, at the very least, succeed West.

A promising young man, West huffs, as they descend from the first floor to the basement. In deference to West's knees, they walk from the center building to the cottages below ground, through the service tunnels. Legions of pipes run through the tunnels, forcing them to walk single file. Light comes at intervals from caged bulbs.

We had hopes for Ingstrom and Mrs. West's niece, West continues, calling over his shoulder. But as you see, he won't be consoled about this dead girl. Could lead to trouble if unchecked: morbid tendencies.

The doctor smiles. We all make hobbies of diagnosing each other, I'm sure.

West nods. And I'm become the senile old fool. He's a good boy, though—your Ingstrom. Reminds me of myself at that age. Curious as a cat and fearless to boot.

Perhaps wanting in tact, says the doctor. He rolls around West's phrase, *your Ingstrom*. But he is not prepared to claim the boy. I don't like what I've observed in the training school.

West chuckles. One wishes sometimes for want of tact when dealing with these ham-handed attendants. Directness, I'd call it—not my particular strong suit. And I confess I was floored when he told me about his cinchonia trials.

The doctor pauses for a moment; he is glad for once of West's dragging pace. What's that? he asks loudly. The tunnel returns his words to him.

Oh, some very nice observations—effects on the sympathetic system detailed and so forth. You haven't reviewed his notes?

The doctor shakes his head. Where did he come upon cinchonia? It isn't stocked in the pharmacy.

Ordered it downtown, I suppose.

He's said nothing to me of the matter. Which of the patients has he been treating? The doctor manages to keep his voice steady.

Oh, no, West says merrily. The boy dosed himself and wrote up the results. It's the kind of trick I'd be afraid to make nowadays, with my health the way it is—and he told me in confidence that he scared himself, doing it. But the result is a lucid little piece for the *Journal of Insanity*, and the hospital will share the credit for it.

Has he submitted it? The doctor feels something like paranoia sweeping over him: *dementia praecox*, he can hear West saying.

Hard to say—the boy seems to always have a project in the works. But you ought to get a look at it—good implications for the treatment of febrile conditions. Of course, Ingstrom himself is most interested in the drug's potential to reduce swelling of the brain—you know what a bug he has for neurology—but that aspect of the paper is only speculative. He fancies it might be suitable as a pre-operative treatment. Very interesting business.

The doctor lays his hand on West's shoulder, so that the older man stops and turns to face him. I will not have articles published about this hospital without my approval, the doctor says, slowly. You will please tell Ingstrom as much.

Oh, the boy means no harm, says West, still smiling. Take him aside and that'll be the end of it. But you won't find fault in his research, Jim—it's a credit to you, having such a doctor on staff.

A *credit* to him, that his medical staff experiment on themselves with new drug treatments! The doctor strides off in advance of West, forgetting to match his pace to his companion's. It's not the spirit of the boy's actions—how often has the doctor asked the state for a larger clinical staff, an allowance to make drug trials? But to go about things in this clandestine way is not scientific; nor is it, in the parlance of the doctor's own era, moral. The sound of West's labored breathing is amplified by the tunnel walls, and the doctor knows he ought to slow down. But the laughable symbolism of his present position makes him walk still faster—to get out more quickly from beneath the vast and labyrinthine hospital. It is impossible to know what's going on here at odd hours—impossible to know what's going on in the 'modern' imagination of a doctor like Ingstrom. *Where has the young doctor gone?* the patients ask, again and again, and it is impossible, now, to hear the question without anxiety. What are they asking for, in asking for Ingstrom?

Through the cold holiday weeks, no word comes from Amy's parents. Other women receive Christmas boxes or new aprons sewn by women's groups. Letitia's is as rough as burlap and lies stiff as a board over her worn skirt. It juts out comically when she sits; it rubs her kneecaps raw. It gathers dust like a windowsill or a bureau top. *The shelf*, they call it; for a week, they make a game of arranging broomstraws, thimbles, and even books upon it, to test its strength. In the dayroom, the other women startle every time the shelf gives way, clattering objects across the floor. Amy and Letitia roar with laughter.

Not until the second Monday of January does the matron bring a box for Amy. Its wrappings have already been removed; Amy only has to lift the lid. On top are sweets, familiar from the other women's packages—cookies, toffee, fudge. Below those, a hairbrush, a pair of mittens, and a box of paper imprinted with her initials, AAU in blue ink.

That's for when the doctor says you can write home, says the attendant Klara, watching. There's some lovely new underclothes, too, miss. And another woolen dress that will suit you nicely. Those have gone to the sewing room, but you'll have them to wear once they've been marked.

Amy nods. Her stepmother used to make her three new dresses a season; she used to mend Amy's clothes as quickly as Amy tore them—or vex herself, trying. *Why should I mend such a rag?* Now Amy's day dresses are stained and sagging at the waists. Her hair is still too short to need brushing. What would Rose say, if she could see?

There is a letter at the bottom of the box. It trembles when Amy lifts it: her first letter.

> Dear Amy,
>
> You must forgive this long silence, which I am hoping has had the effect the doctor wished. Amy, are you happy at the hospital? Surely you must be, or by now the doctor would have sent for us. We miss you very much and pray for you daily.
>
> The biggest trees are gone now from below the house, which your father tells me is for the good of the small ones. Now they

will have room to grow up—so that he can cut them down, too! Still, I should not complain. I ordered a new parlor set out of the present he made to me. Our view now is different—the lake seems an ocean without the trees to hide it—and the cold comes very bitter off the water. Since winter, we've switched to the east bedroom not to freeze at night. (Your things we've moved to the attic for now). Are you warm enough at the hospital? I send another pair of mittens, in case you've misplaced your others.

My difficulties continue. I came down with a terrible fever just after we returned from the hospital. It was not long until my fears were confirmed. I am stronger now and just started on a new regimen, so my hope endures. Your father is well, as always. He helped pull this toffee we send you.

I hope you enjoy these gifts. Please, Amy, don't be angry. We only want you to be well and happy. Write as soon as you can.

With love,
Rose.

What does she say? Letitia asks. She takes hold of the first page when Amy finishes it. I can't make it out.

Her stepmother's handwriting is precise; she recopies her letters until they are clean, no matter how much paper it takes. But still, Amy clears her throat and reads the message aloud.

Rose, Letitia says. Is she as sweet as all that?

Amy shrugs. Sometimes, the letters her stepmother sent her at school would pull her into the past, that forgotten childhood time when they were like sisters. This letter only reminds her of where she is now.

Letitia smooths the letter flat. What 'difficulties' does she mean?

Amy glances around, finds no one nearby. She loses babies, Amy says quietly. She always loses them.

Then you ain't likely to go home until she's got herself one, and maybe not then.

149

It's not my fault!

Letitia clutchs her forehead. Her eyes clamp closed.

What is it? Amy says, putting her arm quickly around Letitia's shoulders. What's the matter?

Leave me be, Letitia says. Leave me be for a minute, can't you?

Amy withdraws. Are you ill?

I'm at a hospital, ain't I?

I meant…it seemed like you felt poorly just now.

Then leave me be. Letitia lowers her head to the tabletop. I've got my headache again. Right here—and she traces a circle on her left temple. Like you could hold it in your hand. And then you go shouting like that.

I didn't know, Amy whispers. She touches Letitia's shoulder. You shouldn't go to the laundry.

If I stay behind, they'll have the old doctor after me.

I hate him, Amy says. I hate him!

Shh! But Letitia raises her head. Has he come after you, too?

He takes things, says Amy. He took away my brother's picture.

You've got a brother? Why don't he come get you?

He's dead, Amy says quickly. He was a lawyer, but his lungs gave out. That old doctor took him away from me.

Letitia's dulled eyes seem smaller than usual. Is that all?

He puts my initials in somebody else's dresses, Amy says. He tied me to a bed for days.

Letitia leans close to Amy. The smell of her mouth is stronger than the chocolate and cinnamon odors coming from the box. What did he do then? Does he come after you at night?

Something used to come to me. It's not so often, now.

Well, he comes after me like a husband would—with his prick. Is that what he done to you?

Amy shakes her head. I don't know.

You'd know if he done it, Letitia says. I've fought and screamed all night for help. That white moustache choking me.

Amy thinks of the lumberjack holding her while the others stared. No one helps you?

That Lil knows why I'm here. She's seen where they cut me open. Letitia presses Amy's hand to her abdomen. There, to keep a baby from coming.

The old doctor did that? Through Letitia's worn dress and the skimpy layers beneath, Amy can feel the raised ridge of a scar.

Back at Pontiac they did it to lots of girls. Ingstrom says they'd never do it here.

Does *he* come after you, too?

Ingstrom? No, he's a good man—too good for this place. And he's too good to blame me for the way I've been used. He'd rather I were someplace else—he says so as often as I see him. If I could just get cured of my headaches, he and I could go any place we wanted. Out West, maybe, and start fresh. But the old man won't cure me. He knows himself, that one. Leaving your sort alone.

He doesn't! He torments me, too.

Not like that; you can't lie after you've told me he don't. And I'd know if he had, too—if he left me alone for once, that wrinkled old dog. He's not likely to bother you until after I'm gone.

Amy grabs Letitia's hand. You won't leave me here!

No, I won't. And you? Letitia draws her hand free. Would you leave me?

If my father came....

He ain't likely to. If he don't want you for Christmas, when would he want you?

Letitia lays her head again on the table and Amy sees that the attendant Klara is watching them. Klara should instead be nursing Letitia, putting her to bed with a cold compress and a dose of patent remedy—as Amy's stepmother would nurse herself during her nervous sicknesses. Days on end, Rose would keep to her bedroom in the house up north, crying out every time Amy slammed a door or a drawer, begging Amy to *be still, be still, be still,* until at last Amy would run to the lake or the woods—away. When she came back, it was always even worse. Amy could never manage to be quiet enough in that tall echoing house. And Letitia is louder than her; Letitia's voice would crack those thin walls. But Letitia is quiet compared to some of the others here.

Don't go to the laundry, Amy whispers.

Letitia lifts her head and her face is angry. *Don't go?* What then—sit here with the crazies? I can't bear to be idle, even if you can.

You're sick....

I can go any time I want, Letitia says. She shoves her chair back from the table. I could go for good. You ain't my keeper.

Letitia crosses the room to Lil with her ring of keys. Amy has not been off the ward unattended in all the time she has been in this place and every day Letitia goes and then comes back again. She goes now, as the other women rock and sleep and rock, and Amy watches for her friend to pass beneath the window, but she sees only snow. Letitia knows how to disappear. Maybe Amy is the only one who doesn't know this trick.

The doctor is distracted at supper—just him and his wife, sharing the kind of simple fare he likes best in the evening: bread and butter, applesauce, beef tea. This quiet would be welcome any other night.

James, his wife says, you will tap a hole through that bowl.

He lays down his spoon. A nervous habit.

She coughs into her napkin, delicately. You've never been nervous in your life.

No. He smiles. Perhaps I am growing suggestionable.

Her lips twitch with humor. She's wearing one of her plain gray dresses and her cheeks seem brighter than usual above her elaborate lace collar. Not bright like a consumptive's—the doctor has seen enough sufferers to recognize that particular flush—but like a girl's. His wife will be fifty-one in February and seems a white-haired child, sitting across from him.

What have you done today? he asks her.

She pats her mouth with the napkin. Nothing out of the ordinary. Read my Bible, answered letters, read Jacob Riis until dinner. You would find his 'other half' very interesting, dear.

Oh? He can't keep up with her reading lists, her interests that flit from the mundane to the scientific.

Yes. The New York tenements demonstrate in the reverse all the architectural principles of your moral treatment—crowding and lack of sanitation that lead to all kinds of degeneracy. Claudia Meijer and I mean to organize a conversation group about it; we discussed it ourselves today at dinner. After that, I had a drive into town and found a good price on buttons. And I took tea with Mrs. Sherman—do you know, that poor woman has not had a word from her husband? She feels it terribly, James.

The doctor shakes his head. He hasn't responded to my letter, either. But hers is an unpredictable case, a transitory frenzy. Mr. Sherman is right to be cautious.

His wife coughs again, more harshly. I think he means to abandon her—and she would be well enough to leave soon, if the shock of his behavior doesn't relapse her.

You haven't told her she seems better? he asks, quickly. You haven't made her any promises?

I only said that I'd tell you about her situation—as I am doing. Still, she *does* seem well to me, James. Isn't there anyone else who could take her?

I am aware of no one else. He taps his foot rapidly beneath the table.

I can't see a reason for her being here…that charming girl.

No. Nor do I wish that you should try to.

She lays her napkin beside her plate. The flush has deepened in her cheeks. I make my observations as you make yours, she says. I know what some of these women are—liars and fanatics and nymphomaniacs. And I know how I'd handle them, too.

But *I* am the doctor! The dishes rattle on his side of the table.

His wife doesn't flinch. And I am only their friend, she says. What rights does that give me?

He stands. I am too excited, he says. It's this business of doing double rounds and dragging around with West all the time. I'm only worn down, dearest—I should finish my notes and turn in early. If you'll excuse me….

She nods and pushes away her saucer, folds her napkin. Does she mean to punish him by not eating, by bringing on a nervous headache? But no: her appetite is always unreliable; he'll mix her a bromide later, if she's still awake. She will perhaps feel contrite, then, for having overstepped her bounds; he will perhaps feel more magnanimous and suggest other ways for her to help Mrs. Sherman. It is touchingly pathetic, his wife's interest in things like the tenement problem or the plight of his women patients. He should be more encouraging of such interests. He *would* be more encouraging under different circumstances. But now….

I only wish that you would speak to me first, he says to her, as he rises, taking a last long sip of his beef tea. So that you and I can always be in accord. As he passes her, he leans down to kiss her cheek. Diana draws away; she's not ready to make up. What can he do, then, but continue on his way, leaving the dining room, leaving their apartment, and letting himself stomp as he takes the broad stairs down to his office?

Calm down, he tells himself, when he reaches his office door. But his fingers fumble uncharacteristically through his keys, and the gleaming doorplates of the other physicians' offices seem to wink at him in the low light. Those offices are dark, with West and Meijer retired to their apartments and the *diligent* Ingstrom hundreds of miles away. Save for his own foolish stomping, the building's administrative center is quiet for the night, except for the occasional passing of the watchman—and, checking the watchclock at the end of the hall, the doctor finds that the guard passed ten minutes earlier. It will be hours before this hall is patrolled again.

The doctor is alone in the center of the building, standing outside his office, standing outside Ingstrom's. He finds the right key, turns it in the lock, and he finds himself alone with the other man's papers. He has never taken such a measure, but neither has he ever heard of such impertinence as this cinchonia affair—and he will know all of it, if he can.

The doctor seats himself at his assistant's desk. Its drawers are secured, but there is no lock in this hospital that can't be opened with his key ring. Fingers steadied, he quickly finds the right fit. He thumbs through Ingstrom's neat ward notes, his old lecture notes from Ann Arbor. The boy's anatomical drawings are impeccable, his handwriting elegant. He has done his work well, it's clear, and the doctor is sorry for what he is doing. Ingstrom's correspondences, Ingstrom's expense ledger—no signs that the assistant physician has been compiling a paper. No clues at all, until the doctor has shut and locked the desk drawers again. He taps his fingers on the desktop…and there it is, in a folio tucked halfway beneath the ink-blotter. "Effects of Cinchonia, C.F. Ingstrom." Hidden in plain sight, like Poe's purloined letter. Did the boy anticipate this search?

The paper is as West had described it, detailing Ingstrom's reactions after ingesting twenty grains of the 'tasteless' stuff. He does not describe how he arrived at such an idea or how he found time to recover from a drug whose nearly paralyzing effects, according to the paper, 'often last' for ten hours. 'Paresis of visual accommodation progresses to almost complete blindness by the end of the second hour.' The doctor shakes his head. If Ingstrom had begun such a trial at seven in the evening…he would only just have recovered in time for breakfast and morning rounds. How many times *could* he have repeated experiment? 'A sense of heat and bloodfullness in the head and upper part of the body is typically accompanied by muscular weakness and waves of nausea.' *Typically.* The doctor feels some of these symptoms come over him now, his stomach shifting. Supposing Ingstrom were to deliver a similar dose to one of the male patients—or one of the female! If the drug debilitated an able-bodied man—a sane man—what might it do to one of the patients? It's a consolation that Ingstrom hasn't experimented yet on anyone else…or hasn't done so with West's knowledge, anyway. But the doctor is a scientist, too; the doctor appreciates that these results must cry out to Ingstrom for further development or implementation. Having made the trial, surely Ingstrom is anxious to take it further. The only way to really test its efficacy is to test it on other people, on patients.

The doctor closes the folio. He slides it back under the blotter. And then he sees something else—a scrap of paper tucked under the blotter's edge, a scrawl of names. *A. Underwood, L. Olsen.* The two girls on ward fifteen: cases of melancholia brought on by pubescence and of periodical mania with delusions of persecution. The doctor examines this enigmatic scrap, written in pencil on what might be the flap of envelope. What business could Ingstrom have with female patients? Does he have questions about these cases, an idea for another insubordinate experiment? Or is it—but how could it be?—a personal interest? What does the boy think about, afternoons in this office, seated here as the doctor is now in his rich leather desk chair, richer by far than the hospital's standard issue? Adjacent to but not communicating with the doctor's own office. The doctor crumples the scrap into his breast pocket. The hospital is and must be a well-ordered community. If Ingstrom is to stay, he will focus his attentions on his assigned duties.

During the rest period between dinner and the afternoon work shift, Amy is allowed to access her Christmas box. Her sweets, shared around, disappear quickly. Within a week, she reaches the last of the candies, a caramel fused to its wax paper wrapping. She peels the paper away carefully, offering the first bite to Letitia, but Letitia shakes her head.

These teeth, she says. When Dr. Ingstrom sends me for my new ones there's nothing I won't eat—toffee and apples and peanut brittle. But those things give me awful pains, now. Isn't there anything else? She turns the box upside-down. A cardboard folder drops onto the worktable, dislodged from the bottom of the box. Letitia opens it to find a photograph of a man and woman, unsmiling, gilt-edged. She touches the faces lightly.

Is this your pa?

It's my mother, Amy says. Her fingers are sticky with caramel, but she draws the photo to her with her knuckles.

Rose, says Letitia. She's not very pretty, is she?

No, says Amy. My own mother, who's dead.

This photograph once stood in a silver frame on a side table in their parlor, next to the brass bell from her mother's teaching days. Objects that were dusted carefully, by girls hired from town.

She has a good figure. But you take after your pa, more or less.

Amy covers her father's image with her palm. Her mother has a square jaw and tense lips; she gapes at the camera like she's straining not to blink. She rode horses astride; she taught school until she was thirty-four. She'd been given up for a spinster before the logging operation moved in. Amy knows these things from her stepmother's stories.

What does your stepmother look like? Letitia says. Your pa's good-looking.

She has yellow hair, says Amy. And she's tall like my mother. They were cousins.

My mother has black hair and violet eyes and a smaller waist than yours, says Letitia. My mother is only thirty-five and she can dance and sing like a queen—and that's what she's probably doing, if she's gotten away from the doctors—traveling with a show until she finds me. When she finds me, we'll go to San Francisco and open a laundry like the Chinamen—and you can be our clerk.

Amy shakes her head. I don't want to go to California. In the picture, her mother looks ill at ease, stiff in her wedding outfit. Her dark hair is parted starkly down the center, pinned at the temples and dangling to her shoulders in brittle ringlets. A high lace collar hides her throat. Her hands hang below the frame. What were those hands like?

Chicago, then—wherever we want. My mother can keep house for us and you and I will have a shop until we get married, and then we can live right next door to each other and my daughter will marry your son. Isn't that what you want?

I don't want to have a husband, Amy says. Or a son.

Letitia shakes her head. Well, you'll have the daughter then, and I'll have the son. But if you don't want a husband, there's no hope for you. How else are you going to get by—do you 'spose your stepmother's going to keep you after she's had her own kids?

Amy shrugs. She uncovers her father. Without a moustache, his face is bare and gaunt; his neck is as thin as a boy's inside its starched collar. But his pale eyes and the set of his lips looked just so in September, when she saw him last. He was part-owner of a sawmill, nineteen years ago, when he sat like this next to Amy's mother. Now he travels all over the state surveying forests and overseeing crews. He may have been in the thick woods behind the hospital or among the trees that she can see from her room, flanking the town. It may be he's planning to take those, too. He took the trees that Amy loved and he left her here alone. But there were good days, once, when he played the piano after supper. Amy can hear him singing still—"The Man on the Flying Trapeze" and "Clementine," the songs that she likes best. On bad days, Amy was shut up alone in her room with nothing to occupy her but her hair and face and instead of music, the sounds of arguing came through the vent. But when her father would let her help him with the horses—Quince and Duster—when he would let her brush them or take her for sleigh rides down the bluff road—those were good days. And sometimes her stepmother would teach her how to make pastries or tell her stories about learning English as a little girl. Her stepmother was born in a fairy-tale forest in Germany; her stepmother came alone to Michigan to be raised by Amy's grandparents after her own parents died. Her stepmother had been like a sister to her, once, back when she was very small, but on bad days they are not siblings or cousins or mother and daughter. On bad days they can't bear the sight of each other, and, thinking of those days now, Amy closes the cover of her parents' photograph. She screws her eyes shut as Letitia plucks at her sleeve. A bad day is stirring within her now.

What are you going to do if they won't take you back? Letitia says. How do you 'spose you'll get out of here?

Amy shakes her head. I don't know.

What else is there to think about? You should write to them and tell them you're better—see what they'll say.

Amy pulls her arm away. Stop bothering me.

Oh—was *I* bothering *you*? Letitia tugs Amy's sleeve again, hard, and a seam gives at the shoulder. I won't bother you ever again, if that's how you see it. She sits back in her chair with her lips stretched open in a broken grin.

Shut your mouth, Amy says. Shut your mouth!

I'll kiss you with this mouth, if you keep sassing me. Nobody here's going to jump when you say so.

Shut your mouth and leave me alone!

Letitia leans toward her. You don't think I'm pretty? Not as fine as your ugly old mother? I can guess what happened with her— worn out old cunt. Having you must've been the death of her.

No, Amy says. The pebbled surface of photo's folder seems to shift as she looks at it, the little lumps rearranging. She lays it by on the table, stretching so that it rests more than an arm's length from Letitia. She ki—

You think I care? Go ahead and keep that photo to yourself. Some ugly old bitch and a little boy—no wonder you came out queer. Came out queer and killed your mother, too. He must hate the sight of you.

You're crazy, Amy says. Pricks of ice cross her scalp. You're crazy, and your mother was, too.

Letitia pushes her chair back from the table, away from Amy's. Your mother's dead! You killed your mother and your father don't want you!

No, Amy says. My father's coming back to get me. And when he does I'm going to leave you here. Nobody is ever going to buy you a new dress or new teeth, or—

Liar! Letitia shouts. She jumps to her feet. You killed your mother, you lying slut!

Your mother is a lunatic. Amy keeps her seat. Even if she *is* still alive, you'll never see her again.

Letitia hurtles herself at Amy, and Amy rises to meet her, drawing on the strength that the Walking Skeleton saw. The daughter of a lumberman, of a horsewoman, she rams her head into Letitia's stomach, knocking her backward onto the floor. She holds Letitia pinned for a moment, but Letitia bucks, and they roll in a clawing mass across the carpet. Amy's nails are sharper, but Letitia is taller, heavier, stronger; she is on top of Amy, her fists making explosions around Amy's eyes—and it is for this reason that Letitia is the one who is dragged away by the attendants, sent to her room, while Amy is only dusted off, bandaged up, and petted with compresses and a seat by the fire. Amy folds her bruised hands in her lap, blood under the nails. Her hands like her mother's, strong.

Chapter Nine

BLIZZARDS SWEEP THROUGH THE MIDSECTION of the state, and the doctor receives a telegram from Ingstrom chronicling the deep snow outside of Detroit, the impossibility of travel back north. Ingstrom is trapped at his not-quite in-laws' horse farm. The trains cannot make it through, he writes…and yet it is manifestly possible for Ingstrom to reach the telegraph office. Still, the doctor must concede that the north country is battened down, too. The hills behind the hospital echo, some afternoons, with gunshot, and the doctor knows that their hardscrabble neighbors are poaching deer and rabbits—even squirrels, if all else fails. Poaching is inevitable when the grocery train is late, though, of course, the groundskeeper does what he can to discourage such activity. If a patient with grounds privileges were to come across a hunter or even to run across the offal that is often left behind… but the hospital's grounds are extensive, and, at their far edges, still quite wild.

By the time Ingstrom makes it back, his week's leave has stretched beyond a fortnight. The doctor first sees him, windburned and smiling, with the Wests at the Sunday night entertainment. He is prepared to resume his rounds in the morning,

Ingstrom says, bowing; he apologizes for the inconvenience he's caused the doctor and the other physicians. The doctor excuses him, graciously, but not without noting a new something in the younger man's eyes: secrecy, calculation, superiority. See me tomorrow evening, the doctor says, after supper. And Ingstrom nods, possibly understands.

Before the interview, there will be the day to get through. The doctor sits at his desk after his morning walk and takes stock of his tasks. Mercifully, he will make only his own rounds through the women's wards with Meijer. The local Women's Christian Temperance Union is scheduled to visit, as well—indomitable women, the snow will not keep them away. The doctor applauds their work, welcomes the wholesome books and pamphlets that they donate to the hospital's library but dreads their scrutiny: he cannot hide that the managers expect rum punch at hospital dances, wine when they come to dine. Nor does he absolutely agree with the temperance party that liquor is a demon, though a good number of cases here at the hospital illustrate the evils of immoderation. He thinks of the tipplers on the men's intermediate wards, of an old woman in the senilic cottage who will not be kept from her bottle. She gets it howsoever she can. Docile when in supply, the woman rages after him when sober—an appalling case of geriatric dipsomania. The doctor's wife will play hostess to the WCTU; though she was over-generous with Mrs. Sherman, he trusts her not to promise too much to this flock of dry old hens.

The doctor straightens his office, already pin-neat. There is where Ingstrom will sit this evening, in his fine clothing that will make the room seem shabby by comparison. But the doctor need not apologize for that or for anything else. Instead, he will offer Ingstrom a chance to make a clean breast of things. He will explain firmly to the young man that the cinchonia trials were wrong. There must be transparency in the hospital's operations; secrets are as contagion in such an environment. Surely the boy will appreciate such a metaphor. The whole interview should—*will*—proceed very simply. Still, the doctor sighs when he remembers how much simpler things were with Ingstrom's predecessor, Kittering. Reliable, keen-sighted Kittering, who devised a new trolley system for the basement, a new latch for the ward windows. Having come to them after a dozen years' work in Ohio, Kittering is now superintendent of that state's criminal asylum. In its upward progress, Kittering's career parallels the doctor's own: the doctor worked through the ranks at Kalamazoo, then received his superintendency. The doctor would want the same trajectory for all of his assistant physicians, if only they wanted it themselves. He cannot fathom what it is that Ingstrom wants—but he will know, if he can. As he strives to know his patients' minds, so the doctor will strive to know his assistant's. *After clouds, sunshine*, he reminds himself. He can never remind himself too often: *Kindness keeps friends.*

Amy waits through long days by the window. Letitia doesn't come back. Amy behaved badly and now Letitia has abandoned her. Letitia has gone. She's on another ward, or the young doctor has married her. She's been cured. The mantle clock ticks incessantly, marking moments without her, and every time the firedoor opens, Amy rushes to see who has come. Finally, the white-haired woman steps through, the old doctor's wife. She smiles when she sees Amy: hello, dear Miss Underwood. Behind her and moving onto the ward is a group of women, all alike in dark woolen dresses and grave expressions. Like a funeral or a Quaker meeting. Amy falls in file with them as they progress down the hall to the dayroom. They greet all of the patients present. They offer their hands.

The doctor's wife brushes off a spot on a sofa and settles herself. She pats the cushion beside hers, smiling up at Amy. Have a seat, she says, as she had said all those months ago, in her apartment. Amy hasn't spoken to the old woman since the doctor caught her with the boy and moved her to this ward. She sits.

Are you well, dear? asks the doctor's wife. Your face has healed nicely since last we visited. And your hair has grown; soon you will be able to put it in a snood.

Amy tugs her cropped hair. The ends don't yet meet under her chin. Under the old lady's chin is a large broach. Its smooth yellow stone glows like liquid, like honey; can it really be solid? Amy's hand rises toward it before she catches herself. The doctor's wife smiles. She unfastens the broach and passes it to Amy.

Just to hold, she says. Just for a moment. I can't imagine what it must be like to be without pretty things.

Amy rubs her thumb over the firm, cool surface of the stone. Like the photograph of the boy, it only seems alive. Does the old woman know that Amy held her brother this way?

Have you heard from your parents, dear? Are they well?

Amy nods again. Another woman has come to sit on the far side of the doctor's wife. She is twice as wide as the doctor's wife and wears her dark hair parted down the middle and pulled back tightly. Her face is a heavy square with a fringe of bang across the top; her face is like Amy's mother's.

We're with the WCTU, says the strange woman, smiling at Amy. Temperance. Glad to see it practiced here. We'd like to help you girls, if we can.

How? Amy says. Her voice scratches in her throat. She seldom speaks, now that Letitia is gone.

With your spiritual health, firstly, says the woman. With rejecting that demon alcohol and helping others to do the same. And with finding other useful occupations.

Amy spreads her hands over her lap. The broach gleams against her dingy apron.

Maybe there's not much you can do in here—but when you're better, you'll want work, and we can help you find it. There's lots of things a girl can do nowadays. You write to us, and we'll show you how. Write to me: Bertha Chapman, vice president. I'll look out for you.

When can I leave? Amy asks the doctor's wife. My mother hasn't written.

The doctor's wife frowns and shakes her head. She lifts the broach gently from Amy's lap. You must speak to the doctor about that.

You write to me, says Bertha Chapman. You have friends outside of this place—all of you do, if you only knew it.

The doctor's wife coughs into a delicate, lacey handkerchief, which she tucks up her sleeve. The handkerchief is lovely. Everything she owns is lovely, and this ward is covered in dust and grime.

Miss Underwood doesn't have letter-writing privileges, at present, the doctor's wife says. Nor do any of the women on this ward. Regrettably.

They will have when we're through, says Bertha Chapman. We mean to make a crusade for letter-writing, as they did years ago back in New York State. We're going to give you a voice, Miss Underwood—trust to it. And remember, too, that you've always got a voice with the Lord.

Amy folds her chapped hands. Do you know the Walking Skeleton?

Mrs. Lovelace, says the doctor's wife in a low voice. The reverend's wife, from Charlevoix—you've read of her, I'm sure, Mrs. Chapman. She is a good example of how letter-writing, if allowed, could compromise a patient's reputation.

Bertha Chapman's wide brow furrows. A pious but misguided Christian, she says. Mrs. Lovelace was a good friend to our organization before her troubles came on. And see here: I've brought this for you, Miss Underwood—the donations of such friends as the honorable Reverend Lovelace make our work possible.

She draws a lumpy satchel from the folds of her skirt. From it, she takes a Bible. But the doctor's wife lays her hand over the book.

We must check with the attendants, she says. In some cases, the patients aren't allowed books of their own. Just to read in the dayroom—isn't that right, my dear?

They've allowed Amy to keep her parents' photograph in her room, that photograph whose flat surface reflects nothing back at her, whose dead images wait for her all day and sit darkly all night on the table beside her bed. But this book, with its impossibly thin pages—Amy's fingers tingle. She shakes her head.

Bertha Chapman's lips lose their smile. Not to have His Word with you must be a great hardship.

Amy leans across the doctor's wife and touches Bertha's hand, as she saw the other temperance women touch her ward mates'. Her fingers are squeezed firmly in reply.

Be brave, Miss Underwood, Bertha says. God will see you through this, and we will not forget you.

Be happy, you ought to say, says the doctor's wife, rearranging her dress. Miss Underwood is receiving the best of care here, without herself having to perform chores or worry about a thing. Be happy, dear girl, and you will soon be well.

But a body wants a purpose, too, says Bertha Chapman. Recover your strength, Miss Underwood, and remember Daniel in the lion's den.

Mrs. Chapman—

It's miss, says Bertha Chapman. You'll excuse me for not saying so earlier, but I didn't like to contradict you. It's Miss Chapman, and I'll hold to my own opinions about scripture and a woman's place, too.

The doctor's wife smiles, her pretty lips stretching strangely. You'll want to share your thoughts with the others, I imagine. You must excuse us, dear Miss Underwood.

Standing, Bertha Chapman bends over Amy and takes both of her hands. You have friends, she repeats. If you forget that, you find yourself a Bible and remember: the WCTU can help you. Our address is stamped right inside the cover: Bertha Chapman, Vice President.

The doctor's wife leads Miss Chapman away and both soon begin speaking with the widows, in their own language. Amy recognizes the sounds from conversations between her stepmother and the hired girls, but she only knows a few of the words. *Vater* and *meine Tochter. Ja* and *nein* and *Guten nacht. Gott sei Dank*, says one of the oldest ladies, and Bertha Chapman repeats it: *Gott sei Dank*. Amy doesn't know how to ask the doctor's wife about the boy, the photograph, but she hasn't forgotten him. What does she have to do all day but remember—and wait? Not for the boy to return, not for flat, empty letters from her stepmother, but for her friend to come back to her. Without Letitia there is nothing to interest her or fill her days: there is nothing.

Across the room, the WCTU woman holds the widows' hands and her crisp bang vibrates above her large, plain face. They are praying, maybe, sitting there with their eyes closed and their mouths moving rapidly. Praying that they will again have the things they used to or else something better. *Dear Lord, bring me my friend.* Maybe somebody answers such prayers. *Dear Lord, let us go free.* Amy folds her hands across her stomach and settles herself again, facing the hall. Maybe.

The shortest day of the year is well behind them, and yet this day seems shorter, to the doctor. He finishes his supper with difficulty. All day he's been dreading his evening's chore, imagining the humiliation Ingstrom will suffer. To be chastised in such a way—it isn't professionally-becoming. The doctor has always been highly sensitive to others' embarrassments; scenes he witnessed in medical school still trouble him. And even a few from primary school.

When he was in the fourth grade, a neighbor girl had been obliged to bring her feeble-minded brother to school—no other way to watch him. The doctor still remembers with shame the way that boy was teased. At the beginning of the term, their teacher had insisted on his reciting along with the others, and he'd memorized the easiest of the primer class lessons. But at the first proper arithmetic lesson, the poor child had broken down, had soiled himself in front of everyone. The accident wasn't attributable to his mental faculties, as the teacher supposed. No—the doctor himself had been one of the bad boys who'd scared the primer class away from the outhouse with stories of snakes and lizards. They'd thought it a good joke, to watch the littler children squirm. But it wasn't funny to see the simple boy's terror and confusion or to know that he had himself been their cause. The doctor carries the guilt of that episode with him yet. After his accident, the boy had been given chores to do around the classroom—tending the stove, sweeping, refilling the water buckets—and, long after the doctor himself graduated to high school, the boy had kept on in this role as the pet and scuttlebutt of the school. Now, the doctor writes regularly to the legislature on behalf of those with amentia, in hopes that eventually a provision will be made for their education and care. His guilt is thus partially alleviated, through diligence.

The doctor wipes his lips and pushes his chair back from the table. His wife is fatigued from her day's exertion with the WCTU; she's taken a bowl of milk-toast to her bedroom and sent word through Matilda that he's not to come to her unless summoned. She doesn't want his doctoring, in other words—no matter that he might need hers. He must both bear up and spruce up without her counsel. The doctor brushes his coat before the hall mirror, adjusts his necktie, combs his hair. He stalls, aware that he's doing so. When the clock begins to strike seven, he shrugs the tension from his arms and strides from his apartment, down the stairs, and to the second floor, where he finds Ingstrom waiting in his expensive suit and his petulant expression at the door to the doctor's office. An apology rises in the doctor's throat—but no, he is perfectly on time, and, even if he were not, this is his hospital; they will keep to his clock.

He nods silently, unlocks the door, admits Ingstrom. They settle themselves on opposite sides of the desk, and the doctor takes a deep breath. He forces himself to begin with pleasantries: how was the journey back? How does Ingstrom find his patients? How is Ingstrom himself bearing up after the strain of travel? Ingstrom makes brief responses, waiting.

It's been some time since you and I have consulted, the doctor says. Have you seen any cases that have especially troubled you? Any matters in which you would seek my advice?

Ingstrom shakes his head. You've reviewed my ward notes? Dr. West and I manage very well together.

Of course. The doctor lays his hands on the desktop. You could not do better than to learn from Dr. West.

No, says Ingstrom, watching him.

The doctor's long fingers tent and fold in front of him. My own first years in medical practice were invigorating, he begins, but also very taxing. Over-stimulated as I often was, I can see now that my enthusiasm occasionally got the better of my judgment.

At the sanitarium? asks Ingstrom. Were your cases so very challenging?

There is a hint of condescension in Ingstrom's question, but the doctor shakes his head—forbears.

I refer to my earlier experience, he says. I interned at a city hospital in Philadelphia after completing my degree. We were understaffed and often quite overwhelmed. I undertook several procedures there that might better have been left to the senior physicians. Though the results were positive, they could easily have been otherwise.

Well, says Ingstrom, you found your calling in the end. I assume you tell this story because you feel I have erred similarly?

The doctor forces a smile. I cannot fault you for lack of perception, Dr. Ingstrom. Yes—I am aware that you have made drug trials without obtaining my permission.

Ingstrom shifts in his chair. I have investigated the effects—upon myself—of a drug readily available from the town druggist. Am I also to tell you when I take an extra dose of cough syrup?

I appreciate a joke as well as anyone, the doctor says. But I cannot see the humor in your publishing these findings behind my back. Your affiliation with this hospital implicates all of us, and myself especially, in whatever work you've done.

I've only written a paper, says Ingstrom. Not published it.

West spoke of it highly, says the doctor. Says it's a very thorough piece.

Then what can be the problem?

The doctor raps the desktop with his knuckles. How did you find the time to complete these trials? How were you able to make your rounds, after dosing yourself as you've described? Our hospital does not have the staffing resources for this sort of experimentation.

Ingstrom shrugs. I made the trials in June, during my week leave—as I explain in the paper.

The doctor doesn't recall this detail, but he won't be tricked into revealing that he's snooped around and read the thing. And even if it's true that Ingstrom conducted the research while on leave, the timing does not absolve him of a worse infraction. Why haven't you shared your findings with me?

Ingstrom rolls his eyes. West told you; where's the difference?

Dr. West quite naturally assumed that I'd heard of the project already. He betrayed no confidence. I wish I could say the same of you. If you keep your ideas secret from me, what practical application can be made of them?

A practical application—here!—of new ideas? Ingstrom shakes his head. I've resigned myself to this hospital's clinical primitivism.

The doctor sucks his teeth. Our standard of care is irreproachable, sir. You will remember that we are among the most modern hospitals in the country.

Electric lights and fire-proofing in the wards—oh yes, very

modern indeed! But what does that matter, if we're practicing nineteenth-century medicine? Ingstrom throws up his hands. We hold two different perspectives, sir. I am a neurologist, both by training and sympathies—and you have managed the farm and buildings capably for the past five years.

You are out of line! says the doctor, his voice rising. I am super-intendent by an appointment from the state medical society—my qualifications are not open to debate. Nor is the superiority of this hospital. It's beyond me how you can speak this way when we have the best surgical facilities north of Chicago.

I mean no disrespect, says Ingstrom, leaning forward in his chair. Neither to you nor your operating rooms—with Dr. West, I've been involved in some fascinating post-mortem work in those rooms. But where is the application of those findings?

What you call *findings* are observations, Dr. Ingstrom, research. We look for patterns—that's the work of science. Finding patterns, we build hypotheses; testing these, we arrive at new treatments. As you gain in experience, so you will gain in patience.

When I've had as much experience as *you*, sir, I hope also to have the humility to yield to those less patient than me—those who see the desperate need for progress in medical science. If we doctors do not meet that need, others will pretend to. I cannot stand idly by while quacks run the show!

Even so, says the doctor, attempting to calm himself. Even so, Mr. Ingstrom, I won't condone your hastiness, and I cannot con-done your secrecy. Psychiatry will advance openly and collabora-tively, if it is to advance at all. Your arrogance is not progressive, and your approaches are not in the best interest of the state's wards.

The doctor hears himself as if from a distance, indignation vi-brating in his voice. He presses his palms to the edge of his desk, presses his anger away. He will not let this interview turn into a farce. He begins again:

We are not properly a research hospital, Ingstrom—as you know. We have not the resources of Ann Arbor or Detroit. If you desire to make drug trials or other such experiments, you must first consult with me. Otherwise, I advise you to seek another position.

Then we are in accord, says Ingstrom. Humphries has offered to back me in founding a private neurology clinic. We begin work in May.

Berthold Humphries? the doctor asks, stupidly.

He's tried to promote clinical work here but had no luck, says Ingstrom. Like me, he's interested in the possibility of surgical interventions in chronic cases. We hope even to attract some of the private patients from this hospital.

The doctor shakes his head. The two of you are partners? And—have you already approached my patients' families?

Without your approval? Ingstrom shakes his head. Sir, I wouldn't dream of it.

The boy sits back, arms crossed. He is smug, self-satisfied—he has no idea the difficulties his project faces. The doctor, too, had once thought that cures could be doled out like penny-candies. Then he'd graduated medical school.

For as long as you remain here, the doctor says, I will expect you to concentrate your energies on your rounds. How long can I expect this of you?

Three months, says Ingstrom. Though, if you wish, I can stay another week beyond that—through your absence for the superintendents' conference. He draws a letter from his breast pocket: his resignation.

Thank you for your considerateness, the doctor says, dryly. He allows the letter to fall open in front of him.

Ingstrom nods. I hope that you'll refer patients to the clinic. It's to be called the Margaret L. Steele Neurological Hospital.

After your fiancé, says the doctor. How apt. He has been pushed too far to keep the sarcasm from his tone.

Yes. Ingstrom stands, leaning across the desk. You'll recall that she died following a head trauma—for several hours she was perfectly lucid before coma set in and then death. And why should that have been so? Why shouldn't *something* have been attempted? You know the histories of those in this hospital—you know how very many have suffered head injuries! Why shouldn't you or I be able to intercede more effectively in such cases?

The doctor closes his eyes. How could the boy imagine *him* as an obstruction to these pursuits? You have my blessing, he says. I ask only that you behave with propriety for the next three months.

With propriety, repeats Ingstrom. And may I expect that you, with propriety, will refer patients to my clinic?

Which of my patients could afford you? The doctor shakes his head. Yes, yes—for what good it will do them, yes.

Ingstrom bows. Sir, I am grateful for your benevolence.

He stalks from the room—and into the office just next door. A preposterous exit: their shared wall reverberates as he slams and locks his door. And yet the cheap theatricality of it befits the tone of the interview. The doctor wipes a hand over his face, half expecting it to come away coated with an actor's thick grease paint. They have enacted a stock drama, young versus old, the handsome hero versus the withered grandee; who would not have seen it coming? If the office walls were cut away, set on a brightly-lit stage, who would not set her heart on Ingstrom's triumph?

The doctor opens the resignation letter, closes it again, slides it under his own desk blotter. The letter will have to be copied and mailed to the state medical society; an advertisement will have to be circulated for an assistant physician. It is imperative that the position be filled before the snow is gone—before the flooding to the hospital of cases kept away by bad weather. This will be the hospital's sixth year of operation, and its admission numbers have increased each year. With every new facility, with every expansion and improvement, new patients have appeared and filled the spaces available. Will Ingstrom's experience be similar?

Long ago, at private health resorts, the doctor tended a class of patients such as Ingstrom's clinic will no doubt attract: an endless stream of ennervated girls, broken businessmen, worn-out aunts. Among the ailing wealthy, the doctor had felt little sense of purpose; what could his advocacy mean to them? The very idea of usefulness was foreign to his patients; having been 'delicate' from birth, they were being preserved for lives of relative leisure. Among them, Diana had been unusual in wanting something else; her ambition, back then, had made him love her. She longed for occupation while the other patients saw life as a long holiday, spoiled temporarily by illness. When their treatments were successful, that set went home to languish in their own parlors rather than the hospital's.

But maybe Ingstrom's contribution could transcend this. The doctor has read of surgical approaches to general paralysis, to epilepsy. All highly unpredictable, but if perfected, what sadness these interventions might alleviate. For the hospital's other patients, those not afflicted by organic diseases of the brain, there remain the methods in which the doctor has vested his career, to which Diana has devoted her fragile energies—and which all of

Ingstrom's progress cannot devalue. There will always be a need for public hospitals such as his; there will always be a need for the moral treatment.

For weeks, Amy waits at the dayroom door, as anxiously as her father's bitch pointer. The dog would have nothing to do with Amy or her stepmother. She would lie at the end of her chain and begin to dance at the first sound of hooves on gravel, her master coming home. Otherwise, she cared only about chasing kittens. Only the fastest kittens grew to cats at the house up north. The rest were buried, broken-necked, beyond the kitchen garden.

At the end of every work shift, women return to the ward, and Letitia is not with them. But finally, one of the others comes to Amy. She sits beside her at the worktable.

I seen your friend back in the laundry today, the woman says. They got her on ward five now. The woman's brown hair is mostly gray and her faced is furrowed all over. Dark stains run down the bib of her state-issue dress.

That's one of the bad ones, the woman says. That's where she is, thanks to you.

Did she send word to me? asks Amy. She turns between her hands the magazine she'd been reading.

She didn't say nothing, says the woman. Not to me, anyhow. You know what beaus she has down there.

No, Amy says. I don't. Will you take a note to her?

You ain't got the right to sit up in here all day while the rest of us works, says the woman. And you ain't got the right to send anybody else to one of the bad ones. I want you to know that if you scuffle with me, I'll kill you. I'll kill you before they take me down to ward five. And maybe I'll kill you anyway.

Tell her that I'm still here, says Amy. Please.

The woman shoves her chair back and spits. A brown stain spreads over Amy's boot.

I ain't your slave, the woman says. You remember that.

She's got tobacco, Amy shouts. She shouts it twice, before Lil and Klara come running. They make the woman spit her plug into a drinking glass: chewing tobacco is not permitted on the women's wards. Klara takes the woman to her bedroom and leaves her there, and Amy is alone again at the worktable, with all the others watching her. The German widows, the sturdy working women, an epileptic or two. Seventeen women ranged about the room, thinking her a tattletale. Some of them, she knows, are crazy.

Amy tears a page slowly from the magazine, finds a pencil in the pocket of her apron. In the margin of a fashion-plate, she begins: *Dear Letitia.*

Her penciled marks fill all of the white space by the time the supper gong sounds. *I didn't mean to make trouble for you. I hope you'll come back soon. I hope your head doesn't plage you too much. I'm sorry. I miss you. I'm sorry.*

That night in the chapel a thin man drones about horticulture. Amy cranes her neck, finding Letitia amidst a row of unkempt women. Letitia whispers now and then to the ones closest her. When Amy sat beside Letitia, there were always jokes. Now, Letitia doesn't look her way. Has she forgotten Amy, like the Walking Skeleton did? Or maybe she's like the girls at Miss Carter's School, who would turn Amy invisible when she fell out of their favor. She was always out of their favor.

When the thin man finally finishes speaking, the rows are released one by one. They're expected to follow like cows one after another, but Amy breaks out of line. Her knees knock against those of Letitia's seated wardmates, who shout with annoyance as she climbs over them. Here, she says, crowding toward Letitia. I'm sorry. Here. The note is a sweaty square in her palm.

Letitia grasps Amy's hand. Her eyes are clear. Saturday night, she says. At the dance.

Amy nods as Lil seizes her left arm, pulling. Look for me, she tells Letitia. I watch for you every day!

You're not likely to see me back there, Letitia whispers, leaning over her companions. Her teeth have not been fixed.

Leave her be, now, says Lil. That's the one blacked your eyes, Miss Underwood. Letty, you be good and turn Miss Underwood loose.

Letitia releases Amy's hand. Saturday, she repeats. Quick as a flash, she kisses Amy's cheek.

That's right, says Lil, there's a good girl. And Amy allows herself to be brought back into the file of women who eye her like wolves as they march through the chapel and down the wards and back to their tightly locked rooms. The other women make their noises after the lights have been dimmed, screaming and moaning and keening after lost loves, dead children, Jesus Christ himself. There have been nights when Amy has added to the din, but tonight she's quiet. At the very most, Saturday is six days away. She lies still and lets the medicine do its work, content now to sleep.

Chapter Ten

O N SATURDAY, ST. VALENTINE'S DAY, the chapel is hung in red and white crepe paper, the pews are again pushed back, the chairs arranged in ranks along the walls. Again, tubs of punch on a long table, platters of frosted cookies. Again, a band of fiddlers tuning on the stage.

Amy's ward spent the whole afternoon making notes for one another, copying out inscriptions from Lil's autograph album. A relic, Lil called it, turning the pages and shaking her head. She'd helped them choose between rhymed variations on 'forget me not': *If the passing years us should part/Hold my friendship in your heart.* Now, in the crowded chapel, Letitia's laugh rises above all others and Amy pushes her way toward that sound. Surrounded by strangers, Letitia stands laughing in her old calico dress.

Amy touches Letitia's shoulder and Letitia twines an arm around Amy's waist, drawing her into the circle. The other women—Letitia's new wardmates?—seem hard-used. One bears a diagonal scar from cheekbone to jaw; another has a milky white eye. A third is missing the last three fingers of her right hand. All of them stare at Amy, looking over her dress, her boots, her short hair.

They shingled her good, didn't they? asks the scarred women.

It suits her. Letitia touches the ends of Amy's ragged bob. At least she's rid of *her* lice.

This is for you. Amy presses into Letitia's hand a Valentine cut from fashion plates and colored paper. She'd printed carefully: *Dearest friend, forget me never/Even if the sun should set forever.* Of all Lil's inscriptions this had sounded the most like Letitia. Now, with these women watching, she isn't sure.

W-what's it say, Letty? asks the woman with the milky eye. W-w-why don't you read it to us?

The others laugh, but Letitia ignores them. Thank you. She kisses Amy on the cheek and tucks the note between the buttons of her bodice.

Just then, the fiddlers strike up a waltz, and Letitia's foot begin to tap. She grips Amy again by the waist, seizes her right hand. Dance with me until *he* asks, she urges. *One*-two-three, *one*-two-three! Move, can't you?

I'm sorry. But the strange women stare after them, still laughing, and Amy's heart clamors in her chest. If the old doctor could hear it now!

Do you think I'm really angry? Letitia spins them. Nothing makes me angry on a dance night; it's almost worth the rest of it.

Amy shudders. Is it very bad, where you are?

It's worse than ward fifteen, that's sure. Noisy all the time and women throwing fits right and left. But I'm gone most of the day and by now, I can tell which ones to stay clear of. Letitia turns them quickly, avoiding the edge of the stage. Those back there are all right—once you get to know them.

I'm sorry, says Amy. She's dizzy already. I'm sorry.

You ain't the only one to blame. But you *could* make it up to me. Letitia leans toward her. Ingstrom said he would post a letter for us.

Amy shakes her head. They won't let me.

Didn't I just say Ingstrom would help? You can write a thank-you note to your parents, for that box. Add to it that you're better and ready to come home.

A thank you? Amy repeats.

They treated you shabby, sure, bringing you here—when anybody can see there's nothing wrong with you. But thank you— they'll like to hear it, and maybe it wouldn't hurt, either, to say you're sorry.

Amy lets go of Letitia's shoulder. The dance parts around them. I can't.

Sure you can. Letitia presses Amy's hand back into place. Your stepmother said *she* was sorry; now you say it back. I'll make up what else to say. They sent you that nice paper—they must want to hear from you.

Write to your own family!

Letitia rolls her eyes. Don't be daft. Your parents might take you back, if you only act like a good girl. And ain't you sorry, anyway? For what you done to me? Here's your chance to make it up.

But what *about* you? They've already got a hired girl.

Oh, you'd like that, wouldn't you? Letitia shakes her head. No, I won't be your maid, but you'll be twenty-one before long, and you can come for me then. By then, Ingstrom will have fixed my teeth and I'll look respectable—like those on ward one.

That's three more years, Amy says. Longer.

Letitia shrugs. Ingstrom will look after me.

The old doctor—

I can manage him. Letitia's face is flushed with exertion. Will you write a letter or not?

Amy ducks her head, watching their feet. If she did convince her parents to take her back, where else might they send her in three years' time? What might they expect her to do or be? Her feet lose the music. Letitia pushes her away and when Amy looks up, the mustached young doctor has come—as if summoned by the mention of his name. Letitia holds out her arms to him, but he shakes his head.

The next song. His voice is crisp, commanding. I haven't danced with your friend. Miss Underwood?

Amy steps backward into moving bodies, into oaths and glares from the other dancers.

Her hands sweat awful, says Letitia. Only feel mine.

The next song, Ingstrom repeats, smiling. He steadies Amy's elbow, as though she were stumbling, not fleeing. Just look at me. You'll be fine.

It is an order as much as an invitation; he begins to steer before Amy can wrest her hand from his. Letitia is alone at the edge of the room and then Amy cannot say where her friend has gone. Ingstrom leads skillfully, executing tidy turns and somehow finding room to make long, gliding passes across the dance floor. Dancing with him is like ice-skating with her father: Ingstrom moves with the same speed and decisiveness. Amy's feet follow his easily, but she sweats more than she ever has, dancing with Letitia.

How do you like the hospital? Dr. Ingstrom asks. You've been here almost six months, I think?

She tries to count: *one*-two-three; *four*-five-six. If they brought her here in September, then he's right.

You're very young, aren't you, Miss Underwood? How was it before? Will you tell me about life at home?

She shakes her head, wiggles her fingers in his grip. But his hand is on her waist and he continues to move.

We don't often see patients your age. Had you been ill, Miss Underwood? Suffered some kind of accident or shock? He doesn't take his dark eyes from hers. What brought you here?

Letitia says you're going to buy her new teeth, she blurts. Her face grows hotter.

Ingstrom nods, unperturbed. It's appalling that patients are still mistreated in this day and age. Force-feeding is not used here, nor any other methods of physical coercion. The music swells, and Ingstrom sweeps them along: Keep looking at me, Miss Underwood, not at your feet. Did you learn to dance at home?

Over Ingstrom's shoulder, Amy sees Letitia paired with a fat man in town clothes. He's the very same pink-faced man that grabbed *her* at the December dance. Has he been lurking all this time in the chapel? Nausea shakes her. There are plenty of places to hide—in the front row during the evening program, at the back of the room during Sunday services…and she sees the fat man nod to the old doctor when they pass. The old doctor's wife smiles and bats her china-doll eyes, but the doctor himself scowls. Catching sight of Amy, he stares after her and Ingstrom.

That old doctor is a liar! Amy says—let him hear! That old doctor is a thief!

Ingstrom grimaces. He lays a finger briefly against his own lips. The doctor is…well-intended, he says. Can you tell me why you don't like him?

She closes her eyes, following the music. The tempo now surges, now falters. When she opens her eyes, Ingstrom is waiting. His clean, smooth face is not a lumberjack's. But like that bearded man by the lake, he grips her by the waist and won't let go. Where could she run if he did?

Letitia, she whispers. He's used her poorly.

Ingstrom raises his eyebrows. She's told you this? Or you've observed something? Think carefully.

Amy shakes her head.

Whatever else his faults, a doctor can commit no greater crime than to mistreat his patients. Do you truly think our superintendent has done this?

She shakes her head again. I don't know.

Well, *I* could not believe such a thing, not without proof. He leans toward her, smelling of lemon and cedar. Miss Underwood, you must know by now that there are women here who tell falsehoods. They do not always mean to—and if they didn't, if they gave up their story-telling, perhaps they might recover and leave. You would help your friend a great deal by not encouraging her stories. Do you have any complaints of your own?

It's not a story!

Ingstrom sighs. Miss Underwood, wouldn't you rather be at home?

Shut up in that house, the trees all gone…. Amy shakes her head again, feels the dull weight of a headache. If he would only let go of her!

Instead, Ingstrom smiles. You're a fine dancer. And a fine friend to Miss Olsen, who has suffered greatly. But what is it that keeps *you* here, Miss Underwood? Do the doctors speak to you regularly?

The old man comes to her with his bag of instruments and asks her questions that she will not answer. She will not tell him or Dr. Meijer about her periods or her stools or, worse yet, her thoughts.

No, she says. We don't speak at all.

Ingstrom gazes over her head. Perhaps you didn't know, Miss Underwood, that the doctors measure your improvement by your cooperation—your ability and willingness to interact with the hospital's staff and with other patients. Do you understand? I think you are more improved than your doctors see. Surely, you do not *want* to remain here another six months?

Amy pulls away from him—the song is nearly over; Letitia is ready to claim her turn. But Ingstrom still holds her hand: Once more, Miss Underwood? His dark eyes hold her, too. We haven't finished our conversation.

Oh no, Letitia interjects, look how you've fatigued the child already! Did you see how I made *my* partner move? She takes Ingstrom's free hand and traces dance steps. And this one a polka— oh, let's go!

If you'll excuse me, Ingstrom says, bowing to Amy. He and Letitia leap into the set, joining the other prancing couples. Laughing, Letitia throws back her head, exposing her terrible teeth. And Ingstrom laughs, too—at Amy?

A hand on her elbow makes her jump, but it's just Lil. Step to the side, miss. You'll get run over, standing there.

How often do we have these? Amy's stomach turns with the spinning room.

Lil shrugs. Every month or so. Sometimes oftener. Did you find a beau?

Amy lets Lil guide her to a chair. He's Letitia's beau.

That Ingstrom? Lil shakes her head. I can't abide a dandy.

On the dance floor, Ingstrom holds Letitia closer than he'd held Amy, their whole fronts touching. Amy turns to Lil, instead. What happened to those girls from your album?

They're all married now. Lil smiles. All except old Lil.

Do they remember you, like they said?

Well. Lil bends to straighten Amy's skirt, the new wool dress from her Christmas box. Well…I been here and there ever since those days, not like the rest of them—but I dare say they remembered me for a while, anyway.

I won't ever marry!

No? Lil dabs Amy's forehead with a handkerchief. I've heard of those who are happy with their men, but I can't say I envy most. How warm you feel, Miss Underwood! Sit tight, and I'll get you some punch.

Amy nods and loosens her collar. If she could lie down, her head would feel better, but then Lil might scold her or send her upstairs. And if she's upright, she can watch the young doctor, the old doctor. Maybe Lil will sit with her for a while and tell more stories about her girlhood and the kinds of friends who copied poems for one another.

But though Amy sits still, the dancing dizzies her. The men, the women, the young doctor—bodies clutched together, revolving. Her heart races and her head feels as Letitia's must, sometimes, like a cage holding a wild creature. The creature lunges, raking its claws down the inside of her skull. She pushes it back, but it is too fierce, it is everywhere inside her—surging through her chest, racing up her throat. Her jaw spasms, a hot red mess splashes onto her knees. Miss! cries Lil, as she hurries back. Amy's throat and nose burn, her eyes stream, and now the doctor will come—the old one or the young one or the stout one or the lame one. There's no getting away from them, here, and her mouth opens again, in a torment of vomit. Red from the dyes of icing and punch; red as though disease was rotting her insides. Her chest heaves, too fast, and Letitia is still dancing.

Someone's hand soothes her forehead; a cloth is passed over her foul lips; someone is lifting her into an old woman's wheeled chair. Rattling from the room she presses her palms to her eye sockets to steady her head against the jolting motion. Her body sways with unfamiliar turns and when she takes her hands from her eyes, she's arrived somewhere new: a clean white dormitory. The chair and the attendant who brought her here are gone already and she won't find her way back to the chapel—no breadcrumb trail, no brother by her side. Her father is a woodcutter and her stepmother, wicked. But the women in this strange room are not witches. They are plump white hens who cluck as they sponge her face clean, remove her soiled dress. They draw a clean white gown over her head, settle her between white sheets with a thermometer beneath her tongue. Don't bite, don't bite, the hens say, and after the effort not to, her teeth chatter uncontrollably when the instrument is removed. The nurses bring her thick drinks, lay cool wings across her brow, hold her upright over a basin when she vomits again—and again. They place chips of ice in her hot mouth. These nurses roost around her, watching, until at last the ward's whiteness overcomes her, the sweet smell of feathers floats her away.

For days, Amy wakes and sleeps at odd intervals, freed from the clanging bells that govern the rest of the hospital. She wakes and sleeps in the grip of pain. Her head, back, muscles, bones, ache all the time; her limbs twitch the bed into disarray. She lies for long spells in the unbroken white of the room, unable to sleep, unfit for any diversions. The nurses bring tonics and bromides. They hold cold compresses to her head, immerse her feet in warm baths, buff her with towels. It's all right, the nurses murmur, you're a good, strong girl.

When they move on to other beds, Amy drifts away, through the halls of the hospital and over the forests between here and home—forests ravaged on their outward edges by men like her father. The trees mutter feverishly as she blows over them. They topple beneath her as though she is an axe or a woodcutter. No way to make them whole again, no way for them to catch her if she were to fall through them in her old game—no way for her to catch them. The trees once her playmates in that lonely house up north; the girls she knew downstate, blurred faces moving away from her. She flings herself after them: forget me never! But instead hot hands seize her shoulders and waist, pinning her. Hot jolts of pain as she struggles: no! And the plump nurses wake her to change her sweated bedclothes. They bathe her gently: don't fret, child. But what happens to her when she closes her eyes? What's happening to Letitia, alone somewhere in the hospital?

The infirmary fills around her. When she is well enough to sit up in bed, Amy can see how much fitter she is than many of the others, wasted women with rattling coughs and bluish skin. New women are brought each day, not just from the wards but directly from town. They arrive weak but raving; two have tried to smash the infirmary's windows; three others rant through the night about murderers, thieves, demons. The nurses are able, somehow, to make them stop. In the daytime, most lie lifelessly in bed, and then the plump nurses lift Amy into a wheeled chair and push her into the infirmary dayroom. The air is fresher, there, and, through the tall windows, she can watch the bustling backyard of the hospital. Carts coming and going; women rushing through the snow to the laundry building. They are too far away for Amy to make out their faces, but she would recognize Letitia's figure, if she saw her—and she doesn't. She has lost her friend again. At least she hasn't found her here, not yet. It's good to sit up in the dayroom with the other convalescents but sad, afterward, to be pushed back past the sufferers to her bed. The sickest women are fed diluted milk through eye droppers, their mouths gaping like hatchlings'. These women fuss feebly, each almost as thin as the Walking Skeleton of Charlevoix. The woman nearest the dayroom door could even *be* the Skeleton, gray-haired and razor-jawed, thinner now than ever. This woman lies with her neck braced up sharply against fat pillows, her red eyes quick in her narrow face. Those eyes lock on Amy.

Child, the woman calls out, as Amy is wheeled past. Miss Amy Underwood!

The plump nurse stops pushing Amy's chair and bends close to her ear. How do you know Mrs. Lovelace? she whispers. Do you know her from here or from home?

I knew her on ward nine, Amy says. She was taken away.

Nurse! calls the Skeleton. I would speak to that child!

Be kind to her, whispers the nurse, but cautious. How nice that you ladies are acquainted! the nurse declares loudly. She pushes Amy to the head of the Skeleton's bed. You can visit for a few minutes, so long as you take care not to bother Mrs. Packer in the next bed or any of the others. The nurse leans over the Skeleton. Are you comfortable, Mrs. Lovelace?

The Skeleton shakes her head impatiently. Her thin hair has been cut short. I am beyond comfort…as you well know.

Oh, Mrs. Lovelace! The nurse glances at Amy, smiling. Dr. Meijer says you're out of danger; only rest now and take nourishment.

Yes, says the Skeleton. I have heard that charlatan's prognosis. Go, please.

The nurse purses her lips, pats the bedclothes. Don't keep Mrs. Lovelace long, she tells Amy. Her white skirt brushes the beds as she walks down the narrow aisle. Amy waits until the nurse is out of ear-shot before turning to the Skeleton. The older woman's burning eyes are already fixed upon her.

It is finished, the Skeleton says.

Amy scoots her chair closer. Why didn't you know me at the St. Nicholas Dance?

The Skeleton closes her eyes briefly. Why didn't Peter know Christ? He was afraid, child, both of the Romans that taunted him and of the Lord's terrible prophecy. He was not strong enough then to proclaim his relationship to the Lord. Not yet sainted. Do you understand?

Amy shakes her head. What should I do?

See here. The Skeleton untangles her arms from the blankets. She opens her balled fists toward Amy. In the center of each palm is a purple bruise, dark and perfectly round. As I've longed…and prayed for.

Amy touches the marks carefully and sees the blood move beneath her fingertips. She's had blood blisters, too, but never in the center of her palms. How did you do that?

It's not a trick, child. It is the Lord's blessing upon me. My feet are the same. You must tell the others. Tell them to…remember me…and live righteously.

The Skeleton's breath rattles between her bursts of speech. But Amy heard what the nurse said. You're getting better, she tells the Skeleton. So did I.

No earthly medicine can countermand God's will. This is my last trial—just see our Savior's marks. The sure sign that my sufferings are holy. He told me that I would come once more to this abhorred place. That I would celebrate His birth between these walls. And He told me that…my efforts would not be in vain. The Skeleton squints at Amy. You've lost flesh.

Amy is only just able to take beef broth, oyster soup. This illness has stopped her monthly period and her cheeks curve in instead of out. But the Skeleton nods approvingly.

The way to salvation is through…mortification of the flesh. Tell the others. Tell them not to let the doctors 'cure' them of their righteousness. The Lord has a plan for each of them. Let them humble themselves to Him or be brought down by pride.

But what should *I* do? Amy asks. You said we would all rise up. You said so!

The Skeleton closes her eyes. When she begins breathing evenly, Amy takes the old woman's hand again, pulsing the dark pool of blood beneath her thin skin. If Amy broke one of these blisters, what would come out? She thinks of her father, lancing boils on the horses; she tucks the Skeleton's hands away quickly. A smell like decaying fruit comes from the bedclothes. Only when Amy is done smoothing the blankets does the Skeleton open her eyes.

My child. She blinks as though bringing Amy into focus. My worldly husband…has his witless flock. So has this doctor. Few can see the wickedness of powerful men. Few can distinguish true doctrine from false. You shall expose them all, child.

How? Amy scoots her wheeled chair nearer.

How? The Skeleton fixes her gaze steadily on Amy. Attend to His word, and you will know how. He will show you the way. Our Lord calls me home…to make way for you.

Amy shivers deeply, as in the earliest hours of her illness. Cold to the core. The Skeleton nods, shivering, too—and then, at once, her neck stiffens, her entire body goes rigid. She seems suddenly to stop breathing, and this must be part of her fame, this ability to turn absolutely white and still. But as Amy watches, the Skeleton's great red eyes roll toward the ceiling, her mouth falls open, her back arches. She flings her hands outside of the bedclothes and her limbs begin to jerk. Amy's chair, pushed tight to the Skeleton's bed, shakes with the Skeleton's body. Her own teeth rattle and she cannot seem to open her mouth, though the women around her have begun to shriek. Mrs. Lovelace! they cry until the nurses come at a run. They move more quickly than Amy has seen before, forcing a knotted sheet between the Skeleton's lips, steadying her arms and legs. The Skeleton writhes furiously in their grip and it is plain that she's not strong enough herself to resist them in this way. It is plain that something else is working through her.

Pushed hastily to the foot of the Skeleton's bed, Amy can see the Skeleton's face flecked with blood and foam, her thin body shuddering. These vibrations are spreading through the floor-boards, through the hospital, the Skeleton infusing everything with an energy that is powerful but fading…and Amy sees before the nurses do that the old woman has gone, as she said she would. Her body quiets and the nurses turn it onto its side, curled as though asleep. They touch the Skeleton's neck and wrists. They lean panting against her headboard.

Heavenly Father, Mrs. Packer intones from the next bed, receive your devoted servant Mrs. Lovelace. The nurses let her pray.

The stout doctor arrives. He stretches the Skeleton flat and folds her hands across her chest. From the foot of the bed, Amy sees his reaction to the marked palms; she sees him raise his eyebrows at the head nurse. But though the stout doctor spends long minutes making notes in his log, no one speaks aloud of the Skeleton's bruises, not at the bedside or as they wheel Amy back to her own bed. The stout doctor himself pushes her chair.

Mrs. Lovelace is in a better place, he says.

This is what everyone would say; the stout doctor is always

inoffensive. He's not like the old doctor. The old doctor hasn't visited the infirmary once since Amy came—and yet he must know that she's here. He must know all about this ward full of suffering women; he must know that one of them has just died. The women are sent here, very likely, at his direction. And maybe it's by his decree, too, that the stout doctor prescribes Amy a warm bath, brisk toweling, a dose of morphia. *Poor stuff next to what the Walking Skeleton's own druggist had given her.* Amy has come lately to agree. Of late, the drink has given her no comfort, only a foggy head. Today the taste of it lingers in her mouth, bitterness stung with alcohol, even after she's been washed and dried and put in her bed.

The Walking Skeleton is gone. She will not reappear in a month or two, remembering Amy or not; she will not draw Amy aside tomorrow with another riddle. She's gone, though there may be others like her, withering away in Charlevoix, uttering proclamations from their deathbeds. There may be others even in this hospital. Certainly, there are other women here who claim to have spoken with God, or even to *be* God. Amy cannot make this claim. She could slam her own hand in a drawer, pierce her palm with a hatpin, refuse to eat at mealtimes. She *has* done such things, in anger at her parents. That is not God. And neither does she know what it is that moves her when she throws herself again and again through the arms of trees or wades ever-deeper into the freezing lake. A feeling builds in her then, a delicious pressure that mounts in her ears, beats at her chest, and vibrates through her core, never peaking. She does not know what to call *that*.

She touches her face, her fingers already gone soft from the sedative, her blunted nails only petting her cheeks. The Skeleton is gone, as she had *longed and prayed for*. Was that what death had been like for Amy's mother—a release? Amy's fingers slide down to her throat. How? she has always wondered. And what happened to her then? She cannot see an answer through the fog that blankets her.

In the confusion of so many cases of influenza, the doctor hadn't immediately diagnosed the symptoms in himself. Only after several long days of rounds, extended by visits to the crowded infirmaries, did he recognize that the dragging feeling in his bones was more than exhaustion.

He's been laid up since February 16, the eve of his wife's fifty-first birthday. Far from being disappointed at the cancelation of her dinner party, Diana received his illness almost as a gift. There's no nurse more attentive than Diana when she's in the mood to be. The doctor has wakened from every nervous nap to find her hovering nearby with a glass of lemonade, a bowl of broth, a male nurse ready to administer an enema. He's been purged or fed, sedated or vitalized as often as Dr. Meijer will allow.

Meijer has taken charge of the doctor's case, maintaining a pretense of deference while quietly implementing vexing rules for the doctor's sickroom. He's not to be troubled with hospital matters (though he did learn that Reverend Lovelace's wife has died, and he can well imagine that the wards are filling with cases of febrile insanity); he's not permitted to read or write. Only by throwing childish fits does the doctor convince Diana to lay aside her latest books—inane accounts of railroad touring—and read to him instead from his medical journals. The most recent issues are filled with debate over whether insanity after influenza should be considered its own strain or whether 'flu is merely a particularly common aggravating cause. These articles torment the doctor with their perfectly impossible timing. What observations might he contribute, if he were able to see the patients himself!

Dr. West comes in the evenings with a backgammon set that he rests across the doctor's knees. He lets the doctor win and tells him gossip from town. Ingstrom sends regards but doesn't visit. It is perhaps better so; this illness creates a distance from which they might learn to appreciate one another. The doctor now feels only benevolence toward his young colleague and imagines in Ingstrom's succinct notes the suggestion of a similar regard. Bending Meijer's rules, West keeps him abreast of the managers' search for a new third assistant physician: notice has been circulated; letters of application, received. The doctor can tease no firmer details from his colleague.

The best of patients from the men's wards come in the afternoons to read him the newspapers. The doctor is glad of their company; robust and cheerful, these men affirm the project of his hospital. (He's glad, too, that Diana breaks off her nursing during these visits). But trapped as he is in bed, he can barely tolerate news of the outside world. He's strangely unmoved to hear that General Sherman has died of crysipelas, that the Pennsylvania coalminers have gone on strike, that startling developments have taken place in the Jack the Ripper case. Mr. Burgoyne, his reader for the afternoon, is fascinated by this last item: two differently-sized women's hats were found near the body of a recent victim. The London police see it as further evidence of their pet theory—that the killer may be a woman.

Can you imagine, sir? asks Burgoyne, a woman so cunning and blood-thirsty!

The doctor gamely agrees to be shocked, but, in fact, it is only irritating to be presented with these tidbits while *real* events unfold around him. The killer is a deviant, a sociopath; is this really news? But:

Do the patients talk of it much on the wards? the doctor asks lightly.

Oh, Burgoyne says, some. He raises the paper between them. Should I read to you about the largest apple tree in New England?

No, the doctor would like to scream, tell me instead about the symptomatology of the 'flu, the progress of Mr. Nickerson's dementia, the reaction to Mrs. Lovelace's death. But—

Our own apple trees ought to have a fine harvest this year, the doctor ventures, instead. And I wonder what our milk and egg yields are like now, with this cold spell?

Hmm, well…I'm sure they're very good. Everything tastes very good, that is. Everything just as it should be. Say—have you heard this about President Harrison meeting with the Sioux chiefs? Mr. Burgoyne clears his throat.

The doctor closes his eyes, interjecting an *oh!* or *is that so?* whenever Mr. Burgoyne's tone of voice suggests the need. But he can't care about railroad consolidations, saloon brawls, a rash of arsons in Texas. Has the newspaper always been so disordered and diffuse? As Burgoyne reads, the doctor quietly examines himself, counting his pulse-rate, testing the heat of his stomach against that of his forehead—has he still a fever? Dr. Kirkbride died of pneumonia in his apartments at the Pennsylvania Hospital for the Insane, falling into a coma in his last days after over-taxing himself. The doctor, in this respect, has no desire to emulate his teacher; he will let himself recover. But how long must he endure this infantilizing treatment? Mr. Burgoyne's interest in the greater world is heartening to him as superintendent, but the doctor is a patient now, too—and does no one see that enforced passivity is the worst sort of treatment for a man of his character? Here is even more evidence against Weir Mitchell's rest cure! Lying by and hearing about others' failings and achievements makes him welter with impatience to resume his own rightful place: as a man of purpose, vision, and authority.

Chapter Eleven

WHEN SHE'S DECLARED WELL ENOUGH to go among the others, Amy walks on the arm of a nurse down the infirmary ward, through a short, curved hallway, and slowly up three flights of service stairs. She is admitted onto ward fifteen, which smells as ever of dust and cabbage and looks slightly dingier than she'd remembered. Her room has been kept open for her— tall and blank and hers alone. Waiting yet on the bedside table is her parents' wedding photograph, flat and unchanged. She sits on her bed and rests them across her knees. Here they are again: her wary-looking mother, her young, bland father. They stare straight at the camera, as if unaware of each other, as if fixated on something else. What? The photo lifts away and Lil helps Amy gently to her feet.

It's good to have you back, miss.

Lil has grown thin, with a slack look about her like an old horse, but Amy is more interested in her mail. Has Rose written? What have they heard about Amy's illness, in the house up north? Will they ever come back for her?

Lil pats Amy's shoulders. They'll be glad to hear you're better, that's sure. Now let's get you settled in the dayroom.

Laboring down the hall, Amy finds small differences: the three German widows gone; a scattering of new faces among the old. Lil steers her through the other women in the dayroom to an empty rocker beside the picture window, under the living bower of houseplants. The view hasn't changed—white snow, black twigs—even though Amy has come to look like an old woman, with a wool blanket tucked in tight around her. She closes her eyes, rocking. Here she is again.

Boo! someone shouts, a hot burst against Amy's ear. The rocker is jogged so violently that she nearly tips out. She clutches its curved arms, scrambles for firm footing. When she turns, she finds Letitia crouched at her side. Letitia presses on Amy's knee and the chair comes to rest.

You're here…. Amy draws the wool blanket back over her wasted limbs. Letitia looks as hale as ever, her velvet eyes glowing. Their warmth spreads through Amy's chest.

They brung me back up when Klara had to go home. It looks like they don't mean to replace her with anyone *but* me.

You're an attendant? It's true, Amy sees, that Klara is gone, and no one new is wearing an attendant's crisp white shirtwaist.

Letitia shakes her head, tucking the blanket around Amy's feet. I'm to help Lil, that's what they said, and no wages to it but no back ward, neither. And no laundry for now.

Then you don't want to leave anymore?

Again Letitia shakes her head. I'm glad to be back here on ward fifteen, but I'm bound to get out of this place. And not like those old fraus did, either—unmarked graves in the asylum plot. No, I'm leaving sooner than later, and I know how to do it, too. She leans close to Amy. I've got the keys to the secretary.

She'll notice, Amy says. Lil walks the other side of the dayroom, dosing women with cough syrup. Lil has a knack for watching without looking.

She don't care anymore. Now come over to the table with me. Letitia braces herself and lifts Amy by the elbows, as ably as any of the real nurses could. She helps Amy to step over the pooled blanket and guides her to the worktable. But once seated in a hard chair, Amy cannot bear to sit upright. She lowers her head to the scored tabletop. Even if she's not ill, the close air of the ward makes her head throb. She isn't well enough, yet, to do what Letitia is asking.

There you go. Letitia places before her several sheets of paper. Sit up and let's write. She shakes Amy gently by the arm.

Amy props herself on her elbows and turns over the stationery: blue-edged sheets with the monogram *AMC*. This is someone else's.

That's an A. Letitia frowns, rubbing her forehead. Don't vex me!

But see, this is an M and a C—look. Mine is blue, but the letters should be AAU: Amy Aurelia Underwood. Not AMC. Amy smiles. Don't you know your letters?

That's all there is, says Letitia. Probably some other woman used yours up—so we'll just use hers. You can scratch out the M and the C.

I can't, Amy says. What would they think? Let me look.

Letitia rolls her eyes but helps Amy again to her feet. Even walking the few steps to the secretary brings a pain to Amy's chest—and the pain sharpens when, once there, she laughs. The compartments of the secretary are organized by last name, and her things are plainly labeled. Here's the fresh box of stationery and a pen and ink bottle she hasn't seen before. She steadies herself against the desktop as she replaces the other woman's stationery.

AMC: is this woman yet among them? That's not a question to laugh over.

Finally, says Letitia, once Amy has shuffled back. This looks just like the other, but if you have to have *your* paper, so be it. The important thing is what we say. So: Dear Mother and Father. Or would you say Father and Rose?

Mother and Father, says Amy. This is how she'd begun her Sunday letters home, during those few long weeks at Miss Carter's School. Miss Carter had taught them how to address a correspondent and what to say: *I am making friends here and learning a great deal.* The other girls seemed to take the lesson easily.

Letitia leans back in her chair. 'Mother' does sound nicer, even if it's not exactly true. So: thank you for the Christmas box, etc.

Amy unscrews the fountain pen and takes up the ink bottle. She has never before been allowed something so messy, no matter how much she admired her father's pens. She suctions a dropper of ink out of the bottle and releases it into the pen's well. Her hand trembles but she doesn't spill.

Did you get that? Letitia asks. Read it to me.

Just a minute. Amy writes the date in the corner: March 4. Days and days have slid away from her. *Mother and Father*, she writes, *Does this find you?* Miss Carter would say it's not right, but it's closer to what she means. What are they doing, what are they thinking? Not questions fit for a letter.

The doctors here are very kind, dictates Letitia, and they take good care of all of us. They've cured lots of women while I've been here, and I think they've almost cured me, too. Please come to visit and see. Your loving daughter, Amy.

The doctors are here, taking care of us, writes Amy. *They did not cure the Walking Skeleton of Charlevoix. I do not think they could. Do you still love your daughter Amy?*

Letitia leans forward, too quickly for Amy to cover what she's written. That's perfect, she says. Seal it up, and I'll give it to Dr. Ingstrom tomorrow.

Perfect? Amy says, and when Letitia nods again, yes, Amy raises her pen to sign the letter. *Write to me*, her stepmother had said. *I will write to you.* But she's only sent one letter—and, even if there were a pile of the same, what good would they do? Her stepmother doesn't seem to remember anymore that they were brought up together, almost like sisters. Amy can't remember those days without Rose's stories. She doesn't need anyone's help to recall the bad days that came later. She presses her pen to the paper, too hard, and a flower of ink blooms from the nib.

I have to recopy this. My stepmother hates mistakes.

Well—add more this time about how much you miss them. Letitia waves her hand. Add that you've been reading your Bible or some nonsense.

My Bible…. Amy nods her head. Find me one, could you? I'll copy a verse.

Something good and pious, Letitia says. I knew you could do it. She hurries to the bookrack.

Amy dates a new page, then scribbles on the back of the ruined letter. The words don't come. Not *thank you*, not *I miss you*. Not any of the flat phrases she'd learned at that school.

Letitia is back quickly. You pick it out, she says, sliding a book across the table. My folks didn't bother much with that stuff.

She's brought back one of the new WCTU Bibles, gilt-edged and fat, unmistakably a Bible—even if someone couldn't read the book's title. Stamped on its inside cover, Amy knows, is the temperance union's address. She glances at Letitia, thinks of Bertha

Chapman's ugly, friendly face, a broader, happier version of her dead mother's. *Write to me,* Miss Chapman had said. *We're going to give you a voice.* Who else would offer this? Amy scribbles again, cleaning her pen, gathering her thoughts. *Dear Miss Chapman, I'd like to know more about how the WCTU can help girls. Can it help them find places to live?*

She holds the letter out to Letitia: How's this?

Exactly, Letitia says. See, you could do it all along.

Yes. Amy's handwriting is very bad; she's been told so often enough. She writes the next lines as carefully as she is able: *I have a friend named Letitia. Can you help her, too?*

What about this? she asks.

Letitia only glances at the page. If she recognizes her name, she doesn't acknowledge it. That's lovely, she says. They'll be sure to come for you now. Don't forget the verse.

Amy flips open the Bible, sets her finger down on the closely-printed page. *Let the enemy persecute my soul.* Is this what the Walking Skeleton meant, when she ordered Amy to attend to His word? She turns again at random, closing her eyes before pointing. Her stepmother would call this superstition. But maybe if Rose attended to His word, she'd write to Amy as she promised; she'd defy the old doctor, like the Walking Skeleton did. *Take thy journey into the wilderness,* Amy reads, *and give them warning from me.* The whole Bible is like this, made up of warnings and urgings. Fit for a letter home, if she were really writing one—a letter to her persecutors. For now, though, she has something else to say: *Letitia is ill-used by the old doctor. And I think by the young one, too.*

Seal that up and I'll give it to Dr. Ingstrom tomorrow afternoon, Letitia says. Now that I don't go to the laundry, I walk by his office special to see him—and more often than not he has me in. He's a gentleman, Dr. Ingstrom; he always asks about my headaches and notes them in his records, too. He even asked after you when you were ill. He said having a dance like that during 'flu season was the hospital's own mistake and that even the old doctor himself was taken down with it—and come to think of it, I haven't seen him since. That old dog.

Amy nods. Can you put this in the stove without Lil seeing?

And when Letitia has carried away the ink-blotted letter, Amy finishes writing to Bertha Chapman. *Please help. This hospital does not help us.* She copies the WCTU's address from inside the cover of the Bible, then slides the letter under a stack of clean stationery. She will not trust it to the young doctor. The envelope addressed to her parents waits for its contents. Somewhere, she knows, this Bible says to honor them. If she flips open to that verse, will she be obliged to obey it? No. If her finger lands on that very verse, just by her thinking of it, it will be proof that the Skeleton was right: Amy is a vessel of God.

But instead, the book's pages fall open to Judges: *he told not his father or his mother what he had done.* She folds a blank sheet of paper, seals it up. Her parents can interpret *this* how they will.

A week into brutal March, the doctor resumes his daily rounds. Dragging up and down stairs, laboring through the subterranean service tunnels, he is for the first time in his life sensitive to drafts. He has a new habit of tugging his necktie tighter, cinching his collar closer to his scrawny throat. His weight loss is otherwise hidden from the patients by layers of woolen underclothes. When he bends over the beds in the infirmary or stoops to speak to pa- tients in the dayrooms, his joints burn. Bundled, they resist like cardboard too thick to fold.

The doctor lay abed for almost three weeks, an absence that would have been disastrous were his staff any less diligent. West and Ingstrom assisted Meijer where necessary with the female patients. Thanks to the reliability of the steward, the hospital remained in relatively good supply; thanks to the care of the matron, order prevailed on the wards, even despite the admission of a dozen or more cases of febrile insanity.

Aware now of all they did, the doctor is especially grateful to the nurses on the infirmary wards. These wards were packed for a solid month with cases of Russian Influenza—or, as it has been alternately named, American Grippe—and the patients were often intractable. Many of the male cases and several of the female had been complicated by the patients' alcoholism, the 'flu treated prior to their admissions either with increased intake of whiskey (in line with old-fashioned attitude that whiskey keeps the blood moving) or by total cessation of drink, combined with massive doses of coal-derived drugs. These patent 'wonders,' these antipyretics, have in past 'flu seasons brought on stupors, deliriums, deaths. Reviewing their case histories, the doctor finds the same pattern among the new admissions. The sick wards are still full of muttering, deluded sufferers brought straight from their family doctors' care. Well, men of medicine may differ in their opinions, *but*…the doctor resists the urge to swear in the presence of his patients. Instead he smiles, bracingly, as he listens to their chests and orders calomel for the digestion, Dover's powder to free up the secretions, strychnine as a tonic. Those newly admitted must be petted and purged, brought back from the jeopardy into which compounded ignorance has placed them. When this crisis is truly past, the doctor intends to hold a special dinner in honor of the infirmary staff.

Though he's managing his rounds, if not quite with his customary pep, the doctor continues to lose moments every day to his own convalescence. His weak eyes ache after just a half-hour's evening study, and so his wife continues to mispronounce her way through his medical texts. No doubt she understands every word she reads to him, but having never spoken the language, she fumbles *amyloid, ecchymosis, glioma.* Diana treats him in all ways as a quasi-invalid, bringing him soothing teas and digestive biscuits, inquiring daily after his stools. She wakes herself in order to wake him in the morning; he cannot quite trust himself, yet. And she holds his arm when they descend the stairs together, not to take support from him, but to give it. Amazing, how she prevails against his illness.

To avoid absolute fatigue by suppertime—to avoid falling asleep, as he has twice, at the evening program—the doctor forces himself to lengthen his afternoon rests. His usual thirty minutes are now ninety, spent not in the grateful relaxation of former days but in an exasperating state of imposed stillness. Bodily stillness, that is, for he can't help but try to make up his lost time by thinking about his hospital: about improvements to the grounds, recreations for the coming summer, particular patients whose cases trouble him. Unfit thoughts for a semi-invalid, but how can he not mull over a case like Mrs. Sherman's? As his wife had feared, the beautiful Mrs. Sherman has taken a turn in the past weeks: she's begun pulling out her hair, and, the attendants suppose, swallowing it. Meijer has moved her to one of the new dormitory wards; he reasons that, with less privacy, she'll have less opportunity to harm herself. The doctor approves the measure, which has proved effective in other cases, but whether Mrs. Sherman will ever be restored to what she was—the belle of their Queen City, her husband's pride—is extremely doubtful. Approaching her this morning from behind, the doctor had taken her for a much older woman, and, like a senilic, she had to be told twice who he was, why he was there. He must remember to ask his wife whether Mrs. Sherman still knows *her*.

The child, Miss Underwood, presents another puzzle. Having weathered the loss of Mrs. Lovelace, having come through her own 'flu without serious complications, she has now developed a trick of sneaking out letters. She'd entrusted the attendant Lil Breithaupt with a letter for the WCTU woman; instead, Miss Breithaupt passed the letter along to the matron. Ingstrom received another—a blank sheet of paper addressed to the girl's parents and carried to him by Miss Olsen. (Again a link between Ingstrom and these two patients. Still, the doctor had thanked him for conveying the letter; he had applauded Ingstrom's diligence, rather than finding occasion for suspicion). The doctor has only gone once to ward fifteen since his partial resumption of duties, and Miss Underwood stared at him then as though he were a ghost. Meijer had tended to her on that visit, but the doctor means to speak with her at length when they're both stronger. He intends to prescribe daily occupation. Private patient or not, she'll improve, he's certain, when given more to do. What can be done, though, to persuade her to trust her doctors?

His wife interrupts his thoughts, carrying in his tray. A dark bottle of cough syrup and, in one of her delicate porcelain pots, more tea—always more tea. It is an invalid's drink, which he resents—as perhaps she does, too, when he presses it upon her. They smile wanly at each other.

James, she says, and lays her hand against his forehead. You look as though you're thinking too hard.

Mrs. Doctor, he says, you wouldn't encourage your patient to malinger?

She sits on the ottoman and lifts his feet into her lap. He's wearing slippers in the middle of the day; he's wearing a ridiculous flannel dressing gown over his shirtsleeves. These are Diana's embellishments, along with the oversized nurse's apron she's now wearing. She begins to rub his feet and ankles, vigorously.

James, she says. It's just over a month until you leave for Washington. Look at you, dearest. Shouldn't we rather take a health trip—out West, say?

Her massaging hands are deft and strong—from crocheting, he reckons. He grunts slightly: Don't judge a man based on his appearance. I've got some weight to put back on; I've spoken to the kitchen about an increasing menu. And I mean to start walking again tomorrow.

In the snow? She shakes her head. Can that be good for your lungs? Think of dry, desert air. Surely that would be better? You know what the air will be in Washington. I can't think why *doctors* would choose to visit such a place.

I plan to walk in the calistheneum, if you must know. I won't be mother-henned, Diana. Who's been tending to *you* this past month?

I can tend myself as well as West or Meijer might. And I don't like to bother Dr. Ingstrom, now that he's decided to leave us. She frowns, his wife, and he feels a pang. She's about to lose her favorite. A dubious favorite, from the doctor's perspective, but he can see things from hers: handsome boy, pining romantically, burning for revenge against the disease that took his beloved. Diana would have avenged her brother just the same, had she been strong enough to study medicine.

You've doctored yourself ably, I can see, but I won't let you prescribe me a rest cure. He leans forward and strokes her cheek. You can take my temperature as often as you please and monitor my mucus levels and all the rest.

Much obliged, I'm sure. She laughs, pouring him a cup of tea. Next, you'll be offering me your chamber pot!

He shakes his head, laughing, too. I hope I'm not *quite* so broken-down!

There's a knock on the door—Matilda. Ma'am, she says, and her face is contorted with displeasure. Ma'am, sir, I've told him that you're not to be bothered, but he won't go away—as always!—and do you want to see him in the parlor?

Parlor be damned, roars a familiar voice, and there he is, as good as clockwork: Humphries, come for a managers' tour. The doctor's wife stands quickly, smoothing out her voluminous apron. She positions herself between Humphries and the doctor, but Humphries can almost see through her. He laughs away her effort.

Having a nap, James? I'd heard you were taken down with this Russian 'flu, but I didn't think I'd see it with my own eyes. Humphries strides across the room and pumps the doctor's hand. Cigar smoke exudes from his clothing when he moves, and the doctor immediately begins to cough.

The doctor is quite restored, says his wife, loudly. As are most of the patients, Mr. Humphries. We're all out of danger, here.

And I'm taking the first occasion to see it for myself. But don't worry about showing me around, James—Corn will see to it.

Corn? The doctor's wife bats her eyelashes, as is her habit when angry.

Dr. Ingstrom, that is, ma'am. And I'm to spirit him away with me tonight to the club, so don't worry about making a place for us at the dinner table.

You and Dr. Ingstrom must be very good friends, says the doctor's wife. Who would have dreamed?

I'm a businessman, ma'am; the boy makes a good proposition. And James here knows full well that I get impatient with asylum politics. Too slow for old Humphries—and too slow for our best young doctors. You're the last of the old guard, Jim, and that's a fine thing, but give me the new guard, every time.

The doctor coughs again and not just for effect: he is surprised to feel sputum in his throat.

You're welcome here, Mr. Humphries—per the hospital's charter. But you must excuse me this afternoon.

Humphries laughs more loudly, mirth rocking his body. Per the hospital's charter—that's hospitality. You'll be my tour guide next month, I'm sure, and Ingstrom and I *will* go over the women's wards today. There's one perk of your being laid up.

You're welcome to tour any of our facilities, at any time, the doctor says.

Please try to be quiet as you visit, Mr. Humphries, says the doctor's wife. This awful 'flu has made some of the women more sensitive than usual, and, as you know, so many have nervous conditions. She tilts her head and smiles at him, almost girlishly. Why not let me go with you as far as ward three? I have an errand there. And I can help you practice your manners.

Er—delighted and all, ma'am. But the doctor can read annoyance on Humphries's broad face, and, when his wife leaves the room to get her things, the brickman turns to him. His voice is quieter now and serious.

You should know, James, that I didn't *ask* Ingstrom to take me through the women's wards. He suggested it. Seems there's a few cases he'd like to share with me.

Dr. Ingstrom assisted Meijer during my illness, says the doctor. He takes a special interest in the younger patients, I believe.

I'm sure he does, handsome boy like that. But it goes beyond spooning, James. He thinks a couple of them might not be crazy. Says they're being kept here as an expedient rather than a necessity.

He and I differ on a number of points.

But if he's right…. Humphries sits down in the armchair beside the doctor's. You're not giving anybody material for a habeas corpus trial, are you, Jim?

The doctor shakes his head. You've read too many dime novels, Mr. Humphries.

I've read Nellie Bly, is more like it. I've read that Packard woman's account of her trouble in Illinois. I'm not an imaginative sort, doctor.

No—only a careful one, and I'm grateful to you for it. But you will please remember that these illnesses are often cyclical or recurring in nature. You will remember that patients beginning the path to recovery may seem more improved than they truly are. The doctor is glad for once of Humphries's amateur familiarity with psychiatry; the little that he's read may now be as much a help as a hindrance.

Humphries nods, but the crease remains in his brow. You've always been prudent, Jim, but you can see how I have to take this seriously. And, well—just remember that I've given you a chance to 'fess up. We don't need that sort of scandal on our hands.

The doctor is prevented from replying by his wife's return. He swallows his angry retort: that diseases of the mind are more complex than bricks; that this hospital is neither a kiln nor a laboratory, but a public institution, chartered for the good of the state. He twists his mouth into a smile for Diana. She's shed her apron now and carries a market basket and a plate of jam tartlets. Offered the cookies, Humphries lifts two daintily, his outstretched pinky like a plump red sausage link. He winks as he stuffs both tartlets into his mouth.

You do a great compliment to my baking, the doctor's wife laughs. You'll have to promise not to eat any more, if you're to carry my basket.

Honor bright, Humphries says, raising one hand in a boy's pledge while the other creeps toward the basket. Diana swats him playfully and takes his great arm. They're an odd couple as they bid the doctor goodbye, one so gross and the other so delicate—and yet both, as the doctor well knows, equally shrewd.

The doctor tries again to find a comfortable position in his chair. His gratitude toward Diana almost surpasses his aggravation toward Humphries. Diana will keep Humphries from harassing the women on wards one and three, keep an ear to his conversation with Ingstrom. But she cannot undo the damage Humphries has done to the doctor's peace of mind.

Ridiculous to mention habeas corpus in connection with Miss Underwood, a minor admitted and maintained by her parents. And, even if the Olsen girl had friends to argue on her behalf, it would be impossible to build a case that she was being kept here wrongly. If the matter went to trial, she'd be sure to say something to implicate herself; she would develop, on the spot, a delusion about the judge or spin one of her wild stories about the doctor. *He comes after me at night.* When he'd first begun treating her, back in Kalamazoo, the doctor had taken seriously her accusations against the staff at

Pontiac and at the county homes where she'd been before that. A poor girl from who knows where, it did not seem impossible that she might have been raped and beaten within the walls of those less-diligent facilities. Certainly she was operated upon: a crooked scar on her abdomen suggests oophorectomy, though she still menstruates. He suspects a botched version of Battey's operation, perhaps meant to ease her monthly migraines, more likely intended to 'control' the hereditary taint. Sterilization is not the doctor's idea of good medicine, and he can't blame the girl for fearing such men as did this to her. And, naturally, those fears exacerbate her illness. The doctor is aware that Miss Olsen's delusions of persecution center now on him; he's the brute who allegedly *comes after her*. Ingstrom would be next, were he ever to cross her.

It's ridiculous for anyone to have mentioned habeas corpus in connection with Letitia Olsen or Amy Underwood, and yet Humphries has, and the doctor is rattled by this evidence that Humphries doesn't respect his judgment.

He gulps the rest of his tea. There's plenty more in the pot, but he's beyond its pale comfort. Humphries is now touring the doctor's hospital while he stays behind in slippers, sipping tea and cough syrup. He takes up that hateful bottle, pours his draught. He tips it back—and then, sputtering and spitting, checks the label. This isn't his cloying, viscous cough syrup, but Metcalf's wine of coca, 'for fatigue of mind and body.'

Did Diana bring this as a joke? The two of them have laughed together over Mrs. West's fondness for such stuff. Of course, the dear old soul doesn't use more than she should…but she does seem to always have a bottle on hand. (Why idle Mrs. West should be fatigued, the doctor cannot imagine). Or is wine of coca Diana's latest foray into doctoring?

The doctor sniffs the bottle: alcohol mulled with spices. It's no worse or better than whiskey—no good at all, then, for an invalid—and what would his father say, if somehow that lean, sober ghost were to appear in the doorway, spying him with his feet up and alcohol on his breath at three o'clock in the afternoon? This scene would confirm all of the old man's silent prejudices against the doctor's profession.

Yet to seize this accident as an opportunity…to make a careful study of the drink's effects…*that* would be a novel experiment, in line with Ingstrom's cinchonia trial. The doctor gropes for his pocket, forgetting that he's wearing a dressing gown. His suit coat hangs all the way across the room; his notepad and pencil are in its breast pocket. Well, he will simply have to remember his observations.

Offensively sweet, the 'wine' improves as he sips it. He takes it slowly, while noting that his frustration with Humphries is mellowing. What will he say the next time Humphries crosses him? What *won't* he say, is more like it. He will have to remember those retorts, too.

Answers don't come to Amy's letters. Though she'd doubted her parents would make a reply, she'd believed in Bertha Chapman. She asks Lil daily, have I had a letter? and sometimes hourly, when the response slips her mind. Each time, Lil only shakes her head, shaking her head when Letitia pesters her, too. Finally she draws them aside.

You've asked and asked, and maybe you don't realize that letters can't get out of here without going through the doctor. I don't know what you put in there, but there's always a chance he didn't like it enough to pass it on.

Letitia shakes her head. Dr. Ingstrom doesn't answer to that old man!

Dr. Ingstrom? I don't see how he comes into it, but I suspect he answers to the doctor as much as the rest of us do—and Miss Amy, I passed your note up like I'm supposed to. If that means you don't like Lil anymore, so be it, but I'm not risking my position for your games. You girls don't know what I gone through to get this spot.

Letitia stares at Lil. *Her* note? What are you talking about?

You've been a help to me, Letty, but if you girls are going to make trouble, I can't be as soft with you as I have been.

Two women begin to shout and flail on the opposite side of the room, and Lil rushes to break up the fight. There are fights here all day long; the newcomers are quarrelsome. Amy shrinks now into the corner of the sofa as Letitia turns to her, frowning.

What note did you give to Lil?

I wrote to somebody else. My brother.

I know you never had one. Why not say a beau? You haven't had one of those either. Was it about me? She jerks Amy's arm. Sly thing! Tell me what you wrote!

Amy pulls away. I wrote to a woman who visited while you were away. A temperance woman.

Temperance! Letitia throws herself back against the cushions. You *are* crazy. Why would you want to get in with them? Picket saloons all day and wind up a spinster.

The woman told me to write if I needed anything.

Sure she did. Letitia sighs. Well, so we're back where we were. Write up another one and I can get it out through the delivery boy—only who knows if he's got sense enough to post it.

Amy shakes her head. What's the use?

Letitia leans toward her, close. I don't want to wither up in here, even if you do. And the old man ain't never going to part with me on his own.

Amy turns away. Why don't you just leave? She speaks softly, but Letitia hears.

It ain't like that. I walked away from Pontiac easy as pie—and then they caught me and put me on the back wards for two months. And to get from here to anyplace worth going I'd have to make my way past all those other hospitals…a body couldn't do it, that's all.

You could sneak onto a boat and get to Chicago, Amy says. Sneak in with the cargo. Maybe that's what the tobacco woman did.

The rough woman who spat on her shoe has been gone for a month now, gone one morning to her position in the laundry and never come back.

Stow away, with the bay all iced over! Letitia laughs. You'd be a fine one at sneaking off. And as for Edda, they're sure to find her when the snow melts. Every year some loon breaks out before the weather's decent. I'd sooner die of boredom than freeze to death.

Amy stands up, stretching her weak legs. She couldn't run away now if she wanted to; she couldn't yet run all the way around the calistheneum. Blood rushes to and drains from her head.

Dr. Ingstrom doesn't think I belong here, she says, slowly. But I don't know where he thinks I *should* go.

Letitia's eyes narrow. Did he tell you that?

Amy stamps her feet, trying to wake them up. I didn't want to dance with him.

No, but looked like he wanted to dance with you—or so *you* think, I 'spose? Won't we all be happy when you're Mrs. Ingstrom and I'm the hired woman? Only, why will my bastard brats all have his dark eyes and hair?

Stop it! Amy squeezes her eyes shut. I don't want anything to do with him!

He's said that to me, too, you know, Letitia says. She spreads her arms across the back of the couch. That all I need is a special treatment, and then I could leave. That I'm a clever girl, and he'd like to help me. You can't always bank on what a man will say.

No, Amy says. On the other side of the room, Lil is braced between two struggling women, who reach around her for one another's eyes and hair. She can't hold the pose forever and still, no one has come to replace Klara. No one but Letitia, who stands.

We're going to write another letter, she says. Don't think I'll forget. She starts slowly across the room. Amy sits again, exhausted.

Letitia is ten steps away, two body lengths away, when someone speaks at Amy's back: *Miss Underwood.*

A male voice, calm and even. It is impossible, but even before she turns to see the dark gleaming eyes, the glossy moustache, the fine suit, she has recognized him. Dr. Ingstrom. Just like at the dance, the young doctor has been conjured up by their mention of his name. Come from his office at the center of the hospital— come quickly through all those narrow twisting stairways to stand here, staring at her. Here as he seldom is, on their untidy ward. How does he hear them or know?

But before Amy can do or say anything, Ingstrom rushes past her, toward the fight. Amy sees Letitia's broad smile, even amidst the tangled women; she watches Ingstrom restore order through just the surprise of his presence. And then her side of the sofa lifts like the lighter side of a seesaw. A fat man weights down its other side. Red-faced, blowing: the merchant from the dances. She leaps away from his face, his hands.

Hello, there! He stands, too. Berthold Humphries. He bellows his name at her, his voice loud and wet, and as he speaks, he reaches for her with his ham-colored hand. He wants to touch her, to grab her by the waist—and Amy *can* run, after all, her flimsy legs propelling her away from the couch and across the room. Letitia has just settled one of the fighting women in a rocker; Letitia swats away Amy's hands, wheels when Amy tries to hide behind her.

Miss Underwood, says Dr. Ingstrom. His voice is like honey even as he restrains the other fighter, holding her arms behind her back. The woman leans forward, panting in his grasp, and he is as cool and clean as ever. Let's all calm ourselves, Ingstrom says. Miss Underwood, Mr. Humphries is one of the hospital's managers, come to tour the wards. Come to see about conditions here among the women.

Letitia pulls away from Amy and holds out her hand to the fat man, who comes puffing now across the room. We danced the German waltz, she says in a strange, careful way.

Yes, well—how do you do? Humphries shakes her hand quickly. He shifts from foot to foot, as though his pants don't fit. Lots of excitement, I see. Some unhappy ladies.

Oh, no, sir; we're all happy here! Letitia smiles without showing her teeth, and Amy stares at her.

Present fracas notwithstanding, I suppose? Don't look like some of these gals want to talk to us much—so what about you then, Miss Underwood? You like it here all right?

Amy shakes her head.

No? Well, now's the time to speak up. Ingstrom and I are on a fact-finding mission. Trying to see where the hospital can improve in efficiency and effectiveness. What's the problem—not enough sweets? Pillows too hard? We're all ears.

I've told you, Amy says, turning to Dr. Ingstrom. What she told him about Letitia and the old doctor she won't repeat to this gaping stranger.

Told him? Letitia speaks in a fine lady's tone of mock surprise. Have the two of you been talking?

Miss Underwood, says Dr. Ingstrom, Mr. Humphries is one of the greatest friends of this hospital; can't you welcome him as a friend?

The fat man shuffles nearer. No need to be shy, my dear; regard me as an uncle—Uncle Berthold, why don't we say?

Amy closes her eyes. This fat man is Ingstrom's opposite—but he has only appeared in Ingstrom's company. Always at the dances he trails behind Ingstrom, an ogre attending a prince, and which of them is really the monster? Ingstrom has done what the other doctors never would—not the old one or the stout one or the lame one. He has brought a strange man onto the ward. Strange men came to see her at her parents' house, two of them separately before she was brought here. Nervous, odd, sweating—they were doctors. This Humphries carries no bag, but he examines her and Letitia. He tries to touch them. For what reason?

She opens her eyes and the fat man is close beside her, his thick lips slightly parted. She sees his heavy tongue twitching in his mouth.

You're not a doctor, she says to Ingstrom.

I'm not a doctor, laughs the fat man. Mark my words, Cornelius is the real thing. The best doctor in the state, I'd wager—and he's brought me here to see and help all of you.

Amy shakes her head. Ingstrom has offered Letitia new dresses, new teeth. He has offered her special treatments—why?

Never mind her. Letitia frowns at Amy. She touches the fat man's arm. Let's *us* talk.

Miss Underwood, says Ingstrom. You're upset. Let me see you to your room.

Amy shakes her head. You're not a doctor, she repeats. She gropes for the word the lumberjack taught her. A word for men who sell women's company.

Now Lil joins them. Sir, Miss Underwood's just come back from the infirmary. Might be you've surprised her.

Is it Miss Breithaupt? Ingstrom smirks at Lil, and, for a moment, he looks neither handsome nor polished but like his real self: cruel. I wasn't aware you'd made it through the training class.

I graduated with top marks, sir. Lil's bun has been torn loose by the fighters and her face is turning redder and redder.

How wonderful, Ingstrom says. Then you will have learned that the doctors determine the patients' course of treatment. While I see to Miss Underwood, you might clean up that mess. He points at a toppled fern, its dirt spilled across the rug.

Lil backs away, biting her lips white in her red face. The room is in shambles from the women's fights, and there is no one but Lil to keep it in order. Letitia fawns now over the fat man; Letitia is not an attendant. Neither is Amy, but she hurries after Lil. She crouches beside her, gathering up broken fronds. Lil's face is damp.

He's not a doctor, Amy whispers. Don't cry over him, Lil. I know why he's here.

I'm sure you mean to be kind, Miss Underwood, but you won't help matters by taking my side. Leave that be, now. Go talk to Dr. Ingstrom, like he asked.

He's not a doctor, Amy repeats, more loudly. She looks over her shoulder at Ingstrom, looking at her. He shouldn't be here with that hulking town man. They shouldn't be here without the old doctor or the stout one—here outside of doctors' hours, examining women who don't need it. Something else brings them here; she finally understands. She musters the word for what Ingstrom is—a strange word, a burst of air. She draws a deep breath.

He's a pimp!

Lil sits back on her haunches, staring at Amy. Struck dumb by this revelation.

Everyone is staring: Letitia and Lil, Ingstrom and Humphries, all the other women in the dayroom. All of them awed by the truth of Amy's words, and in their silence, she repeats herself more loudly: he's a pimp! He's a pimp, and he'll ruin us all!

She could say more—proclaim everything that she has observed about Ingstrom, everything that he has said and done and promised—but Lil cuts her off.

Miss Underwood, she says. You are overtired and…confused.

Then Amy hears the other women repeating her words, alarmed or amused; she sees the two fighting women clutch each other's arms, laughing.

What trash, Letitia murmurs to Humphries, and Amy sees him nod. Staring at her with his popped eyes. Well, well, he says. From the mouths of babes!

She does not know what else to say. How did the Walking Skeleton know what to say next, in moments like this, with everyone watching? She brushes the scattered soil from her hands and stands, in her still-unsteady way.

Miss Underwood, says Ingstrom. His voice is silken but his eyes are cold and Amy shakes her head. She will not let him talk to her or touch her; she will not let him provoke her into saying more. Instead she walks past him, his clean linen and cologne smell nearly gagging her, and then past Letitia, who smells as ever of camphor from her rotting teeth. Her teeth that Ingstrom will only promise to fix. For as long as he keeps promising, Letitia will let him sell her to strange men for the German waltz—and for what else? The fat man's huge red hands touch without asking, just as the lumberjack touched Amy, before he knew who she was. Who is Letitia? Who is there to protect her?

But Letitia doesn't take the hand that Amy holds out to her; Letitia will not come with her as she walks away from the day room and back to her own empty bedroom. Amy wouldn't be allowed to be here during the day, if there were enough attendants to see to the ward properly. If this were really an asylum. But since Ingstrom is a deceiver—a pimp—then this must be some other kind of place. Lewd, piggish men cornering the women on the wards, and the old doctor ignoring it. The Walking Skeleton told her as much—that thin body quaking furiously. Those out-flung hands with their miraculous bruises. What are the women here, if the doctors are liars? What's the use in trying to save Letitia or anyone else? Worse words than *pimp* are screamed by some women, day and night. What if all of those words are true?

Amy crawls onto her bed and turns her face to the blistered wall. She will not speak again until she finds true words.

Chapter Twelve

NOW THAT MARCH HAS TURNED mild and the infirmary returned to its usual capacity; now that the gutters are gurgling and the hills alive with spring melt, all of the buildings' frailties are apparent. Long bubbles rise in the hospital's mineral paint, taut with liquid under the doctor's palpitating fingers. Water damage is endemic on the hospital's topmost floors. In Meijer's and Ingstrom's fourth floor apartments, the wallpaper is working loose, the crown molding moldering. Conditions are even worse in the attic dormitories. The service staff complains that their bedclothes are always damp. Sleeping amongst the hospital's wooden rafters, the kitchen and laundry workers, the grounds crew and the maids aren't allowed stoves but take comfort from hot bricks and thick quilts, sharing beds on the coldest nights like young children in the country. Such dank conditions are unwholesome, liable to aggravate rheumatism, disrupt sleep. The attics are no place for tired muscles to recover, and the doctor will ask the state next year for an appropriation for free-standing staff dormitories, quarters in which his workers might light fires in the evenings, smoke their pipes without subterfuge, stand upright rather than ducking under the eaves. Quarters in which the assignations that take place here, against the hospital's rules but in line with nature's, might be conducted with some dignity.

The poor planning evidenced by these leaking roofs troubles the doctor at least as much as the damage itself. Poor planning in any aspect of the hospital's affairs affects all of its others, like rot spreading through wood. Had he been charged with engineering the roofs, he would have been more methodical: made a closer study of the region's precipitation, interviewed those who had previously built here, visited hospitals in other snowy climates. The doctor would rather adapt a good plan than strike out blindly. He can thank his upbringing *and* his professional training for that kind of vision, comprehensive and waste-averse. If he had been allowed to pick the medical staff, for example, he would have sought as a rule only those assistant physicians with experience at large public institutions. Replacing Ingstrom after only a few years is like repairing the roofs: a necessary act of maintenance, forced too soon upon the board of managers. It is imperative that the new physician be made of more lasting materials—but the doctor is only the managers' advisor in this matter, not their commander.

The good news is that half a dozen viable applicants have so far presented themselves for the position. Their letters of inquiry fan across the doctor's desk, copies forwarded to him by the managers. West and Meijer each have their favorites, hailing from hospitals in Wisconsin or Indiana, Ohio or Illinois. Fresh young doctors who have experience working with the insane, or have not. There are five young men among them and a woman, too; a specialist in puerperal diseases, she took her degree from a homeopathic medical college in Chicago. Women physicians have done good work at other hospitals for the insane; the doctor heard a compelling paper on the subject at last year's superintendents' conference. Then, too, a young female assistant might be more tractable than his youngest male assistant has again proven.

To be fair, Ingstrom came immediately to the doctor with a written report of the incident on ward fifteen; he did have promptness to recommend his handling of the matter. And, as incidents went, it didn't seem such a bad one: how many times have insults and curses been uttered under this hospital's roof? How many times has a patient, in the manner of Miss Underwood, simply stopped speaking after an apparently minor disturbance? But in this case, the most serious damage, about which Ingstrom is characteristically unconcerned, is that done to the ward attendant's morale. Already over-worked, Miss Breithaupt now seems on the verge of resigning her post. As her supervisor, Mrs. Morris had counseled her to meekness but had come to the doctor not quite able to practice what she preached. It's common for the attendants to quit, with or without evident provocation, openly or by slipping off at night, but Mrs. Morris won't lose this attendant without a fight. Miss Breithaupt is a graduate of the training school, a steady, compassionate girl who is *not* prone to assignations or other tomfoolery. To appease both her and the matron, the doctor has agreed to appoint one of the sewing room assistants to ward fifteen. This leaves the sewing room understaffed and puts upon Miss Breithaupt the responsibility of overseeing an insufficiently-trained companion—but at least she has another body to break up fights or watch things when she visits the toilet.

In his careerism, Ingstrom is naturally most concerned with the damage his tour of the women's wards has caused to his relationship with Berthold Humphries. The doctor is determined not to interest himself in their business arrangement—but he could not help feeling a medical concern that afternoon when Humphries had burst back into his study, nearly apoplectic and demanding assurance of Ingstrom's character. Never had he seen the brickman's face so red or his perspiration running so freely.

A fawning hussy and a half-addled child, Humphries had declared the two girls—no habeas corpus about it! What can the boy have been thinking? he'd demanded, pacing about the room.

Energized after all by his wine of coca, the doctor had offered Humphries not the rejoinders he'd been plotting for the past half hour, but instead, support: his own seat, a cup of lukewarm tea, a sympathetic ear. It wasn't that Humphries—or any reasonable person—would believe Ingstrom to actually be a pimp, but that the girl who had declared him so was the very same girl Ingstrom had championed just hours before. The very girl who was supposed to prove the doctor's incompetence and Ingstrom's superiority as a diagnostician.

The whole affair gives evidence that ward tours are imprudent: Humphries has seen what he cannot be expected to understand. Ingstrom ought to have known better than to question his superior's judgment—and, this time, the boy may actually learn to regret his impudence.

The doctor shakes himself out of these ruminations. He files away the application letters, leaving topmost the simple, straightforward letter of Henrietta Firestone, MD. She is a redhead, maybe, this fiery young woman…. No, that is hardly imaginative. Perhaps, then, a demure but keen-eyed brunette, who would naturally be paired with him, overseeing the women's wards. A daughter of sorts, this Dr. Firestone, a young woman of more ability and wit than the attendants but still willing to defer to the doctor's long experience, to *learn* from him.

The picture is pleasing—but it must give way to last week's accumulated ward notes.

On ward two, good eating, good sleeping, continued interest in that macabre case of Jack the Ripper. The doctor has read only thus far when a knock sounds on his office door: Mrs. Morris. Has Miss Breithaupt left them, after all?

But no: There's a man to see you in the receiving room, Mrs. Morris says. He's one of the few that's come today.

The doctor reads in the matron's concerned expression the undisguised perplexity on his own face. He tries to assure her by nodding emphatically and rising quickly from his chair. A rush of blood to his head. It's happened since his illness that he sometimes needs a moment to collect himself, to bring to mind, for instance, all of the reasons that the matron might knock on his door.

It's Saturday, sir, Mrs. Morris says.

Of course, he says, too loudly. Mrs. Morris supervises the receiving room during official Saturday visiting hours. Visiting day!

Mrs. Morris coughs, too polite to remark his lapse but clearly startled by it. She bows as she backs away, hastening to her post. And so he doesn't have a chance to ask the visitor's name. Was he expecting anyone today? The wine of coca still sits there on his desk; his experiment with it was interrupted the other day before he arrived at any insights. Perhaps that potion could perk him up, now…but no: no, he leaves it untouched, and, hurrying down the stairs, he racks his brain. A man, a man—what man is he expecting?—what man is this that he finds in the receiving room, tall, with a dusty brown moustache?

The visitor's thin face is vaguely familiar; the visitor is almost gaunt, and his pale blue eyes seem weak and sore. He stands beside the mantle and watches the doctor cross the room. The visitor's right arm hangs forward in anticipation of their greeting, but his expression is dour, verging on a scowl. The doctor smiles warmly; odds are, this is a former patient.

How do you do, sir? asks the doctor, shaking hands.

Doctor, says the man. His voice rasps. I'm sorry to come without writing first, but I received Mr. Humphries's letter only yesterday, just as I was preparing for a surveying trip east of here.

Ah, says the doctor, nodding.

His visitor frowns, seeming to realize that he hasn't been recognized.

My daughter is in your care, sir—Amy Underwood. I thought you'd know me, but of course I'm changed. The 'flu hit me hard.

I've been laid up myself, says the doctor, smiling anew: Miss Underwood's case, at least, is fresh in his mind. Do sit down, sir, Mr. Underwood. Your wife is well, I hope?

Mr. Underwood lowers himself stiffly into a wingchair. On the whole, he says, she's the same as when you saw her. I didn't tell her about Amy's being sick.

Well, says the doctor. Given how completely your daughter has recovered, perhaps that was prudent. There was no real cause for worry in Miss Underwood's case.

My wife was worried enough about my illness to disorder her nerves considerably—considerably, doctor. And so I haven't told her yet about *this*, either. Mr. Underwood produces a letter from his breast pocket and shakes it out flat, positioning it on the low table between his chair and the doctor's. I'd like you to tell me what it means.

At the very sight of the brick company's stationery, the doctor's nerves spark. Was the letter written while Humphries was yet red and blowing? The contents of the first page suggest so.

It is my bound duty, Humphries writes, *to tell you that the medical staffers of the State Hospital are in complete disagreement over your daughter's condition. Each seems furthermore more interested in defending his pet diagnosis than in treating your poor child. I call that a damned shame.* Humphries's indignant and unprofessional ramblings go on for three full pages, claiming *conflicts of interest* and *incompetent country girls running the wards*. The doctor is spared direct insult, but the letter itself must be taken in that light, as an insult to his medical opinion and authority. Humphries signs off as the *attentive friend* of the Underwoods and of *unfortunates, everywhere.*

Their boorish, lecherous friend, the doctor would add. He scoffs aloud, tries to disguise the sound as a cough—and then must suppress a real cough. How excitable his lungs still are, especially when provoked by such an example of 'friendship'! Mr. Underwood takes the occasion to cough, as well—and, in the chorus that follows, the doctor hears that the other man is much worse off than he is; Mr. Underwood's lungs are still seriously congested.

Well, doctor? demands Mr. Underwood, once he can speak. I'd like to know why some outsider takes this interest in my daughter.

Mr. Humphries is one of the hospital's managers. Perhaps he neglected to mention?

He explains all of that in full. Mr. Underwood jabs the paper with a bony finger. He explains very plainly that he's not a doctor. What I'd like to know is what kind of place is this where brickmakers give their diagnoses freely? One of the benefits of this hospital, or so we thought, was that it might remove Amy from mixed company—keep her away from strange men until she knows herself better. But reading this, I half-suspect that this Humphries is courting my daughter. How else would he know her so well; how else would he even know her name, doctor?

I apologize—

But Mr. Underwood isn't through, only laboring for breath. He jabs the paper again. The presumption of this letter is one thing. But the contents! That's another thing altogether. This Dr. Ingstrom that he's quoting—well, what kind of a doctor can *he* be if his assessment contradicts yours and both of the doctors' we saw up north? We had no trouble procuring those two certificates for Amy's admission, doctor—there seemed no question at all what the best course of action would be. And to hear now that we may have erred—my wife wouldn't be able to bear *that* news, after everything she suffered in coming to this decision.

I apologize that Mr. Humphries has overstepped his bounds—

Mr. Underwood crumples the letter into his breast pocket. I won't have him seeing Amy again, that's the first thing. And, next, I'd like your opinion in plain English. What's your present view of my daughter's case?

The doctor nods his head briskly, clears his throat. Your daughter is more tractable now than when she came to our hospital—I can report progress there. However, having observed her for some months, I consider her to be deficient yet in self-control. Her offenses here have all been of a childish nature: stealing, lying, fighting. It is only through punishment that she seems to understand these things as wrong. She is distrustful, deceitful, and unusually taciturn—qualities which, when indulged, tend to retard the normal development of feeling and intellect. Since she has no history of brain fever or head injury, I take hers to be a case of moral insanity.

Mr. Underwood nods. She's always been a healthy child. But her mother....

Her mother is nervous, it seemed to me?

Her stepmother is, says Mr. Underwood, his scowl deepening. The first Mrs. Underwood was a suicide—did you forget that, doctor?

I'm sorry, says the doctor, shaking his head sharply. Of course not.

Is that what's wrong with Amy?

No, the doctor says. No—we do not consider the girl a danger to herself.

Then you've gotten her to leave off picking at her face?

Mr. Underwood, says the doctor, collecting himself. It is my opinion that, were Miss Underwood receptive to positive moral influences, she would improve. As yet, however, she seems deeply impressed by the disruptive behaviors of those around her, and, our hospital being what it is, we have no comfortable means of removing her from such influences—she would hardly benefit from total isolation, nor is she docile enough herself to make fit company for the women on the better wards. If your daughter took an interest in recovery, the bad influences around her would certainly be outweighed by the good, and she would progress. Instead, she seems not to regard herself as ill—and, until she does, Mr. Underwood, it's unlikely that she'll take steps to correct her impulsive behaviors or develop more productive habits of mind.

Mr. Underwood draws the letter forth again, suppressing a cough as he does so. Then what the other doctor says—that she might train as a nurse's attendant—you regard that as rubbish?

The doctor raises his eyebrows: he missed this item in Humphries's letter. It may be true, he says, that Miss Underwood is more capable that she's shown you or me. But only in rare cases do patients become attendants—and, then, usually, they have been treated on the convalescent wards, not the intermediate wards, where your daughter is and has been.

Mr. Underwood shakes his head, coughing vigorously now. His eyes water as he pages through the letter, able to speak only gaspingly: Not here—downstate somewhere. Humphries isn't for it, either.

The doctor scans the passage at which his guest points. So this is Ingstrom's interest in Miss Underwood: he would, as Humphries puts it, *put her to work not half well.* A shoddy sort of clinic, where a girl such as this would be entrusted with patient care.

The doctor shakes his head: I'm sure Dr. Ingstrom had Miss Underwood's welfare in mind, he says. But as her attending physician and the superintendent of this hospital, I consider it highly advisable that your daughter remain here, as a patient.

Mr. Underwood draws the cuspidor nearer with his foot. He spits, wipes his mouth. My wife talked of hiring someone, he says. She's talked of it, so that we could bring Amy back home, but where are we to find someone suitable—someone with experience and not so roughly-cut as most of the women up here? My first wife…my first wife was a homesteader's daughter who made herself into a schoolteacher. And I guess Amy's like her, doctor, to the extent that she can't be reasoned with when she has a notion in her head. But where do her notions come from?

The doctor resists an urge to pat the other man's arm; after all, Mr. Underwood is not his patient. Instead, he lowers his voice, consolingly: I have peculiar ideas myself, sir—can you honestly say that you do not? The difference is that we've learned how to manage them, how to judge what is prudent from what is freakish or momentarily pleasing. Amy will learn this lesson, too, if we're patient and persistent.

Yes, says Mr. Underwood. He stares at the rug, and the doctor smiles, remembering how the girl had vandalized the very same rug on the day she was admitted. But when Mr. Underwood looks up, his expression is still grave.

Amy's condition—you said it isn't the same thing her mother had. But…what risks are there when a woman has children later in life—what risks to the child?

The doctor answers carefully: The likelihood of mortality increases, for both the mother and child—I'm sure you're aware of that. And we've found that the incidence of abnormalities in children increases with the mother's age. Whether an increased risk of insanity can likewise be traced, we are not certain, sir—but it is possible.

Mr. Underwood's cheeks are now ashen. He does not seem well enough to be traveling.

You're concerned about the current Mrs. Underwood?

The lumber agent shakes his head, sitting up. She and I have been married now for thirteen years.

And you hope yet to have a child?

We've come close, doctor, but things always go wrong toward the end. And she'll be thirty-two this year. The first Mrs. Underwood was thirty-six when Amy was born. Mr. Underwood draws his hand roughly across his face. I'd rather give up the idea than see another child of mine wind up here.

The doctor nods. My best advice to Mrs. Underwood is not to overtax her nervous system or her constitution. And—you will forgive me, sir—but as a physician, I would advise your wife to give up her corsets.

They're therapeutic, Mr. Underwood says. With electrical currents—'guaranteed to stimulate a lazy womb.' He shakes himself. I'd like to see Amy before I leave.

The doctor stands. A visit from home can be very comforting—to both parties. This way.

There's something more he ought to say about the girl's case; the doctor can feel it tickling at the corner of his memory, some other development—but it doesn't come to him as he leads the coughing lumber agent again down the tiled corridor, through the firedoor, onto the service stairs, and up to the women's intermediate wards. It doesn't come to him even once there, as he bids Letitia Olsen fetch Miss Underwood to the visiting parlor, or when he sees the skeptical face she offers in reply. Pert girl: what will she say, in summoning her friend?

Amy stares out her bedroom window and lets her hands move how they will, tearing onionskin pages into thin strips. The sound of shredding paper is like cracking ice or rustling leaves. A sound of things moving, no matter that she is sitting still. The scritching sound is pleasing, the way the words fall into new orders. Words shot through with the Walking Skeleton's energy, with Miss Chapman's—with God's, maybe. She hides the strips in her pockets whenever footsteps pass near her open door. Then, as it hasn't for days, Letitia's head appears around the doorframe.

There's a man for you in the visiting parlor. A real beanpole—probably more temperance rubbish. Doctor said to send you in.

There's only one doctor who would bring a man onto the ward. Amy rises from her chair and paper scraps flutter to the floor.

What's that? Letitia steps toward her.

Amy feels in her pocket and draws forth another page. It may be that Letitia will understand, even if she can't read the words themselves. Amy tears the page slowly.

What *is* that—a Bible? Letitia moves toward her with her hand outstretched. Be a good girl and give me what's left.

Scraps have stuck to Amy's skirt, and she chooses one for Letitia: *Fear ye not, neither be afraid worshippeth it, and prayeth unto it.* Letitia tucks the scrap into her own pocket without a glance. She shakes her head.

You were a lot more tolerable when you were talking, and if I'm right about who that is in the parlor, he's not going to think much of *this* game. Of course, those religious types probably like girls who're seen and not heard—but you're not much of a sight, either. Letitia steps closer—Let me fix your hair—but Amy sidles away.

Is that how you're going to act? Letitia plants her hands on her hips. I knew a girl at Kalamazoo who didn't speak for a full month—probably thought she was teaching the rest of us a lesson—and when she was finally ready to be friends again, all she could do was peep. Is that what you want? She sounded like a chicken from then on. Last time I saw her, that's what she thought she was, and now she's probably alone for good on a back ward. You acted terrible the other day, but I ain't still mad at you! And, if you're mad at me, I'd like to know why.

Amy plucks another scrap from her skirt. If something has been guiding her hands, then Letitia will see these words and know what they mean. But Letitia knocks the scrap away, rolls her eyes. It may be that Letitia is already too ruined to save.

I don't have time to sort through this mess or play games—and that man in the parlor won't wait forever, no matter if he is homely. I'd step quick if there was a man here to call on me—but you never *have* had any sense. She strides from the room.

Amy follows, pausing in the doorway. Letitia marched in one

direction, back to the dayroom and the other women. But Amy has been called in the other direction: a man is here for her. Someone else, maybe, that Ingstrom has brought to examine her. The lumberjacks were kind at first, their whiskey breaths on her face, their whiskers on her neck. Maybe the man in the parlor has brought whiskey. Maybe, after whiskey, he will make her dance with him. She rolls paper strips into balls as she walks, drops them behind her like Gretel did in the forest. Making a trail back this time rather than rushing headlong through branches. She will scream if the man comes too near. If her voice hasn't dried up. She will bite, no matter what.

Amy stops on the threshold of the visiting parlor. Her caller stands by the stove, his hands clasped behind his back. She sees him—and sees that she and Letitia were both wrong.

Her father starts toward her before she can run away.

Daughter, he says. His voice that sang "Clementine" is thin and hoarse now. Maybe he hasn't spoken since they said goodbye. He reaches her quickly.

Her father's hands envelop hers as he pulls her into the room and pushes her gently toward the sofa.

Daughter, he says again, and she sees how changed her father is, deep lines drawing down from the corners of his mouth. He's not at all like the young man in the wedding photograph. Your hair, he says, because she's different, too. Won't you say hello?

She shakes her head. Her mouth is pulling in all directions—laugh, cry, grimace. Her father brushes at her skirt and more bits of paper knock loose. He holds her briefly by the shoulders, assessing her.

I'm sorry I haven't been here sooner. I was at camp a full month up north and then laid up with—ah, a spring cold—and it's only now that I'm called down here to survey. And you—you've been sick, too, I think?

She nods, slowly. The whites of her father's eyes are like an old widow's, pink and wet. The irises are exactly like hers.

You seem well now. Rose is tolerably well, too—that bad 'flu missed her, but she's still bothered by her usual troubles and by worry over me. You can imagine. She nearly nursed me to death—over a cold! He laughs, watching her, but Amy can't laugh back. Then, the sound that he's making turns into a cough. For a moment he can't speak but only stares at her over the top of his handkerchief, his eyes ever wetter and redder. When he finally quiets, he shakes his head: Maybe I need nursing at that. I'll bring Rose with me, next time I come. And, as to that, it's your birthday next month—I'm sure I don't need to remind you!—and we'd thought we'd come take you into town for dinner, if the doctor will allow it, and then have a drive out the peninsula. You can't think how pretty the country is around here, Amy. And you'd like to see your mother—Rose, that is—wouldn't you?

Amy moves her head—yes or no, she isn't sure—and her father rubs his hand across his lips: the familiar sound of whiskers against his rough fingers. Gripping hers, his hands didn't seem so calloused as in the old days of the lumberyard, but lying on his knees, they are still cracked at the knuckles from working in the cold. His thinned face is browned from years spent outdoors but paler now than it used to be.

Rose sends you her love and wanted me to make sure and find out whether you'd received the Christmas box she sent. I'll ask her to make up another box as soon as I get back—she'll know just the gewgaw for your hair like that. And, if there's anything else special you'd like, just tell me. Anything at all!

Amy reaches in her pocket, but it is empty of pages, and she can't say the lumberjack's word to her father, can't tell him outright what she has discovered about the hospital and Dr. Ingstrom. Anyway, he's looking beyond her now, toward the far corner of the room. She follows his gaze to find the old doctor standing there. The doctor smiles at her, but as he draws closer, she sees that his eyes are tired, too. He's an old man, after all. Everyone knows he's been sick.

Good afternoon, Miss Underwood. Your father has come a great distance to see you. You are happy to see him, I'm sure. Won't you say so?

Why shouldn't she? Her father's voice is stronger now. Since when is my child a mute?

Forgive me for not mentioning, Mr. Underwood, but since the incident that spurred Mr. Humphries's letter to you, Miss Underwood has been reluctant to speak. The doctor takes a wing chair beside them. Isn't that right, my dear?

What kind of foolishness is that? Is he serious, Amy?

Her father tries to make eye contact with her, and Amy hangs her head, looks away. That fat man wrote to her father! But she's not a child, to be tricked into answering.

The doctor nods. A not-uncommon reaction to shock or surprise. But I think she's returning now to stability. Miss Underwood, your friends were only upset with you because you said shocking things. They've forgiven you; why not forgive yourself?

Her father takes her hands again, shaking them as though he's holding reins. You can't act wild all your life, Amy. I don't need to know what you've said or done here—I just want to know that you're listening to the doctor. Are you trying to get better—or worse? The doctor says it's all up to you now.

Amy looks at the old doctor—more predictable than the young one, less jovial than the stout one, and now less hale than the lame one. He could not cure the Walking Skeleton; he cannot seem to cure Letitia. Will he not even try to cure Amy?

Miss Underwood, the doctor says, your father has asked after your progress, and I've told him what I've told you: that I know you will begin to improve once you open yourself to the notion of self-governance.

Her father picks one of the paper scraps from her skirt, flicks it toward the stove, picks another. I'd like to have you at home again, Amy—and you know that Rose would like that, too. It's very hard on her, having you here. But you can't come home unless we can trust you to act right—not to run away and all the rest. To be a help rather than a burden to your mother. So here you are, and, when I see you acting peculiar like this, I know this is the right place for you.

Amy pulls her skirt tighter around her legs and closes her eyes. Right this minute, in the house up north, her stepmother is waiting in the sitting room for her father to return. Does she know he's come here? The chair where Amy would sit—when forced to sit—is empty; the woods that once spread around the house are gone. At Miss Carter's School, no one knew that game of falling backward, and the closest she came to the other girls was standing over their neat bureau tops, their pretty trinkets falling into her apron pocket. She thinks of whiskey searing her lips and of Letitia's velvet eyes, bringing her back to herself. She can't muster that clear feeling now, can't muster words to explain why she can't bear the house up north or her father's questions. Both are like heavy blankets thrown over her. She would like to be away from them; she would like to run again through the clutching trees without ever being caught. Those trees are stumps now, waiting to trip her.

Miss Underwood, says the doctor. You'll be staying with us for a while yet. Try to see the good in it. You have friends here, I think, and soon there will be work in the greenhouses that will suit you. Once you're occupied with something other than yourself, you'll be happier, I know.

Her father puts his hand on her shoulder. His touch reminds her of the Walking Skeleton's; her father's hand feels like dry bones against her flesh. Rose will write to you soon, he says. Remember that she loves you. He stares at her, waiting, and then, after a few moments, frowns. What *are* these bits all over you? He plucks one from her hair.

She opens her mouth, but he is flattening the scrap on his knee, squinting down at the small print. He shakes his head, rolls it up again, and flicks it toward the stove. You ought to take care of your appearance, Amy—when Rose spends so much time outfitting you. How have you managed to cover yourself in packing materials?

Amy stands. Her father has not understood, cannot understand. Her father will leave here soon to look for more trees to take. But there is less to him now, too. From above, she can see how gray his hair has grown. Her real mother might be gray-haired, too, if she were still alive and in her fifties. White-haired, like the doctor's wife. Would her father have dared then to send Amy away—or might he have sent them both? If her own mother were at the hospital with her, it could have been a paradise. Or not. Maybe those thin lips pinched together in the photograph would have opened only to scold her. That tall, square-jawed woman raging after her through the wards, reaching for her throat. Or maybe, if her mother had lived, her father would have kept Amy home and sent her mother away. He leaves Rose at home, crying. Where would Rose have wound up, if Amy's mother hadn't died? Who would have taken *her* in and married her? Amy lays her palm on top of her father's head and feels him startle. *You're it*, she might say, and run. But there is no one else to play along. The doctor would not catch him or keep him here.

Goodbye, she says instead, lifting her hand away. Her voice comes out as a harsh croak, as Letitia had warned. Her father looks up and she can see that he is worried. He thinks she's turned into something monstrous and frog-throated, here at this hospital. Maybe she has. Or maybe he thinks she's still as sick as he so obviously is. He reaches up to take her hand again, but before he can catch her, she moves away.

The doctor rises. We're glad to hear you speak, child. Won't you say something more to your father? The doctor edges slowly toward her.

Amy shakes her head. Goodbye, she says again. She walks around the old doctor, away from her father. There's no need to run. Her father couldn't catch her, who once could chop down great trees or singlehandedly defeat both Amy and Rose at lawn tennis. He wheezes now just sitting on the sofa. The old doctor needn't bother to pursue her. There's no place she can go that isn't under his lock and key. She's trapped here more surely than she was at her father's house up north. But here, she's trapped with so many others. The women here don't have to change unless they want to; both of these men have just said so. Here is better than there.

Amy turns from the doctor and her father and follows the trail she made of cast-off words, down the hall, back to her room. Where else could she go?

Chapter Thirteen

APRIL OPENS WITH A RASH of deaths. Three patients brought to the hospital in ill-health quickly die of exhaustion; they are dressed in hospital-made shrouds and sent back to the relatives who committed them. On ward eighteen, Thomas Nickerson—whose case had so disturbed Mr. Humphries in November—succumbs to general paralysis. Death is the inevitable outcome of the disease; it was heralded in Nickerson's case by a paretic seizure, after which he languished for ten days in a semi-comatose state.

Though the course of Nickerson's illness was conventional, the reaction of his friends has been less so. Alerted of her husband's seizure and its likely import, Mrs. Nickerson didn't make the twenty miles' journey to the hospital—and still hasn't come. On the morning after Nickerson's death, the doctor writes to her again. He produces a condoling version of Nickerson's last moments: *After his turn, your husband did not regain consciousness. He was visited regularly by the hospital's chaplain and gave every appearance of resting comfortably at the end. We await your instructions regarding the post-mortem.* Autopsy would allow them to add Nickerson's case to the hospital's growing file on general paralysis. There they might record the condition of his brain tissue—nodules, necrosis, atrophied nerve cells; it is impossible to predict just what changes the disease will have wrought on the meninges and cortex. *Our study of your husband's illness will help us to serve others,* the doctor writes, and who knows but that someday this knowledge might actually inform clinical practice? (Not yet, not haphazardly, not as Ingstrom would have it). But the doctor worries that the widow may be unmovable. Autopsy could reveal proofs of the syphilis with which Nickerson's condition is so often associated—and which may well be her secret, too. If Mrs. Nickerson would rather not acknowledge this husband who made their marriage a hell, the doctor cannot blame her. Dr. West, however, is less patient with the delay. The value of the corpse is compromised with every hour he must wait. *The results of the examination would be kept confidential,* the doctor writes, *and we would take care that our work not delay the memorial services of your choosing.* Will there even be a service, or is Mr. Nickerson bound for the hospital's patch in the city cemetery?

The doctor telephones downstairs to arrange a courier for this letter. He has no sooner replaced the phone's mouthpiece than Meijer's arrival knock sounds on his office door. The other doctor is dressed unusually well for rounds, in his best suit and a new cravat.

The doctor raises his eyebrows: Is it Sunday already? Or are you sitting for a portrait with Madame Neiderer?

Meijer chuckles. Mrs. Neiderer on ward three has taken lately to sketching—quite competently and with no known training—anyone or -thing that will sit still for her. Meijer chuckles, but he also crinkles his brow: I was sure I'd told you about my appointment this morning—with the bank? I'll be leaving you for an hour or so at quarter of ten.

Yes, says the doctor quickly, striking his forehead. Yes, of course. It takes him a moment, however, to actually call to mind that conversation with Meijer, more than a week ago, back when he was still a bit fog-headed, fever-slowed. But yes—there it is: his colleague is buying a house in town. And—how embarrassing—hadn't Meijer reminded him of the fact, only last night, after the evening program? (What had *that* been? Music of some sort, a pounding piano…. Despite the din, the doctor had struggled to stay awake). Meijer smiled, then, in the high-ceilinged chapel, embarrassed but pleased as the wives chattered nearby about pantries. They could hear Mrs. Meijer gloating over her new demesne—a gingerbreaded hulk at the brink of the bay.

Will the doctor walk through it, Meijer asks now, offer suggestions about its final arrangements and sanitary provisions? Yes, delighted—but all of this chatting skirts the obvious implications of such a move. A superintendent is the living core of the hospital, central to its affairs, present at all hours, always. For Meijer to set up housekeeping at forty-eight years of age, forsaking his comfortable apartment in the hospital's center, obtaining the managers' special permission to move off the hospital's grounds, must mean that he doesn't aspire to the hospital's superintendency, at that far-off point when the doctor himself will retire. The doctor has long been aware of West's personal limitations; that Meijer demurs promotion is more surprising.

The doctor smiles now, shaking his head. You'll forgive my lapse. The mind rejects the thought of losing such a neighbor. He pats his colleague on the back as they start down the corridor. For all his bulk, Meijer is agile, athletic; one could imagine him flinging a discus, if the occasion arose. The doctor is pleased to have finally regained enough energy to match the bigger man's pace. His increase in physical strength is certainly more meaningful than his lapses of memory, his inability to perfectly recall the matronly machinations of Mrs. Meijer. A good woman, Claudia Meijer; a good friend these last few years to Diana. With three grown children and a grandbaby soon due, it's no wonder that Mrs. Meijer craves a home of her own to fuss over—and, on holidays, the thunder of so many Meijers in the hospital's stairwell has occasionally disturbed the doctor's wife, sent her to bed with weepy headaches. But for Dr. Meijer to rank domestic arrangements over his career indicates a shocking lack of ambition. The doctor is grateful for Diana's long tolerance of hospital life. And perhaps he is grateful, too, that they have never had family encumbrances of their own.

Meijer departs after they've finished their visits to the first- and second-floor wards. The doctor is left to manage the third floor alone—wards thirteen, fifteen, and seventeen, each the worst of its respective class. These are nice distinctions, however: though ward thirteen is the lowest of the convalescent wards, it is home to the third-best set of female patients at the hospital. Among its present residents are three women recovering from bereavements, two with climacteric troubles, a handful harboring delusions about relatives or neighbors, and several with post-febrile nervous conditions. The doctor raps on a sequence of tidy knees and elbows; many of the patients thank him for his trouble. These women take a social interest in Dr. Meijer's absence.

I hope Dr. M. doesn't have the 'flu now, says a Mrs. Evans new to the hospital. It is so very damp here that it's a wonder we're not all sick!

Dr. Meijer is with my son, whispers her neighbor, young Mrs. Chambers. My Timothy. He sits with him that I might have a moment's rest. Can't you give me something to help me rest, doctor?

She tugs his sleeve. The child, of course, is dead.

The doctor lifts her hand and presses his fingers to the pulse point on her wrist. The attendants will give you something for sleep when it's dark again, Mrs. Chambers—see how high the sun is? For now, I've brought you a tonic. You must rebuild your nerves, so that you can go back soon to your other children. Timothy is gone, try to remember.

She nods, as she does every time she is reminded, and swallows her dose.

Resignation is a virtue, you know, says Mrs. Evans. I've lost as many children as I've kept and I'm stronger for my trials.

Is that so? The doctor raises his eyebrows. I imagine you did not think so directly after your losses, Mrs. Evans. But…perhaps Mrs. Chambers would care to hear about your experiences?

Mrs. Chambers nods, slowly. It is forty-seven days since he went, Mrs. Evans. Tell me about what you did on the forty-seventh day.

And without a trace of the delirium that brought her to the hospital, Mrs. Evans begins.

It is this simple, sometimes, to coax patients out of their inwardness, to spark their interests in the world around them, their realizations that their problems are neither wholly unique nor unbearable. Which of the patients is better-served by their conversation: Mrs. Chambers or Mrs. Evans—who suffers at present not from grief or loss but from their byproduct, over-dependency on chloral? As useful as the sulfonal he has prescribed Mrs. Evans is the interest she has begun to take in her fellow patients' health.

The doctor braces himself with this moment as he makes his way through the firedoors and on to the ward fifteen dayroom. There, the former sewing room assistant, Miss Ellsworth, tends to the ward's lush collection of houseplants. These form a dense bower around the room's picture window and across its high-beamed ceiling; within the bower, Miss Breithaupt sits, reading aloud from a newspaper. Several patients flank her on the settee; others have drawn chairs near. This, the worst of the intermediate wards, looks for the moment like a picture postcard, with only a few patients sitting apart, rocking or chattering or staring stalwartly at the walls. Here is Miss Reed, a blacksmith, recovering from a spell of stuporous insanity; there is Mrs. Pederstuen, a fisherman's wife, who paces the hall, muttering in Norwegian. The doctor's absent-mindedness of late does not extend to the wards. Surveying the tidy dayroom, he mentally lists those who are at work elsewhere in the hospital, then checks this against the shorter list of those allowed to rest in their bedrooms: Miss Randolph, who suffers from insanity of doubt; Mrs. Zimmerman, in the early stages of senile dementia. The girl, Miss Underwood.

She's somewhat more sociable, sir, Miss Breithaupt tells him, after he's examined the women in the dayroom. She and Miss Olsen aren't as thick as they used to be, but they tolerate each other pretty well.

The doctor gestures for Miss Breithaupt to step away from the patients. He screens his mouth with his hand while he speaks: Does Miss Olsen know that Dr. Ingstrom is leaving?

Miss Breithaupt's eyes widen, but she keeps her voice low: None of us knows that, sir.

But I'm right to suppose that Miss Olsen will be upset by this news?

She sets a high store on him, that's certain. Do you want me to tell her—or will he?

The doctor shakes his head. There will be an announcement

soon at the evening program. May I trust to your discretion until then?

Miss Breithaupt nods. She smiles at the patients, many of whom are watching them closely. Of course, sir.

Here's another proof of the attendant's worth, provided she keeps her word. The doctor is glad, too, to find that Ingstrom hasn't leaked the news. The doctor shakes Miss Breithaupt's broad hand and takes his leave of the assembled patients. Down the hall, he finds Miss Underwood sitting at her bedroom window. She's in almost the same attitude as on that morning months ago when he discovered her with his wife's daguerreotype. When he greets her this time, there's no guilty start, just a half-turn, a nod of her head. She's quiet as he listens to her chest; she opens her mouth willingly when asked to say 'ah.' Though she has begun again to speak to him—yes, no, goodbye—she doesn't do so now. He props himself on the windowsill before her, taps his knuckles lightly on the glass.

We don't see yet the great changes to be painted on that canvas, do we, Miss Underwood? Within weeks that melting mess will be replaced by new leaves, snowdrops, crocuses. Spring is my delight.

She glances at him briefly, then scrapes her chair sideways to see around him.

Did you have a garden at home? When I was a boy, I took great pride in tending my mother's kitchen garden—there were so many of us on the farm that we raised an army of vegetables. We'll have new lettuce from the greenhouses soon—think of that!—and the early vegetables are almost ready to be moved outdoors.

Miss Underwood's hands are hidden in her apron pockets, though her face is not bloodied. He can hear something rustling between her fingers. He carries on, in the same chipper tone.

We've allowed you to rest for some time now, Miss Underwood—first, so you could adjust to this new place, then, so you could recover from your illness. But too much idleness is a kind of sickness, and I won't see you fall victim to it. I've asked the groundskeeper to make a place for you in the greenhouses, transplanting the little seedlings that will feed us all. I've asked him to make room for your friend Miss Olsen, as well.

She glances at him quickly, something like interest in her usually sullen expression. Then, she frowns, shaking her head. Letitia....

I know you've quarreled with your friend, but she doesn't hold grudges—nor does your father, who you made to feel so unwelcome. A letter would show him that you're sorry, and you have my permission to write one. The routine of work will be good for your spirits. And Miss Olsen will need your company in the weeks to come.

Again the girl betrays herself with a quizzical look; again she quickly corrects it. She won't let herself ask; what harm is there in telling her? He leans toward her.

Miss Underwood, let me confide in you something the other women will hear soon enough: Dr. Ingstrom is leaving us for another position.

The girl's eyes dart to the door. Shh.

Your friend is in the laundry—she can't hear. Am I right to suppose that she'll feel Dr. Ingstrom's loss keenly?

Don't! She topples her chair, leaping sideways from it and across the room to the doorway. She hauls shut her bedroom door.

The doctor rises from the windowsill: Open that at once!

Rather than obeying, she comes at him, quickly, and, before he can check the impulse, he shields his face with his hands. It is only for an instant that he loses his nerve—only long enough to realize that she's staring at him, harmlessly. He lowers his hands.

He'll hear you, she whispers.

Dr. Ingstrom?

Shh! She nods, vigorously. Is *he* really going away?

Yes, the doctor says, drawing himself up to full height. Very soon, to open a clinic downstate. We'll have a new doctor in his place, who perhaps you'll like better. But let's open your door again and seat ourselves. I tell you about Ingstrom so that—

The girl's hand is suddenly over his mouth, her palm hot and tacky against his lips. He only has to seize her wrist in order to escape, only has to push her from him, but he's shocked all the same that she would handle him so. Still holding her, he uses his free hand to right her chair. He guides her down upon it.

Keep your hands in your lap, Miss Underwood! You will remember yourself—I don't like to think of moving you again to a lower ward.

She perches on the edge of the chair, then sinks back under his stern gaze. He'll hear you, she whispers. He'll come. Her fingers drift nervously over her cheeks.

Leave off that picking, the doctor commands. Try to sit still. What if—*he*—did hear me? Can you tell me why it is that you distrust him so?

She tugs her hair, then catches herself, sits on her hands. She shakes her head.

Good, Miss Underwood—just there you exercised self-control. The doctor crouches in front of her. Miss Underwood, we both know that untrustworthy men exist in this world, but I am very troubled if you have encountered them here. What makes you think the doctors are, as you've said, *pimps*? Do you know the meaning of that word?

She closes her eyes and shakes her head more vehemently.

You don't know—or you won't explain? I suspect you're quiet

because you know the idea is nonsense. I would like to be able to trust you to judge sense from nonsense. And if Miss Olsen will, as we expect, take Dr. Ingstrom's loss to heart, she'll need a clear-headed friend in the coming weeks.

The girl flinches at Ingstrom's name, but the doctor continues: Can I rely on you to be a support for Miss Olsen? Can I rely on you to bolster her when Dr. Ingstrom leaves?

The girl screws her eyes shut, nods her head.

There's nothing to be afraid of—

But she stands: He's here.

Child—the doctor begins, exasperation cutting through his clinician's voice. Then he perceives what she's already heard: heavy footsteps in the hallway. Not Mrs. Pederstuen's constant pacing but the tread of a larger person. The creaking of floorboards stops just outside the closed door of Miss Underwood's room.

Hello? calls a man's familiar voice. Is everything all right?

The girl steps forward, balling her fists, and the doctor places his hand on her shoulder—both as a comfort and a check. So many of the women here pretend at clairvoyance, convince themselves that their hunches and inklings are signs from the beyond. Now, the door is tested, a key scratches in the lock, and he feels Miss Underwood tremble. If, for some reason, she suddenly hates Ingstrom—for his dandyism, his aloofness, his intolerable arrogance—it's possible that Miss Olsen's feelings toward Ingstrom have changed, as well. The affections of the insane are predictable only in their variety, and it may be that there are treatment opportunities to be seized, here, a chance to shift the girls' loyalties toward himself. If Miss Underwood now hates Ingstrom, then perhaps the doctor should restrain her more carefully, but already the door is swinging open, the girl tensing to spring—

—at Meijer. Not Ingstrom, but Meijer, opening the door, returned from his errand at the bank.

Before the doctor can catch her, the girl flings herself forward. The doctor steps after her. By not holding her, he may as well as pushed her toward his colleague, but she isn't attacking Meijer, she's not fighting. Instead, she embraces him. The girl presses her face into Meijer's friendly shoulder, her arms thrown around his girth. He returns the hug awkwardly, one arm pinned by hers, the other freighted with his bag and notebook.

Er, he says. Ah—that's very kind of you, Miss Underwood. But really—it's not quite the thing. I'm sorry to interrupt you, he says, glancing at the doctor. No one answered my knock, and so—well! How are you this morning, Miss Underwood?

Miss Underwood releases Meijer, turning to face the doctor.

I would like to work, she says. With Letitia.

The doctor clears his throat: Very well—but the girl doesn't wait for instructions, rushing off pink-faced toward the dayroom.

Well! Meijer readjusts his jacket. What do you call that? An increase in amativeness—or an outright clinical advance?

Kindness was sure to touch her eventually, says the doctor. His pen shakes a bit as he jots the event in his notes. Perhaps she and I only needed a private interview. We'll see if it takes.

Yes, says Meijer, you've always had a remarkable rapport with melancholics.

Meijer pats the doctor on the back, his broad hand resting heavily between the doctor's shoulder blades. It seems to the doctor as if this heaviness infects his colleague's pace as they proceed toward the worst of the women's wards. Meijer is drained, no doubt, by the unfamiliar exertion of making business arrangements. He speaks in a low voice about his meeting, and the doctor finds it impossible to listen attentively. Though it has been some time since he has felt this sensation, he recognizes his own mental excitement, his sense of surplus energy, as the elation of having made a breakthrough.

In the morning, Lil brings the plainest of Amy's dresses, a flannel skirt, and a thick pair of hose. A laborer's outfit. Wearing these strange clothes, Amy can barely sit still to eat her breakfast. Now she'll leave the ward, see new parts of the hospital, spend her hours doing something other than waiting. She won't have to endure the dull circuit of morning and afternoon walks or the worse ordeal of trotting around the calistheneum. She won't have to talk to the old doctor or worry about what might be happening to Letitia; instead she'll be with her friend and they'll be as close as they were before. And soon enough the young doctor will be gone and they'll both forget all about him. Eating dully at another table, Letitia keeps her eyes on her bowl and doesn't speak to those around her. Amy calculates: it is Letitia's difficult time of the month. But when they're in the greenhouse together, maybe her pains will ease.

After the dining room is put to rights, the women who clean the ward begin their chores, and Amy finds a rocker in the dayroom. The quick thump keeps time with her impatience. Only an infant would find this rhythm lulling. She could go back to her bedroom, settle into a daze before the window, try to tamp down this burning suspense—but what if some excitement broke out on the ward and Lil forgot about her, forgot that she was to leave today, to work?

Finally the other women are settled and Lil draws Letitia aside. Amy tries not to see the two of them glancing in her direction, talking—smiling? Her own mouth betrays her, pulling up at the corners, a feeling in her throat like she might laugh or cry. Their conversation seems to last for hours. At last, Letitia comes to her. She steps on one of the chair's rockers, stilling it.

So, they're putting you to work?

Amy nods, not daring to look up.

Won't the dirt be a shock for our princess! Letitia grabs Amy's hands, pulls her to her feet. Come on—you'll get used to it quick enough.

Lil ties kerchiefs over their hair, outfits them in shawls, and sends them down the service stairs with Miss Ellsworth. Instead of being led as usual into the building's rear, toward the chapel or the calistheneum, they are unlocked into the backyard. They step outside in their work clothes, into the shadowed joint of the hospital's wings. Alone. To their right is the tacked-on tail of the infirmary ward, the big window with its border of stained squares where Amy sat during the long afternoons of her illness. Before them, beyond the outbuildings, is the tall, wooded hill that she can see from the ward fifteen bathroom. A path cuts straight ahead through the snow, running between an icehouse and the outcropping of the chapel; they follow this path to its intersection with a muddy, rutted lane. Dirty heaps of shoveled snow and horse manure are piled in front of what Amy knows to be the laundry building. A cart stands now at the laundry door, the big horse resting on three legs. Amy is pulled in all directions: toward the horse's roan neck, the trees rising up behind the laundry, the frozen lake, far out of sight. The air is wet and cold and new.

What's in those woods? Amy asks, tugging Letitia's sleeve. Which way is it to town?

Letitia shakes her head. There's tramps back in those woods and worse—not a place a girl like you should go. We'll have hikes soon enough with the matron, looking for morels and picking trilliums. And maybe if you're a good worker, they'll give you a furlough into town.

We'll go to a restaurant, Amy says. We'll go to the mercantile.

Letitia laughs. Not me. They'll let me go around the hospital by myself but they won't risk me going among regular folks. We'd head that way if we were taking our own furlough—but the greenhouses are this way, out by the barns. Hurry up, can't you—it's too cold to stand around.

Maybe I could get whiskey, Amy whispers, sliding after Letitia on the wet ice. I could bring it back, and we could hide it somewhere. Then we'd be warm. Maybe it would help with your headaches.

You act already drunk. What's whiskey going to get you but a trip to the back wards? Well—more likely me than you. No, I mean to behave myself until Dr. Ingstrom manages to get me out of here.

Amy winces at the name—a conjuring name, and they are walled in by strange buildings on either side of the lane. Everything made of the same yellow brick, rising up like a fortress around them. The old doctor had repeated Ingstrom's name the other day and nothing happened, but it may be only Letitia who he hears, pursues. Pimp, Amy curses, under her breath, keeping him at bay, pimp!

Come again?

Amy shakes her head: Is *he* taking you with him?

Ingstrom? Oh, sooner or later we'll go away—to Chicago, where he can have a private practice. To California.

No, I meant—Amy glances over her shoulder—Old doctor said *he* was leaving to open a clinic downstate.

Letitia stops so suddenly that Amy stumbles. Dr. Ingstrom?

Amy shudders; even now, he could be nearing. That young doctor, she says. Yes.

Letitia shakes her head. Her eyes are dull, as they are during her bad spells. It's another of the old man's lies. Though, why Ingstrom doesn't leave, I don't know—he's worth a dozen such doctors as the others here.

Letitia hangs her head and begins walking again, quickly. Amy hurries after her. They're in the open now: a carriage house off to the left of the lane, orchards on the long bank to their right, and the big brick dairy barns spreading out ahead of them, across fields of rotting snow. Higher on the right bank, a glass house glints. They turn toward it, up a row of black, bare trees. Someone has cut a track in the snow; there is no one in sight.

Amy clears her throat: Dr.—I.—will be leaving soon, the old doctor says.

Well. Letitia bends forward with the effort of climbing uphill. Other feet have packed the path to slickness. If he *was* leaving, wouldn't I be the first to know? Give me your arm, will you—this steep part bothers me when my head's so bad.

Amy lets Letitia lean on her. It is not like dancing, holding her this way, taking the lead—and then they've reached the greenhouse. *What will you do?* she wants to ask, *What should we do?* But Letitia's features are tight with headache, and she holds her stomach with her free hand. She shouldn't work on days when she's so unwell; Amy should keep hold of her arm and guide her back to the main building, to rest. But if she can keep Letitia here, within these glass walls, there will be no way for the young doctor to creep up on them, no way for him to confuse Letitia with his promises or to spirit her away.

Amy stands on the stone step of the greenhouse and cannot decide what she should do. But before she can act, the greenhouse door opens. A short man in a canvas smock squints out at them, like a gnome in a glass palace.

You're the girls from ward fifteen? He grins with big, crooked teeth. I'm Mr. Schmidt, the head groundskeeper. Come inside, come inside. You don't mind dirt, I hope?

Letitia follows him before Amy can object. The gnome-man shows them to a cloak room and then leads them down one of the long glass wings. Its narrow width is divided by an aisle; to one side are shallow trays of dirt, holding tiny green sprouts; on the other side, wavering rows of small clay pots. There is a delicious green smell here, after the dry must of the hospital, the thawing manure outdoors. Maybe work in this air will be better for Letitia's head than resting would be—no matter that the aprons that Mr. Schmidt gives them are heavy and the floor is hard cement. Maybe the fresh air will finally cure her.

Mr. Schmidt stations them facing each other across a tall wooden table in the center of the wing and brings them a tray of tiny seedlings. Like this, he tells them, and shows them with his brown fingers how to gently loosen a sprout from the tray, press it into a dirt-filled pot. The dirt is cold, dry, and soft and immediately fills the valleys behind Amy's gnawed fingernails. She presses a seedling into a pot, presses another. They have a stack of empty pots, a great box of dirt on casters, and a boy who'll come at intervals with more of both. When they have assembled a long row of plants, they are to fill watering cans at the pump outside and sprinkle the whole lot. These are bell peppers, Mr. Schmidt tells them—and there's something wonderful in the very idea. Amy's stepmother grows peppers, too, but not in a palace like this one. The weak sunlight gains strength coming through the panes above them and the greenhouse is almost as warm as a summer afternoon up north. As soon as Mr. Schmidt sees that they understand, he leaves them to work on their own.

It's awful tedious, isn't it? asks Letitia, after only a few quiet minutes. She stretches, and the bones in her neck click like two marbles striking. There's always noise and fun in the laundry and an accident every now and then for excitement. You work up a terrible thirst and then there's the walk to the water bucket.

Amy shrugs. There are accidents here every time she snaps off a tiny green shoot. She can't work as fast as Letitia, who is as deft with her right hand as her left and fills two pots for Amy's one. How much faster would her friend work if she were feeling well?

Look at that boy staring, Letitia says. She rolls her eyes toward the top of the room, winks. Amy hadn't noticed that anyone else was nearby. Her knees tingle at the thought of who else might have sneaked up on them.

But the boy isn't frightening. He approaches on tiptoe, timidly, a stretched-out version of the groundskeeper. His face is both wider and longer, but his lips part slightly around the same big teeth, and he wears a cap knit like his father's from homespun wool. Up close, he's even more freckled than Letitia. He nods and smiles to them both before trundling away their nearly-full dirt cart.

He should be at school, Amy says, after he has passed out of hearing.

Letitia looks up from her work, raises her eyebrows. That one? If he was right in the head, he'd be too old. I'd be embarrassed to be a great big boy and doing a donkey's work—but it don't seem to bother him at all! She shakes her head, planting even faster: The only male creatures around here *would* be either old or touched!

Amy watches the boy coming back. His smile widens when he sees her looking at him, and he takes one hand off the cart to wave to her. He's a nice-looking boy, but it's plain that Letitia is right. He fell off a wagon or was kicked by a horse: she's seen boys like him before.

Would he know what to do with a letter? she asks Letitia quietly.

Better than he'd know what to do with his prick, Letitia says. She grins, and her face wipes clear of pain. But then, as though a cloud has passed over the greenhouse, her expression darkens. If what you said is true…about Ingstrom leaving…it would make good sense to write a letter now—to anyone you could think of. I hate to think of you stuck here when he takes me away.

Amy chews her thumbnail, feels grit between her teeth. I don't want to go back to my parents.

No. Letitia exhales, ruffling the seedlings in front of her. Once— before they sent me up to this place—I was let go home with my pa. He worked me harder than any hospital would and come at me, too, if he thought I wasn't working hard enough. I wouldn't go back to him for anything.

Not even if your mother was there? If she were back home?

Letitia rubs her sleeve across her eyes, shakes her head: That's about as likely as your ma coming back. Boy, she calls, sharply: boy, come here and talk to us!

And the boy smiles widely and tiptoes closer, taking off his cap to them.

At dinner that day, Amy and Letitia eat flecks of soil with their bread and butter. When Amy takes up her pen and stationery during the rest hour, she's still shedding bits of mica—no matter that she scrubbed her nails with a bristle brush. *Dear father*, she writes, as the doctor has permitted her to, *I am sorry I was cross when you came last month. I hope that Rose is well and the horses, too. Please come again soon.* She uses this empty letter home to shield the other one: *Dear Miss Chapman. They don't want me to write to you, but I need to know what a girl could do on her own. I don't believe in temprance, but I will try if you will help me and my friend Letitia. She's a better worker than me, but I will try harder at that, too. Please come talk to us or send word somehow.* How? A woman like that must have ways to reach them—or else what was the point of her telling Amy to write? *I will wait and hope for your letter*, she writes. It's a phrase from Miss Carter's School, useful at last.

Amy fans again through the WTCU Bible; she has pulled many pages from it, but many remain. Again the pages stutter and stop beneath her fingers. *He healeth the broken in heart, and bindeth up their wounds.* If Letitia could read, this might be her omen, a sign that her teeth will be fixed and her headache cured. Then again, the words might taunt, another reminder of Ingstrom. Amy closes the book, loses the verse. The only lines that are safe to pluck out of the Bible are the ones stamped on its inside cover. Amy copies Miss Chapman's address and slips the sealed letter into her boot.

Chapter Fourteen

F OR EVERY INSTANCE OF PROGRESS, there is one of relapse: this is the economics of asylum medicine—or so the
doctor sometimes thinks. The Underwood girl thrives like a plant
in the greenhouse, the Olsen girl is stable, the Sherman woman is, most days, lucid. But balanced against these cases are all of
the others brought lately to the hospital. A significant number of
spring admittances have been treated here previously, have been
released as 'improved,' and, in several cases, as 'recovered.' Their
loved ones write to the doctor of another illness, another shock,
and so they are returned to reacquaint themselves with the doctor
and with the routines of an ordered life. The doctor will travel to
Washington at the end of the month for the annual meeting of the
Association of Medical Superintendents of American Institutions
for the Insane; in his seven days of absence, he anticipates at least
twice as many admittances.

A letter for you, sir, says Matilda, and the doctor opens his eyes,
breaking his afternoon reverie. The maid managed to cross his
study without his noticing. Has he nodded off, again? She holds
out an envelope: It's another from the managers.

Yes—thank you. Lately, the board of managers has sent daily

updates about their search for the new assistant physician. The doctor skips this letter's opening pleasantries. The body of the note is less pleasant. *Having reviewed their references,* the secretary writes, *we find three of the applicants very accomplished. Indeed, it is a shame we have not several open positions!*

Indeed, the doctor mutters, and Matilda pauses in the doorway before he waves her away. It's nothing, he assures her—but: *These young doctors are peerless in training, versatility, and verve!* The doctor must restrain himself from crushing the note. He's glad that the managers are making progress and that they're enthusiastic about their task of hiring a new physician. But he'd supposed—old fool that he is—that Humphries was the only board member who doubted him…Humphries who has been gone now for weeks. The brickman resigned his position as manager, claiming that his involvement with Ingstrom's clinic constituted a conflict of interest. And now the remaining managers communicate with the doctor like so, through insinuation. Their letter goes on to inform him that the top candidate for the position will visit the hospital after the AMSAII conference; the doctor will not be apprised in advance of the candidate's name. Confidentiality is the surest means of avoiding bias or interference, and, yet, in the context of the letter, this measure feels like another slight. It is without question meant as a slight that Humphries has not written to the doctor directly, has not offered an account of his abrupt disappearance, or even paid respects to the doctor's wife.

The doctor shakes himself. He will find respite from all of this at the superintendents' conference, among his colleagues. What man of the association hasn't been meddled with by his board of managers? A superintendent must be able to see past the annoyances of the hour and work toward the larger goal: treating the insane.

Of course, there will be those doctors at the conference who no longer regard their own asylums as effective, who have come to see themselves as thankless custodians rather than as healers. What can be done, this faction will ask, to stem the rising tide of mental illness? Debates will rage throughout the week, and, though the doctor's illness prevented him from preparing a paper this year, he will have opportunity to respond to others', and to voice his unshaken conviction that the moral treatment is efficacious for *some* patients—when executed according to Kirkbride's principles. The superintendents' conversations will continue over dinner, into the night, during their excursions around Washington. They are to tour Saint Elizabeth's Hospital, built after the vision of Dorothea Dix; they will visit Mount Vernon. The doctor anticipates these outings like a farm boy looking forward to the county fair. His fingers twitch as if to throw a stone across the Potomac, and the managers' letter crumples, falls away.

What makes you smile so? The doctor opens his eyes to find his wife standing in the doorway, unwrapping herself after a midday walk. Seeing her reminds him that he hasn't yet completed his ten daily circuits of the calistheneum.

He sits up straighter. I was just thinking about my trip… thoughts spoiled only by your absence from them.

Ah. His wife crosses the room and seats herself on his ottoman, lifting his slippered feet into her lap. Need that be the case?

It's not usual for wives to attend, dearest. And you hate Washington.

Of course I wouldn't tag along to your medical meeting—but I don't see why *we* shouldn't take a trip. When was the last time? She begins to massage his toes, her fingers icy from having been outdoors. I could join up with you in Maryland, and we could come back through the Poconos.

He chuckles; her fingers tickle. I hope you haven't made any arrangements. I can't be away from the hospital for longer than the week I've budgeted.

I'd prefer a Western tour, anyway. She kneads her knuckles into the arch of his left foot. Everyone says that Southern California is just the place for lung troubles—and, if you'd read it, you'd be charmed by that book I gave you for Christmas. *The Pacific Coast Scenic Tour?*

You inflicted some of it on me during my illness. Very…scenic.

The author recommends embarking from Yosemite in May, in order to get back from Alaska before winter. Diana glances up at him, moving on to his right foot. I don't suppose you could be ready *this* May, but I do wish you'd think about it, dear.

He laughs. I promise to think of nothing else when we're both invalid enough to retire.

No! She shakes him by the ankles, a bit roughly. Look how happy the Meijers are now that they've decided to take a house. We aren't patients, James, who must stay locked at the hospital year in and year out. What sense is there in waiting until we're old to do as we like?

I *am* doing what I like. The doctor withdraws his throbbing feet from her lap. I supposed that you were, too, with your various pursuits…photography, for example.

Ah yes—my photography. Do you know what I take photographs of, James, day in and day out? This hospital! She folds her hands and closes her eyes, calming herself, as he has taught her to do. What I would *like* is to see beyond the walls of this place.

What I would *like* is to look back at it—from a distance! I think that vantage would do us both a great deal of good.

Diana. He inhales, pushing himself up from his chair—what's this about? If you feel suffocated, you ought to vary your routine. Your health doesn't necessitate a Western trip, and I can hardly take five-months' leave on a whim. Looming over her, the doctor totters for a moment. Be reasonable, dearest.

Of course. She stands, too, and thrusts her chin up at him. How could *my* concerns be anything *but* unreasonable? Look at how wild I was for tenement reform, when here we are in the woods! And now I've decided I must travel—only wait a week and the urge will pass. Foolish, fickle Diana—she reads a book, and it goes straight to her head!

Dear. He reaches for her hand, but she crosses her arms. Her mouth is a tight line.

It's not *my* health that concerns me, she says, blinking furiously. I know the limits of my constitution; I have lived with them all my life. But I believe *you* will let this hospital kill you.

Dr. Kirkbride died at his hospital, the doctor says reflexively. The effect of his words is just as quick: Diana's face gone scarlet, her white hands flung into the air. No matter his ideals, he ought to have spoken more carefully. Dearest—

Dearest? She shakes her head, beyond efforts to remain calm. How can you, when you have pledged yourself to this hospital over me? Till death do you part—is that the idea? And think where that devotion led your precious Kirkbride. Your colleagues scoff at him and call him old fashioned—as you have so often lamented to me.

He was systematic to a fault, the doctor says.

But he can never forget those difficult AMSAII meetings, when Kirkbride's idea of a universal asylum architecture was openly mocked. Kirkbride had spent his convalescence after a wasting illness revising *On the Construction, Organization, and General Arrangements of Hospitals for the Insane.* Then he'd taken ill again. He'd died.

Will you imitate him in *every* respect? You aren't in his position, James.

But I am. The doctor manages to catch his wife's hands, folding them in his. No matter how scenic you find California, I am this hospital's superintendent, and—

No! she says. It's not the same at all. You're a soldier, James—not a general, as Kirkbride was. You've followed him, rather than pioneered. There's the difference.

I see. He drops her hands. His own are now shaking. You mean that I'm unimportant? You think that my retirement—my defection—would be inconsequential because I only run a hospital, not a medical field.

Oh, James! Her eyes are wet now; she's upset herself with these insults. Posterity will not love you as I love you—even if you love *it* more than you do me.

Dear—He reaches for her again, but she waves away his hand. Her mouth opens and closes, but what is there that she can say? She hurries away, and the doctor drops back into his chair. He's exhausted, she's hysterical: he won't pursue her, or the subject, any further.

And…he's relieved to be spared Diana's tears. Like rainstorms, her crying spells are now brief, now dousing; when they were newlyweds, she could wear herself out weeping after a quarrel. Her accusations then were of a piece: if he loved her more, he would try harder to give her a child. No matter that his efforts were always timed precisely to her cycles, timed so as to avoid vain testing of her nerves. She would countermand his sensible prescriptions (iron pills, warm milk injections) with all manner of patent freaks, any of which could easily have caused the trouble it was meant to cure. Her disregard—her contempt!—for his calling has not changed in the years since. He might have seen her present accusations coming. Put simply: if he loved her more, he would set aside his work at the hospital.

Or, less tolerable to contemplate, though perhaps more authentic in quality: if he loved her more, he would be content with only *her* as his patient. It has always been the same refrain with her—more, more, more.

Patience! urges his better self; his wife's outburst is almost certainly attributable to the last strains of her climacteric change. He must forebear; he must, within reasonable bounds, comply with her wishes. So: he will look with her later at the photographs in her book—*his* book, his Christmas gift. He will agree that they should travel more some day, so that she too can take such photographs. Some day, when his work is done, impossible as it is to imagine; some day when he can bear the thought of sustained, idle pleasures. 'Some day' has always been his answer to her 'more.'

The doctor slides his feet back into his shoes, straightens his clothing. Diana is right in one respect: he will not be famous for his work, not like Kirkbride, Pliny Earle, Dorothea Dix. But the modest scale of his contribution doesn't devalue it in the eyes of his patients. To them, he's as necessary as Kirkbride was to his patients. The doctor *is* indispensable to his hospital. He lets that certainty draw him downstairs, back to his office. As always, he finds more comfort in work than in rest.

Every other day, Amy is released to the greenhouse. On the days in between, her feet hurt, her nose drips, her neck aches when she's obliged to sit at the worktable and piece together dresses for the upcoming May Day picnic. Letitia spends the between-days at the laundry, and when she's gone, only the line of dirt under Amy's nails reminds her that life is different now: she's a worker now.

Returning to the greenhouse after a day off, she and Letitia find their seedlings carted away or added to by other women who they never see. There are men sometimes, too, working with axes farther up the hill. A crew from the intermediate wards, Mr. Schmidt says, clearing ground for new fields—but in the spring sunlight they carry themselves like lumberjacks. It's hard to concentrate on the delicate seedlings with the sound of ringing blades nearby, the smell of burning stumps tingeing the air. Letitia invents reasons to refill the watering cans and Amy trails after her, watchful. Green wood piling up, men calling back and forth…it could be that some of them once worked for Amy's father. She doesn't go up the slope to find out. Instead, the men call down to Fritz, the groundskeeper's boy; they call to him to bring more drinking water. Fritz finds Amy and Letitia outside, leaning against the greenhouse's stone foundation and staring outright.

Tell them to come talk to us, Letitia orders. Tell that big one there in the red cap.

The boy smiles and shakes his head, pumping water. He seldom speaks. *Yes*, he'd said when Amy asked him to take her letter. *Yes*, he'd said, when Letitia gave him two cents for a stamp and explained where to find the postmaster's house. Now, he shakes his curly head: *no*.

Tell them to look for us at the May Day picnic, Letitia commands. Next Friday, that'll be. Tell them we'll have new muslin dresses and we'll expect a posy from each of them. Can you remember all that, or should we help you carry the water? She bends down as if to grab one of his bucket handles.

The boy splashes water off the top of the other bucket onto the bib of Letitia's canvas apron. Oops, he says, grinning. She stomps toward him, and he runs just out of her reach. This is a game they play, the two of them. Letitia puts her hands on her hips.

If you won't be my go-between, I'll expect a posy from you. And a dance, too, if you can manage not to trample my feet.

Fritz nods his head and squats to settle the yoke of the drinking pails over his shoulders. Letitia had called him a donkey when they first saw him, weeks ago; he's like an ox, too—strong and steady. And there are other things, ugly things, that Letitia calls him when he's out of earshot: *idiot, imbecile, cretin.* He might call them *insane.* He must know that's what they're called. But he touches the brim of his cap before trundling up the hill. When he reaches the work crew, he turns briefly, waves back to them. Not a beckon, not a taunt. He likes them, as his father does—as though they were two nice girls anywhere.

The hours pass with beans, pumpkins, tomatoes, squash. Dull business, according to Letitia. She takes long trips to the privy and fusses again and again with her hair and kerchief. But Amy loses herself sometimes in the planting, startled when the dinner bell rings. Mr. Schmidt shows them a huge plot of land above the dairy barns that's been tilled for their seedlings. Other things are already rooted there: carrots, turnips, onions, radishes. After they're through transplanting food crops, there will be flowers to tend. Meanwhile the air is warming; the ice must be long-gone from the bay. Some days, Amy feels as impatient as Letitia—but there's no choice but to wait for the plants to ripen, and for Miss Chapman to send her answer.

One day after the dinner break, Lil draws Amy and Letitia aside.

There's a note come while you were gone, she says. For both of you.

Lil gives Amy a silver-edged card, delicate against their work-worn hands. It's not in an envelope—but Amy hadn't really expected such a thing to reach her unopened. Every workday, she has checked the dayroom for signs that the temperance woman has been there: a new stack of Bibles, a pile of pamphlets. Maybe she's been watching for the wrong things. She closes her eyes before turning the card over to read the inscription.

Dear Miss Underwood and Miss Olsen, it reads, *Will you please afford me the pleasure of your company this Thursday afternoon?*

What's that? asks Letitia, peering over Amy's shoulder.

Amy passes the card to her friend and looks at Lil. Is this all?

All? I'd call it an honor, miss. The doctors are pleased with the two of you for working so hard and behaving so well these past weeks. I'd be grateful, if I were in your position, invited upstairs for tea with the doctor's wife.

Letitia gasps, and the thick card creases in her hand.

We'll fix you up nice, Letty, don't worry. Lil puts her arm around Letitia's waist. It may be this is the first step to moving you girls up. I'd like to see you on a better ward; I'd like to see you both better off.

Letitia smiles, but she's gone pale behind her freckles. You just want to be rid of us—better ward, worse ward—no matter. Us, the nicest girls you've got!

I'd miss you, that's sure, says Lil, squeezing Letitia. But what good am I to you here, with always a hundred things to occupy me?

It's true that Lil still has no better second attendant than Miss Ellsworth, and there are new women on the ward all the time. Miss Ellsworth wears pretty collars and a waved bang; she's good at sewing and at arranging hair after *Godey's*, but she's very bad at managing women. When someone starts a fight or takes a fit, Miss Ellsworth is apt to stay seated at the sewing machine she brought with her, pumping the treadle and stitching up the long seams of their May Day dresses. Thanks to her, they will all look fine at the picnic…all except Lil, who looks more frazzled and worn by the day. Walking back and forth to the greenhouse, if Amy happens to see new patients arriving, she crosses her fingers that they won't be assigned to ward fifteen—and, usually, they aren't. But only the other day, Mr. Schmidt had been showing them the beds in front of the hospital, explaining the old doctor's design of flowers and shrubs, when a wagon pulled up in the circle drive. Big yellow farm horses and a mud-spattered man helping down a mud-spattered woman. Country people, who'd taken ten minutes to walk to the front doors—not because the woman fought, as Amy has seen some do, but because she stopped to tap every object she passed: the hitching posts, the mounting block, each sapling or shrub in reach of the footpath. Good thing the tulips ain't up yet, Letitia had joked. Now, on their ward, this woman walks up and down the hall, skirting the pacing Norwegian and tapping each of the rockers, tables, paintings, plants that decorate the long corridor. *Bless you*, she whispers with each tap, *bless you*. She does not bless the other women.

Amy shakes her head. There aren't any other letters come for me?

Not yet, miss. Lil smiles. I can guess what kind of letter you're expecting!

Letitia's eyes narrow and she steps free of Lil's arm. What business is that of yours?

I meant that it was getting close to somebody's birthday, Letty—next Tuesday, for a fact—and I'll thank you to watch your tone with me. Lil draws her shoulders up and fluffs her skirt. You girls had better get your things together for the greenhouse; Miss E.'s waiting to take you downstairs.

Lil turns away from them, back to the other women milling about the dayroom; there's no use in Amy apologizing for Letitia's rudeness. There would be no sense in Amy thanking Lil, either—and yet, without Lil, Amy would have forgotten her own birthday. April 28th. Her father had mentioned it, those weeks ago when he came to the hospital. She hasn't heard from him since. She will be eighteen. Old enough to be thought an adult but not old enough yet to have rights, not here at the hospital or anywhere else.

When she was a child, her stepmother baked a chocolate pound cake every year for her birthday and her father set aside the whole afternoon for her. Her father had said that they would visit her, this year, but Amy can't imagine her parents returning together to the hospital. Rose had been scared of the dirt and noise on ward nine—ward nine! She would tremble to hear the women cuss on this ward; she would faint clean away to see the messes some make in their beds. And if she were to see Letitia's teeth….

No—if they remember her at all, it's more likely that Amy's parents will send a box than visit, and her birthday will pass like the others', with a small gift beside her breakfast plate and a note from the old doctor. Maybe she'll be allowed her first furlough into town, alongside women from the better wards. Maybe, just by chance, Bertha Chapman's letter will come on the 28th. Or even Bertha Chapman herself. The temperance lady will help them, however she can; she promised as much. Does the doctor's wife mean to help them, by inviting them upstairs? Amy went alone the first time. Now…have Amy and Letitia become the same girl in the eyes of the hospital? The same things have happened to both of them lately.

Standing before the mantle, Letitia wraps herself in one of the rough-cut black shawls. Amy looks up at the mirror. Letitia's lips purse as she arranges the shawl around her throat; her chestnut hair is never smooth, and the greenhouse has made the loose strands curl tightly. The swell of her bosom is plain even beneath the shawl, the curves of her stomach and hips. Amy's face at her shoulder is a scowling, pale rectangle. She still looks like a boy, not like a grown woman.

Slowpoke, Letitia says. Her glowing eyes catch Amy's in the mirror. Ain't you ready *yet*? Your beau Fritz is waiting.

Amy shrugs into her cloak, which still smells faintly of her stepmother, though it smells also like sweat, dust, the ward's hanging stench of stewed meat. The cloak is too long for her, too fine, and, glancing up again at herself in rich wool and Letitia in rags, she knows that no one could ever mistake them for the same person.

Thursday afternoon comes slowly, even with the new busyness of working. Letitia's fretting seems to slow time further. Do you think she *meant* to invite me? she asks over and over again. Thursday is one of their off-days from the greenhouse; kept back from the laundry, Letitia can't concentrate on her May Day sewing. She talks of nothing but the doctor's wife.

I ain't spoken to her since we come up together on the train when this place opened. Do you think that old lady really knows who I am?

Amy bites off her thread. Letitia sees the white-haired woman at every evening program, during every dull service delivered in the chapel. At any of those times, Letitia could tell the old lady about what she says happens to her at night—how the old doctor comes after her. But Letitia doesn't ever tell these stories. Will she today? Amy spits the thread's end into her palm. I don't know.

What did she have to eat the other time? Letitia asks. She tugs Amy's work until Amy sets it down. I'm half-starving, but my stomach is awful nervous. Do you think she'll have anything nice for us?

Ask old doctor when he comes by. Or just wait and see.

I hope you behave yourself, Letitia says. If you been up there already, maybe you know how to act—*if* you really been up there. That old lady won't stand for the kind of tricks you pulled that day with Humphries and Ingstrom.

Amy flinches, pulling her thread too tight.

Your puffs are awful lopsided. Letitia passes Amy the seam-ripper. I don't think she could have really meant to invite me!

Amy slices the small blade through her stitches. Why did the doctor's wife invite Letitia; why did she invite Amy? There will be hours yet before they know—an hour yet just at the sewing table. Letitia is embroidering bluebells on the bodice of her May Day dress, and Amy cannot even manage sleeves. Not that it matters: tomorrow morning, Miss Ellsworth will lean close to her ear and ask, how do you like your dress? and Amy will see that the sleeves have been fixed, like the yoke, the waist, the hem before them. Her stepmother would have made her keep trying until she got it right.

Letitia heaves a deep sigh. We'll both be good, how's that? You just watch me if you ain't sure how to act.

Finally, after the doctors' visit, the morning walk, dinner, chores, rest hour—after all of this—Lil sends Amy and Letitia to get ready. Letitia wears the less-tattered of her two state-issue dresses, but the clean apron Amy lends her can't hide that the dress is too snug, come back shrunken from the wash. Letitia parts Amy's hair evenly down the middle and tucks it tightly behind her ears, but it never stays put. They look no better than their everyday selves as they follow Miss Ellsworth through the door marked no admittance. Letitia walks carefully behind Miss Ellsworth, not joking or teasing or even looking around like Amy does. The last time Amy visited the doctor's apartment was the first time she'd ever seen Ingstrom, in the center of the building, in his office. And though she knows that they are traveling differently through the building now than she did when coming from her old ward, a floor below, she's still nervous that he might wait along their path, smoothing his dark moustache and pretending to be looking after the women. They cross the length of the convalescent ward adjacent to theirs, pass through another door marked no admittance. In the dim service stairwell, they wait at a door marked 3A. Somewhere below them, quick feet echo on the stairs, but the sound fades away. Amy sighs in relief.

Miss Ellsworth pushes them gently toward the door. Go ahead and knock, Miss Olsen.

Letitia wipes her hands on her skirt before rapping quietly on the door. The maid who'd escorted Amy the first time admits them almost at once, as though she's been waiting. She passes them onto the blue-papered hallway. At its opposite end are sidelights and a foyer, the door Amy was admitted through before. That door leads onto the wide central staircase of the hospital; the door through which they've now come is less grand. It is a door that lets the doctor slip from his quarters into theirs—as now they have slipped into *his*. Is their visit a secret? Or maybe they've been let in through the back door because they're greenhouse workers, hired help. Letitia can't know the difference—but Amy does. They follow the maid into the parlor, where the doctor's wife waits as before.

Miss Underwood, she says. Miss Olsen. I'm delighted to see you. She wears a dark rustling dress with a high collar and a gold watch pinned to the bodice. Her hair is a clean white roll above her pink, child's face.

Letitia curtsies stiffly and drops into the brocade armchair toward which the doctor's wife gestures. The doctor's wife beckons for Amy to sit beside her on the horsehair settee. At Amy's elbow, just within reach, is the octagonal side table, the shallow drawer where she knows the boy is kept. She folds together her tingling fingers, looks straight ahead.

Well! says the doctor's wife. I have heard such good stories lately of the two of you, and, like everyone at the hospital, I'm very grateful for the hard work you're doing in the greenhouse. Matilda will return directly with some treats for us, so please, make yourselves comfortable. I hope we'll have a good chat today.

Amy scoots back an inch farther on the couch; the mauve cushions do not yield beneath her. Opposite, a giant hair wreath hangs just behind Letitia's chair. Amy stifles a laugh at the effect of this odd halo. Letitia squirms as though she needs to use the toilet; her chair looks stiff, too. The doctor's wife clears her throat.

I have made some additions to my albums since you last visited, Miss Underwood; I've even been taking photographs of my own, nature studies and so forth. Perhaps you and Miss Olsen would like to look at them? Or, there on the rack, you'll find some of my new books—can you reach those, Miss Olsen?

Letitia makes a show of examining the books' spines, and at the look of mock-interest on her friend's face, Amy almost laughs again. Letitia lays a few books on the center table and selects one for herself, slowly turning its pages. Taking up another, Amy searches out the illustrations: an ostrich farm, a wild-looking lake, a Bavarian lodge beneath huge, snow-capped mountains. The doctor's wife smiles to see these.

Have either of you been West? Nor have I, but seeing how wonderful it seems, I am wild to go. I try to order some of the new titles every season, you know, in order to compensate for our being so very isolated from the world of fashion and ideas. When I was young, we lived just outside Philadelphia, and I've never—

What's this? Letitia asks suddenly, forgetting to use her strange company voice. Who's he? She thrusts her book toward them, open to a photographic plate—a cramped room with dead or dozing men everywhere: balanced on high bunks, leaning against the walls, covered from their necks down in blankets and surrounded by crates, sacks, pans.

Well, those are 'lodgers in a tenement'; see the caption? Shocking, I agree. The photographs were taken at night in New York's slums—unsanitary places with no provisions for clean air or water. The very opposite of—

This one. Letitia points to a bullish man on the top bunk. He sits upright in his shirtsleeves, his head propped on his fist. It says that this one here is in New York?

Yes, says the doctor's wife. Yes, dear—all of those people are far away. Did he remind you of someone?

Letitia orients the book toward herself again and turns the pages quietly. Her forehead is creased. Who are these? She holds out another photograph, of small children kneeling in prayer. They form a long U opening toward the camera, their faces tiny and blurred, their nightgowns bright white.

They are wards of the city, neglected children. See how sweet and clean they are, now that they are taken care of properly? There are others…well, look here. The doctor's wife pages forward to three barefoot boys sleeping in a pile on a street grate. What chance can such boys have on their own? She hands the book back to Letitia, smiling kindly. Did you grow up in a city, my dear?

Letitia shakes her head, claps the book closed. Her expression is flat. No, she says. No—I've never been to such a dirty place as that. My folks had a big dairy outside Ypsilanti.

Amy's mouth falls open.

We did, Letitia says, staring at her, before my mother took sick and then my pa, too. It was the shock of them dying that landed me here, I guess.

The maid returns then with the cart—cakes and a silver tea-pot—and the doctor's wife begins to serve. Fragrant amber liq-uid gurgling into thin cups; the click of her knife passing cleanly through the cake. That's terrible, she says, quietly. You must miss them very much.

Oh, Letitia waves her hand, picks up a plate, I miss them some. There were so many of us at home I can hardly remember my ma paying me attention.

Amy takes a huge bite of cake. There's no sense in her speaking.

What became of the others? Are they still on the farm?

The others? Letitia sips her tea. I like to think of them like the kids in that picture, ma'am—wearing white nightgowns and taken care of by nice people. Maybe hereabouts, maybe in Heaven. I won't know for sure until I get out. Do they have tenements in Michigan, ma'am?

The cake lodged like a dry lump in Amy's mouth begins to soften.

In Detroit, the doctor's wife says, slowly, I believe there are large apartment buildings. But do you not think, Miss Olsen, that your siblings might have gone to other family members, perhaps there in Ypsilanti?

Oh, says Letitia, what a comfort it would be to think so! But we have some dreadful no-accounts in my family, ma'am—like the men in that other picture. I was startled to see how much that one looked like…my uncle, to tell the truth. The kids will be best off once I have the care of them.

The doctor's wife nods, blinking rapidly. I hope you will have that chance, Miss Olsen—it's terrible to lose a brother or sister.

Amy glances toward the side table, but the doctor's wife does not instruct her to take out the daguerreotype, the brother. Instead, she turns to Amy, smiling brightly.

Now, Miss Underwood, you must tell me more about your family. You have no siblings, if I recall correctly?

Sometimes she has a brother, says Letitia. Or so she'll tell you.

I don't, Amy says. Just a father—and a stepmother.

My brothers would love this cake, says Letitia. Do you think the cook would give me the recipe—before I leave, that is?

The doctor's wife nods without looking at Letitia. Miss Underwood, have you given any thought to what you would like to do when you are recovered? Miss Olsen will take care of her siblings. What about you?

Letitia scrapes her fork against her plate. I might let my next-biggest sister keep on with the others, she says. I might find something else, too. Like working in a big commercial dairy, maybe. Or a factory. What kind of factories are around here, ma'am?

Oh, says the doctor's wife. Wooden things, mostly. Those little bowls you get at the butcher's shop. Handles for tools. Things you might learn to make here in the hospital's woodshop, if you think turning would suit you. Should you like to try that?

I should, Letitia says, her best voice tacked on again over her real one. Only…ain't there an awful lot of men in the wood-turning shop?

The old woman turns her bright doll eyes back to Letitia. Can that really bother you, my dear—having grown up among brothers?

Letitia flushes. I 'spose not, she says, and begins furiously stirring her tea. As long as they're not rough and strange, like those in that book.

The doctor's wife smiles again, but her eyes are shrewd. I think you've been acquainted before with the male patients, Miss Olsen. Whatever they may once have been, those permitted to work are now trying to improve themselves—like all of our better patients. But wood-turning can hardly be a major industry around Ypsilanti. That area was logged eons ago. What *are* the major industries there, dear?

Letitia shrugs and keeps her eyes on her cake. We didn't go into town much.

No? Surely, though, you remember the mills: 'Never a Rip, Never a Tear'—come now, you remember the rest?—'Ypsilanti Underwear'! The doctor's wife laughs; her color is high. Who could forget *that* slogan?

Letitia flips open one of the albums lying there in front of them on the center table. I should like to look at your albums now, she says carefully.

The old lady leaves her place beside Amy and reseats herself in the chair beside Letitia's. Let me tell you about these things, she says, patting Letitia's knee. Such wonderful stories!

Amy concentrates on her chewing to drown out Letitia's dull questions and the old lady's chirping responses: here are trilliums behind the hospital, and a new box of chicks, and and and… Amy cannot tell whether Letitia is truly interested in the photographs or only playing along; she cannot tell anything about Letitia, sometimes. The doctor's wife pities poor orphans, and Letitia becomes one. But she doesn't make a very good show, no matter that her true history is just as sad. Is she working her way around to her stories about the old doctor? Amy finishes every crumb of cake on her plate, then turns her attention back to the hair wreath. Are these people all dead or only missing locks of hair? When Amy attempts to sort out the faded strands, they interweave, blur. She lets her eyes close until the old lady addresses her.

Miss Underwood! Miss Olsen asks to see the arrangement of our apartment. As I told her, this floorplan is the very same as Dr. Ingstrom's above—in fact, when he is home, I can sometimes make out his movements from room to room. It's quite clever, I think, the way the architect designed the doctors' quarters to stack together as they do. Will you join us?

Amy shakes her head, still groggy, and Letitia nods in feigned compassion.

She's just started working, ma'am—must be she's too worn out to stay awake. She works slow enough, afternoons.

Stay, urges the doctor's wife, we'll be back shortly. Call out if you need anything. She stands and rests her hand on Letitia's shoulder, either guiding or pushing her toward the door. Their two skirts brush against each other in the narrow doorway, their voices mingle down the hall, one imitating the other.

Amy sits up and looks around the parlor—alert now that she is alone. The room is a museum of small objects. China and brass figurines, glass prisms hanging from lamp shades, tassels dangling from ottomans and chairs. Things that would be a pleasure to hold, if there weren't something far better in the octagonal table. A small silver face curving under glass; a soft weight that she'd carried as a reassurance. The lost boy with his tiger's eye buttons and his steady, gentle gaze. She has not forgotten him, even if she has a living friend now, another girl. Taking him again would mean being caught by the old doctor, strapped to a bed, sent to a ward without Letitia or Lil. Still, she can look.

She scoots to the edge of the settee, inhales deeply, and reaches for the drawer of the octagonal table. Sticky with spring humidity, the drawer jerks open, but nothing clunks inside, nothing of substance. Only a rattle of stray buttons, the soft slide of fabric. The drawer holds a stack of lace doilies separated by tissue paper. The boy is not beneath or amidst them. He's not there.

Amy slips from the settee to her knees, groping underneath the table's top, around its legs. The boy must have fallen out of the back of the drawer or gotten jammed in its works. She closes the drawer and opens it again—and again, until the table lamp shudders. Nothing. He's been moved; he's in one of the room's many other hiding spots—a drawer of the library table, the shelf of a crowded curio cabinet. She forces herself to look carefully, moving from one piece of furniture to the next, examining under and around everything. Many gilt-edged frames, many small faces, but no other pictures of the boy, no other pictures that seem forged from silver. Rummaging through these worthless knick-knacks, her hands burn. Who needs an inlaid box, an ugly vase? Her stepmother cherishes this kind of junk, too, these ladies made of Dresden porcelain, with lamblike expressions and bright, ugly gowns. How Rose would carry on whenever one broke. Amy fits her fingers into the folds of a china dress. Before she can lift the figurine, she hears voices in the hallway. She's back in her spot in a flash—and then catches, from the corner of her eye, the open drawer of the side table. The drawer slides back crookedly, sticks, sticks again in the other direction, and, then, back on its track, slams shut.

Well! says the doctor's wife, and Amy freezes, twisted away from the door, half out of her seat, her hand still on the drawer pull. What are you looking for, Miss Underwood?

Amy sits back slowly. She can feel her cheeks burning.

The old lady remains standing. Was it my daguerreotype—my brother? I'm afraid he's lost. A great loss to me—a great shock!

Amy nods, swallowing the hard ache in her throat. The old doctor took the boy, she would like to say; she would like to explain that *he* is to blame—but there is no way to do so without exposing herself. The doctor's wife smiles, batting her eyelashes. She seems also on the verge of tears. But when she speaks, her voice is bright.

It's just as well; we ought not spend more time looking at pictures when you ladies are due back to your ward. What a lovely visit we've had! Miss Olsen, I hope you'll let me inquire for you about openings in the wood shop—and Miss Underwood, you must let me know, too, if there's anything you need. Please, help yourselves to more cake, and then Matilda will see you back.

The doctor's wife steps out again, calling for her maid. Amy's hands are empty, her pockets are empty, but despite her self-restraint, the old lady knows her for a thief. Who would help a thief?

The doctor begins to prepare for his trip, assembling his clothing for Matilda to go over and arrange. Normally, Diana has finished packing his trunk before the notion of starting has even crossed his mind, but she doesn't offer her help now, and he doesn't dare ask for it. Since her outburst about the train tour, she has maintained toward him an air of genial indifference, neither asking after his day nor offering news about hers. He learns of her affairs by chance, as today, when the Olsen girl interrogated him about Diana's tea menu. Returning to their apartment in the evening, he finds the parlor still open and Diana still sitting inside it, in the dark. He reaches for the wall button, then thinks better of it. In the dimness, she holds her daguerreotype open on her lap.

Is it Charles's birthday? he asks, remaining in the doorway. She's apt to keep vigil on the anniversaries of her brother's birth and death.

No. She shuts the case and stands. James, why didn't you tell me that Amy Underwood had taken this photograph when it went missing last fall?

He closes his eyes: patience. What makes you think she did so?

Oh, no. His wife shakes her head, her hair luminous in the gloom. I won't be put off. It has crossed my mind before today that Charles's photograph wasn't actually in the settee, where you claimed to find it. Not when I tore those cushions apart three times myself. I have suspected that you found Charles elsewhere—and, after today, I know where. But why didn't you tell me?

Diana…the matter was so easily corrected that I didn't like to concern you or give you a reason to stop your visits with the patients. I *am* sorry. He smiles: I see at least that she hasn't stolen it again.

James! His wife comes toward him, quickly, and he steps back as though she were a patient of uncertain motive. By the hall light he sees that her face is flushed. For how many years have I lived among your patients? I'm not frightened of them. Rather than babying me, you might have let me in on this story—let me help determine the best response to Miss Underwood's actions.

I wouldn't ask you to do my job. The doctor rubs his wife's thin shoulders. The girl understands that she did wrong. She was punished for taking the photograph.

Punished? Did it never occur to you that I might *help* that poor child? Now I've lied to her, instead. Condescended to her like you did to me. His wife sighs and steps away from him, back into the dark parlor. Have you determined *why* Miss Underwood took Charles?

He nods. Her history indicates a long-standing tendency toward kleptomania, and such a disorder of volition supports the initial diagnosis of pubescent ins—

James! Of course you have your explanation. Here's mine: that girl is lonesome. I may not have your training, but I understand *her* case, I think, at least as well as you do. I understand feeling lonely! He can see her watch chain glinting on her breast, rising and falling too quickly with her breath. But when she speaks again, her voice is controlled. Claudia Meijer means to adopt two girls—did you know that?

The doctor shifts on his feet. They'll have room for it, with that new house, and you know Mrs. Meijer has a great deal of experience with children.

Unlike me. Still, I'm struck by the idea. I would like to raise a child. It wouldn't do for me to exert a mother's influence over your patients—I understand that. But if we were to adopt, I think I could do a great deal of good.

He coughs, a surprised burst. Really, dear…Claudia Meijer is some years younger than you, much more robust—and I would caution *her* against adopting, if she asked my advice.

You tend to seven hundred orphans every day; can't you allow me *one*? Diana moves into the hallway again. Her pupils are dilated, both from the darkness of the parlor and from excitement. I wish you would talk to Dr. Meijer about it, James; I think then you would appreciate the great social good that he and Claudia will be part of—and from which you exclude me.

Diana, I— The doctor perceives her imploring look and catches himself: I'll talk to Dr. Meijer when I return. As whimsical as his wife has been lately, it's possible that she'll have forgotten this notion by the time he returns.

While you make up your mind, I intend to do what little I can and organize a sewing project on the women's wards, making underclothes for the orphans out West.

He nods, rubs his eyes. If you will see to having the materials donated and arrange for the shipping of the finished goods, I have no objection.

Of course. She opens the photograph case still clenched in her hand and looks down at the image. I mean to give this to her, you know. Miss Underwood.

Diana, really…. He cradles her hands in his, so that they hold the photograph together. You're generous enough already.

She shakes her head. It's no sacrifice on my part. I don't need a photograph to remember Charles. If Miss Underwood wants him, it seems to me that she should have him—having no brother or sister of her own.

He squeezes her hands gently. Think what lesson the gift would teach her!

She smiles up at him. The lesson is that I'm sorry for deceiving her. The lesson is that I am her friend. Can't you trust me to express that?

As you please. He withdraws his hands and, again, she holds the daguerreotype alone. The last time he saw the thing, it was wrapped up in a handkerchief in his medicine cabinet. He pats his breast pocket, feeling for his keys. Dear…how is it that you were able to retrieve Charles?

She laughs. Do you think I picked the lock? Meijer had another key cut during your illness, so that I'd be able to mix up your doses without sorting through your ridiculous key ring. She shakes her head, closes the daguerreotype case. Things were very different while you were sick, James. Having felt for once *useful*, I cannot resign myself again to my old role.

He looks down at her unlined face, so incongruous under that white hair. You're much more than useful to me, dear: you're essential. I would far rather see you happy than resigned.

She steps toward him. If you mean that, give me more room for influence. Think about adoption. You aren't the sole superintendent of our home, even if it does lie within this hospital. Let me have more that is *mine*.

Your health—

But she puts her hand over his mouth, silencing him as Miss Underwood did. We can worry about my health when it obtrudes itself. She shakes her shoulders back, and her pretty dress rustles. Come, now—let me make sure you've thought of everything for next week. A gentleman should always carry a spare handkerchief, and, with all the toxins in that terrible Washington air, your respiratory problems are sure to flare up. I wonder if you even *own* enough handkerchiefs for this foolish trip! She takes his arm and he yields to her pull, happy for now to cede the management of his steamer trunk.

Chapter Fifteen

ON THE MORNING OF AMY'S birthday, there's no gift beside her breakfast bowl, no note from the old doctor. During his visit the day before, he had announced that he was leaving in the morning for Washington and that they wouldn't see him for a week. But Amy hadn't supposed that this would cause him to forget her. Sitting across the table, Letitia is indifferent, too, focused on her food. Amy stirs her scorched cereal and counts in her head. Maybe this isn't Tuesday, or maybe the 28th actually falls on Wednesday—or fell on Monday! Maybe she's the one who has lost track of time. Maybe she's being punished for going through the old lady's drawer.

No sooner has she settled on this explanation than Lil hugs her by the shoulders, whispering in her ear: guess what Miss E.'s done for you! Letitia grins at her then and without clearing their dishes, she drags Amy by the wrist to the dayroom. Miss Ellsworth positions Amy before the pier glass and holds the finished May Day dress up in front of her everyday clothes. Oh, how pretty! the other women exclaim. They're all looking, and when Amy finally looks up, too, she sees her red face above the clean white dress. Scabbed pimples dot her jaw and cheeks; her light eyes are blanched by the dress's field of white. She hasn't had a special dress since she's been here, a dress sewn for an occasion and intended to make her look nice. She has never looked nice—though maybe she could. Before she can look again, Miss Ellsworth has carried the dress away to the clothes room; when she comes back, she strikes up "For He's a Jolly Good Fellow" on the piano and all the women shout *she!* in place of *he.* The new women, the old women—they all know it's Amy's birthday, they're all smiling. Amy is the youngest of them and today, everyone mothers her, scrambling to help clean her room, vying to walk beside her during the morning constitutional. Miss Ellsworth lets her run the treadle machine by herself during the sewing hour. All morning, the women take turns at the piano, playing whatever Amy wants: "Little Annie Rooney"—*dress'd so neat but quite in style!*—every sad verse of "Clementine." Still, the old doctor has forgotten her, who remembered even the quietest and the most filthy of the other women, and Dr. Meijer has to be told of her birthday when he comes alone on rounds. No one mentions her parents.

When Mrs. Morris comes with the mail, there is no box among the envelopes. Other women get their usual letters full of messages from home and newspaper clippings. Amy gets nothing. And then—One more! calls the matron. Small, wrapped in brown paper, the parcel she draws from her apron pocket is addressed simply to *Miss Amy Underwood.* Sent from the building center, says Mrs. Morris, winking. Not, then, from Bertha Chapman. Amy shakes the parcel, testing it. It is smaller than a book, tied up tightly in coarse string. Unopened. No one knows its contents but the sender.

Amy carries the parcel to the tall secretary, where she can be partially hidden from the others. Whatever's inside the brown paper doesn't feel like a snood or a packet of handkerchiefs, the old doctor's usual gifts. The parcel is too heavy to contain those things, too hard, too flat. She loosens the knotted string until she can slip her fingers beneath the paper wrapping. The object within is smooth with raised impressions across its surface. A leather case: she touches its tiny metal hinges. A photograph case…impossible, but—she rips the wrappings away. He is missing, he is found—inside, the boy.

Amy covers the case quickly with both hands and leans low to the desktop. He was lost, the doctor's wife said so—*lost and gone forever, O my darling!*—and now here he is, with her. She peers beneath her tented fingers. Unclasped, opened, the boy gleams again in his strange, silvered splendor. Everything about him is familiar: his old-fashioned outfit, his shining eyes, the thrill in her stomach at seeing him. Where has he been since she last held him? He can't tell her, and the closer she examines him, the more distracted she is by her reflection. Was this boy ever as unkempt and oily as she is now, three days past bath night and with her menses approaching? Even in childhood photographs, she always looked untidy or blurred, writhing during the exposure, revealing the photographer's brace. She's never been so polished as this boy, never so still and dear and good. And yet looking at him now, she notes something new: an iridescent haze rimming the daguerreotype's copper frame. It reaches just to the fingertips of the boy's curled right hand. The haze doesn't come off when she rubs it. She damps her handkerchief with her tongue, rubs again, but the haze is beneath the glass, a tarnish. Did she cause this when she kept the boy before? Was he hurt when the case fell on the floor, back on her old ward? She closes the case quickly, shutting out air, light, her own imperfections. Shutting in that sweet face. Wraps her fingers around the case to hold it closed more tightly. She won't let the boy disappear. She closes her eyes, holding him in.

What is that? Letitia jogs her arm, reaching around the side of the secretary. Who's it from?

Amy shakes her head, opening her eyes slowly: I don't know. But she does know, even before she finds a sheet of silver-embossed stationery within the photograph's crumpled wrapping paper. The doctor's wife, she tells Letitia. The note is much longer than an invitation to tea:

> Dear Miss Underwood,
>
> When you visited me last week, I told you an untruth. The photograph that you wished to see was not lost but has been kept in a more secure spot since it went missing last fall. I confess that your interest in the photograph made me think that you had taken it. I do not ask whether or not you did this. I write, instead, to ask your forgiveness for my lie.
>
> You have told me that you have no siblings of your own. As I have several, I wish to share with you this one—my brother, Charles. This image has been very dear to me but nowhere near as dear as my memories of our childhood together. Knowing that I will never part with those memories makes it a joy and not a pain to part with this daguerreotype. Charles was the best person I've ever known: faithful, kind, and deeply concerned with the welfare of others. I hope that you desire to be like him. When you look at him, I hope that you will be reminded of his example.
>
> The doctor has entrusted me to express his birthday wishes to you along with my own. Remember that you have a friend in me and do not hesitate to come to me when you need a confidant.

Amy lets the note fall back to the desktop.

Read it out loud, says Letitia. Does she say anything about me, about the wood-turning shop? What's that she sent you— cigarettes?

No. Amy hands Letitia the case and watches her friend open it. Letitia balks, seeing the boy.

Who's that? Not your pa that was in the other picture?

Amy shakes her head. It's her brother.

Letitia frowns. What's he to you?

Amy takes the case back and closes it. She loves him.

You act as though you do, too—a fly-specked old photo.

Amy shrugs. I like how he looks.

How he *looks*? Letitia throws up her hands. He looks like a baa lamb. If I'd known you liked hand-me-down presents, I wouldn't have troubled myself helping Miss E. with your dress. Did you see how I stitched that bodice?

Thank you, Amy says, but she tightens her hand around *this* gift, closes her eyes again. A current of energy moves in her veins. And lying open on the desktop, the letter is just as thrilling—a letter of apology. The doctor's wife has asked *her* forgiveness! She will not dull the old woman's words by reading them to Letitia. She doesn't want to know how Letitia would hear them. Yet neither can she understand them on her own. When her stepmother had written, in January, she'd apologized to Amy for not writing sooner. But what choice did Rose have? She couldn't have written without mentioning all the weeks that she hadn't. The doctor's wife didn't need to admit she'd lied; Amy would've never known. The doctor's wife must know that Amy is a thief; certainly the doctor knows! Still, she has asked Amy's forgiveness. Is it a trick? Or is she truly sorry for her lie—truly sorry for hurting Amy?

Miss E. said you could do up my skirt on the machine, says Letitia, jogging Amy's elbow again. Come on.

Did you really grow up on a dairy farm?

Letitia shrugs. What do you think? The old lady doesn't know any better.

Amy nods.

Oh, and you don't lie! Is that what her letter is about—your bad friend Letitia and all her lies? Letitia reaches for the letter, but Amy tucks it and the case into her apron pocket.

She doesn't mention it. Did you tell her about how the old doctor comes after you at night?

Letitia laughs sharply. Why? She'll either think I'm telling tales, or she'll know it's true—and, either way, I'd be off to the back wards again. I know how this place works, even if you don't.

I suppose, Amy says. I can do your hem for you now.

How very kind of you, says Letitia, in an imitation of the old lady's voice. Be careful you don't make me look *too* nice, or Dr. Ingstrom won't spare you any dances on Friday.

Amy tries to laugh—but in her pocket, her fingers close around the boy. Letitia doesn't speak the young doctor's name so often anymore; he hasn't been to their ward since Amy exposed him. But though he's not near, he's not gone. He sits as ever in the physicians' row at the evening programs; he still hasn't announced that he plans to leave the hospital. And he's still in Letitia's thoughts, ready at any moment to burst forth. Probably, Letitia thinks that Amy lied about his leaving. Amy is a liar, sometimes, but she hopes that she was speaking the truth. Now she follows Letitia to the sewing machine and wishes that the young doctor had never noticed her friend. He confuses Letitia with his moustache and his manners and if he isn't a pimp, what is he? Letitia is beautiful when she keeps her broken mouth closed…and Dr. Ingstrom has no wife. What does the old lady seek in Amy? What might Amy find in her?

* * *

The Virgin Mary. The Queen of the May. They twirl around Amy when she opens her eyes on May Day morning, women from legends that she doesn't know. May, Mary's month. May, when girls in white are crowned with flowers. The sun hasn't risen yet, but in the quiet dark, the day's excitement laps at her, waves stirred by a soft wind. She can't see the lake to tell how the wind is blowing. She's never danced the maypole before.

The woman next door coughs, turns on her cot, and Amy raps the wall: hello, good morning. A rap comes lightly in return. She swings her feet to the floor. The week so far has been mild and sunny, but the almanac calls for bad storms. What do you think? she whispers, touching the boy's closed case. Inside, he's hugged by velvet. She keeps the boy again on her bedside table, again in her apron pocket, but she opens his case rarely now. There are too many threats from air and light; she should not expose him. The alarm sounds, that familiar harsh clang, and the electric bulb switches on above her. Her parents' photograph stands on the table, unaffected by the elements.

The sun rises during breakfast. After their meal, the women rush from the west-facing dining room to the east-facing windows of the dayroom. Pale, clear skies, and a group of men raising a tall pole at the center of the lawn. There will be more men, later, men from all the convalescent and intermediate wards. Amy's fingers scale her neck. She stops them: later, she'll dance with Letitia, holding one of the long ribbons that flutters already from the pole. She touches the scabs on her chin, healed almost to smoothness. She could open them again…or she could try to look nice in her white dress, dancing with her friend.

The cleaning chores are finished quickly, the morning walk a brisk march to the dairy barns and back. The remaining hours before the picnic are given over to what Miss Ellsworth calls *le toilette*. Lil looks after those women who won't wash their faces or button their dresses, while Miss Ellsworth demonstrates the newest chignons in the dayroom.

The hair is a woman's most important adornment, she tells them. The women nod, brushing their long hair one hundred times as she's instructed. Amy lends Letitia her brush; she has no use for it. What will we do with you? Miss Ellsworth asks when Amy's back hair won't go up.

What does it matter? shrugs Letitia. Only that idiot boy would dance with her.

Letty! Miss Ellsworth scolds—but her lips twitch as if she wants to laugh along with the others. Amy shakes the short wings of her hair in front of her face and runs away from that laughter. The others are old, too old to be dressing in white and having a picnic, but in their new outfits, her wardmates have changed into the cruel girls at Miss Carter's School.

In the corridor, the sound of a running faucet is like the lake up north when she is near its edge and Lil's low voice soothes the wild women in the washroom. Little breezes blow through the open door of the sun porch. The country woman and the old Norwegian keep up their steady circuits. They both wear new spring calicoes, though neither can usually be coaxed off the ward. Amy finds a rocker and watches the two women pace in opposite directions, not looking at each other, never colliding. *Bless you, bless you*, whispers the country woman, tapping each item of furniture and skirting Amy. But when she reaches Amy's rocker, muttering as always, the Norwegian woman *does* stop. Her cornflower eyes survey Amy's outfit.

Ditt håret…. she says, patting her own head and smiling. Amy's eyes sting anew. That this toothless old woman should taunt her!

Nenne! the old woman exclaims when Amy stands. She takes Amy's arm, strokes her hand. God jente, she croons. Kommer hit. Her voice is high and lilting. She gestures for Amy to sit on an ottoman and positions herself in the rocker behind it. She plants her strong legs alongside Amy's hips; her hands are heavy on Amy's shoulders. The stench of sweat and urine comes from under her skirt—smells Amy has grown accustomed to at the hospital. The woman begins to part and plait Amy's hair. She hums as she works; every now and then she tilts Amy's head with her blunt fingers. Amy can feel her hair tightening against her scalp, pulled gently at the roots, and little metal nips as it's pinned in place. She closes her eyes, trying to hum along with the Norwegian's song. Finally, the old lady claps her hands: Vær så god! Amy reaches up to feel a braid circling her head and turns to find the woman's own hair hanging loose.

Nenne, nenne, the woman protests when Amy gestures to give back her hairpins. En princesse. She points at Amy. Pen.

Thank you, says Amy. Danke? The woman waves her hand again, smiling. Her kind face is soft as bread dough. What's your name? asks Amy. She touches her chest and says her own. The old woman shakes her head. She rubs Amy's back and resumes her pacing.

Look at the milkmaid! Letitia shouts when Amy steps back into the dayroom. Her face goes hot when all the others turn toward her, but in the midst of them, she spots her reflection in the pier glass. Her dark hair sculpted to her head looks, for once, neat; if the old woman called her a princess, then this could be a crown. The other women are transformed, too, their carefully piled hair making their necks seem longer and more graceful. They look like fashion plates, Lil tells them. Only Letitia's hair has been dressed differently. Pinned up at the sides, it tumbles in chestnut waves nearly to her waist. Perfect for a pagan celebration, Miss Ellsworth says. And though Letitia's dress fits her ill—pulling here and gapping there, as if she's gained weight—her hair is glorious. She twirls so that it fans around her: the Queen of the May.

The women keeping watch at the windows narrate the progress below: the tables are covered now, the fiddlers' stage made up, the doctors and the steward have arrived. When the first patients spill from the building, Lil lines the women up. They surge down the service stairs, through the firedoors, into the celebration.

The lawn is a sea of people, everyone outfitted from the same bolts of fabric, and Amy anchors beside the building as her ward-mates stream away. Soon, she cannot pick out their faces in the teaming crowd; soon, they are lost, and she is sidling back toward the door, toward the quiet empty ward and a view from above. But women still pour out of the building and they push her forward with them, at the edge of their current, until she is caught by a rescuing hand. Over here, goose—and Letitia pulls her toward the maypole. Two circles are forming around it, one within the other. The women stand back so that the ribbons they hold are stretched taut; from a distance, they could be seamstresses, all working on the hem of the same vast skirt. Letitia chooses a red ribbon for herself and a yellow one for Amy.

When the caller says start, we go in and out around those coming toward us, says Letitia. Just keep up with everybody else and listen in case the direction changes. Did you see your Fritz over there, already after the cake?—and of course his old man, too. A pair of horse-toothed pigs. Have you seen Ingstrom?

The opening notes of a fast tune spare Amy from answering. The women around them nod and prance in time with the music, then begin to promenade in and out. Soon, Amy's laughing too hard to talk. Smiling at the women who march in the opposite direction, skipping around them. There are a few men dancing the maypole, too, and men that swoop in and try to snatch the women's ribbons. Many men seem to know Letitia. Some of those that hail her are young or handsome, and maybe they will make her forget to look for the young doctor. There's a man who might be one of the lumbering crew, he's so tall and broad, and when he puts his hand on Letitia's waist, she smiles up at him, lets him dance alongside her. They weave in and out in front of Amy, their hips aligned. Amy would let Fritz dance with her, if he were to put down his cake for a moment; she would let kind Mr. Schmidt or stout Dr. Meijer put his arm about her and kick up his heels. But she cringes whenever a strange man leers at her, passing in the other direction, and she tangles her ribbon, darting out of their reach. The dance goes round and round the pole, then reverses, unwinds, until, finally, the fiddlers stop. Letitia steps immediately out of the lumberjack's embrace. He gapes at her, the way she gapes at him, or someone like him, afternoons outside the greenhouse. Letty—he says, but she doesn't heed. She grabs Amy's arm and drags her away, up the only hillock on the flat lawn.

I saw him now and then, she says, raising a hand to keep the sun from her eyes. I know I did. Help me look.

Amy raises her hand, too, but there are too many people dressed alike, vast quantities of the same fabric milling about in front of the big yellow building. So many men with dark moustaches, so many women with snowy hair, so many people outside all at once. The doctor's wife must be wearing something different from the patients, but Amy doesn't spot her. White, white, white—all of the women look girlish at first glance—and the men are all alike in their dark suits. Still, it's only a moment before Letitia clutches Amy's arm: There! She plunges forward, waving—and then catches herself.

'Spose he don't want to talk to you, she says, squinting up at Amy. Her loose hair plays in the breeze. After what you called him that time. Why don't you go get us some punch?

But the young doctor is already closing in, hand raised, hailing them.

Miss Olsen, Miss Underwood. He stops in front of Letitia, his face as pale as new cream, and Letitia's skin is golden from working in the greenhouse.

Dr. Ingstrom! Letitia curtseys and tugs Amy's skirt until she dips her knees, too. We haven't had a visit from you in so long, I'm surprised you remember our names!

He smiles, positioning himself between them like the third point of a triangle. I'm glad at least to have had the pleasure of *seeing* you at our evening events. You've both been well? Recovered from the 'flu, Miss Underwood? And Miss Olsen—how are your headaches? You haven't visited me lately, either.

I knock every time I pass your office, but seems like you're never there. My head ain't been *too* bad lately…though it does ache with wondering after *you*. Letitia nudges his foot with her boot.

Yes, well. Ingstrom takes a narrower stance. I hope you can forgive me for not seeking you out. I've had a great deal of business to attend to. Spring is a busy season here, as you know…and, as I wanted particularly to tell *you*, I am soon to start my own practice.

Letitia raises her eyebrows, as if she didn't already know this. Your own practice! Think how busy you'll be!

Yes—I'll have a great deal to do between managing the facility and setting up my new household.

And your rounds here on top of all that! Letitia shakes her head.

Ah. Dr. Ingstrom glances at Amy. No. Next week will be my last here.

Don't tease! Letitia cuffs him lightly on the elbow. What would your patients do without you?

Ingstrom rubs his arm, feigning injury. The men will be fine. Think of the fun they'll have, breaking in a new doctor.

Yes…. Letitia tilts her head to the side. A new doctor *can* be fun. But what about all the ladies here, with their hearts set on you? You can't hire *all* of us as nurses…can you?

Ingstrom's eyebrows furrow—and if Amy yelled again, if she carried on, would Letitia stop fawning over him? But before she can shout his true name, his true nature, Ingstrom continues: The clinic will be small, focused on injuries of the brain. Complex cases—and, so, I will hire only nurses with high school educations. Literate women, who can be trained to perform sophisticated tasks.

Not like *our* attendants, then, Letitia says. Not like any of the stupid cows here. She shakes her head and her lips quiver. It sounds *very* grand.

I intend for it to be the finest clinic of its sort, Ingstrom says. Not just in Michigan but in the country. And I would like very much to treat you there, Miss Olsen.

Fix my teeth, do you mean? She smiles with her lips closed tightly.

Fix your headaches. It would require an operation, a simple matter, really, of cutting through the bone like so. With his finger, he traces a circle on the back of her head. Releasing the pressure that troubles you.

Letitia steps away from him. No cutting!

Miss Olsen, I understand your fear, but it's a very simple procedure. I will take good care of you, personally. We can fit you for new teeth afterward.

Afterward? Letitia's eyebrows draw together. Why not before? You think I might not come through it.

No, no. Ingstrom waves his white hands. Before, then—whenever you like. It's all very safe. And my fiancé's family has taken a great interest in your case. They will see to everything.

Fiancé? Letitia says. The word drops from her mouth like a lead weight. That means the woman you're going to marry?

He nods. Miss Eleanor Steele, who takes a great interest herself in injuries of the brain. Her sister died of head trauma. Miss Steele will be very glad that our clinic can help you.

Letitia shakes her head. There's nothing wrong with my brain. You ain't taking me away from here to be cut up for some fine lady's pleasure!

No. Ingstrom looks to Amy, as if hoping for help. You misunderstand me, Miss Olsen. This work, the work of treating you, will be deeply gratifying both to me and my wife—but much more importantly, you'll be free afterward. Able to do whatever you please.

Stay with you, then, says Letitia, stepping closer to him. Get a job at your hospital. I can do anything—you know that. Clean, cook, wash clothes. I can do all that already without getting cut open again.

Ingstrom's lips twitch beneath his silken moustache. But what I especially want for you, Miss Olsen, *is* this treatment. It is nothing like oophorectomy. I would never subject you to some faddish butchery. You know what a study I've made of your case. I *can* cure you.

And then send me off. Where do you think I'd go? If you can't keep me, I'm lost—that's all.

We could see about a position of some sort, if you like. But wouldn't you rather be far from hospitals, my dear?

Your dear. Letitia stares at him for a moment, into the dark pits of his eyes. There's no warmth there—and maybe now she sees that. Letitia shakes her head. I ain't your dear. Not after how you've used me. I might have known.

Ingstrom flushes. Remember yourself, Miss Olsen. I have always been a friend to you.

Oh, I remember. *Shh, keep quiet, my dear.* Letitia shakes her head. You had it about right, Amy. What you called this one. I'm too much a lady to say a word like *pimp.*

I have been a friend to you, Ingstrom repeats. And I will continue to be once you've calmed down.

No, Letitia says. I don't want anything to do with you. Go find some green girl, if you want to play games. Have your fun and then let your fiancé cut *her* up.

Miss Olsen, there is nothing improper in a doctor wanting to help you. If you have mistaken the nature of my interest, I am sorry for it.

Mistake *this*! She lunges toward him, fists clenched. *Get!* Get away from me with your limp prick!

He stumbles backward, raising his white hands. A ridiculous gesture, but Amy can't laugh.

Miss Underwood, says Ingstrom, backing down the hillock. I wish you well. And I hope you will convey as much to our friend once she's calmer.

Amy shakes her head, watching Letitia. *Get!* Letitia yells, stomping again.

Of course, you'd both rather enjoy the picnic than talk to a doctor. I apologize for spoiling your fun. I—I will see you at the evening programs. Ingstrom bows and turns away, walking quickly.

Letitia takes another lurching step after him and stops, wavering, mid-slope. She might be a sleep-walker, with her hair hanging free and her plain gown. Her face is as white as her dress; her arms cross over her midsection as though cradling an ache. When she turns to Amy, her eyes are vacant and wide, and Amy remembers: don't wake them. She guides her friend carefully toward the refreshment tables, finding a spot at the edge of the clustered patients. Letitia accepts the lemonade that Amy hurries to get her. She doesn't drink it, her free hand still resting on her stomach.

He thought of you, says Amy, quietly. Maybe he really could cure your headaches.

Hi! shouts Fritz, and Letitia's dulled eyes shift toward him. He rounds the cake table, grinning. He wears a fresh linen shirt beneath his vest; his freckled face is scrubbed clean.

Hi, Amy says. Fritz's light hair, uncovered, curls like the boy's in the photograph. She smiles to see it.

Here's our donkey. Letitia's voice sounds almost normal, even if her words are cruel. Do you think Ingstrom could fix him, Amy? Cut his skull open and stir up that mess inside?

Fritz shakes his head, still smiling. Hi, he says softly, looking at Amy.

Idiots in love, says Letitia. Well, it's a good thing you posted that letter for us. That letter?

Fritz nods and reaches into the pocket of his vest. He produces an envelope.

Is that her answer? Letitia snatches the envelope from him. A trail of lemonade spills down her white skirt, but she tears at the letter without seeming to notice. Shakes it at Amy: Read it—read it!

Amy's fingers are clumsy. What does Ingstrom matter beside *this*? She unfolds the page—and finds her own handwriting, her own scrawled signature. The temperance woman is frugal; she's re-used Amy's stationery…except that the back of the page is blank. Miss Chapman has sent them no reply. Or else…. Amy looks to Fritz. The boy gropes around on the ground for Letitia's dropped cup, but Letitia sees Amy's confusion.

What? Letitia grabs the letter. What does she say? Even if she can't make out the rest, Letitia has learned to recognize *AAU*. Amy watches her friend's face change when she sees the monogram and realizes Fritz hasn't posted their letter. She feels her own chest quake when Letitia sucks in a great breath. Moron! Letitia shrieks: Imbecile!

Amy shakes her head—shh!—but Fritz rises, just within reach, and Letitia lunges for him. She slaps him hard across the mouth: idiot! He cries out, his smile crumples—and Letitia strikes him again in the nose, the ears, boxing his face with both her closed fists. Other patients turn toward the commotion and begin to laugh when they see a girl beating a boy. But this isn't play-fighting.

Stop! Amy shouts. She throws her arms around Letitia's torso, hauling backward—but Letitia is stronger. Letitia twists out of Amy's grip and seizes the boy's collar. Blood runs from Fritz's lip; caught by the neck, he bawls like a calf. Stop, Amy shouts, Stop it! But though she hangs from Letitia's arms, Letitia keeps on, dragging Amy, shaking her loose to land more blows, and Fritz's face reddens with tears and bruises.

Let *go*! Letitia shouts and shoves Amy away. Amy falls onto her side, her skirts tangling as she crawls after them. She catches the hem of Letitia's dress—the hem she'd finished so carefully with the treadle machine. The heel of Letitia's boot rattles Amy's jaw. She dodges another kick and pushes herself up into a crouch—springs at Letitia's back and catches herself in that long, loose hair. Planting her right foot on the grass, Amy winds her left leg around Letitia's left and jabs her right knee into the back of Letitia's, like the attendants did on ward nine. Jabs again, and when Letitia's knee folds, Amy lets herself fall backward. She drops as though into waiting arms, waiting limbs, as though the ground won't knock her airless when her spine strikes the earth and Letitia's head, shoulders, elbows smash into her torso. Amy gasps, gasps and, even after Letitia clambers upright, staggers off, she feels the other girl's weight on her chest, stopping her breath. She rolls onto her knees, bile searing her tongue, breathless, and sees that Letitia has tackled Fritz to the ground.

Idiot! Letitia screams again and again. She climbs astride the boy's back, pins his arms; she forces his bleeding face into the grass. She will kill him—she will kill him!—and Amy gasps for air as she pushes herself to her feet.

Two male attendants reach them before Amy can. They seize Letitia's arms and lift her, kicking, from the boy's body. She kicks Fritz's ribs as they haul her away, kicks the attendant's thick legs; she tries to kick Mr. Schmidt when he hurries past. Letitia's dress is streaked green and brown, long red stains down her skirt. Her hair is ragged. Broken hanks of it fill Amy's hands. Amy unclenches her fists to find the chestnut strands embedded in her palms. Red smears across her own skirt when she tries to wipe the hair away. The Queen of the May.

Mr. Schmidt is on his knees now beside his son. He clears Fritz's mouth of grass and earth and Fritz begins to sob. Alive—and the relief of hearing him surges out of Amy's mouth as a sob, too. But Letitia raises her voice over the fiddle music, over his cries. Idiot! she screams, useless! I'll put you out of your misery! Mr. Schmidt cradles the boy to his chest and covers Fritz's battered ears. He presses his forehead to his son's. Amy holds herself back from them. The Schmidts will not want to see her; they will not be able to see her anymore as a good girl, a nice girl like any other walking down the street. If they ever see her again, they will see her like Letitia, wild and dangerous. Insane. The sobs thicken in her throat and she retches into the grass.

The other patients, the other picnic-goers, buzz and mill—coming nearer now that their help is no longer needed. Behind Amy, a group of men in town suits is assembled. The pig-like man is not with them, but these men seem like animals, too, making ugly tsking sounds and repeating Letitia's words. Idiots are prohibited by the hospital's charter! says one. The son of a groundskeeper, says another. But is it necessary, asks the first, that he be kept on premises? Amy's fists ball anew, and she turns; she will show them that they have more to fear from patients than from boys like Fritz. But between her and the men is Lil, red-eyed.

She can't help it, Lil says, but you can, Miss Underwood. Be a good girl and keep quiet until we're back upstairs.

Letitia—

Letty won't be there, says Lil. That boy's not hurt as bad as he looks—though, likely, he'll be scared for a while. Come on now. Be good for Lil. It's an awful shame your picnic had to be spoiled, but it's time to clear out and keep things nice for the rest. She puts her arm around Amy's shoulders. We'll go inside and see to your poor hands.

Amy leans against Lil and lets herself be led. She is nearly as filthy and wrecked as Letitia or Fritz. Lil never got a May Day dress of her own; Lil doesn't shrink from Amy's blood and grass and dirt. She braces Amy up. Letitia is gone already from the picnic, and Fritz is being carried across the lawn, safe in his father's arms. Ingstrom has joined the awful town men. The old doctor is far away in Washington. His wife stands with the other doctors' wives and two tiny little girls. Amy had thought she was the youngest at the hospital. She had thought, once, that there were no other girls here at all. But look at how small these girls are, how sad and lost.

When the old woman sees Amy, she breaks away from her group.

I am sorry, says the doctor's wife, repeating breathlessly the language of her letter. That something like this should happen—it is shocking. She takes Amy's torn hands in hers. My dear—you must come to see me soon, whenever you wish.

Amy nods. The old woman's face is kind; for the first time, she sees that the old woman looks like the boy, her brother, around the mouth and eyes.

Thank you, ma'am, says Lil, and Amy nods again. She lets herself be half-carried into the building, back to the calm of the ward.

The doctor is exhausted by the time his carriage reaches the hospital on Monday afternoon. Just four o'clock, but what an agony of travel he has been through since leaving Washington the previous morning: a late-night arrival in Chicago; a cramped hotel too near the depot. All night, trains had blown through the rail yard, reminding him that, after all, he does love the country better than the noisy city.

It is a truth he might forget after such a trip as this has been. Even his beloved grounds look a little duller, now that he has been away—the hospital's lawns noticeably trampled after the May Day celebration, the flowers weeks behind Washington's. What verdancy, there—what stimulation he had found in the company of his colleagues!

The doctor admits himself through the great front door of the hospital. The receptionists are not at hand, no doubt occupied with cleaning chores in these last hours of the hospital's workday. As he crosses the second-floor landing, he sees that his colleagues are likewise busy. Lights are on in every office, and he pictures the other doctors at their desks, working—or, in Ingstrom's case, packing. The boy leaves in only two days. The doctor continues upstairs without greeting the others; he'll be better company later, at the evening program. But in his apartment, in the parlor, he finds company already awaiting him: his wife sits with the Underwood girl. Together on the settee, they turn to one another in surprise when he appears in the doorway. They are not only companionable, it seems, but confiding.

James! his wife exclaims. The girl reddens at hearing his Christian name. Back so soon—I must have lost track of time.

It's no matter. He stifles a yawn and sits down opposite them. I'm happy to see you both. The chairs in his wife's parlor are as uncomfortable as train seats; he squirms against the brocade. Happy to be back.

And we're happy to have you. What times we've had in your absence! His wife raises her eyebrows significantly—but he's had no news during his trip; there have been no emergencies, by West's estimation, nothing serious enough to warrant a telegram. He shakes his head slightly and she continues, her hand a comfort on the girl's knee.

Miss Olsen became agitated at the May Day picnic and attacked that nice Fritz Schmidt. He's quite bruised and cut up—not to mention frightened—but he'll be fine. Dr. Meijer has, of course, re-assigned Miss Olsen to a lower ward.

What a shame, the doctor murmurs. The words are inadequate to the wave of guilt that swamps him—his school-boy guilt compounded. That such an innocent as the Schmidt boy was injured under his protection! He and Mr. Schmidt had both viewed a position in the greenhouse as a perfect opportunity for Fritz to receive training while remaining with his father. But this hospital hasn't proved a haven, either for the boy or for Miss Underwood—who is plainly traumatized. Her palms are wrapped in white bandages and her face is scratched to pieces, her cheeks more ravaged and scabbed than when she was first brought here. Her hair, in contrast, is arranged in a neatly braided crown.

Miss Underwood can't understand, his wife says, and I'm not sure I can explain, why Miss Olsen behaved as she did. She was apparently upset about Dr. Ingstrom's resignation.

And…. The girl twists the hem of her apron. Fritz was supposed to post a letter for us. I don't think he knew how.

The doctor rubs his knees. You couldn't mail the letter through open channels?

The girl shakes her head. I wrote to Miss Chapman, from the WCTU.

The doctor sighs. We restrict your letter-writing to protect you, Miss Underwood. In fact, the superintendents' association has just passed a resolution, affirming our feelings on the subject. The doctor rummages through his travel satchel, then reads aloud from his notes: *The letters of the insane, especially of women, often contain matter, the very thought of which, after recovery, will overwhelm them with mortification and dismay; thus any law which compels the send-*

ing of such letters is, clearly, an outrage on common decency and common humanity.

For example, his wife says to the girl, imagine if Miss Olsen were to write to someone about Dr. Ingstrom. What might *that* sound like?

Miss Underwood shakes her head. Letitia can't write.

It's only an example, the doctor says. If in the future you wish to write to someone, please discuss it with me, first.

Our question, however, was about Miss Olsen's temper. His wife draws him back to the subject. Why is it so very difficult for her to control herself?

The doctor shakes his head. A temper can be controlled. Miss Olsen's excitability is an aspect of her illness. She can no more control her outbreaks than I can my heartbeat. When she's between outbreaks, she seems vivacious, full of fun. That same energy can swell into frenzy. In periodical cases like hers, the attacks will come on quickly—your friend might seem disoriented or uncomfortable for a few moments before an outburst, or you may not notice any outward change. It is difficult for even a trained attendant to catch these signals and manage such a case. What happened isn't new; Miss Olsen has a history of violent outbursts. You yourself have fought with her, haven't you, Miss Underwood?

I started it! says the girl. It was my fault!

But she's had other, more serious incidents, before you came here. She was admitted to the Pontiac hospital when younger than you are now after violently assaulting her father.

The girl shakes her head. Her father beat her.

Well—the doctor glances at his wife—perhaps. But she's made similar accusations against other people, none of whom has been anything but kind to her. And delusions are another symptom of her illness. Be assured that it's not your fault or Fritz's fault or even Miss Olsen's fault that this thing has happened. Periodic mania is usually a hereditary disease—to our knowledge, incurable.

Dr. Ingstrom says he can cure her, says the girl.

The doctor shakes his head. He mistakes the nature of her illness if he thinks so. I wouldn't let him try his new methods on her.

I would like to see Letitia, says the girl. Please.

Yes, the doctor says, nodding slowly. I think you could. You must let me familiarize myself with her case as it now stands and determine when a visit would be most prudent.

His wife clasps the girl carefully by her injured right hand. I'm so very glad you came to me, Miss Underwood. I hope that you'll come and see me whenever you're sad or confused. She glances to the doorway, where Matilda has appeared. The girl stands and so does the doctor.

I'm very tired from my travels, Miss Underwood, but very glad to find you here with my wife. We'll talk at greater length tomorrow.

The girl nods, looking at him directly; her expression is open, rather than fearful or hostile. She offers him her hand to shake, bandaged as it is. This is a pronounced change in demeanor, a continuation of that transformation which began with her assignment to the greenhouse. With care, she will come through this disruption, keep up her progress toward cure.

Oh James, groans his wife, once Matilda has led the girl away. Diana throws herself sideways on the settee. What an uproar these last few days!

He resumes his uncomfortable seat, grimacing upon impact, and steels himself to listen to her elaborations on the picnic, her litany of other small disasters. But instead, she laughs.

I saw that! You'll be in a far better mood to listen, I'm sure, once you've had your supper. She stands, leaning across the center table to take his chin in her hand. It's good to have you home, James. She plants a dry kiss on his forehead; she rustles from the room. The doctor has just time to prop his feet up, settle in, before he hears her coming back, her snowy head popping around the doorframe: Don't be alarmed, dear, if you hear children upstairs; those orphans of the Meijers' came early. And do keep your heels off that table.

Of course, he promises—though, after two days sitting on the train, his knees ache when bent.

Diana's sharp eyes peering back into the room had lingered on not only his heels but also the small disruption of paper he made, digging out his meeting notes. He shoves everything away again in his satchel. Tucked beside his notebook is one of the souvenir photographs he's brought for her. Surely something meant to stay in the parlor cannot be counted as mess, so he places it on the center table. Mount Vernon in '58, before the Ladies' Association rescued it from ruin. In the photo, the great veranda is on the verge of collapse, propped up by tall, roughly-hewn beams. There are of course many such wrecks dotting the South, nowadays, plantations that proved unsustainable once labor—and humanity!—were assigned their rightful values. This home went to ruin ahead of schedule. It's difficult to believe that George Washington's estate could have been so neglected. Of course, Washington left many more important legacies than a farm, and then, too, he had no children to carry things on. They are alike, in that respect, the doctor and the president. But for such an investment of time and thought, such innovations as Washington made at Mount Vernon, to amount— almost!—to nothing…is difficult to calmly contemplate.

The doctor leans back again against the uncomfortable brocade and, first spreading one of his handkerchiefs on the table, dares to prop up his feet again. Between his tour of the rescued estate and the Association's discussions of asylum architecture, he has had plenty of evidence over the past few days of the impermanence of structures. The cottage plan has gained more ground since last year's conference, small, separate dormitory buildings having been found more efficient and fire-safe than large ones. Even at the Pennsylvania Hospital for the Insane, one-story buildings supplement Kirkbride's original design. There's nothing tragic about this turn: it is right and proper that new ideas, if good, should keep company with the old, and the doctor has found cottages useful in the treatment of *some* of his own patients. But how to marry the two approaches? None of the association's members could explain, to the doctor's satisfaction, how to maintain order at a hospital comprised of cottages—each an empire unto itself, each like a household with its own supervisor and attendants, its own needs. How can one superintendent oversee so much?

In Washington, the doctor had been party to the association's annual series of self-aggrandizements. He'd stood with his fellows on the steps of Saint Elizabeth's Hospital, to be immortalized by Mathew Brady—or, more accurately, by the myopic old photographer's keener-eyed assistants. He'd debated with his colleagues whether the qualifications for association membership ought to be grounded more demonstrably in merit (the assumption being, of course, that those debating possessed sufficient merit to decide). And he'd approved, with the other members, a new award: the Dorothea Dix Memorial Prize. The prize is conceived both as a tribute to their late, lamented colleague and as a means of honoring those contributing to the care of the insane.

The doctor couldn't help but think of Ingstrom during discussion of this prize. If successful, the boy's neurological work might prove wide-reaching; generations of doctors to come could, perhaps, know Ingstrom's work. The need for more heroic medical interventions was evident all through the conference, in the papers read and even at Mount Vernon itself. Sitting on the veranda sipping fortified wine, looking across the long green lawn at the broad Potomac, the association members had reminded each other of Martha Washington's great grief—her daughter dying at seventeen of an epileptic seizure. President Washington himself died of what is now generally curable: quinsy. Will doctors a hundred years hence say the same about epilepsy, brain trauma? Perhaps, if Ingstrom and his generation are successful.

The doctor has only a few more moments of quiet before his wife will return with her urgent gossip. He closes his eyes and addresses himself not to medical mysteries or their architectural solutions, not to the plight of boys like Fritz Schmidt, not to the pile of letters that awaits him, and decidedly not to the looming topic of orphans—but instead, to a moment of rest.

Chapter Sixteen

LETITIA'S LEAVING MAKES EVERY DAY seem like Amy's birthday. All of the women on ward fifteen—the attendants, the patients—are kind to her all of the time now, as careful with her as if she'd been the one knocked down and beaten at the picnic. The Norwegian woman draws her aside, mornings, to rebraid her hair and, at every meal, the others quarrel over seats at her table. But this is the up-side of a teeter-totter and Letitia is the down-side, locked away on one of the worst wards. It was Amy's idea that Fritz should post the letter; it's Amy's fault that Letitia became *frenzied*, had *delusions*. The doctor's strange words: *periodic mania*. What does he say about Amy?

The doctor permits Amy to return to the greenhouse the Wednesday after the picnic, but Fritz won't come near her. Mr. Schmidt puts her outside, weeding, with a group of women from ward nine. She doesn't remember them—her memories of that ward are of the Walking Skeleton's unpredictable commands—but they're welcoming enough. On her off days from the greenhouse, she files with her wardmates to the chapel, where they sit at long tables with women from the better wards and sew aprons for the orphans out West. It's a project invented by the doctors' wives. All three of the wives work at the front of the room on these days; they smile and stitch; the old doctor's wife waves when she sees Amy. All three wives have spoken to the sewing group about orphans and their plight. Round Mrs. Meijer even displayed a pair of orphans, who hid behind her and wept while all the women stared or cried out. These are the children Amy glimpsed at the picnic, two tiny girls, not ill (not yet), but motherless, fatherless. They fret and cry when brought to the evening programs, and Dr. Meijer must carry them out, one on each stout shoulder. They will live here until they're grown—longer, maybe—and Amy has been here now for eight months. Where will she be when those little girls are eighteen? Sometimes their crying makes her eyes sting.

The old doctor hasn't forgotten that he promised to take Amy to see Letitia, but for days he shakes his head: she's not settled in yet. Let's wait just a bit longer. And then one sewing day, after checking Amy's pulse and ears and all the rest, he sits down beside her.

Your friend has asked for you, he says. Are you ready?

Amy's legs tingle, but she nods her head.

You've done very well lately, Miss Underwood, and I don't like to expose you to what might be upsetting. Miss Olsen is calm now, but she's not at all remorseful.

I know, says Amy. I would like to see her.

The doctor promises to come back for her after dinner and continues on to the other women. If he checked Amy's pulse again, he would find it racing.

She reaches into the pocket of her apron for her daguerreotype, her cold, still boy. She's never seen one of the back wards, though she's heard stories of them. They are filled with raving lunatics; there's filth everywhere, and the women are locked up naked in chains. Incredible stories, but…there are women in this place who are very wild. Letitia, at the picnic, was very wild. What is she now?

Amy rubs her thumb across the molded leather of the boy's case. The women with Letitia at the Valentine's dance were from a bad ward, ward five. The woman with the scar across her face, the woman with missing fingers. Their ward is the next worse than Amy's—and it didn't seem so very bad. Letitia might be on ward five again, again the star of the show. Amy calculates by the mantle clock: four hours from now, she will know. She will have made her visit, or the visit will have been cancelled. If she were to take a fit suddenly or sound the fire alarm, the day would be too disrupted for a visit. If she were to bolt into the woods during the morning walk, they would have to devote the morning to catching her. But then she might wind up on ward five anyway.

The doctors finish their rounds; Lil gathers the women for their walk. The daily traipse around the grounds—Amy forcing herself to stay in line—the daily newspaper, read aloud. Amy cannot eat at dinnertime; she slips her meat to the woman seated beside her and tents her napkin over her new potatoes. The potatoes were dug from plants she and Letitia handled; she can't bear to slice through their soft skins. Letitia seemed well, most days at the greenhouse. Amy will see her in a different state soon. *Soon* comes nearer and nearer as the dishes are cleared, the rest hour endured, the others sent off to the sewing circle. Amy sits frozen on the sofa, half-praying that she's been forgotten, but Lil stays back to wait with her. Lil straightens books on the occasional tables, nips dead fronds from the ferns.

Give Letty my regards, she says. Tell her we look for her to come back. She beats the cushions surrounding Amy and her long face is grooved and sad. Lil is someone who keeps autograph books;

she's someone who doesn't forget. She hasn't forgotten Klara, even if she never mentions Klara's name. The two of them looked as much alike as sisters with their strong jaws and gold hair shot with grey. Maybe they were sisters. This isn't a question to ask now, not with Lil sweeping furiously and then tracking back through her own dirt piles. She only stops moving when the old doctor arrives. Then, she wipes her face of dust and sweat and gives him a message: Please tell Miss Olsen we miss her, sir.

The doctor leads Amy through the door marked no admittance at the north end of the hall. Beyond the service stairs is ward seventeen, the very worst women's ward in the hospital. Those women come only rarely to the evening programs; they're kept in the back row if they're brought to Sunday services. Amy's knees quiver. Letitia hasn't appeared in the evenings or on Sundays; can she really be on seventeen? But the doctor turns, taking her down a flight. He pauses at the door to ward eleven. There's a steady din already in Amy's ears.

You will find that the accommodations here are not what you're used to. The doctor smiles at her. There isn't a visiting parlor or a dayroom, so you'll meet Miss Olsen in the dining room. I'll wait in the corridor—so as not to agitate Miss Olsen by my presence—and an attendant will keep watch. When you're done, I'll be there to take you back. Are you ready?

Amy nods. The doctor unlocks the door, and the two of them step over the threshold.

No one rushes up to them or falls upon them—as Amy had most feared. No one appears at all. Amy stays close to the doctor as he relocks the door. The rooms opposite the firedoor are all shut tight like her own attendants' rooms are during the day. When they step around the joint of the hallway, into the main corridor,

Amy sees that every single door is shut. She can hear women cry-ing or crying out; their sounds echo off the plain, bare floors. Amy shies away from the barred windows set high in some of the doors. She doesn't want to see these women, or worse, let them see her. The rooms on this ward are cages, but cages can break. The air reeks like a privy and like wet, rotting wood.

The doctor draws Amy forward by the elbow, guides her slowly down the narrow throat of the corridor. Ahead, the hall widens, brightens; heavy wooden furniture is ranged opposite a bay win-dow. There's nothing soft or comfortable here. But Letitia has been in the crib, she's been fed with the tube. Her stomach has been cut open and sewn shut. What's a hard-backed chair to any of that?

Amy lets the doctor show her into the dining room. It looks like the dining room on her ward—except that the dish cabinet is front-ed with wire mesh, not glass, and the windows are uncurtained. She sits down at one of the tables, facing the door. The edge of the table is covered in curved gouges. The doctor leaves; Amy touches the boy, solid in her pocket. The gouges, she sees, are teeth marks.

In a moment, there's noise outside the door. Go on in and see your friend, a woman says loudly. She speaks as though to a child, but Letitia appears in the dining room doorway. Letitia stands still, seeming to sway, then pitches forward. A hulking attendant follows behind her. She pushes Letitia again: Don't be shy now, Letty. The attendant folds her arms and leans against the door-jamb, keeping them in.

Letitia sways for a moment longer, staring at Amy. She still wears one of her state-issue dresses but it fits more loosely now. Her face seems thinner, too—her cheeks sunken, her pretty eyes laced with red and popping from her face. She doesn't blink, her mouth doesn't move, her hands hang open at her sides. Amy watches those hands closely. Then Letitia comes toward her.

She wraps her arms around Amy's head before Amy can stand. Squeezes her tightly, the smell of her unwashed body filling Amy's nostrils. Just when Amy is about to squirm, Letitia releases the hug.

You're here, she says. She sits down opposite Amy as though it were meal-time back on their ward. They kept you away long enough!

I'm still on fifteen, Amy says slowly.

I know that! I meant I was surprised you hadn't come to see me sooner. Letitia toys with the edge of the table, frowning. They don't let me off the ward for anything…they don't even exercise the poor bats in here, except to let them out in a fenced-in yard.

What do you do all day? Amy tries to keep her voice low— though the big woman doesn't seem to heed them. In the doorway, she is pulling up her stockings, as though no one can see.

They had me resting and taking tonics after I bled so much, but just since yesterday, I've been getting 'round. Helping clean—that passes some time.

Blood had smeared Amy's white dress and Letitia's. Did Fritz hurt you?

That idiot? No. No, it turns out there was a baby coming. The fight knocked it loose. And *did* I bleed!

Amy shakes her head. What?

Letitia laughs. That's what I said! I thought they cut everything out of me back at Pontiac.

No, I meant…how can that be? Who—

I told you and told you: that old man comes after me at night.

He ain't been after me yet down here, but I keep an eye out for him. You should, too, now that I'm gone.

Amy presses her hands to her forehead, as dizzy as when the 'flu hit her. Letitia—

There's lots you don't see, but that don't mean it don't happen. Those doctors are bad sorts. What goes on down here—you wouldn't believe it.

But—

Fancy this. Letitia leans across the table. They have a girl down here younger even than you. Do you know what she does all day? She draws on the walls with her own shit! Letitia grins, sitting back. They give her a pallet of straw to sleep on and hose her room down three times a day.

Amy shudders, as she knows Letitia wants her to. *You* have a bed, though—don't you?

Just the same as yours, Miss Priss. The food, though…ugh! Vegetables and crackers, every blessed meal. Was it meat that made me a maniac?

I'm sorry, Amy says. No matter what else is true, there had been blood on Letitia's skirt. I shouldn't have given Fritz the letter.

Letitia laughs and waves her hand. I would've punched him sooner or later—I couldn't stand him staring at me all the time. It's against the law for old doctor to keep idiots here, did you know that? Sarah told me—that big one there that's watching us. He's snuck a couple of 'em back here, too, but they didn't last. By law, we ain't supposed to have to live with idiots. That means it's against the law for me to be on the back wards. That old dog ain't got any right to put me back here.

Amy shakes her head. You tried to kill someone.

Letitia grins. Not that time I didn't.

Amy closes her eyes. She concentrates on the weight of the boy, an assurance against her leg.

Letitia pats Amy's hand: Look here. She twists around in her seat so that the back of her head is facing Amy. Her fingers search through her hair. She parts it beneath her bun to show Amy two scabby bald spots, each the size of a dollar coin. That's what you done to me!

I'm sorry! Amy's throat gathers.

There's a lot of it broken off, too—I look like a regular witch. See? Letitia pulls the pins from her hair, and it is no longer the gleaming mantle of the May Queen but a ragged, dirty mass that tumbles over her shoulders. She rattles the hairpins together in her palm. Can you believe they still let me have *these*?

Amy glances at the big woman. Her head is craned out around the doorframe, looking after others down the hall. When Amy scrapes her chair against the floor, the attendant turns to watch them again.

It'll grow back soon enough, Letitia says. She piles her hair again on top of her head, jabbing the pins back in place. Nobody can tell unless I show them.

Amy's mouth is dry when she speaks. Do you need anything?

Anything *you* could bring me? No. But—Letitia smiles and leans forward—I'll tell you what I *would* like: that big Elmer Johnson who danced the maypole with me!

Amy shakes her head. I don't know him.

Did I think you did? None of the men come around much when you're with me, but don't they flock otherwise! If you see Elmer around the greenhouse, tell him to wait for me. Wouldn't *that* get to Ingstrom, if I had a regular beau!

He's gone, Amy says, though at his name, her knees still tremble. He's been gone for days.

Letitia frowns. Ingstrom? He was here only this morning. Likely you mean that lame doctor—I hear he's gone away.

Letitia, Amy says. You've known for weeks that *he* was leaving. Remember at the picnic? He said he'd take you with him for a treatment.

But Letitia grips her forehead. Right here, she says. You're giving me that headache again, right here.

Amy stands. It's a lie—this isn't how Letitia's headaches come on or when. But there's a note in her friend's voice that she's learned to heed.

The attendant catches Amy's movement: Do you want the doctor, miss?

Leave me be, says Letitia. I don't want that old dog. Come to cut holes in my head.

But Amy nods to the attendant and steps closer to her friend. Touching Letitia's shoulder, she feels her sharp bones beneath the thin dress.

I hope you'll be back on fifteen soon. Lil hopes so, too. And it doesn't matter about the letter to the temperance woman—the doctor's wife will help us.

Is that so? Letitia looks up at her, baring her terrible teeth. That old doctor ain't ever going to let me out. He cut a hole in my skull so that he can stick his pecker in it. See? See back here where he shaved my hair?

Letitia—

His old bitch likes it this way—doesn't have to pry open her legs anymore. Neither of them will let me go, ever. Letitia shakes her head, and her great eyes well. How am I going to last that long?

No—Amy begins, but the big woman is there beside her and

Letitia has turned away. I'll come back again, she says. We'll get jobs together in the wood-turning shop. We'll get positions at the bowl factory when we leave. But Letitia doesn't look at her, doesn't seem to hear. Letitia, Amy calls, stopping in the doorway. Letitia ignores her, running her finger over the marked edge of the table.

In the hallway, the old doctor smiles at Amy. He's calm, unbothered by this terrible ward. Used to it. Are you ready, Miss Underwood?

Amy nods but can't smile back. What if the old man does go after Letitia at night? Who is there to stop him, or care? He's the one who let Ingstrom near her. And Ingstrom has hurt Letitia with his promises and maybe in other ways, too. Her baby—was it a baby?—where did it come from, if not one of the doctors?

Amy trails behind the old doctor down the service stairs to the ground floor and through two unfamiliar wards, wards three and one. These wards are empty, with the women away sewing; the rooms are orderly and fresh: the best intermediate ward, the best convalescent ward. Wards for women who wouldn't attack each other—or wouldn't, anymore. Wards for women who may as well be at home, so different are they from Letitia. Does that difference keep them safe? The boy thuds against Amy's leg, and the old doctor glances over his shoulder now and then, to make sure she's following. Why does he keep women here on wards one and three? What do *they* need to be cured of? What does she? Amy cannot tell—she cannot tell!—whether the old doctor is kind or cruel. When they reach the chapel, Lil spots them at once, and the doctor simply says goodbye.

How did you find her? Lil asks, guiding Amy through the women to her regular sewing machine.

The doctor stands at the front of the room now, talking to his wife. Amy is free to tell Lil: Letitia will not change.

The doctor is in his office one morning, two weeks after his return from Washington, when the receptionist announces the arrival of the board of managers. They have brought, at last, their top candidate for the open position. The doctor puts aside his letters—he's not yet quite through his backlog of correspondences—and straightens his clothing. He's wearing his finest collar today; he has shined his shoes. He's eager to see which applicant has come.

Downstairs, he finds the managers' parlor readied for this visit, a silver coffee service gleaming on the sideboard and his two assistant physicians already shaking hands with a chubby young man. Not his Dr. Firestone, after all; not the girl-doctor. He relaxes his posture slightly to avoid the shoulder-ache that standing upright on a hard floor sometimes causes him. This young man is instead Dr. Chase, West's favorite. Despite his baby face, Chase has been two years already at the Northern Indiana Hospital, where he made a special study of epilepsy. Chase smiles now, presented to the doctor.

A great honor, sir. I've heard so much about this wonderful facility and your judicious management of it.

The doctor smiles stiffly; will this boy, too, emphasize his 'management' over his medicine? But he likes the looks of Dr. Chase: stringy yellow hair oiled across a pink forehead. This is not a doctor to fall in love with.

The receptionists pour coffee and everyone helps himself, milling around the central figure of Chase. He is married, they learn, with a son and daughter nearly the ages of Meijer's new charges. The doctor sees Meijer's broad face light up at this coincidence:

playmates would surely improve the spirits of the orphaned girls. One of the managers proposes to move the Chase family into Meijer's apartment, once the Meijers are settled in their new house in town. The second bedroom of that apartment has already been partitioned off into two small chambers. Everyone nods at the prudency of this plan; everyone acts as though the boy has already been appointed.

What medical questions are put to Chase are elementary in nature. The managers ask him ignorant questions about his work with epileptics: ought this class of patients have separate quarters? (Of course, the doctor thinks impatiently, as I have urged from the start!). What are the best treatments for their condition? (The bromides! thinks the doctor as Chase begins to explain this basic clinical fact). But the boy can hardly be blamed for the stupidity of the board. Nor can he be blamed, exactly, for his personal interests so neatly overlapping with West's; somehow they have discovered their shared fascination with Lincoln's brain injury. They launch into a game of arcane one-upmanship, during which everyone else consumes quantities of coffee. There is much raising of eyebrows across the cups, many pleased nods. This is the managers' man, then—and the doctor can see no obvious objections. If Chase is not as personally impressive as Ingstrom, not perhaps as original in his thinking, these limitations will no doubt better qualify him to be a third assistant physician. The doctor shouldn't be troubled to hear Chase plunging into the past with Dr. West, diagnosing a condition that cannot be proved or treated. His work with epileptics is, after all, grounded in the present.

The doctor has drifted from the conversation back to the coffee pot when one of the receptionists appears. We're fine, he tells her, hefting the full pot, but she shakes her head.

There's a woman here for you, she says quietly. In the receiving parlor, in mourning. She says she won't speak to anyone but you, sir.

At such a moment!—but he abandons his cup and saucer. Makes his excuses to the assembled men: a business matter, please continue without me. If he can resolve the visit quickly, he might be able to catch up with their tour of the hospital. And if this can't be done, he will hopefully have other opportunities to correct the managers' misrepresentations of his hospital.

He crosses the hallway. Did the receptionist ask for the woman's name? She did, but the woman wouldn't give it—and so the doctor announces himself to his guest by clearing his throat. The visitor gazes out one of the far windows. She is tall and tightly-corseted, with sleek blond hair knotted at the base of her skull and her front hair dressed in a high cloud of curls. When she turns away from the window, her face looks bloodless above her black dress.

The doctor had forgotten her husband, those months ago, but he recognizes her.

Mrs. Underwood, he says. Good morning.

Good morning. She doesn't move toward him. I have had no reply to my letters, she says. Seeing me, can you guess their subject?

He shudders: she is very cold, very angry. I am sorry, he says. Deeply sorry. I have been away—

Does no one answer the mail while you're away? She bites her lower lip, rolls her eyes to the ceiling. I did not like to send a telegram—there was no emergency, only the question of how to approach my child. How should I do that, sir?

He moves nearer to her, negotiating the clustered furniture between them. May I know what happened?

She looks again out the window. Pneumonia. Mr. Underwood

never entirely recovered from that 'flu. It kept coming back—and all the time he was staying in those filthy logging camps. The doctors up north…not once have those doctors helped my family. My husband died just after Amy's birthday.

I am very sorry. The doctor extends his hand toward her.

She doesn't take it; she doesn't even seem to see it. He did not want me to send for Amy—and, when he finally understood that he was in danger, there wasn't time. I did as he asked, but it is awful that she didn't know…still does not know.

You would like to tell her, I'm sure, now that you are come all the way here.

I would like to take her away. Mrs. Underwood faces the doctor. Her eyes are bright but not, he thinks, with tears. It may be that she has drugged herself—or it may be that she has more resolve than he would have guessed. What must I do?

Your daughter has made great progress in these last months, the doctor says. Even since your husband last saw her. I would not advise you to remove her just yet—and especially not after receipt of such a shock.

Mrs. Underwood nods. I thank you for your opinion, but I am Amy's guardian now. I do not wish that she should stay here. It torments me to think of her shut away without friends.

You mistake our hospital, if that is what you think of it, says the doctor. Miss Underwood is well-liked here and has done very good work this spring in the greenhouses. I expect she could be ready to leave by the end of the summer.

And yet, sir, I will not leave her here. I do not think you could make a legal case for retaining her against my wishes—and I hope you will be good enough not to try. She and I have only each other now.

The doctor reaches again for Mrs. Underwood's gloved hand, this time managing to catch it. I am very sorry, ma'am. Of course I would not make things more difficult for either of you. After you see her, if this is still your intention, I will honor it. Let me only remind you that, if you remove Miss Underwood unrecovered, we will receive her again within six months without requiring new bonds or certifying documents. After that, the process for admission must be initiated anew.

Thank you for the information, says Mrs. Underwood, pulling her hand from his grasp. It is not necessary to say more. If you would bring Amy to me or tell me how to find her, I would be greatly obliged.

Of course. Please make yourself comfortable. I'll be back soon. The doctor bows, and Mrs. Underwood gestures at him limply, as if disgusted. I am very sorry, ma'am, he says again. She doesn't bend, braced upright by her brutal corset.

The doctor strides quickly from the room, his blood moving hot and fast in his addled head. It is a damnable oversight on his part that has allowed this news to take him by surprise! He has lost track of one of the patients who has been most on his mind—how? If this has happened, what vital pieces of news has he overlooked concerning the other seven hundred? And now, walking, it's as though his feet are also out of his control, lifting up and down without sufficient forward momentum; he positively staggers once out of Mrs. Underwood's line of vision. Does he catch his toe on a loose tile or turn too quickly, vertiginously? Or is it mental confusion that overwhelms him, causing his legs suddenly to buckle?

The doctor stumbles into the wall, his left knee hitting the floor. His vision is spotted, sounds suddenly compound in an indistinct rush. The voices, the clinking cups, something like music from a distant room. It pulls him, that music, pulls him, lulling and lovely, not quite decipherable…but no! The melody resolves into the hum of the basement trolley system, clear and flat now that his ear is against the floor. He's snapped back to himself by distinct thoughts: of Miss Underwood, Dr. Chase, the hard tile against his cheek.

The doctor blinks, scattering the black spots to the periphery of his vision, blinks rapidly to clear his eyes as he draws himself up onto one of the club chairs lining the corridor. He hangs his head between his knees. No pain or shortness of breath: not a heart attack. Fingers and toes flexing: not a stroke. No real muscular derangement. A simple swoon, then, a loss of blood—brought on by the shock of his own incompetence! He tries to focus on his breathing, on returning his systems to normal, but the refrain of self-reproach is thunderous. It's always been his practice to assign funeral announcements the lowest priority—those black-bordered missives that arrive at the hospital so steadily. But in the weeks that he's been back, how is it that he hasn't even noticed the Underwood return address? Why hadn't he delegated some of his letter-writing—why but simple stubbornness, having always been able to manage the load alone, in the past? He draws deep lungfuls of air, daubs his forehead with his handkerchief. Anyone in charge of so much must have such moments. It's impossible to be perfectly in control of everything. And yet hadn't he felt invincible at this time last spring…and the springs before and before?

Meijer pops his head out of the managers' parlor. Seeing the doctor, he hurries to his side. What happened? he asks quietly, loosening the doctor's tie. I thought I heard something drop. Have you fallen? May I take you upstairs?

The doctor shakes his head, pushes away Meijer's huge hands. It's nothing. I'm likely overstimulated—two cups of coffee already! And I'm surprised, very surprised. Nathan Underwood has died— the lumber agent from up north? The widow is here to see about her child.

Meijer draws his hand over his broad face, surely feeling, as the doctor does, the bad timing of this news. Let me go for her.

No, says the doctor. At this hour, the child is in the greenhouse. The air, the walk—they'll do me good. Make my excuses, please, to the managers and to Chase. And see to Mrs. Underwood while I'm gone.

Of course. Meijer pats him on the shoulder, then bends lower. And since you've mentioned him…how do you like our new colleague?

He has his youth to recommend him. The doctor laughs. Nothing to sneeze at, as I begin to see.

You'll outlast us all, says Meijer, patting him once again. The doctor manages not to flinch under his colleague's kind but heavy hand.

Amy nudges her trowel into the soil, leans against the resistant roots of another dandelion. Sometimes she isn't patient enough to work those roots free; sometimes she hurries down her rows, snapping off the visible parts of weeds, leaving the roots to regrow. But whether she's careful or hasty, there's always another row ahead of her and no friend to share the work. She's in the field with strange women, and Letitia is locked inside the hospital. Letitia will not change.

She walks to the water bucket more often than she needs to, taking deep drinks to pass the time. No one goes with her or shares jokes. She drinks until she needs the privy. They're working at the far end of the field today, where it's quicker to duck into the woods than to walk back down the long slope to the barns and the outhouses there. The new leaves are bright and small, just unfurled, but already thick enough to screen her at a few paces beyond the treeline. She gathers up her dress and underskirt, lets down her drawers. Squatting, she peers out at the other women bent over their work. No one sees her or guesses what she's doing as she watches them through the leaves. The soft air blows under her skirt, over her skin. She finishes urinating and holds her crouch. No one is looking for her. No one misses her and won't, until the midday break. The woods spread out behind her, alive again.

She pushes through last year's damp, fallen leaves, her hands outstretched to the low branches as she climbs the hill that steepens beyond the field. The trees are friends she's missed. They've waited for her while she sat for all these months shut up behind the hospital's windows, or circled the lane under the attendants' watch. She clasps the sharp, low branches, tugging them as she goes. Their clutch draws blood from the healing scratches on her hands. Like the Walking Skeleton, she bleeds from her palms. She licks away that trace. Her blood is a reminder of Letitia, not of any holy mission. Letitia wild with anger because Ingstrom betrayed her. Letitia *frenzied* because Fritz failed them. Amy failed; that's what this blood means. But she's free now. All along, has it been this simple?

She follows the crest of the hill as it curves behind the hospital's yellow buildings. There are two sides to this hill, not like the bluff at home; she could throw herself down either side without being hurt. She turns her back to the hospital. For a moment, her knees waver, unwilling to plunge. Run, fall, catch: she closes her eyes, feeling those long-ago hands. Reminding herself of that thrill—then letting go. Running faster, faster with every stride, leaping to keep her balance on leaves still wet with snowmelt. Her skirts tangle in deadfall, and she slips, slides between saplings and thick trunks. Throws her arms finally around a slender tree and laughs, breathless, as she swings to a stop. Catching herself rather than being caught. At the bottom of this hill, at the base of the next, she crouches, panting. These hills might go on forever. She will run until she drops.

Letty? someone calls. Letty—wait up!

A man's voice. Rising, she sees a man coming up the narrow valley behind her, his face not familiar yet in the dappled light. A patient, by his clothes, a tall man walking fast. Her footsteps must have been as loud as his now are in the dead leaves. She touches her head, the kerchief that covers her hair and confuses him. She begins to walk away—to run.

Letty? The man closes the distance quickly and grabs her by the shoulders. I been waiting for you every day, girl. Don't play games.

He turns her to face him, and it is *him*—her father's man who held her by the lakeshore. Tall and broad and clean-shaven now, wearing a shirt and vest instead of flannel. But even so, he's followed her here.

No! she shouts, pulling away.

Oh. The man's tanned forehead furrows as he draws his hands back. You? Those hands hang between them, huge and calloused. I been watching for Letty.

Amy shakes her head. This is her father's man or one just like him; this is the man who danced with Letitia at the maypole—or maybe not.

Letitia's on a back ward now.

I heard that. After what happened at the picnic. I like a girl with some fight in her. He takes a step nearer to Amy. Did she send you?

Amy shakes her head, backing away.

You come back here on your own? He grins at her. Were you looking for somebody?

No! Amy says, backing more quickly.

Slow down, girl. I ain't going to hurt you. You come back here just like we always do, so I figured…. Well, why else would you be in the woods? You ain't running away, are you?

No, Amy whispers. I don't know. Do you have whiskey?

Whiskey? The grin grows across his big face. Might be I've got some stashed near abouts. Is that what you like?

Amy nods.

Reach through here first. He unbuttons his pants. Go on.

No—

He grabs her wrist, dragging her the few steps toward him. Shoves her hand through his open pants flap. Feel that? Give a tug on that, girl, if you want whiskey.

She's pressed tight to his chest, suffocated by his smell of sweat and tobacco, and the smooth firmness that he forces her to touch is what came so near her at the lakeshore. She balls her fist against it. There are tramps in these woods, Letitia said. Would a tramp help her, if she screamed? A sound leaves her mouth, not loud enough, and the man presses her down to her knees.

There it is, he says. It is right in front of her. Her loose hand claws at her throat.

Hello? someone calls. Who's there?

Footsteps again in the leaves, and the lumberjack steps away from Amy, his hands covering his open pants. Shh, he tells her. Just stay still.

But another man is coming, another man is close by in the woods, and Amy scrambles to her feet, running. Running down the valley, through low scrub, over downed trees. Running until those thunderous feet are behind her again, and the lumberjack's great arms seize her, stopping her. I got her, doc, he shouts, as he swings her around to face the other man. Familiar at first glance, even in the shifting light. White-haired, trim, frowning beneath his great white moustache. The old doctor, too, come into the woods, come after women, coming closer and closer.

I'm here for Miss Underwood, the doctor had told the attendant overseeing the women's field crew. His embarrassment—his horror!—over the whole affair had steadily increased as they searched the fields, the greenhouse, the barns without finding her. Mrs. Underwood's blue glare hardened in his imagination with every passing minute. Meanwhile, his sense of competency shriveled. Amy Underwood isn't a particularly difficult patient, and yet her case in this one day has revealed multiple failings in his superintendency. Finally, one of the field workers had remembered something: Last I saw, she was relieving herself in them woods.

And so the doctor found himself tramping up and down the hills, bruised knee burning, weak lungs laboring. He didn't want someone else to find her, not any of the many others also combing the woods. He wasn't so foolish as to compound his folly by searching alone, but he was determined, if he could, to fix this himself.

Hearing her voice, he'd thought the problem solved, and he'd hurried toward her, quickened by relief on this terrible morning. But she'd bolted as he neared; she stands before him now only because Elmer Johnson managed to catch her. Johnson is a convalescent patient, one of the febrile cases, maybe—or was his a case of simple mania? The doctor is grateful for the man's help, though he doesn't remember enlisting him to the search crew. Another disturbing lapse of memory. And now the girl is wide-eyed and quaking. What triggered this relapse, this urge to run? Does she somehow sense the bad news waiting for her?

My dear, he says—and, at the words, she shrieks. A rough, crow-like sound, as aggressive as it is fearful. Even from three paces, he can see that her pupils are dilated; she seems close to hyperventilating. Could she be a hysteric, after all? If you will calm yourself, Mr. Johnson can let you go. I've been searching for you.

Get away! She strains against Mr. Johnson's grip. I don't want your old prick!

There now! says Johnson, shaking her. The mouth on her, doctor—she said the same to me.

Mr. Johnson! The doctor steps closer, and the girl shrieks again. Mr. Johnson, do *not* handle Miss Underwood so. And Miss Underwood, of course I am not here with sexual designs—as you would surely realize, if you would calm yourself. Your friend Miss Olsen makes such claims against me, I know, but they are untrue: delusions, Miss Underwood, as I have explained, as we have discu—

He came after me, she shouts, thrashing. *Him!* He came after me with his prick like he came after Letitia! I saw it; I saw it!

Dr. Ingstrom? Will you still not say his name aloud?

No! Her voice is a broken wail. This one, *this* one! He's the one!

Mr. Johnson? The doctor shifts his gaze to the big man, who's gone red in the face, sweating. It's a more satisfying explanation of Miss Olsen's pregnancy than the doctor himself has been able to reckon…but this is the man he asked to catch Miss Underwood for him; this is a man he mistook for a helper. He shakes his head briskly. Mr. Johnson—

Not me, says Johnson. Not me. He rattles Miss Underwood again, viciously.

Mr. Johnson! Let go of the girl at once. You will return to ward eight. Mr. Johnson!

The man pushes Miss Underwood away from him. They're all lying whores! he shouts. All of 'em!

Mr. Johnson! But the big man charges off, up the next hill, away from the hospital, toward the forest beyond and the country beyond that. Johnson bolts as heedlessly as a runaway horse, and it seems unlikely that one of the other searchers will be able to catch him. Here's an elopement to add to the day's embarrassments. In the man's running, however, one mystery is solved—that mystery whose solution could not possibly have been Ingstrom…and yet the doctor *had* wondered, ever since he learned from Meijer of Miss Olsen's miscarriage.

The doctor turns now to Miss Underwood, scrambling in the leaves. Are you hurt, child?

No, she says. No! when he reaches out for her. She rises to a crouch, wrapping her arms around her knees.

I'm very sorry. The apology is an echo of others he has made so lately to the girl's stepmother. Very sorry that this man frightened you. Can you tell me how it happened, how you came to be in the woods with him?

She shakes her head. She has raked her throat with her nails, he sees—or Johnson scratched her. Her fingers hover there now. He checks an impulse to restrain her hands; he must not frighten her again.

Please, Miss Underwood. Will you come with me back to the hospital? He squats down on his own groaning knees. I'm your friend. I hope you know that. Miss Breithaupt, my wife, the Schmidts: we're all your friends.

Then why are you here? she demands. Why did you come after me like that one did?

I was looking for you, he says simply. You were missed from the fields. If you listen, you'll hear others still searching.

She nods but won't look at him. You never went after Letitia, like she said?

No.

That man did! Miss Underwood presses her face against her knees. He came after me! Her voice is muffled by her dress.

I'm very sorry for it. I would like to take you back to the hospital, where you can rest.

The searchers move closer, or the wind carries their words; the girl raises her head, listening to her name. He follows her gaze as it moves from tree to tree. Looking for the search party, or looking at the trees that surround them? The woods are coming back to life at last; the mid-day sun filters down around them. Her eyes travel over the brush, and his do, too, finding sprouts of green here and there among the grey leaves. Trilliums coming out of their dormancy. But along with these signs, as she sees, as he sees, are other evidences. A flurry of feathers, scattered. A charred log. An empty bottle.

Will you come back to the hospital with me? he asks quietly.

Her body sways, and he wouldn't be able to catch her, if she were to run. Instead, at last, she nods.

Chapter Seventeen

BACK ON THE WARD, LIL washes Amy's face and hands and helps her into a fresh dress. Call for me when she's ready, the doctor had said before leaving. Ready for what? Amy asked. Lil only tells her that a visitor has come.

My father again? Amy sits over a cold lunch sent up from the kitchen: ham and rolls, applesauce. She just missed the mid-day meal. Her wardmates, sitting with Miss Ellsworth in the day room, find reasons to pass the dining room and peer in. Concerned about her—or only curious? Lil has treated her scratched neck with salve. Why didn't the doctor say so?

I don't know, miss. Did you need butter?

Amy shakes her head. She isn't hungry; the pink slab of ham makes her stomach clench. There was a man in the woods, she tells Lil. She pushes her plate away.

It's all right, says Lil. You're all right now.

I've seen him before, says Amy. By the lake, she would like to say, back home, up north—but is this true or *delusional?* He danced the maypole with Letitia.

Lil passes her a buttered roll. Letitia knows how to handle herself around men—but you're better off staying away from that sort.

Eat a bite of this. What were you doing in the woods, anyway?

Relieving myself. Amy pushes her applesauce into a mound.

Doctor said you were way back behind the laundry. That's a long ways from the fields.

He followed me! says Amy. He thought I was Letitia.

Lil looks at her steadily. Just keep your distance from the rough ones, miss—you remember that once you leave here, too.

The hills roll away from the hospital and that man is hiding somewhere among them—or other men are…. Amy puts her hand on her stomach. I think I have the 'flu again.

Doctor just checked you over. I'll ring down for him while Mrs. P. braids up your hair. Do you want to keep your photo with you, now that you're not off to work?

Where am I going? Amy asks again. Did the temperance woman come?

Like I told you, there's a visitor. That's all I know.

The doctor tells Amy nothing more as he takes her downstairs. She keeps her hand closed around the boy. When they reach the receiving room, the doctor gestures for her to go first—but she stops on the threshold. Inside, sitting on the settee as if she never left, is Amy's stepmother. Rose.

Rose rises upon seeing Amy. *What did you do*, she'd shouted in August, *what did you do?* She'd forced Amy to drink purgatives the last time a lumberjack held her. She'd locked Amy up, sent her away. Amy backs toward the door; how can Rose already know? How is she here already? But the doctor stops her: Steady, he says. Hear why she has come.

And Amy sees then that Rose's eyelids are red. Rose's black dress makes the stains under her eyes seem darker. Black crepe doesn't suit Rose at all, despite the dress's fine jet trim and narrow sleeves. Amy knows about these things now, about what the magazines are urging for this season—just the sort of pleated underskirt that Rose is wearing. But not in black. A dull pain clogs Amy's throat: there's only one reason for a black dress in the middle of May.

Amy, her stepmother says. She crosses the ugly rug and holds out her arms. She smells as always of lavender; her torso is still rigid when she pulls Amy against her. Her stepmother takes Amy's hand and holds it tightly, drawing her farther into the room.

You missed my birthday, Amy says.

Her stepmother nods. I am very sorry not to have sent word to you then. But your father—

Father said he'd visit and we'd have supper in town. Were you too sick to come?

Her stepmother shakes her head. Amy, let me tell you.

Amy pulls her hand out of her stepmother's grip. He's dead.

Her stepmother raises a black-edged handkerchief to her mouth and turns her face away. She nods. He had a very serious case of the 'flu back in winter, and he did not recover as he should have, never got over his cough or regained the weight he'd lost. He never quite recovered, and then he took sick again—it happened a week or so after he saw you here. His lungs could not bear it. She sits down again on the settee, pulling Amy beside her.

I had the 'flu, too, Amy says.

I did not know, says her stepmother. I am sorry—oh, Amy, I am so very sorry!

Amy lets her stepmother cling to her hand, so tightly that her rings pinch Amy's flesh. Her father is dead. Her mother has almost always been dead. Her mother is a flat homely face in a wedding photo, and now her father is dead and flat, too. She already knows how it feels to be without him—here, and in the house up north. Will it feel different now?

It will be all right, says her stepmother, patting Amy's face with another black-bordered handkerchief. I've come to take you home.

That house is a rattling trap. Amy looks to the old doctor seated opposite them. She doesn't want to live in that house up north, hemmed in, always nervous. Afraid now to go into the woods; afraid to stay inside.

I don't want to go.

The doctor glances at her stepmother. I think it's a good sign that you have such feelings, my dear—feelings of attachment to this place. You were indifferent to many things when you arrived.

Rose squeezes her hand. I have closed up the Petoskey house. We will go back to Ionia, for now, at least, and figure out our way from there. We will have help there if I am sick—or if you are.

There were other girls, when they lived downstate; the cold wasn't so terrible there; the lakes and trees were smaller. There was a lumberyard, before—but it's sold and gone. Amy thinks of the man who bought out her father. She shakes her head. You'll marry—

I will not! The traces of Rose's lost accent come out on 'will'—a German 'v'—as happens when she's especially serious. If we cannot bear to live together, we will find some other way. I will not force you to stay with me if you hate to. And, if you are ill, there is a private hospital being built at Flint—

I won't go to *him*! Amy shouts. She jumps to her feet.

No, my dear, says the doctor, stretching his hand toward her. A different place. A small hospital like a ward unto itself, like one of our cottages—not a surgical clinic. Not Ingstrom. Think, too, of all the schools and seminaries downstate, where you might go when you're ready.

Amy shakes her head. I won't go to school. But she can imagine the kind of place that she might like—where girls keep autograph books and help each other with their sewing. Where girls look like Lil or Miss Ellsworth. Another sob nearly chokes her. No one at a school would look like Letitia.

My wife will not forget you, says the doctor. You must write to her regularly after you leave. If you ever should need anything, you have only to ask.

Your cousins—*our* cousins—look forward to seeing you again. Won't that be nice, Amy?

Amy shakes her head. She's still not the pretty orphan girl from the book, from *Eight Cousins*. Not a prize that anyone would protect or fight to keep. Nor was her stepmother such a child. Her stepmother was an orphan, too, named Rose, but not tended like the story-girl. Her stepmother was sent alone to a strange country and married off early to a widow. Now, all of that is over. The trees are gone in front of the house up north; the piano is quiet; her father's dog will have gone mad with waiting. Where are the horses? Quince—

Shh. Her stepmother draws Amy against her shoulder, rubs her back: He loved you very much.

Amy pulls away. Do *you* want me to go? she asks the doctor. She's only on ward fifteen; there are so many other wards that she is supposed to pass through before she is cured. And she has had a shock. Such shocks as she had today often bring women to the hospital. How can she leave?

The doctor smiles. I want all of my patients to leave.

But—she thinks of the Walking Skeleton, appearing and disappearing—I could come back?

The doctor nods his head. The hospital will always be here, of course.

Amy closes her eyes. The boy in her pocket is not a comfort now. He's a reminder of the doctor's wife, who she will miss, a reminder of the other photograph in her room upstairs. Both her father and mother now as unreachable as this boy who she will never know. This dead boy. She draws the case from her pocket and opens it. Her tear-stained face is mirrored on his. He's supposed to help her be good. Can he?

Would you like to speak to my wife? the doctor asks. Or to any of your other friends?

You should, says her stepmother, standing. Say goodbye to all of them. I am staying at a hotel in town. I will come back for you tomorrow morning—send for me if you want me sooner. Things will not be what they were before, Amy—you may trust to that. She bends from the waist and takes Amy's head in her hands, kissing her. With your hair braided so, you are very like your grandmother Boehm, who raised us. You and I are left to each other now.

Rose waves away the doctor's attempt to show her out. Her black silk hisses as she brushes through the furniture and from the room. The doctor takes a chair opposite Amy, watching her.

I am very sorry, he says quietly. Shall I take you back upstairs?

Amy shakes her head. I would like to go to the greenhouse.

Wouldn't you rather go back to the ward and see your friends? Or I could take you to my wife—or to the chaplain?

But Amy shakes her head again. When her father was alive, she was made to stay here at the hospital; now that he's dead, she will be released. There's the whole world out there for her to feel adrift in. One last time she would like to feel strong and useful, before she is taken away.

Tonight will be a celebration of Dr. Chase—to whom the managers have already offered the position of third assistant physician. Engaged all afternoon with the Underwoods, the doctor missed the chance to debate the matter. His vote wouldn't have mattered, in any case. The others were unanimous in their favor, and so Chase accepted the appointment without having had even five minutes of conversation with his new superintendent. Now, the boy has returned to his hotel in town, the very same hotel where Mrs. Underwood is presently staying. What different attitudes toward the hospital are housed tonight under that roof! Mrs. Underwood sees this place as a prison; what can Chase really know of it, having spent all day in the company of its dullest boosters? Chase will return in a matter of hours, wife and children in tow. They are a brave little family, come all the way from Indiana without knowing what they would find. Come all that way, moreover, upon the conviction that they would be invited to stay.

The doctor adjourns to his private study for the several hours leading up to dinner; the doctor is exhausted. His left knee is swollen and throbbing now, his conscience throbbing too with the terrible bruises inflicted by this day. He deserves Mrs. Underwood's anger, and worse. The widow put on a brave face in front of her stepdaughter, only glaring at him when the girl was looking elsewhere. How could he blame her? Mrs. Underwood had remained steadfast in her decision to remove the girl. Perhaps she is equal to the task of raising her. The widow's nerves seem now the very opposite of what they were in September. And the girl herself has grown more accountable during her time at the hospital, has developed what seem to be real affections for things and people. She's gone through those phases of shallow pretension that mark pubescent insanity—as when she tore Bible pages into strips or tried to join the Temperance movement—but of course, such freaks are not unknown among the sane during pubescence. And the doctor must share the blame for Miss Underwood's outbursts, her thieving, having not sooner arranged a more productive outlet for her energies. He must bear the blame for what happened to her today in the woods, and for what nearly happened. When he thinks of it, the doctor's knee twinges more sharply.

He limps from his chair to the sofa, stretches his leg. He should return to his office downstairs, make his way to the bottom of that treacherous stack of mail before another disaster strikes…but the day has taken much out of him already and will yet take more. He thinks briefly of the wine of coca—thinks he must throw away that bitter temptation!—but as soon as his head meets the cushion, all thought is gone.

Jim, someone says, shaking him by the shoulders. Jim, you're snoring to wake the dead.

Bending over him, the excess flesh of his red face distorted by gravity, is Bertold Humphries.

What are you doing here? The doctor sits up quickly, grimacing when his knee spasms.

There's hospitality! Humphries settles his bulk into the doctor's own customary chair, hitching it nearer to the couch. The board invited me, seeing as I had a hand in the search for the new doctor. I didn't mean to startle you.

The doctor nods and wipes his eyes with his handkerchief. He's dazed, drowsy; had he really been snoring? He is also resentful, as ever, of the big man's liberties.

You must forgive my informality.

Since when have I minded that? We'll have enough ceremony later on. But it isn't the prospect of a good dinner that brings me here, if you can believe it, or even the company, which, Lord knows, I miss. I came to speak to you. Humphries draws from under his arm a large leather folio. These are the plans for the neurological clinic.

The doctor manages not to fall off the couch in his eagerness to receive the folio. Inside its rich cover is a stack of immaculately-drawn architectural plans: full-color renderings of the clinic from the outside and from above; plans for the basement, first floor, and attic; cross-sections of the fireproof stairwells. The plans have been prepared by a Chicago firm whose name the doctor cannot help but recognize.

Humphries rises from the chair and plants himself on the sofa, close beside the doctor. See here, Jim, in the center—these are the surgeries and offices and such, and those of course are the male and female wings…these smaller rooms are nurses' chambers—Ingstrom means to have one nurse per patient around the clock.

Very costly, murmurs the doctor. To find and keep so many qualified attendants!

Yes, but bear in mind the small scale of the thing. The clinic will hold just twenty patients at a time, between those under observation, those undergoing surgery, and those convalescing. There will be—Humphries rummages for a drawing at the back of the pile—a guest cottage, for the patients' families. The idea is to devote just as much attention as possible to those patients admitted. It's a sound plan, medically-speaking, but I wonder about some of the arrangements.

The doctor turns each page carefully, the delicate vellum trembling in his hands. Construction is underway, isn't it?

Humphries snorts. We aim to break ground in June, but there's no telling when the thing will be finished—it grows like a weed. I haven't brought you the plan for Dr. Ingstrom's own house or the caretaker's cottage or the carriage house and etcetera, etcetera. But look here at these elevations, that's what I most wanted your opinion about. And the pitch of these roofs. After all the trouble we've had here, I want to take especial pains on that score.

The doctor squints at the architect's stylized handwriting, making out the measurements. It all seems in order. You have a well-drained site, I'm sure, with access to a clean water supply? And, as for materials—will you use your own good brick?

Ah— Humphries shakes his head. I'd offered to absorb the cost of shipping it by rail…but the boy wants to use stone instead. He finds it 'statelier.'

Surely not! The doctor twists his neck to see whether Humphries is joking, but the brickman's expression is stolid. He ought *of course* to use your fine yellow bricks or whatever is nearest and most economical. How can he think of doing otherwise! And, even if the exterior is stone, he ought by now to see what a great supply of brick he will need for the inner walls!

I can't say whether he understands any of that. Humphries leans closer. If you can believe it, he proposes to hang wallpaper in the patients' rooms.

No! Does he know the first thing about upkeep or sanitation? The doctor flips quickly through the plans, searching for the surgical facilities. He groans upon seeing them. Look at these angular corners—perfect traps for germs and filth! You must tell Ingstrom to round *all* of the corners in his operating rooms and to take care that the rooms' surfaces be covered in cement, tile, or enamel.

There seems to be plenty of natural light, which is prudent.... I wouldn't have been surprised, after what you've just said, to find the rooms outfitted with crystal chandeliers!

Well.... Humphries sits back, shrugs. He's extravagant enough to think of it. I've only had a peek at the plan for the doctor's own home, but this Mrs. Ingstrom-to-be is Corn's match for spending.

The doctor gapes. Is there already a new fiancé?

Humphries nods, pressing his lips together like an old lady's. Seems, all along, that dead gal had a sister—just as rich as the late Margaret and nearly as pretty.

As is so often true of such sisters, says the doctor, shaking his head. My wife will be inconsolable.

Humphries claps him on the knee—the bruised knee, but even so, the doctor smiles. It's good to see you, Jim. Good to have a laugh—like old times.

The doctor claps Humphries on the shoulder: remarkably, it *is* good to see the brickman—not at all like in old times.

I'll let you rest up a bit now. I'm expected upstairs to admire these foundlings of Meijer's. Tell your missus *I'm* still her beau, even if Ingstrom's off the market.

The doctor rearranges the plans to hand back to Humphries, but Humphries waves them away.

I had an extra set made up for you. Hang onto them, and, if you notice anything else amiss, let me know. Or toss them in the stove—as you prefer. I'll see you in an hour or so. The brickman stomps out, the doors rattling behind him.

The doctor swings his legs again onto the couch. Again, he removes the topmost drawing from the folio: *The Margaret L. Steele Neurological Hospital.* It's a handsome, healthful-looking building, with none of the silly gingerbread that the managers have insisted on adding to his hospital's new cottages. Such superfluous frills might be 'homey,' but they're a fire hazard and an embarrassment. Ingstrom's clinic will be entirely his own to outfit and manage as he wishes. To think of treating just twenty patients at a time! With so few to see to, how could one fail to succeed, and quickly? If the doctor had oversight of a mere twenty patients, surely his cure rate would be inverted: eighty percent instead of twenty. Surely, then, he would always be able to attend to things as he ought and not commit such a grave and indecorous error as he has in the Underwood case. He will not burn these lovely drawings but keep them in view, a reminder of the standard of care to which he, as superintendent, must every day recommit himself.

The officer's dining room is spectacle tonight, with all of the leaves fitted into the long table and spring blooms from the greenhouse spilling across the sideboards. For the first time in the hospital's history, a children's table has been arranged, too—at the head of the table, at the doctor's insistence. Chase's two towheads are a bit older than the Meijer orphans and markedly more hale; overhearing their conversation, the doctor decides that they are kind children, too. Have you ever been to a circus? they ask the little girls. What kinds of cake do you like best? He can't hear the orphans' answers, but glancing back, the doctor for the first time sees them smiling.

The six managers have so disrupted the balance of sexes that Chase is seated to the left of the doctor. The young man proves as amiable a conversationalist as his offspring. He was raised just over the Indiana border, educated at the Illinois College of Physicians and Surgeons. Chase discusses his own affairs modestly and he succeeds, unlike his predecessor, in asking questions without sounding combative. The doctor finds himself describing his own early career: his course of study at Penn, his years tending invalids at Bedford Springs, his hard campaign for the position at Kalamazoo.

From the beginning, I wanted to help the broadest range of patients, the doctor explains, but I found city hospitals rather too hectic and impersonal and the resort too removed from the rest of the medical field. Notwithstanding that I met my wife while installed there, the value of that work seemed insignificant compared to caring for the insane. I hoped to help those who were most vulnerable.

Chase nods. Then you've found asylum work rewarding? I've heard different opinions on that score, and being so new to the field, I haven't quite determined for myself.

The doctor shakes his head. I've sometimes found it the very opposite of rewarding: there are always more patients, every year, and more theories about how they should be treated. It's difficult to take satisfaction in those I *have* helped when so many more are suffering.

Of course…. Chase chews his meat vigorously, swallows before speaking. You specialized in melancholia while at Kalamazoo?

The doctor chuckles: the boy has done his due diligence, to have unearthed that dusty fact! All of us back then specialized in whatever was at hand. But I published several papers based on my observations and a series of case studies, too, on katatonia.

Circumstances also had much to do with my work on epilepsy…my circumstance of being lowest in rank at Northern Indiana. It was interesting work, to be sure, though so nearly hopeless. Dr. Chase shrugs. And what about now, sir—what do you consider your specialty?

Now…. The doctor pushes himself back slightly from the table, spreads his hands: Now my specialty is as broad as the moral treatment itself. I've been working for some time on a response to Dr. Weir Mitchell, arguing that the occupational therapies we pursue here are more efficacious than his rest cure.

The moral treatment! Chase smiles, shaking his head. It's been a long time since I've heard *that* phrase! Well, I hope my coming will afford you more time for your projects. You were very good this morning to endure my talk with Dr. West about Lincoln and physiognomy. But it didn't seem like you shared that interest. What are your hobbies, sir? I can see by looking at the grounds that horticulture might be among them.

The doctor looks down at the uneaten asparagus on his plate, grown by good Mr. Schmidt and his poor son Fritz. Arguably, the doctor's decision to let that boy work at the hospital set off this whole string of recent accidents. He shakes his head, focusing. Maybe the young doctor will bring fresh insights.

I leave hobbies to my wife. However, from the time I was young, I've been highly interested in the challenges of amentia, or feeble-mindedness, if you will. Michigan makes no provisions for those individuals' care, as you may know. They are, in fact, specially prohibited from hospitals like this one. I have written letters to the governor on that subject…and I've sometimes bent the rule and admitted patients whose circumstances were dire. But more must be done.

Hear, hear! Chase waves his butter knife, his round face animating. In Indiana, we've just established a School for Feeble-Minded Youth. The state hopes to train up its idiots and to take strict measures to control the hereditary taint, cut down on natural increase. The adult idiots remain at large in the general population, but plans are underway for *them*, too. Mental hygiene demands it, don't you think?

No, the doctor says bluntly. Certainly not.

He recognizes in his new colleague's language a god-like ideology that he abhors. Miss Olsen is just one victim of its flawed logic, suffering now from a failed oophorectomy and the paranoia it exacerbated in her. The doctor has heard Chase's language, too, from a certain faction at the superintendents' conference.

It is well to make special provisions for those with amentia, says the doctor, as we ought for any class of citizens with distinct needs—epileptics, say. And it would hardly be prudent, at any large custodial institution, to allow unsupervised interaction between the sexes. He closes his eyes briefly against the irony of *that* remark. But I do not think that the states or medical professionals should have the authority to sterilize anyone, for any reason.

The boy shakes his head. How are we to combat the problem of idiocy—or insanity, for that matter—without going after the hereditary causes? Should medicine sit by while such people propagate and marry? You wouldn't breed one of your cows, would you, if she were defective?

Breed a human? People are not cows, Dr. Chase, without aspirations or affections. Medicine should play *no* role in such matters, the doctor says firmly. That is what I believe. It is what this hospital practices.

I see. Chase smirks slightly, swallowing the last bite on his plate. And, of course, the cost of a sterilization program will be tremendous for Indiana. But tell me, in these letters you've written about the feeble-minded—what solution *do* you propose?

Schools, homes for the dispossessed. In truth, the doctor hasn't ever proposed any solutions, only documented the problem. Now, thinking of Ingstrom's clinic, he continues: I don't imagine a large institution such as ours would suit. I imagine the best situation would be a very small facility, home-like, where at most a dozen individuals could be cared for and educated.

Chase's brow furrows. The counties couldn't be trusted to manage such places properly, and the state would never invest that kind of capital. You can't imagine that idiots would be able to pay for their own care or that their families would be willing to?

The doctor shakes his head. I imagine, for example, a small farm, privately funded.

And run by?

By a doctor, the doctor says. He looks down at his plate. It's a notion of mine. One that I even consider for my retirement. His heart clamors: why not? But the word *retirement* sits strangely in his mouth, a foreign term, calling to mind only the dimmest of corresponding images.

The managers mentioned that you'd been in ill-health, says Chase. They said in a year or two there'd be a good chance of promotion for the third assistant physician.

For a *suitable* candidate, the doctor says, promotion could eventually be a possibility—eventually. Let's find out first whether you're suited to this work.

The receptionists begin reaching over everyone's shoulders, lifting away the last traces of dinner and presenting ample slices of rhubarb pie. Chase takes a great bite before turning to amiable Mrs. West, seated on his other side. The doctor tastes the tart filling—he's never cared for crust—and watches his wife. She's talking to Humphries about orphans; he can read her lips, even from across the table. Diana is filled with good intentions; is it possible that the hospital will not be the last recipient of them? He couldn't leave his hospital in the hands of a pitiless boy like Chase, but there are other young physicians in the world who subscribe to more enlightened principles of care. He read some of their résumés only lately. If Meijer means to resign, or if West should retire, the doctor could find a way to exercise more influence than he has heretofore on the search for their replacements. He could find a true heir to his superintendency, someone excited to oversee a place so large and shifting. Meanwhile, the woman in front of him clamors to take on more responsibilities. The doctor has resisted all these years the terrible intimacy and private rewards of family life. Might there yet be a compromise between Diana's dreams and his?

Through her last afternoon in the fields Amy tells no one that she won't be back. She works steadily, shaking her head when asked where she went earlier in the day, never venturing to the water bucket now. Mr. Schmidt assigns her to weed the cabbage beds. Doing so, she digs her fingertips deeper and deeper into the dirt, forcing grains far below her short nails, so that the hospital will be with her for a long time to come.

After the evening meal, Lil draws Amy aside: If you want to stay back from the entertainment, Miss E. can take the others and I'll sit with you. If you'd rather.

Amy shakes her head. This filing down the stairs, this assembling in rows, this looking around at all the other patients: she won't do these things again. This place will go on without her as it has without the Walking Skeleton or Letitia; it will forget her. She wants to remember it.

In the chapel, she sits beside Lil. The old doctor introduces Ingstrom's replacement, Dr. Chase, who Amy will never know. The new doctor has brought along with him a treat for their evening entertainment, a magic lantern show about the Great Chicago Fire. These pictures would be captivating any other night. Now, Amy cranes her neck to see if Letitia is there at the back of the room. But though the big attendant from ward eleven sits at the end of a row, blocking in a line of squirming women, Letitia isn't among them. Letitia isn't well enough to be here, or she doesn't want to leave her place on the bad ward. Letitia doesn't know that Amy is leaving, or why.

When the show is over, Amy files for the last time down the center aisle. The old doctor's wife stops her.

I had hoped especially to see you, says the old woman, breathlessly. To tell you how deeply sorry I am for your loss. Will you walk with me around the lane?

Now?

The doctor's wife nods. I would like to say goodbye.

When's the last time Amy was outside at night? She lets the old woman lead her from the chapel through the center lobby and out the hospital's great front doors. The pebbled lane gleams in the moonlight; their skirts are dark stains moving over the lighter ground.

I was older than you when my father died, says the doctor's wife. It was difficult, even though I was grown and married. My father meant a great deal to me, as I'm sure yours did to you.

He left me here, Amy says. The words tear at her throat.

But do you not think he did so for your own good? Now that you are leaving, do you think he was wrong to bring you here?

She shakes her head. I don't want to go.

No, my dear—that isn't what I mean, either. This is not a place for you to make your permanent home. But who among us wouldn't like some time away, now and then, from our regular lives…some time to scream, if we want to. The old woman throws back her head and lets out a small howl.

Amy laughs, but her throat is tightening again. *My stepmother won't like for me to act so.*

I understand she means to take you back to Ionia—where you have family? That will be very good, my dear. And the two of you will have means, I suppose, to set yourselves up or embark on a train tour…or to go abroad, perhaps.

Amy shakes her head. *I don't know what she'd like.*

Think then of what *you* would most like. The old lady squeezes Amy's hand. In coming here you had an opportunity to start over— it was forced upon you, I know, but you've made something of it, dear girl. I think you now have another such opportunity. I would give a great deal to be in your position. I dare to hope, even, that the doctor might consider leaving, with this new physician come at last.

Amy thinks of that pink face at the podium and shakes her head. *Who would take care of Letitia?*

My husband is not indispensable to the hospital, no matter if he thinks so. I think he begins to see another way. At the table to-night, I even heard him use the word retirement. And for my part, I would like to adopt a girl…a daughter.

I'm an orphan, says Amy.

The old woman squeezes her again. Your stepmother is alone now, too.

They circle around the lane. As on her first afternoon here, Amy cannot tell when they will stop or why they're walking. The doctor's wife shivers a bit in the cool breeze off the bay. Amy follows that lakeshore north to her father's empty house; she follows it south to Chicago and tries to peer past the blazing images from the lantern show. There must be hundreds of towns and cities along this lake. And there are a million places in the world that don't touch this lake or any other.

In front of them, the hospital is lit like a great boat at anchor, like a city unto itself. Amy tries to pick out her window. Who will be given her room when she is gone? Who slept in it before she did? She and the doctor's wife near the portico.

I will miss you, child, says the old woman. Miss Breithaupt will miss you very much, I think. You must remember her when you are gone.

Amy nods. *Forget me never.*

And I have this for you, too, which I hope will help you to recall the good times with your friend.

From her string satchel, the old woman draws a cardboard folder, square, the length of her hand. Inside, a round picture floats like a dark bubble against a white background. Amy brings it nearer to her eyes and sees it's a photograph of herself, bending over the transplanting table, and Letitia, opposite. Letitia's face is tilted toward the glass ceiling, her eyes closed; Amy can hear the click of her friend's stretching neck. She can smell the green shoots, the dirt, their sweat. This is how they looked, not so long ago. Two girls wearing rough aprons and handkerchiefs over their hair. They are small figures, grey and black—captured in profile, content.

The dim light spilling from the portico wouldn't harm even a daguerreotype, but Amy quickly closes the folder, presses it to her chest. How—?

The doctor gave me a box camera for Christmas. It requires a great deal of light to get good shots. A greenhouse is just the place to practice. You girls were so intent about your business that I'm sure you never saw me—and the pictures come out better that way.

Thank you, Amy says.

The old doctor and Lil are waiting for them in the foyer; they are visible now, through the sidelight windows, standing beneath the cheerful electric lights. Lil is waiting to take Amy for the last time to her room, and Amy lets herself sob—as the doctor's wife had let herself scream. No one in all the rest of the world has ever petted her or pried at her secrets—or loved her?—like Lil has.

The doctor's wife stops walking. Write to me, she says. She puts her arms around Amy.

Amy shakes her head. What would I say?

My dear, says the doctor's wife. You will have everything to say. You will have everything.

Amy closes her eyes. The bright after-image of the electric bulb floats inside her dark eyelids, a version of what she just saw. What else, what else will there be?

I'll try, she says. She hugs the old woman, and then lets her go.

The doctor draws his wife's arm through his. Her eyes are wet now, watching Miss Underwood walk away with Miss Breithaupt. She shakes her head and smiles up at him.

It is best so, she says. Silly to be sentimental when things go well.

He pats her hand. How did you find Mrs. Chase? he asks, as they mount the stairs together.

Devoted to children and husband; rather more pious than the rest of us wives. Bland and blond—but on the whole, tolerable. I can guess what you think of that smug little doctor. You even seemed bored during his evening program!

The doctor shrugs. I was thinking of other things.

What happened today was just a series of freaks, dear. Don't let it upset you too much.

Thank you—but something else was on my mind. The doctor stops climbing, surpressing a cough. I was drafting a letter to the managers…one that I think you'll like.

James. She turns to look at him squarely. I thought I overheard you at the table, but I scarcely believed my ears. Do you really mean to resign?

Not yet, no. I couldn't release myself from the hospital as it is now, in its current state. I suspect my letter to the managers could take years to write.

You know I'll be delighted to help you. She shakes her head. Still…don't take this step because you feel overwhelmed, or sorry about the Underwood case. Those feelings always pass—unlike your ambition.

Perhaps, the doctor says. In the days to come, perhaps he'll present to her all of the reasons he's come to question himself, and even to question the viability of one person superintending a hospital of this size—or of any size. Now he pictures Henrietta Firestone, MD, in his imagination a younger, haler version of his wife.

It's *because* of my ambition for the hospital that I'm considering such a step. I would leave to make room for other, brighter doctors.

Is that all? Diana asks, and he feels the muscles of her arm tighten, her arm tucked now through his, her arm that carried him through his illness and convalescence.

Well, he says. It seems to me that there are other things that *we* have left to do.

Oh James. She laughs. That has always been my fear—and my hope.

Acknowledgments

THOUGH THE CHARACTERS AND EVENTS in *Moral Treatment* are fictional, the novel's setting is closely modeled after the Northern Michigan Asylum, a Kirkbride hospital opened in 1885 in my hometown of Traverse City, Michigan. Many of the hospital's original buildings are still standing, and in describing this space, I have drawn on my own familiarity with the campus, as well as the historic and contemporary photographs included in Heidi Johnson's *Angels in the Architecture*, and the additional archival photographs in Chris Miller's *Images of America: Traverse City State Hospital*. I am also grateful to Ray Minervini of the Minervini Group for taking me on a hard-hat tour of some of the hospital's buildings in the winter of 2003, before wide-spread redevelopment of the property began.

For details about patient demographics, common mental and physical illnesses, and hospital maintenance, I drew extensively from the biannual reports (1886-1896) of the Northern Michigan Asylum's Board of Trustees. Earle E. Steele's memoir, *Beauty is Therapy: Memories of the Traverse City State Hospital*, provided me with a sense of everyday life at the hospital between 1922, when he arrived as the child of the head gardener, and 1984, when he retired as Superintendent of the Grounds Department. I am also grateful to the late Mr. Steele for organizing and curating a museum at the hospital in the late 1980's—and for his hospitality as curator toward unaccompanied thirteen-year-olds. Those visits were the beginning of my unofficial research on this hospital; my official research began at the Traverse City Public Library, which maintains a collection of newspaper clippings and other materials related to the hospital.

The American Journal of Insanity, the publication of the Association of Medical Superintendents of American Institutions for the Insane, was an invaluable primary source for this project. Not only did it provide me with a sense of current medical and legal issues in the 1880's and 90's, it also gave me a sense of the language of the profession, which was not as specialized or scientific as that of psychiatry today. The schism between the doctor and Dr. Ingstrom is a reflection of the kinds of generational tensions I saw fomenting in the pages of this publication. Dr. Ingstrom's experiment with cinchonia, described in Chapter Eight, is based on Joseph G. Rogers's "Some Peculiar Effects of Cinchonia," found in the July 1882 issue of this publication. The resolution about letter-writing, from which the doctor quotes in Chapter Fifteen, was printed in the "Proceedings of the Association of Medical Superintendents of Institutions for the Insane" found in the July 1891 issue. Other medical texts vital to my project included Thomas Story Kirkbride's *On the Construction, Organization, and General Arrangements of Hospitals for the Insane* (1854; rev. 1880), the founding text of the moral treatment, and Edward Charles Spitzka's *Insanity: Its Classifications, Diagnosis and Treatment* (1889), which was useful in depicting the doctors' diagnostic practices.

Accounts of patient life in the 1890's are less readily available than are medical texts, but Elizabeth Packard's *Modern Persecution or Insane Asylums Unveiled* (1873) provided me with one individual's impressions of the gender politics and hypocrisy of institutional medicine. *The Letters of a Victorian Madwoman* (ed. John S. Hughes) offers an account of how female deviance could be constructed as insanity within the nosology of institutional psychiatry. Clifford Beers's *A Mind That Found Itself* (1908) provides a glimpse of the mistreatment that male patients endured during this era.

For information about commitment laws in Michigan in the late nineteenth century, I turned to John Koren's *Summaries of Laws Relating to the Commitment and Care of the Insane in the United States* (1912). For an account of early mental health care, epidemic diseases, and medical equipment employed in Michigan, I relied on the *Medical History of Michigan*, compiled by a committee of the State Medical Society in 1930 and examining the years 1820-1910.

Historical newspapers and magazines were vital to my understanding of the fashions, popular literature, and medical and quasi-medical practices of 1890, like the treatment of Russian Flu (or American Grippe). The most useful of these included *The Michigan Farmer*, *The Detroit Clinic* and the *Medical and Surgical Reporter* (all available through the American Periodical Series Online database). To get a sense of small-town newspaper content during this era, I looked to the national and international news included in the Saugatack, MI *Commercial Record*, a semi-local source available electronically from 1868-1958.

Among critical treatments of nineteenth-century mental health care, I am especially indebted to Ellen Dwyer's *Homes for the Mad: Life inside Two Nineteenth-Century Asylums*, which profiles the

New York State Lunatic Asylum at Utica and the Willard Asylum for the Chronic Insane and offers, among many other things, an excellent study of the qualifications of and conditions for attendants working in isolated, rural mental institutions. Nancy Tomes's *The Art of Asylum-Keeping: Thomas Story Kirkbride and the Origins of American Psychiatry* helped me to appreciate the principles of the moral treatment and their enduring influence. Gerald Grob's histories of mental health care in the United States (including *The Mad Among Us: A History of the Care of America's Mentally Ill* and *Mental Illness and American Society, 1875-1940*) were also very useful references throughout this project.

I began work on this project many years ago, as an MFA student at Syracuse University. My thanks to my classmates and teachers there, and to my thesis advisor, Brian Evenson, who read early versions of some of this material. I completed the first full draft of the novel as my PhD dissertation at the University of Missouri, where I am grateful for feedback and support from my director, Trudy Lewis, and my committee members, Pat Okker, John Evelev, Speer Morgan, and Kristin Schwain. For their generosity in reading and commenting on the full manuscript, I thank Robert Long Foreman, Michael Piafsky, and Heather Jacobs. I am also grateful to the Society for the Study of Midwestern Literature, which recognized the Chapter One of this novel with a 2008 David Diamond Prize for Student Writing and publication in *MidAmerica: The Yearbook of the Society for the Study of Midwestern Literature*.

Many, many thanks to Mika Yamamoto, for pointing me toward the Summit Series contest; Erin Smith, for her brilliant cover design and layout; Kevin Morgan Watson, for his advocacy and advice; and Matt Roberson, Director of the Central Michigan University Press

Summit Series, for creating this prize and being such a responsive, respectful, and collaborative editor and publisher. Thank you to the editorial board of the Summit Series, Steven Bailey, Jeffrey Bean, Darrin Doyle, and Robert Fanning, and to the 2024 contest judge, Eric Torgersen. For their kind words about *Moral Treatment,* thanks to the brilliant writers Laura Kasischke and Clare Beams. Deep thanks to my publicist, Caitlin Hamilton Summie.

Thank you to those with whom I've explored the Traverse City State Hospital over the years, especially Ann Carpenter, Mark and Karl Snyder, and Peter Richards. As I developed my fictional hospital, I had in mind the experiences of my own family members who once worked at the TCSH, including my grandmother, M. Iris Carpenter, who earned her nursing degree there; my great-uncle, Robert Carpenter, who was one of the dairy farmers responsible for the hospital's famous cow, Traverse Colantha Walker; and my great-uncle, Len Burr, who worked in the upholstery shop. I also did my best to imagine and honor the many people who were institutionalized at TCSH over its 104 years of operation—and at so many other hospitals like it.

Finally, thank you to my partner, Tim Havens, namesake of poor Timothy Chambers, for never forgetting about this book, and for your support in bringing it into the world.